BLOOD OF THE RAVEN, BOOK 3

Ravenflight

ELIZABETH
SCHECHTER

For more information contact:
Riverdale Avenue Books/Circlet Imprint
5676 Riverdale Avenue
Riverdale, NY 10471

www.riverdaleavebooks.com
Cover design by Scott Carpenter
Design by www.formatting4U.com

First Edition, October 2025

Digital ISBN: 9781626017221
Paperback ISBN: 9781626017238
Hardcover ISBN: 9781626017207

Riverdale Avenue Books would like to thank you for purchasing book three of the Blood of the Raven series, *Ravenflight*. Please, consider signing up to our newsletter where you can find the latest on us and your favorite authors, along with free copies of books from each of our imprints, at the link provided:

https://preview.mailerlite.io/preview/1098983/sites/136486432257607665/0kJ9TD

If you are interested in being in our ARC reader/reviewer program, you can sign up here. Re-views are the life blood of the independent author and publisher and every single one counts to getting books into the hands of the right readers.

Chapter One

How could four months last so long?

There had been a month of healing and slowly regaining strength as the winter rains eased and passed, until Lorcan came out of the bedroom one morning to find the springtime garden a riot of color and scent seemingly overnight.

Once Livia pronounced him hale, his days were filled with training, starting with wooden blades that felt strange in his hand as if he'd never before held a sword. Relearning what he knew. Growing as a fighter, and learning how best to teach what he knew. Finally walking back out onto the sands of the arena and hearing the screams of the crowd as he fought and won, hearing them call his name as he saluted the Emperor–*Corax Princeps*!

Once it was known that he was now a *doctor* of the *Ludus Manius,* teaching filled the days when he wasn't in the arena, as young Roman noblemen clamored to learn from the undefeated Corax, the hero who had saved Rome. And evenings were spent planning. He learned accounting, keeping careful tally of his arena wins and his earnings from teaching. He learned how to negotiate with traders and merchants, slowly laying the groundwork for the long trip home. He learned to read maps and traced the routes of the Roman roads toward the north. Toward the port where they'd take ship for Alba and Eire.

Four months that led to one last day.

Corax's final fight.

* * *

"He's asleep? He can't be asleep! How can he be asleep?"

Lorcan opened his eyes. He was stretched out on the bed-shelf in the arena cell where they waited before a fight, and he'd been just drifting off when Nona's voice banished sleep. He shook his head. "I'm awake."

1

Nona snorted. "You were snoring. Lorcan, you're going to fall asleep on the sands and get killed."

"He's newly married," Yaroah murmured. "He does not need sleep." But as teasing as the words were, the tall Carthaginian looked worried. "You do look tired," he added. "Perhaps you should not fight today."

"We've already been announced," Lorcan said. He could hear the roar of the crowd in the arena. Odd how the sound had become almost comforting after nearly a year in the arena. Would he miss it, after today? "You're the ones who told me that if I didn't fight, there would be riots." He pushed himself up on his elbows. "I'm fine."

Yaroah growled at him, "Ghost…"

Lorcan sat up and grinned. "You haven't called me that in ages. You're that annoyed at me? Why?"

"Because Livia will poison all of us if anything happens to you," Ennius answered. "She told us that herself. All of Rome knows that this is your last fight. It's the last chance someone has to try and get at you on the sands. That's why Nona and I are here—so there aren't any surprises like that mercenary your cousin sent. So, why don't you tell us what's really going on? You're not sleeping, and it's not newlywed games. I know. My rooms are closest to yours since we moved out of the cells. So, what is it?"

"You've been listening?" Lorcan snorted, more amused than annoyed. "Have we been entertaining?"

Ennius made a rude gesture, and Lorcan laughed. Then he sighed. "The truth? Visions. I've been having visions. They started before the Emperor's birthday games, and they've been coming more and more frequently. Sometimes multiple times a night. I'm seeing things that are happening in Eire, and there's nothing I can do about any of it until I get there. But I can't leave yet. Gaius told me that the weather to the north is still too poor to travel. He says I need to wait at least until the next full moon." He rubbed his face. "He's annoyed with me, too. Because I wanted to leave as soon as the rains stopped."

"Have you told the Flamen Dialis about your visions?" Nona asked. "You see him every few days."

"I did, and he's talked to other priests on my behalf. Even the ones who speak visions for your gods have no advice." Lorcan shrugged and got up. "We need to prepare. That was the third bout, and Yaroah and I are fifth."

2

By the time the crowd roared the end of the next bout, Nona and Ennius had finished helping Lorcan and Yaroah into the coordinating *ocrea* and *manica* that Manius had commissioned for them. The cell door creaked open, and Manius and Livia entered. Livia went straight to Lorcan's arms, kissing him, then stepping back and studying his face.

"You didn't sleep again," she pronounced. "Lorcan, I haven't been a wife long enough for you to make me a widow."

Lorcan kissed her again. "So little faith in me?" he asked. "I slept."

"You just told us you weren't asleep!" Nona protested. Then he yelped when Ennius slapped the back of his head.

Lorcan rolled his eyes and pulled Livia back into his arms. "I'll be fine," he said. "This is my last fight. You know that."

"I also know that you said that about the last one." Livia rested her hands flat on his chest, her fingertips on the chest strap of the *manica*. "Promise me," she said. "Promise me that you'll walk off the sands today and not look back."

Lorcan took her hands in his and kissed each of her palms. "I swear it, my Livia."

"Manius, who do we fight today?" Yaroah asked.

"Another pair of *murmillos*," Manius answered. "A matched pair. Their *lanista* promotes them as twins. They're from one of the eastern provinces. Thracia, I think. I've never heard of them before."

"Twins? This city was founded by twins, wasn't it?" Lorcan asked. "Would it be a bad omen to trounce twins in the arena?"

"You've been spending too much time with the Flamen Dialis," Manius scoffed. "They are gladiators like any others. And I'm sure that they are no more twins than you and Yaroah are. It just makes for a good spectacle."

Lorcan nodded. Then he held his arms out to the sides. "Livia? Am I ready?"

She looked him up and down with the critical eye of a gladiator's daughter. Then she nodded. "You're ready. Be careful."

* * *

Given their status as *rudiarii,* Lorcan, Yaroah, Nona, and Ennius were no longer confined to the cells between bouts, and weren't escorted by guards to the gates that led to the sands. Nona and Ennius walked Lorcan and Yaroah to the gates instead, where they were met by one of the familiar arena guards.

"They're nearly finished raking the sands," Julius said as they joined him. "And your feathered friend is out there, Corax. I saw her perched on the wall after the last bout."

Lorcan chuckled. "I'd wondered where Corvina was. She doesn't like the cells, so she usually stays with Livia."

"I agree with her," Yaroah muttered. "I have never liked the cells."

Julius looked out the gate. "Linus is one of your officials today, Corax. He says he's looking forward to seeing your last fight. And if you could please not make it as exciting as your first?"

"I have no intentions of being exciting," Lorcan answered. "I'll miss him. And you, my friend."

Julius knocked his fist against Lorcan's shield. "Just be sure you're alive to miss me, Corax. I don't want your last time on these sands to be your last fight in this world. Keep your helmet on."

Lorcan chuckled. "But the crowd loves it when I throw my helmet."

Julius snorted. "Yaroah, keep this idiot alive, will you?"

"I will do my best," Yaroah promised. The gates rose, and Julius gestured for them to go out into the bright sunlight. Yaroah went first, and the crowd roared. Then Lorcan followed, and the voices grew louder. He turned and waved, and the people started chanting.

Corax! Corax! Corax Princeps!

Lorcan waved again, and the flowers started falling like snow.

"They love you, Corax," Linus said as he and Yaroah approached him. "And they'll miss you when you're gone." He nodded toward the other official. "This is Titus."

Lorcan smiled. "They'll find someone else to cheer for," he said. "It's time and past time for me to return to Eire. It's a pleasure to meet you, Titus." He turned to the other two fighters, who did look enough alike to be twins. "May your gods smile on you today."

"And yours, Corax," one of them said.

"Salute the Emperor," Linus called. Lorcan drew his *spatha* and raised it toward the box, but his eyes weren't on Lucanus. He searched the faces of the people seated behind the Emperor, looking for dark skin and curling hair.

Tavi wasn't there.

Lorcan dragged his attention back to the sands, stepping back and planting his blade in the ground, handing his shield to Linus so that he could put on his helmet. He took the shield back and picked up his sword, moving to the side so that Yaroah could finish arming. Then they walked back toward the other gladiators, and Linus held his staff parallel to the ground, separating the pairs of fighters. He paused, and the screams of the crowd grew louder. Then he swung his staff out of the way and shouted, "Begin!"

Lorcan's world narrowed. The sounds of the crowd faded away, and he only knew the weight of the *spatha* in his hand, the shield on his arm. The bone-jarring impact and rattle of metal on wood. The pounding rush of blood in his ears, and the sweat running down his face. The twin that he faced was good, as good as any fighter that Lorcan had faced in the past year. He found himself struggling to guard, to find an opening to attack. How had he never heard of these two before? The crowd noise was a constant roar that almost drown out his own panting for breath, but there was no space to breathe or take off his helmet. He saw an opening and took it, hearing the other *murmillo* howl. A heartbeat later, Lorcan felt the pain in his right side, the rush of blood over his hip and down his leg. At the sight of blood, the crowd screamed their approval.

"Ghost!"

"I'm fine!" Lorcan shouted. He was lying, and he knew it. He could already feel his head spinning. It was the same side where Tiernay had stabbed him, and nearly the same place. How badly was he hurt? He staggered back a step, trying to ignore the pain. The *murmillo* attacked again, and Lorcan heard Yaroah cry out a bare instant before a blade glanced off his *manica*. Both fighters closed on him, and in the breath before they engaged, he caught a glimpse of Yaroah kneeling on the sands. Bleeding on the sands.

Lorcan had practiced fighting two opponents before, but that had been in the relative safety of the *ludus*, and against Nona and Yaroah. That was play. This was real, and he knew that his practice hadn't prepared him for the real thing. He blocked a strike from one of the twins while trying to stop the second, then both twins rushed him and carried him to the ground, a move that Lorcan knew was illegal.

"Hold!"

Lorcan heard Linus' voice, but neither twin stopped, ignoring the officials. One of them dragged Lorcan to his knees, pulling his arms behind him while the other pulled off Lorcan's helm and threw it away.

5

"Make it fast!" the one holding Lorcan growled. "We don't have time!"

The other nodded. He grabbed a handful of Lorcan's long hair and pulled his head back, raising his sword...

A white rod splintered over the attacker's back, making him stagger and let go of Lorcan's hair. It was enough of a distraction that he was able to break free of the other twin, rolling clear. He caught a glimpse of one twin stalking toward Titus as he grabbed up his *spatha* and Yaroah's *gladius*. He hadn't fought as a *dimachaeri* while wearing a *manica* before, but he didn't have a choice. He had to do something.

The second twin rushed at him, and Lorcan blocked his thrust with one hand, stabbing with the other and leaving the man screaming and bleeding on the sands. The remaining twin turned, and started back toward Lorcan. He grinned behind his helm, his teeth flashing in the gap of the faceplate.

"Should have known you wouldn't lay down and die," he called. "They told me when they hired me that you'd be hard to kill."

"Who told you?" Lorcan demanded. Behind his opponent, he could see guards rushing out of the gates, Nona and Ennius with them. If he kept the remaining twin's attention on him, they could take him alive. "Did my cousin hire you?"

"Does it matter?" He raised his sword. "Dance with me, barbarian."

Lorcan shook his head to clear it, and stepped back. The entire arena was starting to spin harder. The crowd noise was a distant buzz. Lorcan thought he heard the other man laugh but ignored it. All that mattered was in front of him...

"Ghost!"

And maybe something behind him. "Yaroah?" he called without turning. "How badly are you hurt?"

"I will survive this," Yaroah answered, coming up next to Lorcan. "The other one is dead."

"Good," Lorcan said. The guards were close enough that he lowered his blade and raised his voice. "He says he was sent," he called. "Keep him alive. I want to know who hired him."

The remaining twin turned toward the guards, then stepped to the side before turning to face Lorcan again. Lorcan couldn't see his face, but his voice was steady. "Be disappointed." Then he turned his *gladius* so that the point pressed underneath his breastbone.

"No!" Lorcan shouted. Two of the guards lunged forward, but neither was close enough to catch the man before he threw himself at the sands; the point of his sword punched through his back, and he didn't move.

Above them, the crowds roared their approval.

"Corax!" Linus ran up to them. "You're hurt!"

"I'll live," Lorcan muttered. "What… Linus, how do we end this? What do we do?"

"I…" Linus looked up at the Imperial box. "Salute. Let him know you live. Don't let the people know this wasn't planned. We'll get a litter— "

"No litter," Lorcan said. "I promised my wife I'd walk off the sands. I'm keeping that promise." He leaned on Yaroah and limped away from the carnage that the guards were already cleaning up. Every movement hurt. Breathing hurt, and walking a straight line was nearly impossible, but he forced himself to raise his sword to the Emperor. Even at this distance, he could see how angry Lucanus was.

"I think I'm tired of having the crowd love me," Lorcan said as Linus and Yaroah started to lead him toward the Victory Gate. Ennius and Nona joined them. Ennius took Lorcan's arm and draped it over his shoulders. Lorcan winced and muttered, "Even if this wasn't my last fight, it would be my last fight."

"He's fading," Ennius said. "He's lost his Latin."

"We'll get him to Livia," Nona said. "He'll be fine."

"We need a litter!" Ennius called. Livia appeared in the Victory Gate, Corvina on her shoulder. She looked shocked, and he wondered why.

"No litter," Lorcan repeated. "I will walk off these sands on my own two feet."

The walk to the Victory Gate had never seemed so long. But finally, he stood in the arch, with his Livia in front of him. His wife, his mate. He rested his forehead against hers and sighed.

"No more," he whispered. Then he smiled. "I promised. I'm here."

"Get a litter!" Julius called. "He's to be taken to the Palace."

"What?"

"The Emperor ordered it," Livia said. "We're to go under guard to protect you, and his own *medici* will take care of you."

"I want my own *medicae*," Lorcan grumbled. He turned, and the room kept turning.

"Catch him!"

* * *

7

Lorcan woke up on his back and moving, seeing a low stone ceiling over him. He shifted and groaned in pain.

"Easy, Corax."

Lorcan blinked and looked up, seeing a shadowy figure next to him. The voice was familiar. "Gaius?" He tried to raise his head, but abandoned the effort as too much work. "Where's Livia?"

"Next litter over," Gaius answered. "With Yaroah, who was more badly hurt than we thought. Ennius is with her, and Nona and I are keeping an eye on you."

"Yaroah is hurt?" Lorcan turned his head, recognizing Nona's profile. "How badly?"

"Not as badly as you are," Nona answered. "How are you even talking?"

Lorcan closed his eyes. "Stubborn."

"Is he awake?" Livia said, and Lorcan felt her cold hand on his cheek. He sighed at her touch. "How do you feel?"

"Dizzy," Lorcan answered. "Hurts."

"That's not surprising," Livia said. "I wish I could pray to your grandmother to put you to sleep the way she did the last time, so you don't have to feel this. The wound is deep enough that it needs to be stitched. We're going to the *valetudinarium* near the Palace. They'll have what I need."

Lorcan frowned, trying to translate the word and failing. He heard Gaius chuckle.

"Where the *medicos* who serve the military treat the legions," Gaius said. "And I'm coming with you to smooth the way… and as a guard." He glanced over his shoulder. "Manius has gone to find the *lanista* who brought those two to the arena. They were sent?"

Lorcan nodded and winced, closing his eyes. The movement of the litter was too much like the movement of a ship, and he knew that if he vomited now, he'd be in agony.

"It won't be long, Lorcan," Livia said. "We're almost there."

The tunnel ended, and Lorcan blinked in the bright sunlight. He could hear shouting, the sounds of people coming closer.

"Clear the way!" Gaius shouted. "The *medicae* needs to get to work immediately!"

The swaying got worse as the men carrying the litter picked up speed, but they quickly slowed and entered a cool, dark building.

"Bring him here," Livia said, and Lorcan felt the litter sway and rise, then felt something hard under his back. Opening his eyes seemed too much effort, so he listened as Livia spoke to a man whose voice Lorcan didn't recognize.

"When the Emperor told me to come see to an injured man, I wasn't expecting it to be Corax Princeps," he said. "And you... I remember you from the Temple. You're Manius' girl."

"Yes, sir," Livia said. "I am Lorcan's wife."

"I see. Do you feel competent to treat him? Tell me, how would you approach this?"

"The wound is long and deep, but doesn't appear to have damaged the intestines. There's no smell of corruption or effluvia. I intend to clean the wound with vinegar, use *fibulae* so that there's drainage, and dress with honey and clean linen."

"Very nice. I'll assist, if I may?"

"I would be honored, *Comes*."

Movement all around him, then Lorcan heard Livia's voice. "Lorcan?"

He opened his eyes to see her holding a cup. "You need to drink this," she said. "It will make you sleep so I can work without hurting you."

Lorcan nodded, and she held the cup to his lips. It was a cloyingly thick syrup—wine and honey and something bitter he couldn't identify. He swallowed, coughed, swallowed more, then grimaced as Livia took the cup away. She chuckled, no doubt at the look on his face.

"I know," she said. "It tastes terrible."

"Too sweet," he mumbled. His already heavy limbs felt leaden and warm, and he couldn't keep his eyes open.

"And you don't like sweets," Livia said. She kissed him on the forehead. "Go to sleep, Lorcan."

Lorcan listened to his wife. His last thought was that if he'd listened to her earlier, he wouldn't be on this table now

Chapter Two

When Lorcan woke again, it felt as if he was being dragged out of a pit of tar. His mouth tasted awful, and what parts of his body didn't hurt didn't seem to want to move. It took him what felt like years before he realized that he couldn't move because he was bound to the narrow cot on which he lay. He squeezed his eyes closed, then opened them again to a room that seemed to be gently rotating. Or maybe he was the one rotating. He couldn't be sure. There didn't seem to be anyone else in the room, but there was a curtain covering the door, and he heard movement outside.

"Is anyone there?" he croaked. He heard an answering croak, and Corvina landed on his chest, making him gasp at her sudden weight. She cocked her head to the side and croaked again, a gentler sound this time. The sound of a mother looking over her nestling. Lorcan smiled.

"Thank you," he murmured. "Where's Livia?'

Corvina croaked again, then launched; Lorcan winced as she took to the air. There was a small window, an air vent high up on the same wall as the door, and she landed there and started calling. There was more movement outside the curtain; it parted, and Livia came inside, followed by an older man. Lorcan ignored him for the moment; Livia came straight to the cot, knelt, and kissed him hard enough that the room started spinning harder.

"I'm sorry," Lorcan whispered when she let him breathe again.

"You've lost Latin," Livia murmured. "I shouldn't be surprised. How do you feel?"

"The room is spinning," Lorcan answered, forcing himself to speak Latin. "I hurt, and I feel… slow. I can't think."

"That's common after drinking Cretic wine," the man said. "You haven't asked, but you're bound because when you started to wake, you were violent. Also common after drinking Cretic wine. We didn't want you to hurt anyone, or to tear your side open again." He smiled. "Are you going to try to take my head off again?"

10

"I'm sorry if I did it before," Lorcan answered. "I don't remember it."

The man laughed. "Apology accepted, Corax. Or should I call you Albus?"

"Lorcan."

The man nodded and picked a small knife up from a table. "I am Laris, and it's a pleasure to meet you, Lorcan. Let's get you comfortable, then you can have visitors. Manius is waiting, and the heir."

Lorcan nodded, watching as Laris bent to cut the cords binding his arms to the frame of the cot. "When can I get up?"

"A few days, once the wound starts to heal." Laris answered. "And the sooner the better, I think. There's a rumor in the streets that you're dead." He straightened up. "There. Now, I'm sure your wife will reinforce these directions, but you're to stay flat on your back for the next two to three days. Then we'll see how you're healing, and about taking out the *fibulae*. Shall I send people in?"

"Please."

Laris stepped to the side and peered out through the curtain. "He's awake."

The curtain opened again, and Gaius came inside, followed by Manius. The two men looked at each other, then Gaius gestured, standing back as Manius came to the cot.

"They were hired to kill you, you said?"

Lorcan nodded. "One of them said he was told when he was hired that it would be hard to kill me."

"Did he tell you who told him that?"

"No." Lorcan frowned. "My cousin, I suppose?"

Manius looked back over his shoulder at Gaius, then sighed. "Not that we can tell. Did anyone tell you I went to talk to the *lanista*? We found his body. He'd been dead at least a day." Manius sat down on the cot near Lorcan's feet. "There was nothing in his records or his papers that indicated he had any contact with Hibernia, or with your cousin. Nor any large amounts of money. But he might not have kept that in his records."

"But we can't question him, and both gladiators are dead," Gaius added. "I have men following their travels back to the eastern provinces, but I don't think we'll learn anything."

Lorcan frowned, grunting softly as Corvina landed on his chest again, then hopped off to nestle next to his ear on the cot. "If not my cousin, then who?" he asked.

"A rival *lanista*?" Laris suggested. "Someone who lost money because of you?"

"We'll find out," Gaius said. "And once you're able to be moved, you'll be staying in the Palace." He held up one hand to silence Lorcan's protest. "Father ordered it. Better not to argue."

"Just Lorcan?" Livia asked.

"No, we've all been invited," Manius answered. "Nona and Ennius will be staying at the *ludus* though. Someone has to take charge of the slaves and train the students. I'm not certain what that will mean for the lessons Lorcan and Yaroah are supposed to teach, but neither of you will be teaching until you've recovered anyway." He paused. "And by the time you've recovered, it will be time for you to sail."

"Ride," Lorcan grumbled. "No boats."

"Not until you don't have a choice?" Gaius asked. "I understand. I get sick at sea myself."

Lorcan smiled. Then he winced as Corvina started to preen his hair, tugging on it painfully hard.

"Corvina, stop that." Livia came around the bed and reached for the raven, only to pull back when Corvina stabbed at her hand. Lorcan croaked at her, but Corvina only croaked back and tugged on his hair again. Lorcan closed his eyes, remembering the pull as the *murmillo* held him in place by his hair. He grimaced.

"Let her be. I understand what she's telling me," he murmured in Gaeilge. He clicked his tongue at Corvina. "I understand," he repeated, and smiled as the raven rubbed her bill against his cheek.

Manius patted his leg. "You held your own against a pair. That's impressive, Lorcan."

"I almost spilled my guts against a pair," Lorcan corrected. He still felt dizzy, but he wasn't sure if it was the Cretic wine, or the pain. "How is Yaroah?"

"He also almost spilled his guts out there," Livia answered. "But his wound wasn't as deep or as poorly placed." She moved around the bed. "When will the bearers be here?"

"As soon as you tell me that he's able to be moved," Gaius answered. "They're in the courtyard. *Comes*, can we move him?"

Laris folded his arms over his chest and tucked his chin, giving the impression that he was scowling. "Let me answer your question with a question," he finally said. "Does the Emperor want him moved now? Or can I keep him here until morning?"

Gaius chuckled. "Father wants him safe in the Palace as soon as he can be moved. But he'll defer to your experience as to when that should be. If moving Lorcan will cause him pain, then we'll post guards and wait."

Laris nodded. "We have flexibility, then. Good. Livia, what are your thoughts?"

"I'd rather not move him until the wound has a chance to start healing," Livia answered. "Tomorrow. Perhaps the day after."

"So be it," Gaius said. "I'll tell Father." He took a deep breath, then blew it out like he was blowing out a candle. "Lorcan—"

Lorcan winced and shook his head. "No more talking."

"Enough," Livia added. "He's in pain. Let him rest."

The cot shifted as Manius stood up. "Livia, I'll be back," he said. "I want to look in on Nona and Ennius."

"Father, you put them in charge," Livia said. "Let them be in charge."

"I will." Manius grumbled, then sighed. "I want to see what Nona might have heard. And see if any of my sources have information. I'll be back."

"Be careful," Lorcan mumbled. He closed his eyes, so he didn't see who patted his leg. But when he opened his eyes again, he and Livia were alone.

"I can give you something for the pain," Livia said, sitting on the cot next to his hip. "Do you think your grandmother will help?"

Lorcan shook his head. "She said I wouldn't see her again for a long time. I think healing me is yours to do." He took a deep breath and felt a pang for the first time in months. "I want my mother," he murmured.

Livia took his hand and squeezed it. "Let me get more wine. You'll sleep, and you'll heal."

* * *

The days passed in a blurred haze of pain and Cretic wine. Lorcan didn't remember being moved—he closed his eyes at dusk in the tiny room in the *valetudinarium,* and opened them to a bright morning in the Palace rooms overlooking the garden where he'd awakened the last time he'd been attacked. He turned his head from side to side, but saw no one. Where was Livia? He frowned, considered his options, then slowly pushed himself up on his elbows and from there to a sitting position. His side still hurt, but he wasn't in excruciating pain anymore. How long had he been asleep?

The door opened, and Livia came into the room. She stared at him for a moment, then gasped, "What are you doing?"

"Wondering where you were," Lorcan answered. "Where anyone was, really. And how long have we been here?"

Livia closed the door and came to perch on the bed next to him, leaning close to kiss him. "We've been in the Palace two days," she answered as she straightened. "And there's a guard in the gardens, and one outside the door. I went out to talk to my father and Laris. How do you feel? You shouldn't be sitting up. You shouldn't be healed enough to sit up."

Lorcan looked down at himself and the bandages wound around his body. "I still hurt, but not as much, and the room isn't spinning anymore. And I can think. What is in that Cretic wine that you've been giving me?"

"*Papaver*, and I wasn't going to give you anymore. Too much, and you start to crave it. Did you know that? Do you even have *papaver* in Hibernia? I don't know what you'd call it."

Lorcan thought about his lessons at his mother's side, then shook his head. "I don't remember Mother teaching me about *papaver*, but that doesn't mean we don't have it. It just means that she didn't tell me the Latin name. What plant is it?"

"Poppies."

"Poppy syrup? We call it *meilbhaeg*, and Mother did warn me about it. She didn't use it."

Livia's brow furrowed. "Then what would you give someone for pain?"

"I don't know the names in Latin. *Saileach*, usually. *Gafann* if the pain is very bad. But Mother taught me that *gafann* is dangerous, so it's probably like *papaver*."

"*Saileach* is *itea* in Latin. *Gafann*... oh, I know that one. One of the healing references calls it *bilinuntiam*. And it's what I was going to start using if you were still in pain."

Lorcan chuckled. "I'm not in that much pain. I want to get up."

"Not until I take out the *fibulae*," Livia said. "Now lie down."

Lorcan lay back down, but reached out and caught Livia by the wrist, tugging her closer. "Lay with me."

"Lorcan!" Livia laughed and tugged against his grip. "You're not healed enough for that!"

14

"I didn't say that!" Lorcan tugged her again. "I said lay. I want to hold you." He let her go when someone knocked at the door. There was a sharp flare of hope that it might be Tavi, but that faded away as the door opened and Laris came inside.

"I wasn't expecting you to be awake," he said as he closed the door. "I came to see how you were faring and… and you're not happy. You're disappointed that it was me?" He looked back at the door. "Who were you expecting?"

"It's nothing," Lorcan murmured. "I'm feeling better."

"I can tell." Laris came to the side of the bed and tipped his head to the side. "Livia, you said something about him being a *semideus*. Does that mean he heals faster?"

Livia looked at Lorcan, who shook his head. "I was told that, but the last time, my grandmother got involved. So, I'm not certain. Why? Am I healing faster than I should?"

"You're healing," Laris answered. "That in and of itself is extraordinary. And, I think, a credit to how stubborn both you and your wife are. Now, let's look at that wound. If you're healing this well, we may need to take the *fibulae* out today." He stepped back and folded his arms over his chest. "Are you able to sit up?"

"He was sitting when I came in," Livia said. "On the bed, or in a chair?"

Laris nodded. "On the bed," he answered slowly. "In case he faints."

Lorcan snorted. "Faints?"

"There are 16 *fibulae* in your side," Laris answered. "Taking them out won't be painless."

"You keep saying *fibulae*," Lorcan said as he sat back up. He held his arms out of the way as Laris and Livia started to unwind bandages. "What do you mean? Because the *fibulae* I know are the pins Livia uses on her gowns."

"Those are exactly what we're talking about," Laris said. "Here, look down. You can see what we mean."

Lorcan looked down, and could see the uncovered wound, and the first four of a neat row of pins that looked exactly like the ones that littered Livia's dressing table in their bedroom in the *ludus*. There was a cord laced around them, crossing between pins to lace the same way Lorcan would have laced the bracers he wore after Gnaeus attacked him and broke his arm.

15

"Why this way?"

"The slash was deep along the side," Livia answered. "I wanted it to be able to drain. This is the best way to do that."

"You're going to have to teach me this," Lorcan said. Then he yelped as a sharp pain shot up his side, feeling as if something was being ripped out of his skin. His stomach twisted, and he swallowed hard to keep it in place.

"Livia," Laris said. "A bowl, or a basin? These definitely should come out now. It's healing nicely."

Livia stepped away, coming back with a metal bowl. Laris dropped a bloody *fibula* into it, making the bowl ring like a bell.

"How many did you say?" Lorcan gasped.

"16," Laris answered. Then he paused. "You're looking a little green, Lorcan. If you want to do this lying down, it will be easiest if you face the windows and look out at the garden. Livia, can you steady him?"

"I… just a moment," Livia answered. Her voice sounded shaky, but Lorcan didn't get a good look at her before she hurried out of the room. A moment later, Nona came inside.

"Livia sent me to help," he said.

"Thank you." Laris rested his hand on Lorcan's shoulder. "I need to take the *fibulae* out. Lorcan, lay down. And you… what's your name?"

"Nona."

"Nona, hold him still."

Lorcan lay down on his left side, facing the window. Nona came around and knelt down in front of him, taking his hands. "Squeeze hard," he said. "And… distractions. The Emperor will be coming to see you. Later today or tomorrow, or so I've heard. So, you need to be awake."

Another tearing pain, and Lorcan squeezed Nona's hands hard enough that the other man winced. He swallowed again as his stomach threatened once more to rebel. Then he asked. "Have you seen Tavi?"

"He's not in Rome," Nona answered. "The word is that he's in Carthage. And the word is that Gaius sent messengers, telling him to come back. But it's only been a couple of days since the ship left. It'll be a few days before he can get here."

Lorcan winced as another *fibulae* made the bowl ring. "Carthage?"

"Something for the Emperor," Nona answered. "Haven't been able to find out what. I tried. I knew you'd want to know. Lorcan, why is Livia green?"

16

"She did look a bit green," Laris murmured, just before he pulled another *fibula* free and made the bowl ring. "You're doing very well, Lorcan."

"Green?" Lorcan gasped as another *fibula* was added to the bowl. "What do you mean green?"

"Like she was going to be sick. Which isn't like our Livia," Nona answered. He shifted his grip on Lorcan's hands. "I've seen her stitch up wounds that made me want to throw up last week's meals. That long scar on Yaroah's leg? That one. She made sure he could walk and fight again."

Lorcan nodded, trying not to pull away as Laris worked. "How is Yaroah?"

"Officially retired from the arena," Nona answered. "He says he's too old for this. When you're on your feet, you need to let people see you. See that you're alive. There are rumors that you died."

Lorcan nodded, panting as another—or was it two?—*fibulae* were dropped into the bowl. How many were left? He'd lost count, and was afraid to ask.

"Who sent them?" he mumbled. "The twins. Manius said you'd find out."

"He said that?" Nona chuckled. "He has a lot of faith in me. I couldn't find anything. All I could find was that they were real gladiators, that they'd made a name for themselves in Thracia, and their *lanista* was talking about bringing them to Rome to try against you months ago. Everything agreed with what we'd heard. No one can say who paid them or when, so we don't know. But we're fairly certain it wasn't your cousin. Thracia is east by a good distance. We're also not sure if they killed their *lanista*, or if he killed himself. Or if someone else did it."

Lorcan nodded, moaning as another *fibula* was pulled from his skin. He squeezed his eyes closed and tried not to move.

"You're doing fine, Lorcan," Laris said. "We're almost done."

"*Comes*," Nona said. "Is there a reason that he's awake for this? I mean… why torture him?"

"He's had far too much Cretic wine," Laris answered. "And I don't want to dose him with anything else unless there's no choice. He's a gladiator. Pain isn't a new experience."

"You could have asked me," Lorcan growled through gritted teeth as another *fibula* was dropped into the bowl. "I could have told you how much *gafann* I could take. *Bilinuntiam*. Livia called it *bilinuntiam*."

Laris sniffed. "What does a gladiator know about *bilinuntiam*?"

"Livia didn't tell you?" Nona asked. He sounded horrified, but when Lorcan looked up at him, Nona winked and squeezed his hands. "You didn't know?"

"Know what?"

"We call Lorcan *Corax Princeps* when he's in the arena, but that's because it's true. He actually is a prince. In line for the throne of Hibernia. And he's a fully trained *medici*. He's been working with Livia since before he could even speak a full sentence in Latin."

"A fully…" Laris' voice trailed off. "No one told me!"

"Why does it matter?" Lorcan demanded. "Healer or slave? *Medici* or gladiator? If you treat them different, then you're no real healer. Now finish and leave."

"Do you want something for the pain?" Nona asked.

"Livia can give me something when she comes back." Lorcan closed his eyes and tightened his grip on Nona's hand. "I want this done."

The remaining *fibulae* were removed in silence, and Lorcan was sweating and shaking by the time Laris left.

"Lorcan?" Nona asked. "What do you need?"

"Livia. And a basin."

Chapter Three

The sun had barely risen the next morning when a servant announced the arrival of the heir. Gaius came in, carrying a basket. He looked surprised to see Lorcan out of bed, sitting near the window.

"Good morning," he said. "How are you feeling?" He brought the basket over and placed it on a table, taking out three cups. "Wine? And... you're alone? Where's Livia?"

"Still in pain, but not as much," Lorcan answered. "And yes to wine, please. Livia... I'm not certain. She excused herself almost the moment we were awake." He gestured toward another chair. "Sit. I wasn't expecting to see you quite so early."

Gaius smiled and looked around. "You don't have a servant or a slave in here, do you?"

"No. Why?"

"Because the fewer ears hear this, the better. But I trust you as I trust my own brother." Gaius looked out the window, then turned back to Lorcan. "I know we discussed it, but it's long past Saturnalia, and you haven't gone to Drucilla's bed. You're not going, are you?"

Lorcan nodded. "I gave it more thought, and I realized that I can't risk a child of mine the way... well, what the rumors say she's done before." He picked up the cup of wine and sipped it. "Why do I think you're not surprised?"

"I'm not," Gaius admitted. He sipped his own wine and nodded. "I think I've known since I asked you the question. So, I have another question for you. I think I know the answer to this one as well, but it was my father's idea and I promised I would ask." He set his cup down. "Stay. Stay in Rome. Let me adopt you."

Lorcan sputtered on his wine. "What?"

Gaius burst out laughing. "You heard me," he said. "Lorcan, I've been married to Drucilla longer than you've been alive. Our first child would have been about your age now. If you stayed, and allowed me to adopt you, someday you'd be Emperor—"

"You mean, someday I'd have a knife in my back because of the people who would object to a barbarian on the throne?" Lorcan asked. "I've been reading your history, Gaius. My people may be barbarians by your standards, but at least we're honest about it. And I do have a father. I need to go home." He drained his cup. "Was that truly your father's idea?"

"Yes," Gaius admitted. "And I told him you'd say no. And I have made my own plans accordingly." He picked up his cup, looked at it, then set it down again. "I'm up this early because I haven't yet been to bed. I've been away from the Palace making arrangements, and then…" He paused. "I'm divorcing Drucilla," he said, his voice quiet. "You made me see Antius' true face. You were talking about a knife in the back? That would be my fate if I kept Antius at my side. So, I need an heir. A true heir. A child of my own. And…" His voice trailed off, and he turned to look out at the garden. Lorcan leaned forward to set his cup down, and realized that there was a bruise where Gaius' neck met his shoulder.

No, not a bruise. A bite-mark.

Lorcan coughed. "You'll need to keep that covered," he murmured. When Gaius looked at him, he tapped his own throat. "She marked you. I assume she?"

Gaius looked startled. He reached up and touched the mark, then blushed. "I hadn't realized. That would have been a disaster. And… yes. Her name is Claudia Valeria. She's the widow of a Carthaginian general who was chosen for the Senate. He was a friend, and he died two years ago." He smiled slightly. "She has a son who is almost three. And…" His blush deepened.

"Gaius," Lorcan asked in a quiet voice. "Is she pregnant?" The luminous look on Gaius' face was answer enough, and Lorcan laughed. "Congratulations!"

"Juno has finally smiled on me. I just have to go carefully," Gaius said. "I cannot let Drucilla or her brother know about the baby. Not until Claudia is safely my wife. But my father knows. And Decus knows." He raised his cup to Lorcan. "And now you, Lorcan. If you won't let me call you son, at least may I call you brother?"

"That I will agree to, and gladly." Lorcan raised his own cup to Gaius. "I hope I get to meet her before I leave." He paused, then lowered his cup. "Thank you."

Gaius arched a brow. "For what?"

"Sending someone after Tavi. He's in Carthage, Nona said?"

Gaius nodded. "Ah. Yes. He's there for me, actually. I trusted him to be discreet in speaking to Claudia's father on my behalf. He's an excellent diplomat."

Lorcan shrugged and looked out the window. "If you say so. I'm realizing that I don't understand Roman diplomacy. Or Tavi."

"He's confused," Gaius said. "And... well, running because he doesn't know what to do. And honestly, Lorcan? I don't really understand why. He loves you. We all know it."

Lorcan sighed. "And yet you helped him run?"

"Not quite," Gaius replied. "I sent him to Carthage because I can bring him back from Carthage. Am bringing him back from Carthage. If he'd gone anywhere else, I might not be able to do that." He looked out the window. "He'll be back in Rome... tomorrow, I think. Perhaps the day after. Once he's back in Rome, then I'll do what I can to make him face his fear. And you."

Lorcan met his eyes, then blurted out the first thing that came to mind, "I'm going to miss you."

Gaius smiled. "I'll miss you, Lorcan. Perhaps one day I'll come and visit you. I'd like to meet your uncle the High King. Perhaps we can speak of alliance. He has a daughter?"

"Siobhan. She's my cousin Ronan's mate," Lorcan answered. "She's my age, so perhaps a little old for your new son?"

Gaius chuckled. "Perhaps. And yes, that's what I was thinking. Perhaps if they have a daughter, and she recognizes him as her husband." He nodded slowly. "I'll think on it. And perhaps I'll come and see Hibernia. I've never even been to Alba. I think the farthest I've been from Rome is Aquae Granni."

"I don't even know where that is," Lorcan admitted.

"North of here." Gaius looked thoughtful. "You might go that way, if you're going by road. There are *thermae* there... you like the baths here in Rome?"

Lorcan blinked. "I... I could wish for soap, but yes."

"Stop in Aquae Granni," Gaius said. "The hot springs in that area have made the *thermae* something to experience. I think Livia would appreciate it after being on the road for nearly a month, and it will give you a respite from travel before you have to get on a ship."

Lorcan grimaced, making Gaius laugh. The door opened, and Livia came inside, followed by a pair of slaves carrying trays. She stopped as Gaius stood up.

"Good morning, Livia Corvina," Gaius said. "I've been keeping Lorcan company."

"Thank you for that," Livia said. She turned to the slaves. "Leave the trays." Once the slaves had gone, she turned back to Gaius. "There are people looking for you, Gaius." She glanced over her shoulder. "Your wife is looking for you."

Gaius sighed. "Of course she is. She's been avoiding me for weeks, and now she wants me." He shook his head. "Livia, may I impose on you as a *medicae*?"

"Of course. I presume this is about the bruise on your neck?" She looked at the door again. "That you did absolutely nothing to hide in front of the slaves, who are going to gossip?"

Gaius winced. "If I'm going to see Drucilla, I need to hide it."

"Or you can flaunt it," Lorcan suggested. "I presume that she'll know soon that you're here. And that you've been here. The slaves will tell her that you're keeping me company. So let her think I bit you." Gaius and Livia both turned to stare at him, and he blinked. "What?"

"It might be better if she thought I did it," Livia said slowly. She went to the dressing table, opened the large bronze box in which she carried her medical tools and remedies, and came back with a small jar. "Sit, Gaius. If she thought it was me, there would be less... damage to Gaius' reputation. For you to mark him like that... no. No, you absolutely cannot hand that much of a weapon to anyone."

Lorcan frowned. "How is it a weapon if I bite? Or is it just a weapon if a man bites?"

"It's... complicated," Gaius murmured. "And it may be part of what Tavi is afraid of—"

"Oh!" Lorcan nodded. "Valerius explained that when I asked him why men can't marry men in Rome. That bending for another man damages your status, or something like that. I didn't understand."

"Perhaps this will make more sense," Gaius said. "If we do as you propose, and start a rumor that you're bending to me, because I absolutely cannot bend to you, then what do you think Tavi will say? Did you give any thought to how that would hurt him?"

Lorcan scowled and shifted, wincing as something pulled in his side. "I haven't," he admitted. "But that would make me the only one of the pair of us caring about how I might hurt my mate." He turned to stare out the window. "My uncle told me that he tried to deny his mate. All he ended up doing was torturing the both of them for months. Once the bond exists, the only way it can be severed is death. Wishing it away doesn't do anything but make everyone miserable." He looked up at Livia. "I'm sorry. You know I love you, too."

"I know. And I know you're hurt, and it makes you feel more vulnerable in all ways," Livia said. She put the jar down and came to him, resting her hand on his shoulder. "I do understand. His denying you—denying us—it's tearing you to pieces, and time is running out. And I can't do anything to heal that, or make it stop hurting. But I've never doubted you."

Gaius sighed and sat down across from Lorcan, putting one hand on Lorcan's knee. "I'm sorry. He'll be back in Rome in a day or two, and I'll try to make him hear you."

Lorcan smiled. "Thank you, Gaius. And… forget that suggestion. Now, let Livia see to that bruise."

Livia leaned down and kissed him, then picked the jar up and tugged out the cork. Gaius tipped his head back as she delicately dabbed salve on the bruise, then wrinkled his nose.

"Drucilla is going to be able to find me by scent," he muttered.

"What is in that salve?" Lorcan asked. "I can smell it from here. I smell… is that *an lus liath*?" He leaned forward in his chair and winced again.

"Lorcan?" Livia glanced at him. "What is it?"

"Just a twinge," Lorcan answered. "I moved wrong."

"I'll put some of this on you when I'm done." She went back to her work. "This is a blend I haven't shown you yet. Yes, there's *an lus liathe.* We call that one *stoechas*. The rest is *isop, itea, solidago, euphrosinum, hyssopus, arnoglosson,* and *acantha*. I'll have to think of their names in Gaeilge, but you know them all. We've used them, just not in this combination. It smells strong, but it will draw out the swelling and the redness," Livia answered. She stepped back, corking the jar.

"You're going to use that on Lorcan?" Gaius asked. "He'll need more of it, so I might be able to hide behind him if Drucilla gets my scent."

"Oh, absolutely not!" Lorcan said with a laugh. "I'm hiding behind you!"

"You can both hide behind me," Livia said as she put the jar back into her box. "Gaius, go change. If you drape your toga right, it will hide the bruise until the swelling goes down. And once the swelling goes down a little, you can tell anyone rude enough to ask that you were bitten by an insect. Whoever did this didn't break the skin."

"I hope I can make it to my rooms without being seen." Gaius stood up, then turned to the window as Corvina flew in. Lorcan sat up at the shrill, alarm calls she was making, then looked at the door.

"Gaius, go out through the garden. I think we're being warned."

Gaius blinked. "Thank you, Corvina!" he whispered, then rushed out the garden, with Corvina taking off and following him. As soon as Gaius was out of sight, Lorcan reached out, grabbed Livia's wrist, and tugged her into his lap.

"Lorcan!" Livia gasped. "Your side!"

"I'm fine," he assured her. Then he wrapped his arms around her and kissed her. She melted against him, running her hands up his chest. He could feel the warmth of her hands through the fabric of his tunic. She shifted in his lap, pressing closer, and he felt her fingers in his hair. She tugged, hard enough to make him shudder, and he felt her laughter against his lips…

And the door opened. Lorcan forced himself to turn, knowing what he was going to see. Drucilla, framed in the doorway. To his surprise, she wasn't wearing her usual heavy cosmetics or elaborate clothing. Her hair was pulled into a simple tail, and her gown was simple and unadorned. When she saw them, her face turned bright red.

"I…"

"Is there some reason you're barging into my rooms like this?" Lorcan asked softly.

"I…" Drucilla shook her head and visibly gathered the shreds of her composure. "I'm sorry, but… my husband… the slaves said he was here?"

"He was here." Lorcan shifted his armful of wife, glancing up at Livia. She had her lips pressed together hard enough that they were near invisible, and he could feel her straining to keep laughter at bay. He looked away before he started laughing with her. "He came to see how I was faring, and then he left."

Drucilla looked around, as if she expected Gaius to just appear because she wished it so. For a moment, she looked lost and alone, and Lorcan wondered why. Then the mask slipped back into place. This time, though, Lorcan could see the cracks in it.

"Where did he go?" Drucilla asked after looking around once more.

Lorcan shook his head. "I don't know. I haven't even left these rooms in days. I barely know where I am, let alone where he's gone. And speaking of rooms, you barged into mine without leave. Apology not accepted. You can go."

Drucilla sputtered, then snapped, "You're ordering me around?"

"Does he have to?" The voice came from behind Drucilla, and the Emperor stepped into the doorway. "Or do I have to?"

Drucilla turned, fast enough that she nearly fell. "Father—"

"Is something wrong with your hearing, Drucilla?" Lucanus asked. He came into the room and gestured to the doorway. "Prince Albus told you to leave."

Drucilla swallowed, then bowed. "Yes, Father." She hurried out, and Lucanus lingered by the doorway for a long moment.

"How long were you there?" Livia asked. "How much did you hear?"

"Most of it, I think," Lucanus answered. "So... my son is where?"

Lorcan nodded toward the window. "He went that way. If he's not still out there, I'm not certain."

Lucanus chuckled. "I'll see him eventually. And I can see that Drucilla interrupted something, so I won't stay. You're feeling better, I see."

Lorcan laughed and looked up at Livia, who blushed. "Yes, I think so. Please, come and sit. And... was it truly your idea for Gaius to adopt me?"

"What?" Livia gasped. "He what?"

"He asked me just before you came back," Lorcan told her. "And I said no."

"He told me that he thought that would be your answer," Lucanus admitted as he sat down. "I regret it, but I do understand."

"I am honored that you both want that," Lorcan said. "I truly am. But I can't stay here. My family needs me. I need to go home. But I will miss you." He smiled slightly. "I never knew my grandfather. He died long before I was born. But I imagine that he'd have been a lot like you."

Lucanus laughed. "Your grandfather was the beloved of a goddess. He must have been an extraordinary man indeed."

Lorcan nodded. "That's what I said. He'd have been like you."

Lucanus blinked. Then he smiled and stood up, coming to put one hand on Lorcan's shoulder, and the other on Livia's. "My children," he said, his voice shaking slightly. "I regret that I must lose you both, and so soon after I found you. I know that once you leave Rome, we will not see each other again. You are immortal, and will grant Livia your immortality, correct?" He waited for Lorcan to nod before continuing. "I, unfortunately, am not immortal."

"Yet," Lorcan said. "I was told that you'll become a god. So, you're not immortal yet."

Lucanus laughed. "Not yet," he agreed. "But since I have never been visited by my immortal ancestors, I'm not certain I can say that I will be able to visit with you in Hibernia when it's my turn. So, when you leave, it will be our final goodbye." He squeezed Lorcan's shoulder, then rose, laughing softly. "I'm being… terribly morbid, aren't I? I shouldn't be talking of death. Not today. Will you remain in the Palace until you leave for home?"

"No," Lorcan answered. "I want to go back to the *ludus*. It's more…" He glanced at the door. "Private."

Lucanus snorted. "Then I'll see myself out. And I'll post a sentry at your door to make certain that you have no further unwanted guests." He paused, then looked at the window. "Are you going to go through the gardens, or would you like an escort?"

Lorcan looked over his shoulder to see Gaius step back into view. Corvina sat on his shoulder, and launched herself in the air. She landed on the back of the chair that Lucanus had just vacated, and croaked at him.

"Oh?" Lucanus held his arm out, and Corvina took off again, landing on his upper arm and sidling to sit on his shoulder. Lucanus chuckled and reached up to ruffle the feathers at her breast with one finger, and Lorcan watched in surprise as the raven rubbed her heavy bill against the Emperor's cheek.

"What a lovely surprise," Lucanus murmured. "I am honored, Lady Corvina." He sighed. "Now, I don't expect that you'd be willing to stay?" Corvina launched herself off Lucanus' shoulder, and landed in Livia's lap.

"There's your answer, Father," Gaius said. "I'll walk with you. And we'll talk. In private."

Lucanus nodded. "The plans are laid?"

"Yes."

"Then let us walk, my son." Lucanus turned to the door. Gaius followed him, pausing only long enough to squeeze Lorcan's shoulder before leaving. The door closed behind them, and Lorcan tipped his head back and sighed.

"How healed do I have to be before we can leave?" he asked the ceiling.

"Let me take a closer look at the scar, and we'll see."

Lorcan raised his head and met his mate's eyes. "Just the scar?"

She smiled, starting to run her fingers through his hair. He closed his eyes in pleasure as she preened him, until she closed her fist and pulled. He shuddered, trying to pull away, and she let him go.

"What is it?" she asked, sounding alarmed. "Did I hurt you?"

Lorcan sighed. "You didn't. But he did. In the arena. He held me in place by my hair and he was going to kill me. If it hadn't been for Titus—"

Livia smoothed one hand down the front of his tunic. "I'm sorry. I didn't know. I didn't see all of the fight."

Lorcan stared at her for a moment, pulling her closer, resting his hand on her thigh. "You didn't... but you always watch me fight. Is that why you were so surprised when I came off the sands?"

Livia nodded. "This was the only time I ever looked away. I took my eyes off you, and I almost lost you."

"It was not your fault," Lorcan said, rubbing his hand up and down her thigh. "I shouldn't have been out there. I should have listened to you and the others and not gone on the sands. But I was a proud idiot, and I paid the price." He sighed, then ran his hand up Livia's side. "Now, you were going to examine me?"

Livia chuckled, then caught her breath as Lorcan slid his hand further up and cupped her breast. He rubbed his thumb over her nipple, watching the flush bloom in her skin and stain her cheeks. She bit her lip, and Lorcan shivered as the heat that Drucilla's interruption had quenched rose once more.

"Bed?" he murmured.

Livia hummed softly and stood up, but only long enough to pull her gown up so that she could straddle Lorcan's legs. He laughed, running his hands up her bare thighs as she tugged the hem of his tunic up to his waist. She pressed against him, trapping his cock between their bodies as she kissed him. He closed his eyes and ran his hands up her thighs, cupping her arse, pulling her tighter against him as she started to grind her hips into him, the curve of her belly warm and solid against him. She pushed back, and tugged the folds of her gown aside to reach between them; Lorcan moaned as she ran her fingers down his length.

"Bed," she whispered. "Now."

"I can't carry you," Lorcan whispered back. "You need to move."

They stumbled to the bed together, and Livia pushed Lorcan onto his back, his tunic pushed up to his armpits. She straddled his legs, then leaned down and kissed the still-livid scar.

"You're not allowed to move," she ordered as she moved up his body. Her gown hid her body from view, but he felt the heat radiating from her, and he could smell her arousal. He reached underneath her gown and ran his hands up her legs as she rose up on her knees, then lowered herself onto his cock. Lorcan shivered all over, trying to fight the desperate need to dig his heels into the bed and thrust into her, to roll over and pin her beneath him and thrust until they were both screaming. She rested her hands on his chest and started to move, and he twisted his hands into her gown and closed his eyes, straining, feeling her heat building, feeling the pressure and the need growing as they soared together, as they crested and fell, crashing together on the bed in a tangle of arms and legs and clothing and hair. Livia rested her forehead on his shoulder and sighed happily, and he tightened his arms around her, ignoring the pain in his side from her weight on him.

"I think we're ready to go home," she murmured. "I think you can finish recovering there."

Lorcan nodded. "When we get back to the *ludus*, I want you to do something for me."

"What?"

"Cut my hair."

Chapter Four

Lorcan lowered his *siccae* and wiped sweat off his face. This had been the first time in the 10 days since they'd come back to the *ludus* that he'd felt strong enough to practice, and even though he was winded, he thought he'd done passably well.

"Not bad." Manius confirmed his assessment. "You're a little slower, and a little stiff, but that's understandable. You'll gain it back, and probably faster than you did the last time. Enough for today. Go soak or you won't be able to move." He sheathed his own blades and glanced to the side, then looked again and smiled. "Livia."

Lorcan turned, going to meet his mate as she came out onto the sands. "Good morning," he said, kissing her cheek. "I didn't wake you when I got up, did I?"

She shook her head. "No. How was practice?"

"Good." Lorcan dug his blades into the sand and twisted at the waist. "Nothing hurts or pulls. I'm just stiff from not moving." He looked at her as he tugged his blades free and started toward the armory. "And you're dressed to go out."

"Which is why I came to find you," Livia said, falling in next to him. "Once you're bathed, I was hoping you'd come to the temple with me."

"It's been some time since we went last," Lorcan said. "We should go. You should do whatever you need to do for your gods before we leave."

"Which will be soon, I warrant?" Manius asked. "You're healed enough, I think."

Lorcan put his weapons in the rack and turned to face his mentor. "I think it will be soon, yes."

"We can start laying those plans tonight." Manius walked away.

Lorcan held his hand out to Livia, and pitched his voice low to ask, "Any word yet?"

"Nothing yet," she answered. "Gaius promised, Lorcan. He'll keep his word."

"I know he promised, but we're running out of time. Most of the plans your father mentioned are complete, and they're just waiting for the final word to set in motion. We'll be on the road out of Rome soon. If Gaius doesn't convince Tavi in the next day or two, it'll be too late." Lorcan sighed and ran his hand over the short, soft fuzz of his hair. Livia had shorn him near-bald, and the feeling was something he was still getting used to. He wasn't sure if he liked having his hair so short, but he wasn't going to let it grow out until this was over.

"Let me go get cleaned up. I'll meet you in the garden."

* * *

The walk from the *ludus* to the Temple of Apollo was so familiar to Lorcan that he walked three steps alone before he realized that Livia had turned to go down a different street. He caught up with her and looked around.

"Where are we going?" he asked. "We're not going to Apollo's Temple?"

"Not today," Livia answered. "Today, we're going to Diana's Temple."

Lorcan thought about his lessons with the Flamen Dialis. "Diana is… Apollo's sister. Goddess of the moon, and the hunt and… I'm missing something. Why are we going there?"

"Goddess of the moon, the hunt, and childbirth." Livia didn't turn to look at him, but her cheeks flushed as she spoke.

"Childbirth?" Lorcan repeated. Realization hit like a blow, and he staggered to a stop, turning Livia to face him. "Childbirth?"

She bit her lip and nodded. "I… yes. Yes, I'm certain. I'm pregnant."

Lorcan stared at her, letting the words settle into his skin, into his bones, into his very core. They burned through him, and he had to laugh as the heat transformed him into something new. A person he had never expected to be.

A *father*.

He whooped with joy and picked Livia up in an embrace that took her off her feet and left her breathless and laughing. Then he kissed her, and the tears on her cheeks left his own face damp.

"And I thought you wouldn't be happy!" she gasped when he let her go.

"Not… how could I not be happy?" Lorcan asked. He took her hand. "Where are we going?"

They started walking again, and Livia leaned into his arm. "That temple. The little one."

Lorcan looked where she was pointing and coughed. "That's a little one?"

"You've seen the Temple of Jupiter."

"True." Lorcan nodded. "So, we'll make the sacrifices here for your gods, and when we get to Eire, we'll speak to my grandmother's sister."

Livia chuckled. "And that would be… who? I forget."

"Brigid. The healer, the smith and the poet. She's well-loved in my family."

"And well represented? You have several of each."

Lorcan nodded. "Two healers. Three, with you. Two smiths. A harper, a poet and an *ollamh.*" He paused. "Three smiths. But Cormac…"

"Isn't family anymore."

"No, he isn't." Lorcan sighed. "Livia, I don't want to kill him. I've killed enough people, and I'm tired of it. But I have to kill him, or this will never end. And now… I have you to think of. And a fledgling of our own on the way. I have to end this." He took a deep breath, raised her hand to his lips, and kissed her knuckles. "I wish he hadn't set us on this path, but if he hadn't, I'd never have found you. So, I should thank him."

Livia grinned, her look one of pure mischief. "Right before you kill him?"

Lorcan chuckled. "Yes. It will make him even more angry. He tried to kill me, and instead gave me everything I ever wanted."

Diana's Temple wasn't what Lorcan was expecting. He'd seen sacrifices at the Temple of Jupiter, and at Apollo's Temple. He was expecting either some sort of animal sacrifice, or at the least a sacrifice of cakes and incense. But at Diana's Temple, he found himself making an offering in coin and receiving in return a pair of terracotta figures. Each was a rough semblance of a swaddled infant, and would fit into his palm. Lorcan cradled his in one hand and used the folds of his toga to cover his head, remembering Gaius' instruction from their triumph—*we go before the gods with our heads covered.*

The priest also wasn't what Lorcan was expecting. He'd never seen a Roman priest bearing arms, but Diana's priest wore a sword was easy familiarity, and the leather belt and scabbard looked well-worn. He had a pleasant voice, but his Latin was colored by a thick accent, and Lorcan's guts twisted when he realized within a few words that he wasn't going to be able to follow. And a few words after that, his Latin abandoned him completely—he glanced at Livia in panic, and she smiled softly.

"Just follow what I do," she whispered.

Lorcan nodded and watched her, letting her cue him to what he needed to do and when. The priest lit lamps, burned incense, said things that Lorcan couldn't have remembered if he'd tried, then took the little figures from them and passed them through the fragrant smoke before laying them in a basket. He spoke more words, then gestured for them to follow him out of the Temple. In the courtyard, he uncovered his head, so Lorcan did the same. The priest studied Lorcan for a moment and laughed. Then he spoke.

In Gaeilge.

"If I thought you'd be in Rome in a year, I'd tell you to bring the babe to be blessed. But you'll be going home soon, won't you, Morrigan's son?"

Lorcan stared at him for a moment. "You're from Eire?" he gasped. Then he looked at Livia. "Is that what I sound like when I speak Latin?"

The priest laughed. "I learned Latin in Sarmatia, which is north and east of here. I speak it the way they do there." He glanced at Livia. "Does he know about Diana's priests?"

"I didn't tell him," Livia answered. "The Flamen Dialis might have."

"No, I know nothing about Diana's priests," Lorcan said.

The priest nodded. "Those who serve Diana do so by right of arms." He rested his hand on the hilt of his sword. "Diana's priest is always an escaped slave. And we always take our place by killing the priest who served before us. Eventually, someone will kill me."

Lorcan blinked. "And they call us barbarians," he muttered, and the priest laughed.

"I think to these Romans, barbarian just means 'anyone who isn't us,'" he said. "I've lived as Diana's priest in this shrine for seven years now. I think it's seven. I've killed five men to keep my place. I think Diana favors me." He looked up and smiled. "I've told her the stories that I learned as a child of Brigid of the Three Faces, and I think they would like each other very much." He laughed again and shook his head. "Now, I wish you the best of luck, and all of the favors Diana can offer. Go well, Morrigan's son."

"Why did you never go home?" Lorcan asked. "And what's your name?"

"I was born Bressal," the priest answered. "I renounced that name when I was sold into slavery by my own kin. My owners called me Tiro—"

"You were a gladiator?" Lorcan asked.

"I was just the newest slave," Tiro answered with a shrug. "Why did I never go home? Because Diana took me in and made me hers. I have a place here that I never had in Eire." He smiled again. "This is my home. I wish you well, Morrigan's son."

"Lorcan." Lorcan offered his hand, and Tiro clasped it tightly.

"I wish you well, Lorcan," Tiro said again. "When you next see to your grandmother, tell her that Diana's priest sends his regards. I haven't seen her for some time."

Lorcan blinked. "You've seen my grandmother?"

Tiro laughed and pointed. "I see her now. There, behind you."

Lorcan turned and saw a familiar raven sitting on top of the wall. "Corvina? She's mine. We found her injured, and took care of her. She stayed with me. I…" He looked back at Tiro. "She's not my grandmother. She is my friend."

Tiro shrugged. "Are you sure they're not the same? Regardless, she's been here before, and I've told her the stories of Diana. And I think they'd like each other as well."

Lorcan chuckled. "From what I've read, I agree with you. And when I do see her, I'll tell her. Thank you, Tiro."

* * *

Lorcan barely remembered a step of the walk back to the *ludus*. Just outside the door, he stopped. "Livia, does your father know?"

"Not yet," she answered. "I wanted to tell you first. He may have guessed, though. I've been… well, you've seen me."

Lorcan frowned. "Oh, is that why the sight of blood has been making you ill?"

Livia made a face. "I'm a *medicae*. It's frustrating not to be able to take care of my patients. I would never have hurt you the way Laris did—"

"I didn't tell you about that."

"Nona did. I was so angry… I think most of the Palace heard me when I cornered Laris."

"I didn't!" Lorcan laughed. "I'd have liked to hear it. My fierce little Livia. Let's go tell Manius." He led Livia into the *ludus*, and stopped just inside. Nona, Ennius and Yaroah were all standing in the atrium, and they all straightened as Lorcan closed the door.

"What is it?" Lorcan asked. "Why aren't you with the students?"

"Manius called a break while he is busy," Yaroah answered. "And you both have visitors. Manius has them in your workroom." He paused, and Lorcan realized that the big man was trying not to laugh.

"Yaroah?"

"Manius told us not to say anything, and to send you on in," Nona said quickly. "So go on."

Livia took Lorcan's arm. "This is not like Father at all. Let's go see." She tugged him out of the atrium, and behind them, Lorcan heard the other *doctores* start laughing. He looked at Livia, who shook her head and kept walking.

The door to the workroom was closed, which was another surprise. Lorcan went first, tapping on the door before opening it, then walking inside.

"Manius?" he said. Then he stopped.

Tavi.

Disheveled, dressed only in a tunic, and clearly furious, Tavi was sitting on one of the stools, flanked on either side by his father and his uncle. Manius stood nearby, his mouth covered by one hand. He, too, looked as if he was trying not to laugh.

"What..." Lorcan sputtered. "What is this?" Decus and Gaius looked at each other, and for a moment, Lorcan was reminded of his younger cousins, Cullen and Regis. The twins always looked at each other just that way before they started trying to talk their way out of being in trouble. "Morrigan's tailfeathers, what did you do?" he demanded.

Tavi growled softly, then snapped, "Tell them to untie me!"

"What?" Livia gasped.

"We... well, we kidnapped him," Gaius said.

"It was his idea," Decus added, pointing at Gaius. "But I helped, because he's right."

"I promised I'd get him here. And I've been trying to convince him ever since he got back to Rome. He wasn't going to listen to me, so..." Gaius sighed and spread his hands. "He's here now. And now he's going to listen. And if he doesn't listen, Manius is going to lock the three of you in a cell until he does listen!"

"There's nothing to say!" Tavi blurted. "They're married!"

"So?" Livia demanded. "You know how we feel about you!"

Tavi snorted. "And which of us gets to be immortal?" he asked.

"All of us, or none of us," Lorcan answered, his voice soft. Tavi stared at him, clearly shocked. "Tavi, if that's the choice I have to make to have both of you by my side, then I will give up my own immortality and live as a man for the rest of my days. Because that's how much I love you. I'm not choosing one of you over the other. I told you that in your rooms, the day I was freed." He paused. "You told me that you met my uncle Petran. He tried to deny his mate. All he did was make himself and Turlach miserable. For months. The bond is there, Tavi. You know it as well as we do. You probably knew it before I did, because you bonded with Livia before I ever knew you existed, long before I ever was brought to Rome! We're all a part of each other and right now, the only thing keeping all of us miserable is you being stubborn and selfish."

Tavi looked at him, then looked away and whispered, "You left out scared."

"Scared?" Lorcan blinked. "I... we scare you? Why?"

"Because I can't lose you," Tavi answered. "I... I can't. I *can't*! And every time..." He glanced up at his father, then stopped talking and hunched over, a defensive gesture that made Lorcan's blood boil.

"Tavi?" Decus asked. "What is it?"

"Do you remember Gisla?" Tavi asked, not raising his head. "Or Catia? Or Illica? Or any of the other girls in whom I showed even a hint of interest? Or the boys? Didimus? Or Wulf?"

Decus frowned. "I—"

"How about the weapons?" This time, Tavi did look up. "Or the horses? You gifted me with weapons and horses every year. Did you ever see them again? Never mind that I didn't really know how to fight until a few months ago. Did you ever see them?"

Decus looked at Gaius. "I... don't remember."

Tavi snorted. "Of course you don't. You never saw them again. Not in my hands, anyway. Because I never had them for more than a day. You never once noticed that any time I had something worth taking, Antius took it. It didn't matter if it was weapons, horses, or lovers. Once he noticed I had something or someone worth having, I never saw them again. Antonina was just as bad about the boys. The both of them said the same thing—I didn't get to have anything good. I didn't deserve it. And Galius..." He swallowed and

35

looked down. "I... when I tried to go to you, you never listened. You never believed me. You barely saw me. Not until I was useful to you."

Decus went white. "I... I did that?" He looked at Gaius. "I did that?"

Gaius shrugged. "How am I supposed to answer that, Decus? You went from Numidia to Britannia, and I didn't even know you'd remarried and had another son until you brought all of the children to Rome. Tavi was... 10?" He waited for Tavi to nod before shaking his head. "Don't look at me for advice. I can't tell you how to raise your children. I don't have the experience. But I do know that Tavi wouldn't lie to you. If he says it, it's so." He glanced at Lorcan. "And I think we're done here. The gates are open. They'll talk now. Let's leave them to talk." He reached across and grabbed Decus' arm, dragging him toward the door. Manius followed them.

"Wait!" Tavi called. "I... someone untie me!"

The door thumped closed, and Livia went and barred it, then turned back to face them. "Why?"

Tavi blinked. "What?"

"She has a point," Lorcan said. He crossed to stand in front of Tavi, close enough that his toga brushed against Tavi's bare knees. "You seem to be listening far better now than you were the last time we tried to have this discussion. Which, if you'd told me this months ago..."

"I wouldn't have wasted so much time," Tavi murmured. "The thought had occurred. I'm not proud of it. I'm not proud of being a coward." He looked up. "You told me you loved me. That you wouldn't leave me. You said you couldn't. But..."

"They all told you the same thing, didn't they?" Livia asked. "And... and I started it, didn't I? When I told you I wasn't going with you to Britannia?"

Tavi smiled slightly. "No, you were honest about it. I asked you to come with me and you explained why you couldn't go, and you promised me you'd be here when I came back. You didn't betray me. I didn't find you in my brother's bed. Or in my bed with my brother."

"Your brother has that little respect for you?"

Tavi looked at him. "You have no idea. Galius..." He paused, then shuddered. Livia sighed.

"You're better off with us."

"I am. And I'm sorry. I shouldn't have run. I should have told you. I was so afraid I'd lose this that I almost ruined it myself." Tavi shifted in place. "Will one of you untie me?"

"And again, why?" Livia asked. She came around behind the stool and pressed against Tavi's back, running her hands down his chest. "I think this has potential. Don't you, Lorcan?"

Lorcan stepped back. He smiled, watching as a tent started to grow in the front of Tavi's tunic. He let his toga slip from his shoulder to puddle around his feet. "Oh, yes. I seem to remember something being discussed about being bent over a bench?" He looked around. "No bench in here. How about a table?"

Tavi moaned softly, and Lorcan looked back at him and smiled, watching as Livia scraped her nails up his chest and over his nipples. Tavi tossed his head back against her shoulder and whimpered, then moaned as Lorcan pressed against his front, leaning down and kissing him, tasting his lips for the first time in months. He could feel Tavi shaking, straining against his bonds, and he knew that neither of them would last very long.

"We should thank your uncle," Livia murmured. "For delivering you so nicely wrapped." She ran her hand up Tavi's neck, then caught him under the chin and held his head in place. "Lorcan? You've never had a pair before, have you?"

"No."

"Do you mind if I take command?"

At the question, Tavi whined, a sound Lorcan felt in his bones. He shuddered, and croaked, "Please."

Livia laughed. "Then kneel, and give Tavi what he wants," she said. "And Tavi?" She pulled his head back a little further. "Don't move."

Chapter Five

Lorcan licked his lips and slowly lowered himself to his knees. He ran his hands up Tavi's legs, pushing his tunic up and freeing his cock. Gently, he started massaging Tavi's legs, digging his thumbs into the muscles, brushing closer to Tavi's cock and balls but not touching them. Tavi whimpered, but didn't move, and Lorcan stole a glance up to see that Livia still had his head pulled back. He could see the cords in Tavi's throat standing out, watched as he swallowed. Then he moaned again, and Lorcan shivered. He wanted—*needed*—to hear that sound again. He lowered his head once more, breathing in Tavi's scent as he exhaled softly on the head of Tavi's cock. He heard the soft gasp overhead, one that turned into a sharp whine as he licked Tavi's length from root to tip. Then he hesitated as a sudden wave of grief washed over him. For a moment, he was confused. Then he realized what it was—the last time he'd pleasured a man like this, it had been Bran, on their last day together. The day that Bran had been murdered.

"Lorcan?"

He looked up to see Livia looking at him, her brow furrowed. She hadn't released Tavi's chin, and his head was still tipped back. He shivered, then whispered, "What's wrong?"

"Nothing," Lorcan answered. "I'll explain later." He closed his eyes and wrapped his arms around Tavi, holding him tight for a moment, his ear pressed against Tavi's chest so he could hear his heartbeat. Then he slid his hands back over Tavi's ribs, down his body, resting them on his thighs as he moved back into position. He licked Tavi's length again, then slowly swirled his tongue around the head of his cock, hearing a tortured whine from overhead as Tavi struggled not to move. Fighting his own desire to swallow Tavi completely, Lorcan closed his eyes and lowered his head with tantalizingly deliberate movements that left Tavi straining against Livia's orders. He was moaning, whimpering, making guttural sounds that might have been words in some other language. Lorcan didn't know. It didn't matter. What mattered was here and now, and turning his mate inside-out with pleasure. He swallowed again, and his nose brushed against Tavi's belly. He could hear Tavi panting now, feel the tension in him, and slid one hand between Tavi's legs, cupping his balls. At the touch, Tavi seemed to forget every order Livia had given him—he thrust forward into Lorcan's mouth, and howled and shot as Lorcan pushed him back down into the stool.

Lorcan swallowed and swallowed again, hearing Tavi groan and whimper and wheeze above him. Then he slowly sat back on his heels, hearing his jaw pop as opened and closed his mouth. He licked his lips, and tasted Tavi.

"I'm out of practice, I think," he said, trying not to think of the reason why. Trying not to think of Bran.

"That's out of practice?" Tavi wheezed.

"If you can put that many words together in a sentence? Yes." Lorcan shoved aside memories and forced himself back to the now. He got to his feet and pulled Tavi up off the stool, wrapping his arms around him again, his cheek pressed against Tavi's shoulder. When he let go, Tavi staggered. Lorcan caught him and steadied him, then looked at Livia, nodding toward the table. She smiled, and walked around to the far side. Lorcan looked up at Tavi, who blinked owlishly.

"Do I get untied now?" he asked.

"Oh, I'm not done with you," Lorcan said. He took Tavi's arm and steered him toward the table; Tavi's arm tensed.

"You were *serious* about putting me over the table?" he whispered.

"If you're going to make an argument that it'll damage your status, then I have two questions for you." Lorcan waited until Tavi looked at him. "How is a mortal's grandson of higher status than the grandson of a goddess?"

Tavi licked his lips. "And the other question?"

"Why do you care what they think?" Lorcan waved his free arm toward the window. "You're coming with us to Eire. Rome's rules don't matter. What they think doesn't matter. The only people who matter are in this room. How we love each other is our business and our business only." He moved his hand from Tavi's arm to his back, between his shoulder blades. "Do you want this?"

Tavi closed his eyes and nodded, then stepped closer to the table. He frowned. "I think I'm too tall for the table."

39

"The bed, then," Livia said. "On your knees next to the bed." She picked up a jar and walked to the bedroom door, and Lorcan steadied Tavi as they followed her. Tavi sank to his knees next to the bed, then grinned as he looked up.

"Livia, this seems familiar."

"It should." Livia laughed and ran her fingers through Tavi's curls, then sat down facing him. "This is how you said goodbye to me."

"Is it?" Lorcan asked. He sat down next to Livia and put his arm around her. "Then perhaps you should say you're sorry the same way?"

"I'm sorry, I love you, and I'm coming with you?" Tavi grinned. "That's a lot to say."

"It's not how much you say, Tavi. It's how you say it," Livia said. She drew the hem of her gown up and spread her legs, and Lorcan laughed.

"Oh, is that how you're apologizing?" he asked. "And it's my turn to watch?"

"If you only watch, I'll be very disappointed." Livia chuckled and leaned into Lorcan's side as he put his arm around her. He took her chin in his other hand, turning her head and kissing her, running his fingers down her throat and underneath the folds of her gown. Through half-lidded eyes, he watched as Tavi kissed his way up the inside of Livia's thigh, then leaned in closer. Livia gasped, and reached down with one hand to run her fingers through Tavi's hair. Lorcan shifted, moving so that he was sitting behind Livia, his arms around her.

"You like this?" he whispered in Livia's ear. "Having your men play with you?"

She whimpered and tipped her head back against him, moaning as he cupped her breasts in his hands and started stroking her nipples. Her breathing was coming faster, and Lorcan bit down on a laugh—clearly, Tavi wasn't only good with languages. Livia turned her head toward him, and he kissed her again, holding her tightly as Tavi worked his magic and made her scream until her body went limp in Lorcan's arms. She whimpered as he let her go, and Tavi straightened, grinning.

"I haven't forgotten how to speak Livia," he murmured in a husky voice.

"My turn now?" Lorcan asked.

Livia laughed and stretched out on her side as her breathing slowed. She waved one hand languidly and Lorcan ran one hand down her side as he shifted off the bed and onto his knees. He moved behind Tavi, pressing him into the side of the bed and gathering up the hem of his tunic. He pushed the fabric into Tavi's bound hands, then ran his hands over Tavi's arse. Tavi tensed and shivered.

"Oil in the jar," Livia murmured. She propped her head up on her elbow, smiling. Lorcan picked up the jar and tugged the cork out, pouring some of the contents into his hand. A thought occurred, and he set the jar down.

"Tavi, have you ever done this before? Had someone take your arse?" he asked. "And how are your hands?"

"I... I'm fine." Tavi's voice was muffled by the bedclothes. "And... I want this. I want you."

"I'll be careful." Lorcan trailed his fingers down the cleft of Tavi's arse. "Spread your legs."

Tavi shifted, spreading his knees as wide as he could, and Lorcan rested his free hand on Tavi's bound wrists, pressing against him with oil-slicked fingers until Tavi gasped and tensed.

"Easy," Lorcan crooned, twisting his fingers in Tavi's tight heat. Too tight, and... was that *scarring*? He forced himself to slow down, to go even more carefully, and realized that Tavi hadn't answered his question. The scars were answer enough. "Easy. If you can't take this, you can't take me. And I don't want to hurt you." He crooked his fingers gently, and Tavi whimpered, pushing his hips back against Lorcan's hand.

"He likes it," Livia murmured, running her fingers through Tavi's hair. "Easy, Tavi. He won't hurt you."

"I noticed him liking this." Lorcan slid his fingers out just far enough to add more oil, then began to pump, pressing down on Tavi's wrists. Tavi strained against him, gasping and moaning, forcing his knees even further apart as he tried to open himself even more.

"Oh, you're ready, aren't you?" Lorcan leaned over Tavi's back and kissed him between the shoulder blades, then slowly pulled his fingers free. Livia handed him a rag, and he wiped his hands before he picked the jar up again. He poured more oil into his hand and smoothed it over his cock, biting his lip to try and rein in his reactions to just his own touch. He set the jar down and shifted to kneel between Tavi's legs, putting his hand back on Tavi's wrists. With his other hand, he positioned himself against Tavi's arse. He could feel Tavi shivering, and wondered which of them would shoot first. Wondered if the shivering was lust... or fear?

Only one way to know. He pressed. Gently, slowly, feeling the resistance as Tavi's body tensed. "Easy. Relax. I won't hurt you." He ran his hand down Tavi's side, over his hip and down his thigh, long strokes as if he was brushing a horse. "Easy."

Tavi sighed, and his body slowly relaxed, only to tense again as Lorcan pressed into him; he gasped, then whimpered and pulled away, tugging against the ropes binding his wrists. Lorcan fought the desperate, animal instinct to keep going, to pound Tavi's arse until they were both screaming; he stopped moving, and Tavi whimpered again and pushed back against Lorcan.

"Tavi?"

"…more." Tavi's voice was soft, muffled in the bedclothes, and he had to turn his head and repeat himself. "More. Please."

Lorcan leaned over Tavi's back and kissed his open palm, then started moving again. He started slowly, watching Tavi closely for any signs of distress or pain. Livia ran her hand through Tavi's hair and stroked his cheek.

"He likes it, Lorcan," she murmured. "I'll tell you if you need to stop." She smiled. "Easy. Relax."

Lorcan chuckled to hear his own words repeated back to him. He rested one hand on Tavi's hands, gripped his hip with the other, and let himself fall into the sensation. Tavi's body didn't just feel good against him, around him, it felt *right*. The little grunts and gasps and moans harmonized with his own perfectly and in ways that he'd only found with Livia. A random thought—what would the three of them sound like together? He couldn't wait to find out. Then Tavi pushed back against him once more, and Lorcan stopped thinking. There was no thought anymore. There was only Tavi, moving with him. Moaning for him. Screaming for him, with him, until they collapsed into a limp pile that slid from the bed onto the floor, where they lay panting and cooling.

Lorcan blinked, trying to focus his eyes, and found Livia looking down at him from the bed.

"I think I'm jealous," she said. "You never fell off the bed for me."

"You've always been entirely on the bed," Lorcan croaked. "When we were on the bed. And you're usually on top." He rolled toward Tavi, who had curled up on his side. "Are you awake?" he asked, running his hand up Tavi's thigh, wondering how to ask about the scars. He'd talk to Livia, he decided. He ran his hand back down Tavi's thigh, and he shivered. "Awake?"

"No," Tavi answered. "I've been pleasured by the gods, and I'm dead." He looked over his shoulder and grinned. "I thought the Elysian Fields would be greener. Less… indoors."

Livia laughed and reached down to poke Tavi in the ribs, making him yelp. "We've been pleasured by a *semideus*. I don't think that counts."

"Considering I have no idea what you're talking about, I'm fairly certain it doesn't," Lorcan added. He reached over and pulled Tavi into his arms. "And you're not allowed to be dead. No dying. Understand?"

"No dying? I can agree to that," Tavi said with a nod. He looked over his shoulder again. "Do I get untied now? I need to tell my father I'm going to Hibernia with you."

"I'm fairly certain that he already knows."

* * *

The garden was empty, as was the atrium. They walked side by side through the quiet halls, looking into empty rooms.

"Where are they?" Livia murmured.

"They wouldn't have left," Tavi answered.

"Would it be a bad thing if they did?" Lorcan took Tavi's hand. "Are you ready to tell them?"

Tavi chuckled. "They knew I was going with you before I knew. This isn't going to be a surprise to anyone. Honestly, I think my father will be relieved that I'm not flailing around avoiding a decision anymore. He already thinks you're the best thing to happen to me because you got me to fight."

"You've put on muscle," Livia said. "I noticed. Your arms are larger, and your shoulders are broader."

Lorcan chuckled. "I want to see you fight. You told me you were practicing, but that was months ago." Lorcan looked up at Tavi. "Want to show me?"

"Now?" Tavi asked. He paused, then laughed. "I'll have to borrow those clubs from Manius. My *dolabrae* are in my room, and… well…" He laughed again. "I just realized. It's my uncle and my father, and they're here. That's where they are. The practice ring."

"How did they manage to kidnap you?" Livia asked as they started down the passage to the ring. "And how did they get you here?"

Tavi snorted. "Father told me he and Uncle wanted to talk with me in private. We got into Uncle Gaius' rooms, and the next thing I knew, I was trussed up and gagged. They put a cloak and hood on me and threw me into a *lectica*. No one saw me, I don't think." He paused. "Nona won't gossip, will he?"

"No," Livia said. "You're part of us now, and the *familia* protects our own."

"Especially since I know that if I so much as sneeze your name, Lorcan will turn me into paste."

Lorcan looked over his shoulder. "I wouldn't. I'd just make you wish that I had."

Nona chuckled. "That's worse. It'll hurt longer. Everyone is in the ring. Gaius wanted to play, and Yaroah agreed."

They left the shadows of the hall for the bright sunlit ring, joining the others ranged against the wall. Decus glanced over, then smiled and held his hand out to Tavi, who went and stood by his father. They started talking, too softly for Lorcan to hear, so he turned his attention to the fighters on the sands.

Both Gaius and Yaroah were wielding wooden practice swords and shields, and both of them were laughing like children as they struck at each other. Gaius saw them first, and stepped back, lowering his sword. Yaroah glanced over his shoulder.

"Ah," he said. "So, have your differences been settled?"

"Yes," Lorcan answered. "How are you feeling, Yaroah? You looked good."

Yaroah swung his sword, then sighed. "Old. I am feeling old. I think I will not fight again."

"Thank you, then," Gaius said. "For honoring me with your last fight. I enjoyed it." He tucked the wooden sword under his arm. "Albus, we never did have our fight."

"And we're not going to," Lorcan called back. "I want to see what Tavi can do. Manius, do you still have those clubs?"

"The ones you started him with?" Manius nodded. "Yes. I'll fetch them." He headed for the armory.

"What made you think of using *dolabrae* as weapons?" Decus asked, coming closer. "Because, I'll admit, it's nothing any of us thought of, but they work."

"You said your cousin made throwing axes?" Tavi asked as he joined his father. "But they were different?"

"Ronan's throwing axes are smaller than a *dolabra*," Lorcan said.

"When we get to Eire, I'll have him make a set for you." He grinned. "A mating gift."

Tavi flushed, making Decus chuckle.

"It wasn't the axes, though," Manius said as he came back. "Lorcan saw what we were missing. That Tavi had to learn how his body fit. I think that was the true key."

"Only a little. It was mostly the axes," Tavi corrected. His dusky skin turned even more pink. "I'd already been declared hopeless with everything else. Once you hear that enough, you believe it. So having something entirely new? That helped. And... well... it was mostly because I wanted to impress Lorcan, because he thought I could do it."

Lorcan laughed. "Well, let's go, then. Impress me."

Tavi took the clubs from Manius, and walked out onto the sands. Manius handed Lorcan a pair of wooden *siccae*.

"I thought you'd want these, and not the real ones."

"Thank you." Lorcan took the swords and followed Tavi. Tavi had already turned to face him, and Lorcan studied his stance, the ease with which he held the pair of clubs. "You have been practicing," he said. "They're part of your arms."

"Not entirely," Tavi replied. "But almost. And I practice with the guards every day. I told you. They think I'm insane. But some of them have started trying to fight with *dolabrae*, too."

"So, your insanity is catching," Lorcan said, and was answered by a laugh. He took his place on the sands and raised his swords. "All right. Impress me."

Tavi grinned. Then his face went slack, and his entire demeanor changed as his body tensed, muscles flexing. And, to Lorcan's surprise, his eyes never moved. There was no warning before he struck. The attack didn't come from above, with Tavi taking advantage of his height. Instead, he struck from the side, sweeping his right-hand club level with Lorcan's ribs—Lorcan had to jump back to avoid the blow. Tavi's expression didn't change. He just advanced, and Lorcan launched himself into the fight. He kept having to remind himself that this was practice—Tavi had clearly been pushing himself, and he fought with a single-minded intensity that Lorcan usually only saw in the arena. Lorcan blocked an overhand strike on his right, and as he struck with his left-hand sword, Tavi did something completely unexpected—he blocked the strike, and kept moving, spinning and dropping to one knee...

And slamming his club into Lorcan's right side.

The world faded to pain-filled black, then snapped back into brilliant focus. Lorcan was on his back, and Livia and Tavi were both kneeling over him.

"What happened?" Tavi's face was ashen. "What did I do?"

"Wasn't your fault," Lorcan wheezed. "I'm not as healed as I thought." He grimaced and sat up. "You did it. I'm impressed."

"Never mind that!" Tavi snapped. "What happened?"

"You don't know?" Livia asked. "No one told you?"

Tavi sat down in the sand. "I... wait. You were hurt. That's why Uncle Gaius told me I needed to come back from Carthage. But that was... that was a month ago, wasn't it?"

"And he only just got back on the sands this morning," Livia said.

"I'll show you the scar," Lorcan added. "Which you managed to target without even knowing it was there."

Tavi crumpled. "I didn't know! I'm sorry! I didn't mean to hurt you!"

Lorcan reached out and caught Tavi by the back of the neck, pulling him closer and kissing him. "You're forgiven. And I want you to show me what you did. Slower. I want to see if I can do it. Now help me up."

Tavi stood up, and helped Lorcan back to his feet. Lorcan leaned on his arm for a moment, then shook his head. "Manius, I'm not going back on the sands. Not so close to us leaving."

"That's something I wanted to discuss," Manius said as he joined them. "Go and bathe. We'll join you there. We have... much to discuss." He turned and walked away, and Lorcan looked at the others, who were still standing by the wall.

"Does anyone know what he's talking about?" he asked. "Nona?"

"Why does everyone ask me?" Nona asked.

"Because you have all the best sources?" Gaius answered.

"Maybe, but they failed me this time. I have no idea." Nona reached up to scratch the back of his neck. "So... who wants a bath?"

Chapter Six

The heat of the *caldarium* pool made Lorcan's already-sore scar ache even more. He winced as he settled in the hot water, then smiled as Tavi lowered himself into the pool next to him.

"You said we had things to discuss," Lorcan said, shifting closer to Tavi so that their legs were pressing together. Manius was across the pool from him, his head tipped back and his eyes closed. He looked up and nodded.

"Yes. I'll yield to Gaius, though."

Gaius turned to face Lorcan. "Father is having a small feast to bid you farewell. You're all invited to stay in the Palace tonight."

"How small of a small feast?" Tavi asked. "Grandfather's sense of proportion is… strange. So please tell me just family?"

"Yes, just family. And not even the entire family. Just those in residence at the Palace. However, that includes Antius."

"And Galius," Decus added.

Tavi tensed. "Galius is in Rome?" He sounded shocked. "I thought Grandfather said he wasn't allowed? That's what you told me!"

"He arrived from Thracia this morning," Decus said. "And I'm as surprised as you are. Apparently, he has business here, and he reported to Father this morning and said that he would only be staying a few days. Father allowed it with… conditions."

"Why is your brother not allowed in Rome?" Lorcan asked.

"Galius made… some poor choices," Decus answered. Tavi made a soft gagging sound, but Decus didn't seem to hear. "And it was deemed best to have him away from Rome. Permanently." Decus shook his head before Lorcan could ask anything else. "No. I won't say more. He's not your problem. He's mine." He snorted. "Although Tavi will probably tell you all about it when you're alone."

"I can't tell him anything about why he's not allowed in Rome," Tavi protested. "I don't know. I know all too well why he was exiled from Britannia. All I know about this was that you had to come back to Rome, and I wasn't allowed to come with you. No one would tell me why. Not that I really cared. He deserved whatever he got, I'm certain." He paused. "He probably deserved worse than he got."

Lorcan studied him for a moment. "Tavi?"

"Later," Tavi murmured. "I… I'll tell you later."

"When you're ready, love. What about Drucilla? Gaius, have you…" Lorcan stopped, hoping the heat of the pool was enough to cover his flush of embarrassment.

"Don't worry, Lorcan. I trust everyone in this room," Gaius said. "Remember, I am part of the *familia*."

"I keep forgetting that," Lorcan admitted. "When are you telling her you're divorcing her? Or have you?"

"I told her already, and she's agreed that it's for the best. It's odd. I sat down with her a day or two after I told you. I told her the truth—I do care for her, and I always will. But Antius cannot become Emperor. He's not fit. I need a son of my own. And she just… accepted it. Thanked me for being honest with her. She already knew about Claudia, and that she's carrying my child. I don't know how she knew, but she wished us well. It's her brother that's the problem. He refuses to accept her dower back to finalize the divorce. And I can't publicly defy the Pontifex Maximus. But I can't help thinking that there's something more going on here, and I'm not sure what. I don't understand." He sighed. "Don't worry about that. You have other things to worry about. How are your plans progressing?"

"Go back to Drucilla for a moment," Lorcan said. "When she barged into my room in the Palace the day we left, she looked different. Is she ill?"

Gaius frowned. Then he shook his head. "No…" he said, drawing the word out. "Unhappy. She knows Claudia is pregnant, and that our problem wasn't just with me. She knows now that it was never meant to be, no matter how we tried. Or what we tried." He sighed. "When we go back to the Palace, I'll see if she'll talk with me. I do want her happy. And she's been unhappy for a long time, and I just never noticed." He shook his head. "Your plans, Albus?"

"Everything is ready," Lorcan answered. "We can leave within a day or two of saying the word. We're traveling by road to… I forget the name of the place. But we'll take ship from there to Alba."

"Itius Portus," Decus said. "And I'll have a letter of introduction for you to give to Arcus. Manius told me a little of what you're planning, so

I've already sent messengers on to him. There will be mercenaries waiting for your approval."

"Mercenaries," Gaius said. "Why? Lorcan, I could put legions behind you. For everything you've done for Rome, and for my family? You've earned a few legions."

Lorcan licked his lips. The idea was tempting. With even a single legion, he could end this quickly. But how would Eogan react to Roman legions on his shores?

Roman legions who answered to someone who could also claim his throne?

"I can't," Lorcan said. "I appreciate the offer. But... it's complicated."

"Is it ever not?" Ennius asked.

"You said things were simpler in Hibernia," Nona pointed out. "Why is this complicated?"

Lorcan sighed. "This goes no further than this pool."

"Naturally," Manius replied.

"High King Eogan is my uncle. My father's brother." Lorcan paused. "My father's younger brother."

"Oh," Gaius breathed. "Oh, I see."

"I don't," Tavi said. "Lorcan, why isn't your father High King?"

"Because neither he nor my uncles knew their fathers. They were the Morrigan's sons, and that was all. Their fathers had no claim to them," Lorcan answered. "Da told me that he didn't know the High King was his father until long after Eochaid died, when Eogan told him. He renounced any claim to the throne then. It was before I was born."

"But if you showed up in Hibernia with legions at your back, it would make your uncle nervous. Because your father may have renounced his claim to the throne, but not yours." Gaius nodded. He looked at Decus, who nodded.

"Send them to Britannia. I'll tell Arcus." He turned to Lorcan. "We won't send them on with you to Hibernia. But know that they're there, if you need them. And since this cousin of yours intends to move on your uncle, then perhaps your uncle would be amenable to help from a... friend of his nephew?"

Lorcan tipped his head back against the edge of the pool, thinking. He nodded slowly. "I can bring that to him, if it becomes necessary. Which... I hope it won't. Because that's the other part. I need to do this on my own. I need to take back what's mine without Rome behind me."

"Or they will never believe that you can stand and hold your throne alone," Yaroah murmured.

Tavi shifted next to Lorcan. "Lorcan, why waste the time to go by land? It'll take a month or more. By ship, it will be half that. If it even takes that long."

"Lorcan and I share an affliction," Gaius said.

"Mine may be worse." Lorcan laughed. "I get sick in the *lectica*."

"And on the litter," Gaius said with a nod. "I remember. But Tavi may have a point, Lorcan. We know your cousin knows you're here. If the word that you've left Rome gets to him before you even reach Itius Portus, he'll be ready for you. Possibly even waiting wherever you come to shore. If you want the element of surprise, then it may be worth the discomfort."

Tavi put his arm around Lorcan's shoulders. "If you want to be back in Eire before your cousin knows, you have to move fast. That means going by ship." He looked across the pool. "Father, you're sending those messages to Arcus by courier ship?"

"I am," Decus said. "Lorcan, by courier ship it's only 14 or 15 days from here to Britannia."

Lorcan growled softly. "Fine," he grumbled. "Manius, how do we change the plans so we're going by ship?"

"I'll arrange it," Decus said. He turned. "Yaroah? Do you have passage to Carthage arranged yet?"

Yaroah chuckled. "Are you offering me passage on the courier ship?"

Decus smiled. "If we do this properly, then no one will realize that Lorcan is on board the courier ship. We'll send the legions on overland as planned, with whatever baggage and such that you were planning on taking that way."

"But we'll actually be on the courier ship?" Lorcan asked

"That way, if your cousin does have eyes in Rome, which I do not doubt, they'll be looking at the group going overland, not the courier ship on a scheduled trip to Britannia." Decus smiled and looked at Gaius. "So?"

"So, I'm glad you've agreed to stay in Rome," Gaius said.

"You're staying?" Tavi blurted. "Father—"

Decus nodded. "Arcus and I discussed it before we left Britannia, and I talked to Father once I was here. Arcus will be officially named

provincial governor of Britannia, and I'll be staying here and being lazy."
He sighed. "I'll miss the grandchildren, but perhaps it's better I be here."
He looked at Gaius. "If nothing else, I can guard your back from my son."

Tavi coughed. "I—"

"I am sorry, Tavi," Decus interrupted. "And Gaius. I owe you an apology, too. If I'd been a better father, Antius and Galius wouldn't be the way they are."

"My uncle Niall is a good father. His youngest son is my best friend." Lorcan paused. "And his oldest son murdered my lover, sold me into slavery, and turned on our entire family." He felt Tavi tense next to him and rested his hand on Tavi's leg under the water. "He's a man grown. He's made his choices."

"Perhaps, but that doesn't change the fact that I'm learning that I've apparently sired a number of bullies." Decus frowned. "It's galling. We weren't like that. We weren't raised like that."

"Arcus and Decia Lucania were Julia's children. And there was never a kinder and more generous woman born," Gaius said. "Antonia, now…"

"Antonia… was poisonous," Decus murmured. "I saw it far too late, and Antius and Galius were both too old to change their ways when I did. I appear to have been lucky with Decus the Younger, and the girls and the twins were too young."

"Antonina wasn't," Tavi murmured.

Decus shook his head and sighed. "Antius won't stand down quietly, will he?"

"He always knew that he was only my heir if I didn't sire a child of my own." Gaius frowned. "Which… we're in for quite a few problems, aren't we, Lorcan?"

Lorcan snorted. "Just a few. Hopefully your son won't share mine."

Gaius sighed. "That's for me to deal with, and nothing for you to worry about, Lorcan. Will you go by courier?"

Lorcan grimaced. "I can't argue with the logic. We'll go by the courier ship. There has to be something Livia can brew for me that will make it bearable." He glanced at Tavi, then smiled as he turned back to Gaius. "I want to hear from you when the baby comes. I want to know if it's a boy or a girl." He paused, considered, then decided that Livia would forgive him. "And we can discuss possible alliances. Because by then we'll know if our baby is a boy or a girl."

Manius' jaw dropped. "What?"

"Albus-Corvus-Lorcan-you-have-too-many-blasted-names," Gaius sputtered. "You... Livia is pregnant?"

"Oh..." Tavi breathed, his voice very quiet. "That's why..." Lorcan looked at him, and his face turned dusky-red.

"How long have you known, and why didn't you tell me?" Manius demanded.

"I found out this morning, when we went to the Temple," Lorcan answered. "And we were going to tell you when we got back, but... ah... you distracted us." He grinned up at Tavi. "Not that I'm complaining."

"Well..." Manius murmured. "This makes my news that much more... appropriate." He turned to Nona and Ennius, who had been sitting and listening with rapt fascination. "The pair of you have come a long way in the time you've been mine. And even longer in the months you've been free. You are both exceptional *doctores*. So, my question to you both is what are your plans for the future?"

Nona coughed. "I... hadn't made any, yet," he admitted. "I wake up every morning and I think I'm dreaming. I'm a free man. And I'm a rich man. I could do... well, I could do anything. But I don't know what I want. I've been a slave and a gladiator almost my whole life. What else do I know?"

Ennius nodded. "I keep thinking I might want to take a wife. I want children of my own. I want them to have what I never had. But... I haven't gotten any further than that." He frowned. "Why?"

Manius smiled slightly. "As I said, you are exceptional *doctores*. What would you think of being *lanistae*?"

"What?" Ennius sat up with enough force that Lorcan was splashed in the face.

"*Lanistae?*" Nona repeated. His face was chalky white. "Are... Manius, are you... are you kicking us out?"

"No, of course not," Manius said. He waved one arm, spraying water across the surface of the pool. "If you agree, this is yours. All of this. I'm not kicking you out. I'm setting you up as *lanistae* in your own right."

"And you'll be doing... what?" Lorcan asked. Then he blinked. "Are you coming with us?"

"If you've no objections, and if you think your father will have me?" Manius answered. "I've been thinking on this since we started laying the plans for you and Livia to leave. Ever since her mother died, it's been her and I. Nona says he doesn't know how to be anything but a gladiator? I don't know how not to be Livia's father." He stopped for a moment, then sighed. "And I'm getting old. I felt my years more this winter than I ever have before. Going with you means spending however many years I have left with my daughter, the man I've come to care for as my son, and now… grandchildren." He smiled. "I like the idea of grandchildren."

"I think you and my father will get along quite well," Lorcan said. "But are you sure? You'll be leaving behind everything."

"Livia is my everything." Manius tipped his head back. "You've made her very happy. And you respect her and her work. You respect our gods, even though you're not Roman."

"I understand her work," Lorcan said. "I was training with my mother to be a healer, and I was supposed to go to the druid college to finish my training." He realized something, and laughed. "I was supposed to go this year."

"And instead, you trained with Livia," Nona said. "How different is it?"

Lorcan considered the question. "There's a lot that's very similar. But there are things that Livia knows that I never learned. That technique with the *fibulae* that they used on me, for example. But there are things my mother can do and that I was going to learn that I haven't seen here."

"Such as?" Gaius asked. "I've heard stories, but you never know what to believe."

"I keep telling you. All those reports are by people who have never once set foot in either Hibernia or Britannia," Decus said, and Tavi snorted.

"There are chroniclers who seem to thinking that accurate reporting is synonymous with storytelling," he said to Lorcan. "None of their stories match. And all of them are at the best insulting."

"And at the worst, outright lies?" Lorcan asked. "Why lie?"

"Because as wondrous as your people are," Decus said. "The people of Rome must be better. So…"

Lorcan shook his head. "That's silly. Why make my people look bad to make yourselves feel better?"

Decus shook his head. "I don't know. I've lived among the people of Britannia for years. I've had contact with the Hibernians. I've even spoken to the Picts, for all that they don't like Romans. There's very little in the writings I've seen here in Rome that show the truth."

"So… back to my question," Gaius said. "What do your healers do in Hibernia that ours don't do here?"

"I'm not certain if you don't do them, or if I've not learned enough to know," Lorcan answered. "It may be something that only Apollo's priests do. But we have healing chants that speed healing. My mother taught them to me, but I haven't learned how to use them properly. That was something I was supposed to learn at the druid college." He looked around the pool to see the others looking... skeptical. "What?"

"That's real?" Decus asked. "I mean, I've heard that. But... I've never seen it, and I just assumed it was another... fabrication. Like the story about your people eating fallen heroes to gain their power—"

"What?" Lorcan gasped. "They say that?"

Tavi nodded. "They say that. And... no, the priests of Apollo don't have that sort of thing. That I know of, anyway. Livia would know better than I."

"If they did, I imagine that Laris would have used them on you," Manius said.

"Laris is incompetent, and an insult to the name of healer," Lorcan grumbled.

"The *Comes* thought that because Lorcan was a gladiator, that he didn't need anything for pain when he took the *fibulae* out," Nona added. "That tune changed when I told him that Lorcan was a healer, and that he was a prince."

"And I took that out of his hide when I found out."

"Livia?" Lorcan tipped his head all the way back to look up at her, and smiled to see both her and Corvina looking down at him. "I didn't think you were joining us. And... you're dressed, so you're not joining us?"

"It's not proper," Livia said. "No, I came to tell you all that I've dismissed the students, and that I've arranged for a meal. When you come out, things should be ready."

"Why dismiss the students?" Lorcan asked. "They have training to do."

"And they're standing around with weapons while their instructors are turning into wrinkled old men." Livia folded her arms over her chest. "We've already had one slave uprising this year. Let's not start the seeds of a second."

Lorcan blinked and looked across the pool at Manius. "You told me we weren't teaching slaves. That all of our students were paying for us to teach."

"And that is true, for now," Manius said. "Especially for your students. But it's not sustainable. If Ennius and Nona want to remain *lanistae*, there isn't much choice. They need slaves to turn into gladiators, because it's the purses from those fights that keeps food on the table."

"So, you were holding off on buying slaves until after I was gone?" Lorcan asked. "I... thank you, I think?"

Manius chuckled. "You're welcome. I think. Now, shall we go and eat? Then we'll arrange to close the house so we can all go to the Palace."

* * *

"So, you can sing healing into someone?" Livia asked as they shared their meal in the *triclinium*. Normally Lorcan didn't care for eating reclined, but today it meant that Livia's bottom was pressed against his stomach, and Tavi's long body warmed his back. Corvina sat on the end of the couch, accepting morsels from anyone who offered. Lorcan gave her a piece of cheese, then pulled his attention back to Livia.

"My mother can do it. I know the chants, but I haven't learned how to sing them properly." He sat up and held out his left arm. "When Cormac challenged me the first time, he broke my shield with an iron club. Mother thought from the bruising that I might have broken a bone. So she sang the chants over me while I slept. When I woke up, there wasn't even a bruise left behind."

Livia's brows rose. "It's not something I've heard any *medico* in Rome speak of being able to do. And if I asked Laris, he'd laugh in my face. You should ask the Flamen Dialis."

Lorcan nodded. "Gaius, will he be at this feast? You said it was family, but—"

"Father invited him," Gaius answered. "He knows you've been spending time with Valerius and Cordelia, and he thought you'd want to say a proper goodbye. They're already at the Palace."

Lorcan smiled. "Good. I do like him. I've met the *Ard Ollamh*, and Valerius reminds me of him."

"*Ard*... that sounds important," Gaius said.

"The head of their religion," Decus answered before Lorcan could.

"Not quite," Lorcan corrected. "The *Ard Ollamh* is the head of the druid college. He's the leading bard and scholar in Eire. The *Ard Ollamh*, the *Ard Drui*, and the *Ard Brehon* all sit on the Council with the *Ard Ri*." He smiled at the blank expressions. "The High... Bard, I think you would say. But there's more to being an *ollamh* than just being a bard. The

Council is the High Bard, the High Druid, the High Brehon, and the High King."

"And the druids are the priests?" Decus asked.

"Priests and sorcerers, yes," Lorcan answered, and was again met by blank faces. "What? You... don't have sorcerers in Rome?"

"The stories we've heard about sorcerers in Britannia and Hibernia are true?" Tavi asked. "No wonder we've never gained more than a foothold in Britannia." He frowned. "How do you learn?"

"There's... something. You're born with it. My uncle Petran said that my uncle Oscar called it a fire in the head. Uncle Oscar was a druid and a sorcerer. If you have it, you go to the druid college to learn to use it. And if you don't learn to use it properly... well, not using it properly killed my aunt Muirenn. Uncle Oscar's mate. He died... not long after." He rested his hand on Livia's leg, leaned back into Tavi's warmth. "We... don't last long after the death of a mate. Not once it's sealed."

The silence in the *triclinium* grew heavy, until it was finally broken by Nona. "But... you're immortal," he said softly. "I mean... when you have your cloak. You told us that."

"And that's true," Lorcan answered. "We're immortal, yes. But we can die. Just not... naturally. We can be killed." He looked over his shoulder at Tavi, then took Livia's hand. "My grandmother's gift is that we won't spend eternity alone. We can give part of that to our mate. And we'll know them when we find them, so there are no mistakes. If you'd found the missing part of your heart, Nona, would you want to live without that forever?"

"And you're giving that up?" Tavi asked softly. "For us?"

"I'm not giving up anything." Lorcan tipped his head back to look at Tavi. "I'll have you both for the rest of my days. There might not be as many of them, but you and Livia will be there for all of them."

Chapter Seven

"All I'm saying is that I'm jealous," Nona said as they approached the Palace. Tavi had taken Livia on ahead with Manius, Gaius and Decus, but given the choice between riding in the *lectica* or walking, Lorcan had insisted on walking. The other *doctores* had opted to stay with him, and they'd talked the entire way. Corvina rode on Lorcan's shoulder, occasionally interjecting croaks or clicks or burbling that sounded like laughter.

"I can see how one could be jealous of a *semideus*, yes," Ennius said.

"It's not even that!" Nona protested. "It's that when you find your wife, you know it's her. Absolute certainty. And then she's with you forever."

"Or he," Lorcan said. "My uncle married a man."

"And that's another thing! You can *do* that in Hibernia! I couldn't marry a man here, but you can do that!"

Ennius turned, walking backwards so he could face Nona. "You'd want to?" He frowned slightly and stopped walking. "Wait… how did I not notice? I've known you how many years? And I've never once noticed that you never wanted a woman outside the ones who came to the arena looking for a gladiator. Nona…"

Nona blushed. He looked down and shrugged. "I… yeah. I never was interested. You really didn't know? I mean… Yaroah knew."

"I knew because you asked to share my bed," Yaroah said. He draped one arm over Nona's shoulders. "I remember how shy you were then."

Nona's face went even more red. "And… you were nice about it. You said no, but you were nice about it."

"How did I not know this?" Ennius demanded.

"You never asked?" Nona answered. "And I never told you. You were there, but you were always talking about women. You were talking about taking a wife not even an hour ago. So I just thought…" He paused. "Ennius? Was I wrong? Should I have asked you?"

57

Ennius smiled. He held his hand out to Nona and said, "Let's take a walk. I think we have things to talk about." He glanced over his shoulder. "Tell them we'll be along… later. We won't miss the feast." They walked away, and Lorcan looked up at Yaroah. The big man looked amused, and it took Lorcan a moment to realize why.

"You've been waiting for that to happen, haven't you?"

"For three years now," Yaroah answered, laughing. "I kept wondering when Nona would finally find the courage to ask, or if I should just push him in Ennius' direction."

They started walking again, and Lorcan saw the Imperial Guards waiting at the gates. "How did you know Ennius would be willing?" Lorcan asked. "I never guessed that he was interested in men, and I usually notice when someone is… well, like me."

"Because finding someone like you is something that doesn't happen often?" Yaroah asked.

Lorcan laughed. "I'm used to being the strange one. When I find someone who is… strange in one of the ways I am, I notice." He grinned. "It's nice, not being the only strange one."

Yaroah nodded. "I understand. Manius owned another Carthaginian slave, before Nona and Ennius came to us. Gebal and I were partners in the arena. It was good to have someone who understood. He fought well." He paused, then smiled. "Like you do."

"What happened to him?" Lorcan asked.

"Sickness. The same that took the rest of the gladiators in the *ludus*, and brought Nona and Ennius to us."

Lorcan nodded. "What are you going to do now? You're going back to Carthage. I know that much. What then?"

Yaroah shook his head. "I don't know yet," he answered. "I have wanted to go home for so long, and now that I am going, I realize I haven't thought of what I will do when I get there. I was…" He paused, then chuckled. "I was your age when I was brought to Rome. I am not the same person. Not anymore. And I do not know what the man who is going to Carthage will want when he gets there." He shrugged. "I'll know when I set my feet on the land that gave me birth. Until then? I need to get there, first. Look, Tavi and Livia are waiting."

* * *

Tavi led Lorcan and Livia to his suite of rooms. "I thought we could stay here," he explained as he opened the door. "It's more comfortable than the rooms you were given, and... well, the bed is bigger." He stepped into the room, then stopped. "What are you doing here?"

Lorcan stepped around Tavi, then moved in front of him. Inside the room, a woman stood up, smoothing the front of her simple gown.

Lorcan blinked. "Drucilla? What are you doing here?"

"Oh. You cut your hair," she said. "You look older." She blushed slightly. "I'm sorry. I was waiting... I wanted to talk to you, Albus. Please."

Lorcan looked at Tavi. "Close the door. And stay by it." He held his hand out to Livia, leading her in to sit down. Tavi closed the door and leaned against it, his arms folded over his chest. Lorcan nodded, then turned back to Drucilla. "How did you know I was coming here? And... I didn't say it the last time I saw you, but you look so different without all the paint. Better. You look better without it." He gestured to his own face, and she laughed.

"Thank you," she answered. "And... do you know? You and Gaius are close. Did he tell you? About the divorce?"

Lorcan nodded. He gestured to another chair, and waited until Drucilla sat down. "He told me. I... I hope that whatever happens now brings you happiness. I know he does, too."

"Thank you," Drucilla said. She looked down. "You're very kind. And I've been very horrible to you. That was why I came. To apologize." She looked up. "Tavi, I apologize for invading your room. Apparently, invading rooms is becoming something of a new habit of mine."

"Apology accepted. But how did you know I'd be bringing them here?" Tavi asked as he came to Lorcan's side.

Drucilla paused. "Two reasons," she said softly. "First? You're not exactly subtle. Either of you. I don't think there's a person in the Palace who doesn't know how you feel about Albus, or how he feels about you."

"And second?"

Drucilla blushed. "Gaius didn't know I was in the next room when he and Decus brought you in this morning. I promise, no one will ever hear a word of it from me." She smiled. "And I'm very glad it worked. You're smiling, and you haven't been. Not for months." She folded her hands in her lap and looked down. "So, that's why I knew to come here. And that's why I'm here, Albus. To apologize to you and your wife. I am sorry. Truly. I... there's no real excuse I can give, or reason. I was terrible to you both, and I am sorry. I… don't like the person I was, and I'd like to start again, in the time that we have left before you leave."

"Thank you," Lorcan said. He glanced at Livia, who nodded. "We accept your apology. And since we're starting over, my name is Lorcan."

"Thank you," Drucilla murmured. "I… I think it's for the best that the divorce happens, that I get out of Palace. Away from this life. I don't like her very much."

"Who?" Lorcan asked.

"The woman I am when I have to be the heir's wife. The woman who'd be Empress. She's horrible, and I don't like her. In truth, I'm afraid of what she'd be if she did become Empress. So, it's better that she doesn't." She smiled slightly. "Gaius deserves better."

"Drucilla, may I ask you a question?" Livia added. She waited until Drucilla nodded before continuing. "Gaius is a good man. He'll be Emperor, and you clearly care for him. Why did you…"

Drucilla's face went pale. "I… know what you're going to ask. You're a *medicae*. You know the tales. I promise you, they're not true. I always wanted his child. His children. I… I know the rumors. They're lies. I never…" She looked away, and when she looked back, Lorcan could see the tears starting to fall. "I wanted… and I don't know why…" She paused, then shook her head. "And if you're asking that, you know the rest of the rumors. Those were lies, too. I was pregnant four times. They were all of them by Gaius, no matter what the rumors say." She sighed. "Gaius had his lovers. I had mine. He even arranged some of them. He liked to watch." She reached out and tapped the back of Lorcan's tattooed hand. "I was going to surprise him with you, Albus."

"You said that in the arena. I was wondering what you meant," Lorcan admitted. "Why me?"

Drucilla blushed slightly. "Your first fight was… intoxicating. I wanted to be the first to have you, because I knew you were going to be in demand. Gladiators are… exciting. New gladiators even more so. I won't deny that. I don't think there's a matron in Rome who would."

"Roman matrons are terrifying," Lorcan said. "And I don't think there's a gladiator in Rome who would deny that."

Drucilla blinked. "Terrifying? Me?" She started laughing, full peals of laughter that almost muffled the sound of someone knocking. Lorcan glanced back at the door to see that Gaius had come in, and was staring.

"Which of you broke my wife?" he asked slowly.

Drucilla caught her breath, then asked, "Gaius, did you know I'm terrifying?" Then she collapsed into giggles.

"Terrifying? No," Gaius answered. "But I will admit that right now you're frightening me, just a bit. Who said you were terrifying?"

"I did," Lorcan answered. "The first time we met, I was certain she was going to chew me up and spit out the bones."

Drucilla burst out laughing again, and Gaius chuckled as he sat down next to her, waiting until the giggles finally tapered off before speaking.

"I can't remember the last time I heard you laugh like that," he said as Drucilla caught her breath. Drucilla nodded.

"I can't remember the last time either." She took a deep breath, then smoothed the front of her gown with one hand.

"You're very different than you were when I first met you," Lorcan said. "You're..."

"Real?" Drucilla interjected. "Not the painted doll? That's what I was. A painted doll on display, acting the part of the proper Roman matron. All that awful behavior, that's what was expected of me by the other wives, by the other nobles." She looked at Gaius. "But not you. You never asked it of me. You always told me I didn't have to dress that way. But..."

"You insisted because it would have reflected poorly on me." Gaius nodded. "I just never realized how unhappy it was making you."

Drucilla shook her head slightly. "I was never unhappy with you, Gaius. Never." She paused, then asked, "But... I'm clearly not the right person to be your wife, no matter how I feel about you. Now, you were looking for me?"

"I was," Gaius answered. "I was going to come find you after I welcomed Lorcan and Livia. Welcomed them and warned them, and I was going to warn you." He paused. "The Pontifex Maximus is in the Palace."

Drucilla went still. "He is? Why?"

"I don't know why he came today. Neither does Father. He wasn't invited the way the Flamen Dialis and the Flamenica were. Father knows that Antonious doesn't like Lorcan—"

"The feeling is mutual," Lorcan muttered, and saw Drucilla's lips twitch. Gaius snorted.

"Regardless, he's here, and he knows about the feast. I'm not certain there's any polite way for Father to get around inviting him." He paused.

"And Father said that the reason he came was to formally accept the return of your dower."

Drucilla paled. She closed her eyes and let out a long breath. "He finally listened. I've been asking him to see reason since you and I talked. His petty... tantrum isn't fair to any of us. You need an heir, it cannot be Antius, and I'm not going to be able to give you one. However much I want to. I'm too old." She paused, then looked around the room. "Now that it's done, I don't know what to say."

"What will you do now?" Lorcan asked.

Drucilla frowned slightly. "I... I don't know. I don't want to stay in the Palace. But I don't know what to do now. I could go back to my brother, but... well, I'd rather not."

"Will you let me arrange things for you?" Gaius asked. "If you agree, I'll speak to my father, and arrange everything—a place, servants. Anything you might need." He rested his hand on hers. "I'm thinking that villa in Ostia. Remember how much you liked it there? If you want it, it's yours."

"I..." Drucilla stopped, pulling her hand out from under Gaius'. She laced her fingers together in her lap. "May I think about this?"

"For as long as you like," Gaius answered. "Drucilla, I have lived with you and cared for you for a long time. I still care for you, and I want you happy. So, I want to know what you want. Take your time. You're welcome here. And when you know what you want, let me know and I'll make it happen."

Drucilla sighed. "What I want? I can't have. You can't give yourself back to me, or we'll be in the same tangle we're in now." She took his hand. "Gaius, I want you to be happy. I hope she gives you what I couldn't. Will you come and visit me, if I take the villa in Ostia?"

"If you want." Gaius smiled. "You'll still be part of my family." He stood up. "Let's leave them, and we'll go lay some plans. And clear the air. I think that perhaps there are too many things that we never said aloud, and too many rumors that we believed instead of trusting each other."

They left, and Lorcan waited until they were gone before looking at the others. "Everything we thought about her was a lie, wasn't it?"

"Or a mask," Tavi agreed. "I never really knew her well. When I first met her, she started to welcome me, then closed me out. And the Pontifex just scared me."

"He doesn't like me at all. So, I'm really not sure how tonight is going to go." Lorcan leaned back in his chair. "Now, I'm taking Gaius' example. I told you I'd explain what happened before. Why I stopped." He paused and swallowed. "His name was Bran." He looked down at his hands. "I mentioned him in the bath, Tavi. He was my lover. We both knew it wasn't forever. He wasn't mine. He knew it. But we liked each other. We were friends since we were boys, years before we were lovers, and… he told me that he was ending it. That our last tryst was the last time, because he was going to marry. I told him I was happy for him. For them. And a few hours after, my cousin killed him. He was trying to save me, and Cormac killed him." He looked up to see almost identical looks of horror on Livia and Tavi's faces.

"You never talked about this," Livia murmured. "This is the first time you've said anything about him, I think."

"I didn't talk about him. I don't think I ever really mourned him," Lorcan said. "I never had a chance. And… it all came back when I realized that the last time I was with a man, he died for me." He looked at Tavi. "You're not allowed."

"Yes, sir," Tavi replied, his voice somber. "I will do my best not to follow his example. And if the baby is a boy, name him Bran?"

"You know?" Livia asked.

"Lorcan told me."

Livia smiled. "We might. I like the name." She rested her hand on Lorcan's arm. "Are you all right?"

Lorcan shrugged. "I don't know. I… I'm not sure why this is so close to the surface now. It's been a year."

"And you said it yourself. You haven't mourned him. You haven't talked about him. You haven't grieved. So now it's time. I want to hear more about him," Tavi said. "All about him. Later." He cocked his head to the side. "You know, Drucilla was right. You do look older with your hair cut short. Why did you cut it?"

Lorcan reached out and ran his fingers through Tavi's curls, then gently grabbed them, making Tavi moan. "One of the gladiators sent to kill me held me like this when he was going to slit my throat." Tavi shuddered, and Lorcan let him go. "I'll let it grow out again once I know it's safe. Now, it's your turn to explain something."

Tavi blinked. "I thought I did."

"No, about something you said in the bath. When I told you Livia was pregnant, you said that explained something. What?"

Tavi's brows rose. "You haven't noticed?" He grinned, reaching across Lorcan to take Livia's hand. "You haven't noticed that Livia... ah... tastes different?"

Lorcan blinked. He looked at Tavi, then turned at looked at Livia. "Tastes different? I... oh!" He laughed. "I... it's been a while. I haven't... not since before I was hurt. And possibly before... Livia, when is the baby going to be born? I don't even know. I can't think when... well..."

"Too many possibilities?" Livia asked, then laughed. "It's still too easy to make you turn red. If I'm counting correctly, late fall. I've been... distracted, so I'm not certain."

"Having your mate try to die twice would do that." Tavi kissed Livia's fingers. "And having your other mate be a bone-headed idiot. Which, no more of that. Now, we should get ready for the feast. Your things have already been moved here, so the only question is if we want to bathe again."

* * *

"Lorcan, I've been thinking," Livia said as she helped him drape his toga. "About Diana's priest."

"Tiro? What about him?

"Do you think Corvina is really your grandmother?" Livia asked.

Lorcan turned to watch Livia as she moved away to finish her own preparations. He considered the question, then shook his head. "I... we're so far from Eire. So far from the people who call her their own. I don't know. I don't know if she's there in every raven and she's watching over me. And if she is watching me, then who is watching Eire?" He frowned. "I don't know."

"How many relatives do you have on that side?" Tavi asked as he came back into the bedroom. "Maybe one of them is watching Hibernia for her? Livia, there's a girl here. Drucilla sent a gift for you."

"For me?" Livia turned as the girl came into the bedroom. She bowed, then placed a casket on the table.

"My lady asks that you accept this gift," she said. "She thought it would please you."

Livia went to the table and opened the casket. "Oh!" she gasped. She looked down, then up again. "I..." She reached into the casket, and took out a necklace of heavy gold and lapis lazuli beads. "This is beautiful." She put it on, turning toward Lorcan and Tavi.

"That's lovely," Lorcan said. "And the color suits you."

Tavi nodded. "It looks very nice on you."

"I will tell my lady her gift pleases you," the girl said. She bowed again, and backed out of the room.

Livia ran her fingers over the beads. "Why would she send something like this to me?" she asked. "As an apology?"

"No, I think she just wants to make you happy," Tavi said. "She used to do that a lot, when I first came to the Palace. If she thought something would make me smile, she'd gift it to me. I hadn't thought about that in ages."

"Why did she stop?" Lorcan asked. "And are you ready?"

"I'm ready." Tavi looked down at himself, then laughed. "This is the last time I have to wear a toga! I can go back to wearing trews!" He grinned as Lorcan started laughing. "Why did she stop? I... I don't know. She lost a baby around that time, and she was very sick afterward. Then she... was different. She didn't want me to be around her."

"That's understandable," Livia said. "She'd lost her own child; someone else's child would be painful to be around."

Tavi shrugged, then adjusted his toga to drape properly. "Probably. We went back to Alba before she was fully recovered, so I didn't see her again for years. And when I was in Rome the last time, I was more interested in Livia than in why my aunt had changed." He came over and leaned down to kiss Livia's cheek. "Are we ready?"

"I think so." Lorcan looked down at himself. "Lead the way."

Chapter Eight

Lorcan heard Lucanus' laughter echoing through the cooling night air as he and Livia followed Tavi through a garden to the *triclinium.* Tavi paused just outside, and an older man Lorcan thought looked familiar came to meet them.

"Good evening, Lucanus," he said, bowing slightly. "Albus Corvus, I don't think you'd remember me?"

"You're right," Lorcan said. "I don't. I apologize."

"Lorcan, Marcus Sextus is my grandfather's *dispensator*," Tavi said. "And since I'm not sure you know what that means, he runs the Palace."

Marcus smiled and bowed his head. "I looked in on yourself and your lovely wife when you've stayed in the Palace, but you were hardly in any condition for an introduction. Now, I'm to understand that all three of you will be sharing a couch?" He gestured. "This way."

"Are my brothers here yet, Marcus?" Tavi asked in a low voice as they followed Marcus up a step and into a room that was far more ornate than the *triclinium* in the ludus. This room was enormous, with a high, vaulted ceiling that glittered with gold and large windows that looked out into more gardens.

"Just arrived," Marcus answered, equally quiet. "At your father's request, I've put them as far from you as I could and still have them in the same room." He glanced to the side. "They are... deeply affronted to have been placed at the foot of the hall. But with the arrival of the Pontifex Maximus, what could I do?"

"Of course," Tavi murmured.

"And the Flamen Dialis and the Flamenica?"

"The couch next to yours, Albus."

Lorcan was about to ask the man to use his name when Tavi caught his eye and shook his head. Lorcan fell silent and looked around. Lucanus was standing with a group that included Yaroah, Gaius, Decus, and Manius. To Lorcan's surprise, Manius was wearing a toga.

"I've never seen Manius in a toga before," Lorcan said to Livia.

"Neither have I," Livia replied. "I didn't know that he had the right to do so."

"A courtesy, granted by the Emperor," Marcus said. "Now, as you can see, the *doctore* Yaroah is here, but we're missing *doctores* Ennius and Nona. Will they be joining us?"

"They didn't come?" Lorcan looked up at Tavi. "They told us that they'd be late, but they'd be here. I wonder what kept them?" He turned to look around, and yelped and backed up a step in shock—the Pontifex Maximus was standing behind him. He swallowed, them bowed. "Apologies, your Holiness. I didn't hear you come up behind me." He paused, then gave in to the urge to needle the man. "You're very quiet. Honestly, I've heard louder cats."

"Lorcan," Tavi whispered. "Behave."

Lorcan fought the urge to grin. "Is there something you needed, Holiness? How may I serve?"

"Walk with me." The Pontifex turned and stalked away. Lorcan looked up at Tavi, then at Livia.

"I'll be back," he said. "And I'll behave." He touched Tavi's arm, then leaned over to kiss Livia's cheek before hurrying after the priest. They left the *triclinium* and walked out into one of the side gardens. It boasted a large, central fountain, and was full of fragrant herbs and night-blooming flowers that were just starting to open and release their fragrance. Lorcan paused by one that boasted brilliant pink blossoms that he'd never seen before.

"Holiness, do you know the name of this one?" he asked, reaching for one of the flowers. He jerked back at the priest slapped his hand.

"*Nerium*," the Pontifex said. "It's poisonous. Your wife will know how it's used. She can tell you more." He sniffed. "It is ornamental, but it's known to not allow children to handle the flowers. I thought you were a *medico*?"

"I am," Lorcan answered. "But this isn't a plant I know. And I should know better. My mother taught me never to touch a strange plant. Thank you for your correction, Holiness." He straightened, turning to face the priest. "You wanted to speak to me, Holiness?"

The Pontifex studied him for a moment, then sniffed. "I do not like you."

Lorcan coughed, then laughed. "Well, if we're telling the truth to each other, I don't like you, either."

That drew a laugh from the priest. "You are refreshingly honest; I will give you that."

"It's considered a virtue where I'm from," Lorcan said. "And since I'll be going back home soon, you won't have to worry about me annoying you for much longer. I am curious, though. What did I do? You disliked me before we'd even met, and I don't understand why."

"You are an upstart barbarian—"

"That's prince upstart barbarian, thank you," Lorcan replied, and saw the man's lips twitch. "Prince *semideus* upstart barbarian, if we're being specific."

"And you set a bad precedent."

Lorcan blinked. "You said that at the Temple. I remember. I set a bad precedent by being raised to the ranks of patrician. Which... I didn't have a say in that. You're laying blame at my feet when I had no choice."

"Truly?"

Lorcan snorted. "Truly. I asked for none of this. I wanted none of this. All I did was defend a good man, and people I have come to care about. Is that a fault in Rome?" He paused, then continued, "All I have wanted from the moment I arrived was to go home. Holiness, I am here in Rome because I was kidnapped and sold as a slave. My cousin betrayed me. He wanted what was mine, my inheritance and my place as my father's son. My family is in danger, and I'm here, unable to help them." He looked around. "I didn't want to be a Roman citizen. I didn't want to be the darling of the Roman people, and have them scream their love for me with every drop of my blood that paints the sands of the arena. I didn't want to be honored by the Emperor by having him take my name from me. The only things that have come to me in Rome that I will forever be grateful for are the people I've come to love. And all I want is to take my wife and go home." He held his free arm out to the side. "You said I was refreshingly honest? That's the entire truth."

The Pontifex frowned. "Took your name?"

"When I was named a citizen, the Emperor renamed me. I will never tell him he was wrong, but... Albus Corvus Torvus? That's not my name. My name is Lorcan, Holiness. Lorcan Lachtna mac Diarmuid mic Morrigan."

"Does it mean anything? Barbarian names usually mean things, or so I'm told."

Lorcan chuckled. "Mine does, yes. Lorcan means little fierce one. My parents told me they chose it because I was the only one of their children to draw breath. Tavi… sorry, Lucanus the Younger said that Torvus is a close translation. And Lachtna means milk-colored."

The Pontifex barked with laughter. "Truly?"

Lorcan grinned. "Truly! It was supposed to be an insult, but I like it. The rest means son of Diarmuid of the line of the Morrigan. She's one of our gods. We call her the Battle-Raven." He heard a croak from above. Looking up, he saw Corvina on the edge of the roof. He called back to her, and she flew down to his shoulder. He reached up and ruffled the feathers at her breast, then looked back at the Pontifex. "I'm sorry. I've forgotten your name. Or rather, I keep thinking that your name is Holiness."

"My name is Antonious."

Lorcan nodded. "I should keep calling you Holiness, though. You're the high priest of high priests. Am I remembering that correctly? It's been some time since the ovation when Gaius explaining things."

"It's close enough." He paused, then nodded toward Lorcan. "Your raven. Is that your grandmother? Or her emissary?"

"This is Corvina. We found her in the *ludus* with a broken wing, and nursed her back to health." Lorcan rested his hand on Corvina's back, and she leaned down to worry at a fold of his toga. "The priest of Diana thinks she's my grandmother. Livia asked me tonight if he was right, and I don't think so. But I don't know. If you and the other priests think she is, then perhaps I'm wrong. Honestly, if Corvina is my grandmother, she's a long way from home, too."

Antonious nodded. "A fair answer. Another question—the necklace your wife is wearing. Where did she get it?"

"Drucilla gave it to her," Lorcan answered. "Just tonight. We were all surprised by it—it's a princely gift."

"That's truer than you know, I think. It was given to her by a prince. One of the men who wished her hand in marriage." He paused. "I think it suits your wife very well. I wish her joy of it."

"Thank you," Lorcan said. "Shall we go back in?"

"I do have one more question. You broke Antius' nose. Why?"

"Because he hurt Lucanus the Younger," Lorcan answered. "Tavi is mine, as much as Livia is mine. He'll be coming with us when we leave." He frowned, then turned his head slightly. "Corvina, go to Tavi, please." The raven rubbed her beak on Lorcan's cheek, then launched off his shoulder and flew away.

"Why did you do that?"

"Because Antius is a coward and a bully. He is in the *triclinium* with the two most important people in my life, and I'm out here."

Antonious nodded and gestured back the way they had come. "Then we should return." He started walking, and Lorcan fell in next to him. The priest glanced at him, then sniffed. "I think that perhaps I do not dislike you quite so much."

Lorcan smiled. "Considering that I was told that the only person you truly liked was your sister? I'll take that as the highest compliment. I am honored."

Antonious chuckled. "They were not wrong, whoever told you that. What do you think of my sister?"

"When I first met her? She terrified me," Lorcan answered. "Now? I like her very much." He glanced at the Pontifex. "Why is she afraid of you?"

"We… disagree. On many things, but I only want what is best. And Gaius was what was best for her. Or so I thought." He frowned. "Did you share her bed?"

Lorcan stopped walking. "That's a very personal question."

"And if there's a chance that she's bearing your child, I need to know. To protect both her and the child."

"She isn't," Lorcan answered. "Because I haven't, although both she and Gaius invited me to do so." He looked around to check that they were still alone in the garden. "Protect her? From what?"

"You know about the divorce? And you know that she cannot bear a child?"

Lorcan nodded. "Yes. And I know that she wanted those children."

"I am not entirely convinced that what happened was the will of the Gods." Antonious pitched his voice low. "Drucilla is… generous. She loves with her entire being. And she trusts far more than a noble woman should. It is, I think, her greatest fault, and I worry that this was another case of her trusting where she should not." He looked around as Lorcan had. "If she was bearing your child, people would think Gaius was the father. Which I assume was the plan?" When Lorcan nodded, the priest continued, "With her divorced, there would be those who would attempt to use her against the Emperor. I won't see that happen. As I said, I want what is best, and having my sister be a puppet in a war against the Emperor? That is not to anyone's benefit."

Lorcan looked back at the hall. "You're thinking Antius."

"I did not say it."

Lorcan nodded. "I understand. If I thought there was a chance Drucilla was carrying my child, I'd ask her to come with us. Especially since I don't know if a child of mine sired on someone who is not my mate would share in my family inheritance from my grandmother." When Antonious arched a brow, he shook his head. "It's… not something I'll discuss. Not where the night can hear." He glanced around again, then looked up at Antonious. "We were going in?"

"Yes," Antonious started walking again.

Lorcan fell in next to him. He smiled slightly. "Since we're being honest with each other? I don't dislike you as much as I did when we came out here, either. I understand wanting what's best for someone."

Antonious chuckled. "Thank you."

They walked on in silence, and as they approached the door, someone came outside. Lorcan stopped, then smiled when he realized it was the Flamen Dialis. The older man laughed when he saw them.

"And here I was worried you'd left him underneath the *nerium*," he said.

"Valerius, really!" Antonious sighed. "That's far too obvious."

Lorcan burst out laughing. "I'm fine, Valerius. You were looking for me?"

"I wanted to congratulate you, my boy!" Valerius sounded jubilant as he pulled Lorcan into a quick embrace. "Cordelia noticed, and Manius confirmed it for us! I'm so happy for you and Livia!"

Lorcan smiled. "I just found out this morning. She took me to Diana's temple to make an offering, and that's when she told me."

"Told you…" Antonious paused, and his eyes widened. "Well! Congratulations, indeed!"

"Thank you." Lorcan glanced toward the door. "We were going back inside."

"Your Tavi is with his father, uncle, and grandfather," Valerius said softly. "And has your Corvina with him. Cordelia and Drucilla have taken Livia off for a private conversation. They will rejoin us later." He glanced at Antonious. "You're in a very mellow mood this evening. You haven't growled at me once."

Lorcan laughed, and they walked back into the *triclinium*. Standing in the doorway, Lorcan could see two groups—the one that included Tavi, and a group of two next to the wall. Antius scowled at him and turned his back. Lorcan assumed that the man with Antius was his brother, Galius. He looked like Antius' twin.

"Albus!" Lucanus called his name, then came over to greet him warmly. "Congratulations!"

"Thank you, Sire," Lorcan said. "I'm still… well, stunned."

"Of course," Lucanus agreed. "Of course. Now, are you still set on leaving? You could wait, stay in Rome until the baby comes? Return to Hibernia next spring?" He laughed. "The look on your face, Albus!"

Lorcan chuckled. "You're very kind, sir. And very generous. And I very much need to go home. My family needs me."

The Emperor nodded. "I understand. Once your family is safe and your inheritance secured, I wish to hear from you. And perhaps, from your uncle?" He smiled. "When you are ready, send to Arcus in Britannia."

Lorcan bowed, and Lucanus moved away. When Lorcan straightened, Tavi was coming toward him, Corvina on his shoulder.

"Did you send her to me?" he asked as he reached them.

"You and Livia were in here, and I wasn't." Lorcan nodded slightly in the direction of Tavi's brothers. Tavi nodded. Then he bowed to the priests.

"Holiness," he said. "You honor us."

"Antonious, come share a couch with me until Cordelia returns," Valerius said. "I had a thought about Corvina, Lorcan. I was going to tell you when we met next, but we can discuss it now. I'm interested in what the Pontifex thinks. I was reading a Greek text that I wanted to introduce to you, and it all became clear." He reached up and stroked one of Corvina's wings, and she clicked at him. He smiled. "She's a *daimon*."

"Oh, that would make sense," Antonious murmured.

Lorcan frowned. "I don't know the word. I'm still learning Latin, and we haven't done much with Greek yet."

"A *daimon* is… a spirit," Tavi said. He led them to their couches, but no one sat. "Not quite mortal, and not quite a god. Something in between."

Lorcan looked up at Antonious. "You asked if she was an emissary. Would that be the same thing?"

Antonious nodded slowly. "It would be very close to what I meant, yes. You will be leaving us when?" he asked.

"Within a week," Lorcan answered. "Possibly sooner."

"A pity. This is a conversation that requires time, and research, and exploration."

"And if you hadn't been a stubborn jackass, you would have had that time," Valerius murmured. Tavi coughed, turning pink.

"Holiness!" he gasped.

Both priests just laughed. They settled onto the couches, and Lorcan stretched out on his left side, feeling Tavi behind him.

"Holiness, by chance was the text Plato? *The Symposium?*" Tavi asked. Valerius beamed at him.

"It was! You've read it?"

Tavi chuckled. "It's been a few years, but yes."

Lorcan settled against Tavi and listened, letting Corvina nest in a fold of his toga as the others discussed the text, and what the existence of *daimons* might mean for Corvina. Was she a normal raven, a *daimon*, or even Lorcan's grandmother herself? Corvina contributed to the conversation with clicks and croaks and an odd, gurgling bark that Lorcan had never before heard from her.

"I feel as though I should be sitting at your feet," he said at length. "The three of you. I have no idea what you're talking about."

"I'll teach you Greek," Tavi said. "And you can read it yourself. Or I can read it to you."

"Is there a Latin translation?" Lorcan asked.

Antonious shook his head. "It must be read in the original Greek. Translating it to another language would be vulgar. Greek is the language of the educated."

Lorcan sniffed. "And I thought I was getting an education by learning Latin." He tipped his head back. "Tavi, I'm ignorant."

Tavi chuckled and kissed Lorcan's forehead. "But you're decorative. I think I'll keep you."

Valerius chuckled. "And what does Livia Corvina say about that?"

"She hasn't said anything yet, but if she were to complain, I think it would be to say move over," Lorcan answered. "Because our bed is too narrow for three." Valerius burst out laughing, while Antonious looked shocked.

"Thought I told you to behave," Tavi whispered in Lorcan's ear. "You've scandalized the Pontifex Maximus. I don't even know what that's going to mean to the Gods."

Lorcan burst out laughing. "I've read your stories. Your Gods don't seem to be shy about loving. Why should loving someone be forbidden, then?"

"An interesting question," Antonious said. "Shall we change the subject, then? What are your thoughts on the matter, Albus?"

Lorcan propped himself up on his elbow. "I spoke to Valerius about this. I don't understand your restrictions on who can lay down with who. So long as those involved agree and no one is hurt, why should it be forbidden? And having rank come into the question? That makes no sense. I would think you would celebrate love, not try to control it. Trying to... Tavi, what's the word for making laws? I can't think of it."

"Legislate?"

"That's it, yes. Trying to legislate love? That's ridiculous. I thought laws were supposed to keep people from being hurt, not inflict hurt on them."

Antonious nodded slowly. "You have an interesting logic." He turned toward Valerius and asked, "Are conversations with him always like this?"

"Albus is a wonderful student, and I will miss him," Valerius said. He looked past Lorcan and blinked, sitting up on the couch. "What—?"

Lorcan turned to look, and saw Livia. The look on her face was one of rare fury, and was enough to make him clamber awkwardly off the couch, trying not to trip over his toga. Corvina barked out her outrage, and took to the air, settling on Lorcan's shoulder. Livia passed him without looking at him, didn't stop until she'd reached the Emperor. Lucanus turned to smile at her, but the smile faded from his face as she said... something. Lorcan couldn't hear what. He glanced toward the door, and saw Cordelia standing with her arm around Drucilla's shoulders.

Drucilla was in tears.

"Tavi," Lorcan said softly. "Go tell your uncle to see to his wife. Now."

"What..." Antonious breathed. He started forward, then stopped as Livia passed in front of him, closely followed by the Emperor.

"Lorcan," Livia said. "I want you to smell this. Do not touch it." She held up a cloth wrapped flask. She had more cloth wrapped around her hands, and Lorcan looked at her in shock for a moment before leaning forward. He stopped himself before breathing directly from the bottle, remembering the plant outside. Instead, he closed his eyes and waved his hand over the flask, trying to waft the scent toward himself. He breathed it in, coughed, then straightened and stared at her.

"Where did you get that?" he demanded, horrified. "Give it to me! Now!"

"Why do you think the bottle and my hands are wrapped? I know how dangerous this is for me," she said. She handed it to him, and he corked the bottle before wrapping it entirely in the cloth.

"Go burn those wrappings," he said. "You didn't spill any, did you? Where did you get this?"

"Albus, what is it? What is in that bottle?" Lucanus asked.

"My people call it *pulegium*," Lorcan said. "And… wait… *glechon*. In Latin this is called *glechon*." He looked down at the bundle.

"Sire, this is a tonic that was given to Drucilla during her last pregnancy. She still had it, and offered it to me to see if it was still effective. She tells me that the same tonic was given to her for each pregnancy after she lost her first baby, to help strengthen her so that she might bear a healthy baby," Livia said, her words clipped in her anger. "But that was a lie. *Glechon* is used to end a pregnancy, and could very well kill the woman as well."

"No!" Antonious murmured.

"Livia, are you saying someone poisoned my wife?" Gaius said, his voice shaking. He'd brought Drucilla to join the group, holding her to his side. "Someone… someone *murdered* our children?"

"The potion was given to her by the *Comes* Laris," Livia answered. "He needs to be questioned, because I do not think this was something he did on his own."

Chapter Nine

Lucanus' expression hardened, and he turned to Marcus, who had appeared at his elbow as if summoned.

"Marcus, order the *Comes* Laris brought here immediately. Be... circumspect. I do not want this spread around the Palace." Marcus nodded. He bowed and hurried away, and Lucanus turned to face Lorcan and Livia. "Until such time as I announce this, you will keep this secret. Am I understood?"

"Yes, Sire," Lorcan said. "Livia, why don't you take Drucilla someplace..."

"Our rooms," Tavi said from behind Lorcan. "We'll join you there as soon as we can."

Gaius hugged Drucilla closer to his side. "Father, I'd like to go with them—"

"Not yet," Lucanus said. "I need you to stay. I want you here when they bring Laris in. This won't take long, I don't think." He took a deep breath. "Livia, if you would?"

Livia nodded and went to Drucilla's side. Cordelia joined them, and the three women left the *triclinium* together. Lorcan reached up and ruffled Corvina's feathers. She clicked her beak at him. When he clicked in return, she launched from his shoulder and flew out after the women, over the heads of guards who started to file in and take positions around the perimeter of the room. Lucanus nodded and returned to his couch. That seemed to be the signal for the rest of them to disperse—Manius and Decus took Gaius off in one direction, while Yaroah went to speak to one of the guards. When Lorcan and Tavi returned to their couch, Antonious was sitting with Valerius. The Pontifex was ashen. Lorcan crouched in front of him.

"Holiness?" he asked. "Are you all right?"

"I... I feel ill," Antonious answered. "I can't... Drucilla has never hurt anyone. She would make a wonderful mother. Why do this to her?"

76

"Why indeed?" Tavi muttered. Lorcan looked up. Tavi wasn't looking at him. He was looking across the *triclinium*.

At Antius, who was pacing back and forth in front of his couch. Galius had reclined, and was watching his brother with a bored expression on his face.

"Tavi?" Lorcan kept his voice low, and spoke in Gaeilge. "You think he did it?"

"If Aunt Drucilla bears a child, he loses his place as heir and his path to becoming Emperor," Tavi answered. He glanced back at Lorcan. "You should know better than any of us what a man will do in that situation."

Lorcan snorted and stood up. "We have no proof," he murmured.

"Yet." Tavi looked at him. "I'm going to go and talk to my grandfather, then see how my uncle is."

Lorcan nodded. "I'll stay here. I want to keep an eye on Antonious. He's not looking well." Tavi touched his arm and walked away, and Lorcan turned back to the priests, moving to sit on the ground at Antonious's feet.

"Are we doing that again?" Valerius asked.

"It's appropriate," Lorcan answered. "If I'm to learn at the feet of the Roman *Ard Drui*, I should act like it."

"That means what?" Antonious asked. "What you called me."

"The High Druid. The high priest of our religion." Lorcan considered adding the high sorcerer as well, then decided against it. He wasn't sure how the Pontifex would react to learning that sorcery was real, and that Romans didn't have it. "It's a rough comparison, though. The positions aren't... quite the same."

"You called me something different," Valerius said.

"I called you the *Ard Ollamh*. The leading bard and scholar and the head of the college where the *ollamhs* and druids learn their craft."

Antonious sniffed and looked sourly at Valerius. "Why do you get to be the scholar?"

Valerius smiled. "It's almost as if he knows me."

Antonious glared at him for a moment, then shook his head. "And what would you learn from me, Albus? No. It's Lorcan. You wanted to be called Lorcan."

"Thank you," Lorcan said. He looked down at his folded hands, trying to think of a question. "Why Greek?" he blurted, looking up. "From what I understand, Rome is considered the... the highest of the high. Rome is civilization, according to your people. All the rest of the world are barbarians. So why is the language of the scholars Greek?"

Antonious blinked. Then he smiled, and Lorcan watched as he visibly relaxed. "Because before there was Rome, there was Greece."

"Isn't there still?" Lorcan asked. "I mean… Greece is a place, isn't it? Is it not there anymore? Was it conquered, or… or destroyed? Is it gone?" He frowned, trying to remember long-ago lessons. "I don't know much about Greece. My tutor was… not a good man. He was more interested in shouting at us than he was in teaching us."

Antonious straightened. "A horrible teacher is a crime indeed. Us? You have siblings?"

"I have a cousin who is only a few months older than I am. When I fostered in my uncle's court, we shared a tutor."

"Who is the reason Lorcan had so much trouble learning Latin." Tavi's voice came from behind and over Lorcan; he looked up and saw Tavi looking down at him. "What are you doing down there?"

"Learning." Lorcan held his hand out. "Help me up? I'll trip on this otherwise."

"First lesson?" Tavi said as he helped Lorcan to his feet. "Don't sit on the ground in a toga."

Both priests burst into laughter, and Lorcan smiled. "What did you learn?"

"Nothing yet," Tavi answered, speaking Gaeilge. "Grandfather agrees with both of us. He suspects Antius, but he wants proof." He sighed. "Uncle Gaius looks… broken. Father and Manius are with him, and they have wine. I think they're trying to get him drunk." He looked around. "And Yaroah looks worried."

Lorcan turned and saw Yaroah coming toward them. "Yaroah?"

Yaroah stopped next to him but didn't say anything. He glanced back the way that he had come, then softly said, "How has no one noticed that these are not the right guards? Or that some of them are not wearing the right armor?"

Tavi blinked and stood a little straighter. "What?"

"I went to speak to one of the guards. I thought he was one that I knew. It was not him. I looked closer and I do not think any of these are the Emperor's guards. And there are three wearing the wrong helms. How has no one noticed?"

"Because no one looks past the armor to see the person wearing them," Tavi said. He looked at Lorcan. "Now what?"

Lorcan looked across the room at the guards, silently counting, seeing the three closed-faced helms that Yaroah had mentioned. "Twenty-four," he murmured. He turned to Valerius. "Holiness, perhaps the Emperor would appreciate your wisdom right now?"

Valerius nodded. "Twice the wisdom is always a good thing. Antonious, come with me." They stood up and walked over to the Emperor's couch.

Yaroah narrowed his eyes and growled softly. "None of us are armed."

"Let's go talk to Manius," Lorcan whispered. He touched Tavi's arm, and they walked over to where Decus and Manius were plying Gaius with wine. Manius glanced at them, then blinked and straightened.

"What is it?" he asked.

"Yaroah says that the guards aren't the right guards," Lorcan murmured. "So maybe don't get Gaius drunk?"

Gaius looked up at them, his face ashen. "Did... are you saying someone has subverted the Praetorian guard?"

Tavi answered before Lorcan could ask what a Praetorian was. "Yes. And we're all of us unarmed."

Decus shook his head slightly. "But not for long. Look at Father's couch. The one in the alcove. There are two chests on the table behind it. See them?"

Lorcan glanced over to where Lucanus was talking with the priests, near an alcove set between two doors. There was a couch in the alcove, and a low table beyond the couch, on which rested two long cases made from polished wood. He nodded. "I see them."

"Father wanted to give you both something to remember him by, since he doesn't think he'll see either of you again in this life." He sat up straight. "Antius?"

"How's Uncle?" Antius asked from behind Lorcan. "And... I know you probably all think I had something to do with this. I did not, and I'll swear it before all the Gods if I have to." Lorcan turned to look at him. He was sweating, looking around like he was terrified of something. "I promise, I didn't know!"

Decus stood up. "What do you know?"

Antius took a deep breath and shook his head. "Nothing, Father. I just know it's going to be laid at my feet, because I'm the one who benefits the most if Uncle has no child of his own." He sniffed. "I know you have no reason to believe me. Or trust me. Or even like me, to be honest. But it's the truth."

"You know, some of us might like you better if you were less of a prick," Tavi grumbled. "Or less inclined to take anything you felt entitled to. Or stopped trying to get information out of us by any means you think necessary."

Antius winced. "I had debts," he muttered. "Gambling debts. I needed... but Corax won, and I paid them off. And..." He reached up and ran his finger down his crooked nose. "Well, I know better than to even sneeze at either you now," he finished.

"Good," Lorcan muttered. "Because if you touch my Tavi again, you won't finish the sneeze. So, if not you, then who? Who else would benefit?"

Antius shook his head. "I don't know. I need to speak to Grandfather. I need to make him believe that this isn't me."

Gaius stood up, swaying slightly on his feet. "I believe you," he said. "You're a bully. You're not a murderer."

Antius frowned. "I... thank you? I think? Uncle, sit down before you fall down." He frowned as Gaius flopped back down onto the couch. "I've gotten drunk with you. And you haven't had nearly enough wine to be that drunk."

Decus stared at his son for a moment, then looked at the pitcher of wine. "Manius, did you drink any?"

"I hadn't finished my first, and it came from the other pitcher," Manius said. "You?"

"No." Decus dropped to his knees. "Gaius, stay awake," he ordered. He glanced over his shoulder. "Father!" he shouted, then turned back to Gaius. "Gaius, I need you to stay awake." He looked up. "Lorcan, you're a *medico*. What do we do?"

Lorcan stopped for a moment, his mind racing. Then he reached for the pitcher and sniffed it, almost gagging at the rank odor rising from the liquid. "You drank this?" he gasped. That smell... what was that smell? He knew it... it was dangerous... it was... *fealla bog!* Ah... Latin. What was it in Latin?

"*Koneion.* It's *koneion*." He tried to fight down the fear—there was no antidote for *koneion* poisoning. He knew that. But he had to try. "He needs to purge and he needs to purge now. We need... blast it... *searbh luibh*. Ah... *apsinthion*. It's a purgative. It may be early enough that it will help. Laris will have it. Where is he?"

"We don't have time," Manius said. "Decus, take him off and stick your finger down his throat."

Decus nodded and dragged Gaius back to his feet, trying to hold him steady. Lorcan hurried to take Gaius' other arm, seeing the big man was covered in sweat. Gaius looked at him for a moment, then looked past him.

"Father." Gaius' voice was quiet and sad. "I'm sorry."

Then his eyes rolled back in his head, and he dropped like a stone.

Lorcan dropped to his knees, shrugging his arm out of the toga so that he was surrounded by folds of wool. He needed to be able to move. He felt Gaius' throat for a pulse, found it racing. "Tavi, I need Livia now," he barked without looking up. "And the *Comes* Laris. I need *apsinthion*, however they have it prepared, and as fast as they can get it to me. Decus, try to make him vomit. Your hands are bigger than mine." The sharp cry of an angry raven made him jerk and look up, but there was no sign of Corvina or of any other raven. Had he imagined it? A moment later, there was a loud crash, and the discordant scrape of metal on metal.

"What is this?" Lucanus demanded. "Prefect, what are you doing? Why have you barred the door? We need the *Comes* at once!" He brushed past Lorcan, then stopped, looking around. The guards had all come away from their posts, and they had all drawn their swords. Lucanus drew himself up to his full height and turned to face them. "So…" he said slowly. "Has it come to this? Am I to be assassinated? Are we all to be assassinated?"

"You know, you never should have trusted a barbarian. Truly, it's a shame, but honestly, you should have known he'd turn on you." Lorcan didn't recognize the voice. He glanced across at Decus, who had gone pale.

"Galius," he growled, getting to his feet. "What are you doing?" He moved to stand in front of the Emperor, touching Tavi's arm as he passed. Lorcan wasn't sure what passed between father and son, but Tavi started slowly backing away from the crowd. Backing toward the Emperor's couch. Toward the chests.

Manius took Decus' place next to Gaius' still form, pulling Lorcan's attention back to his patient.

"What do I do?" he asked in a low voice.

"Make him vomit, however you can," Lorcan answered. To his surprise, Manius shuddered and turned pale.

"I have no trouble with blood," he muttered. "But vomit…"

"Do the best you can," Lorcan murmured, getting to his feet. Galius walked into view, with one of the guards behind him.

"Galius." Antius pushed forward to stand in front of his father and grandfather. "What are you doing? You promised to support me! I told you; you could choose your position once I was in power, and everything would be forgotten. What are you doing?"

Galius smiled, reaching out with his draped arm to rest his hand on Antius' shoulder. The drape of his toga hid his movement from view, but Lorcan heard the wet impact, heard Antius grunt. Watched him fall forward. Galius stepped back, and dropped the bloody dagger on top of his brother. "I am choosing my position," he said. "Yours."

"Galius," Decus gasped. "No!" He stepped forward, and was pushed back by the closest guard.

Galius just sniffed. "Galius, yes," he answered, clearly mocking his father. He wiped his hand down the front of his toga, leaving streaks of blood on the white wool. "After years of Galius, no, it's finally Galius, yes. Finally, I'll have what should have been mine. And I'll have all of you out of the way." He glanced around. "Oh, I promise you all wondrous funerals. The most amazing funeral games ever. But really, you should never have trusted a barbarian, Grandfather. They're wild things. They're like wolves. Likely to turn on you when you least expect it."

"No one is going to believe that Albus turned on me," Lucanus said. He looked back to see Lorcan standing behind him, and gestured. "This man saved my life. He was honored as a hero in front of all of Rome. No one is going to believe that he would turn on us, that he would murder all of us. Or that a single man would be able to overpower all of the guards. Galius, this is madness. Stand down, and open the door, and we will talk."

"Talk?" Galius snorted. "You don't want to talk. You want to lecture. You'll lecture, then I'll get banished to the darkest corner of the Empire, just like before. No, Grandfather, we will not talk. And the people will believe whatever I tell them. Because I'll be their Emperor." He smiled. "No one will ever say no to me again."

"You didn't listen to anyone who said no to you before."

Lorcan looked over his shoulder to see Tavi standing with Antonious. His face was ashen, and even at a distance, he could see that Tavi was shaking.

"Tavi?" Lorcan whispered. All at once, he remembered scarring under his fingers. He growled, and heard someone behind him gasp.

Tavi looked at him and shook his head. He spoke in Gaeilge, "It's not what you're thinking, Lorcan."

"Did he force you?" Lorcan spat.

"He... tried," Tavi admitted, a flush creeping up his throat. "He was exiled. Which... that was a mistake."

He was lying. Lorcan knew in his bones that Tavi was lying. But this wasn't the place to press. "I won't make that same mistake." Lorcan snorted and looked back over his shoulder. "Do you want him gelded across, or lengthwise?"

Galius burst out laughing. "I do understand the pair of you, you know," he called. "And really, are you planning on using your bare hands, boy? Your teeth?" He grinned. "Now, that would be an experience..." He shook his head and laughed. "I'm getting distracted. Guards, secure them all. I need—" He paused and looked around. "Where did the Carthaginian go?"

Lorcan turned and looked around the *triclinium*. Yaroah had vanished. So had Valerius.

"You!" Galius pointed at one of the guards. "Search the garden. Find them and..." His voice trailed off as Lucanus started to laugh. "What's so funny?"

"If they've gotten out into the gardens, then they can easily reach the rest of the Palace. I doubt you've corrupted the entire Praetorian guard, boy. They'll be here momentarily, and there's no way to completely secure this room." He shook his head and turned away. "You did not think this plan of yours all the way through."

In the distance, they could hear shouting, and bells starting clamoring. Galius glared at his grandfather, then started barking orders. Three of the guards herded Lucanus, Lorcan and Tavi into one group, leaving Antonious, Manius, and Decus near Gaius' still form. Galius nodded, then pointed at Lorcan's group. "Secure them and bring them through to the library." He scowled at Lorcan. "Behave yourself, or I'll kill all of them in front of you, and I'll start with him." He pointed at Tavi, who closed his eyes as a guard rested his sword against his neck. Lorcan let another guard bind his wrists behind him, and watched as Lucanus and Tavi were similarly bound. As the guards started pushing them toward the doors that flanked the alcove, he heard Galius's voice.

"Kill the others. We don't need them."

Chapter Ten

The door opened to a dark corridor, and the guards pushed Lorcan forward. He could hear shouting behind him, but it was quickly cut off by the door slamming closed. He had no idea where they were going, and was surprised when they came out of the corridor into a room that he knew.

"This is the library in Apollo's Temple," he said, looking around. Livia had brought him here, to this room specifically, so that he could practice his reading. She'd told him that there was another room where the books were all in Greek, but hadn't shown it to him. The guards spread out, barring the doors. Galius stalked around the room, then stopped in front of Tavi and shoved him, hard enough that he fell. Lorcan surged forward, only to stop with the point of a sword pressed against his chest.

"Sit down," the guard snarled. "And behave."

"Yes, barbarian. Sit and stay, like the good dog you are." Galius snapped. Lorcan ignored him, looking at the guard. It was one of the three who he'd seen wearing the wrong helms, and all three were in this room.

Was his voice... familiar? Lorcan couldn't tell. He scowled at the guard, then looked at Tavi. "Tavi?"

"I'm fine," Tavi said. "Do what he says. Sit."

Lorcan sat down on a bench, and one of the guards pushed Lucanus down next to him. Lorcan glanced at the Emperor, then licked his lips. How were they getting out of this? He twisted his wrists, trying to find some slack, but there was no play in the ropes.

Galius ignored them, going to stand over Tavi, who was lying in the folds of his toga on the floor. Galius sneered, then spat, "This is your fault. If you'd just kept your mouth shut and taken it like the whore you are, none of this would have happened."

"Don't blame him for your crimes," Lucanus said. "The only reason you were never charged and punished was that no one could find the girl."

Tavi sat up. "He did it *again*?" he asked in horror.

"And was exiled to Thracia—"

"Where he became someone else's problem, and you could ignore him," Lorcan interrupted Lucanus, who just glared at him. "Tell me I'm wrong," Lorcan added. "You didn't make him face his crimes, or do anything to stop him. You just sent him away so you didn't have to see it. And now…" He paused. "I've read your books here. Killing your own brother? Your father? That's a crime against your gods, isn't it?"

"Not when you're the Emperor," Galius answered, laughing. "When you hold all the power, you make all the rules. And I will be a god among men." He smiled. "And since this will all be laid at your feet, Prince Raven, I'll have every reason to take the legions and destroy Hibernia completely."

Lorcan licked his lips, realizing something. Wondering… "You were in Thracia. Did you send the twins to kill me?"

"Twins… oh, the gladiators!" He chuckled. "Yes, I did."

"Why?" Lucanus asked. "He'd done nothing to you. If you'd let him have his final bout in peace, he'd have already left. There would have been no one to stop this."

Galius leaned against a table. "One? He hasn't stopped anything. Or have you not noticed that you'll all be dead shortly? Two?" He gestured toward Tavi. "This little whore is mine. He gets what I give him, and only that. And I do not share what's mine, especially not with filthy barbarians. And… well, call it a favor for a friend."

"A friend?" Lorcan tugged against the ropes, again, growling in frustration. He glanced at Galius, who was pacing back and forth like one of the arena's caged beasts. "You mean Cormac? What do you have to do with my cousin?"

"I have some… dealings with… men of a certain reputation. I met your cousin through them, and helped him to lay his plans to take what was rightfully his. And I… suggested men to support his claim. Some of his men are mine," Galius answered. "And when the time is right, they'll be my wedge into the impenetrable Hibernia. And all I had to do was kill one little slave." He snorted. "But you're incredibly hard to kill, Raven. I should just slit your throat right now and be done with it." He stopped moving and frowned, idly stroking the folds of his blood-stained toga. "I need to think."

Lucanus snorted. "There's nothing to think about. You failed. And now you're trapped. You have nowhere to go, and by now, the entire Palace knows that you're a traitor and a murderer. They know where you are. Even if we die here, you'll follow. So now, the only question is are you going to die by your own hand, or will you survive long enough to be executed." He raised his voice slightly. "A question, I might add, that applies to everyone in this room. By assisting him, you are all condemned as traitors to Rome. It doesn't matter that we can't see your faces. You'll be found."

Galius sniffed and turned to one of the guards, taking his sword from him. "Perhaps. But you'll die first." He smiled, then glanced at Tavi. "Or last. I think that you're going to watch your precious namesake and your pet barbarian both bleed out before you die." He pointed at the guard closest to Tavi. "Get him on his feet," he ordered. Then he looked past Lorcan. "And keep them in place. I don't want to be interrupted."

Lorcan started to get to his feet, but froze with a blade against his throat.

"Be still, Corax," the guard murmured, and Lorcan finally recognized his voice. "You're not alone."

Lorcan fought the urge to turn or say something, feeling cold metal against the inside of his arm. The ropes around his wrists tightened for a moment, then fell loose.

"Don't move. Don't let him know you're free."

Lorcan gave a slight nod, looking out the corner of his eye at Lucanus. The Emperor was sitting still. He glanced at Lorcan. Then he winked. Lorcan relaxed slightly, keeping his hands behind his back as he watched the other guard hauling Tavi to his feet. There was something familiar about how he moved...

The guard steadied Tavi, unwinding his disheveled toga and letting it fall. He must have said something, because Tavi's eyes widened. Lorcan watched as his eyes darted to look at him, then back at the guard.

"I can't decide," Galius said, walking over to Tavi and tapping him on the chest with the tip of his sword. "Do I have you first, and then slit your throat, or do I slit your throat and fuck your corpse?" He snorted and looked at Lorcan. "Tell me—how is your woman, slave? Does he scream for you?"

Lorcan blinked. Had he translated that wrong? "I... what?"

"He means me," Tavi called.

"Oh, does he mean that?" Lorcan swallowed, trying to stay still and play along. The sword resting on Tavi's chest made him want to kill, but he needed to keep his head. "Calling you a woman? Is that supposed to be an insult?"

"Don't tell me you haven't fucked him," Galius said. He laughed. "Does he scream for you? Should I gag him? Tell your Emperor everything."

"You expect me to tell your grandfather?" Lorcan scoffed. "Because you're no one's Emperor. You're nothing but a petty little bully, and if you ever somehow managed to become Emperor, you'd be dead before a year was up. Probably from one of your own guards, because they were tired of listening to you prattle and fuss like a child." He paused, seeing Tavi nodding. The guard gestured with one hand, his meaning clear—*keep going*! So Lorcan looked Galius up and down, then did his best to leer. "I'll tell you what, though—if you want to know how a woman screams, come over here and get on your knees." He paused again, waiting until Galius was staring at him, outrage clear on his face. He smiled and finished, "I'm a gladiator. I know how to make a woman scream. You're hardly worth my trouble, but I expect you'll thank me very prettily for the privilege of swallowing my cock."

Galius' face went white, then purple with rage. He wheeled toward Lorcan, clearly forgetting all about Tavi as he raised the sword…

Which was just what the guard was waiting for—he drew his own sword, sliced the ropes binding Tavi's hands, then shoved the sword into Tavi's right hand.

"Julius, get the Emperor out of here!" Lorcan dove off the bench, catching Galius around the knees and driving him to the ground. He heard a hollow thump, and Galius stopped moving. Lorcan crouched over him, seeing the growing pool of blood underneath his head. He checked Galius' throat for a pulse, and found one.

"Lorcan?" One of the guards held his hand out. "Are you hurt?"

"I'm fine." Lorcan let himself be pulled to his feet. "The blood is all his. Ennius? Nona? What are you doing here?"

Ennius tugged off his helmet and grinned. "You know how you're always saying that Nona has the best sources? One of them caught us when we were on our way back to the *ludus* to… ah… to talk." He blushed slightly as Nona came up next to him. "We didn't know which guards were in on the plot, so we went to Julius."

Lorcan nodded and closed his eyes. "We need to get back. Gaius… he may be dead by the time we get there." He looked at the door that led back to the Palace. "They... they might all be dead by the time we get there."

"Yaroah would have gotten the real guards," Tavi said. He nodded toward Galius. "Is he dead?"

"He hit his head on the table when Lorcan took him down," Ennius said. "He might be."

"He isn't," Lorcan answered. "It just knocked him out." He rubbed one hand over his face. "A small family feast, your uncle said."

"And I seem to remember telling you that my grandfather has a strange sense of proportion, so this is completely in line with other small family feasts," Tavi replied.

"Ghost!" Lorcan turned to see Yaroah in the doorway that led to the Palace. "You're safe. Thank the gods. You have to come now. They need you. Gaius is still alive, and Livia says that they need you."

"Nona, Ennius, deal with my brother!" Tavi grabbed Lorcan's hand, and they joined Yaroah, running back through the corridor to the Palace.

The *triclinium* was full of guards and people. Couches were overturned, and there was spilled wine, broken glass and pottery shards all over the floor. A guard stopped them before they could enter, then looked at Lorcan and blinked.

"You've cut your hair, Corax," he said. "I didn't recognize you."

"Centurion, the traitor knocked himself cold back in the Temple library," Tavi said. "He'll need to be taken into custody."

"Of course," the guard saluted, then turned and shouted. Two more guards joined him, and they disappeared down the corridor, closing the door behind them. Lorcan looked around, then saw the group gathered around a couch. He headed toward them.

"Lorcan!" Decus came out of the group at a run. "You're here. Please..."

"What?" Lorcan looked past him. "How is he still alive?" The group had parted, and he could see Gaius on the couch. His face was deathly pale, and even from this distance, Lorcan could see he was barely breathing. Manius sat on the couch next to him, and Drucilla was on her knees holding his hand. Livia was on the far side of the couch. She looked up, met Lorcan's eyes, then shook her head.

"He's stubborn," Decus said. "Lorcan, you told us about singing the healing into people. You told us you knew how." He looked back at the couch. "Please."

"I… I know the chants," Lorcan stammered. "But I haven't been taught how to use them. I might make things worse!"

"What's worse than dead?" Yaroah asked from behind him. Lorcan turned to stare at him, then realized he was right.

"I'll try," he said. "There's… there's no promise that I can help. But I'll try."

"That is all we can ask." Decus put his arm around Lorcan's shoulders and escorted him to the couch.

"Was anyone hurt?" Lorcan asked. "When he took us out?"

Decus snorted. "I would not have given the Flamen Dialis any credit for being a fighter before today. But he fights like a *cestus*. And your wife knows how to use a sword, so do not make her angry."

"My wife what?"

"I'm a gladiator's daughter!" Livia called. "Of course I know how to fight." She came around the couch and into Lorcan's arms, studying him intently. "He didn't hurt you?"

"No," Lorcan answered. "I'm fine. We're fine." He looked back to see Tavi behind him. "Tavi might have a bruise, but he was ready to take Galius' head off." He looked past Livia to see Corvina on the couch next to Gaius. "Let me see if I can do anything." He kissed Livia's cheek, then went to kneel next to the couch. He took a deep breath, then looked across at Drucilla. "Let him go. No one touch him."

"What are you going to do?" Drucilla asked.

"Something that I haven't been properly taught how to do," Lorcan answered. "And… it may not help. I don't know. But if it works…" He stopped and swallowed. Then he reached out and rested one hand on Gaius' chest, the other on his forehead. He took a deep breath, and started to sing the healing chant.

* * *

A fire in the head, they'd told him. The power inside a healer or sorcerer was like a fire in the head. This didn't feel like fire. It was ice, pouring through him, pouring out of him and into Gaius. His body went numb from the inside out. He couldn't feel the floor under his knees, Gaius under his hands, the warmth of the room around him. He couldn't hear his own voice, even though he knew he hadn't stopped singing. There was nothing but ice, flowing out of him, surrounding him. It was hard to concentrate, hard to think at all, and he could feel himself starting to falter…

Something that burned like a brand settled on his shoulder, driving back the ice. A hand? Lorcan didn't look. He needed to focus, needed to keep singing, keep working to heal the damage and keep the man who called him brother alive. The warmth helped, and he felt his strength returning.

"That's enough, little raven," a man said. His voice was as warm as his hand, deep and musical. "He'll live."

Lorcan nodded, but continued the chant. His mother had taught him never to stop in the middle, never let the power run free. Close the circle, bring the spell to a close, thank the gods, and release the power. That was how it was done. So he finished the chant, feeling his throat burning like the brand on his shoulder. He let his hands fall into his lap, and realized that he was no longer kneeling next to the couch. He was kneeling in the middle of a field, surrounded by gently blowing grass and wildflowers.

"Where am I?" he croaked, and looked up. A golden man looked down at him, smiling. Lorcan blinked twice, but it wasn't his eyes. The man was glowing.

"Well done, little raven," the golden man said. He was young, beardless, and beautiful, and his voice was wonderful. Lorcan wanted to close his eyes and just listen. "No sleeping now. You won't wake, and you have work to do."

"I… what?" Lorcan looked around again. "Won't wake? Where am I?"

"Elysium, but you're not staying. You don't belong here." He squeezed Lorcan's shoulder, then gestured. "No, this is just so you can recover, and as a favor. You've pleased me greatly, little raven. I could wish you were one of mine. Your grandmother must be very proud of you."

Lorcan coughed, realizing who this man was. Who he had to be. "Lord Apollo, I…"

"You caught my interest when you came to my temple. A healer who happens to be a white raven? How could you not catch my eye?" Apollo grinned. "And then you turned out to be a hero. Exceptional! But you're spoken for already, so I can't claim you. And she's coming for you." He looked distant, then frowned. "Oh, calm yourself, cousin! He's hale. And he's done me a great service."

"He's a blasted little idiot who should know better than to play with

90

power he doesn't have the training to use!" Lorcan staggered to his feet as the air to his left rippled, then tore open. His grandmother stalked out. She didn't slow until she was on him, and her barehanded slap across the face drove him back several steps. "You could have died!" she wailed. "What then for your family? For your kin?"

"Cousin!" Apollo stepped forward, extending an arm between Lorcan and his grandmother. "Honestly, did you think I would let a talented healer die? Especially one who has served me well? He was safe."

"Grandmother, I'm sorry. I had to try," Lorcan added. "He's a good man. He's like a brother to me."

Morrigan sniffed. "So for the sake of a good man, you'll condemn your own father?"

Lorcan went very still. "Is… is my father dead?"

"No," Morrigan said. "But you must return to Eire as soon as possible."

Lorcan nodded, feeling a tightness growing in his chest as he realized what this might have cost him. "How badly is this going to hurt me? Am I going to need to delay again?" He looked up at Apollo. "I should have left a month ago, as soon as the weather changed. But…"

"You risked a great deal for me. So I'm not going to let this hurt you, little raven. You will wake up hale." Apollo smiled. "Hale and hungry. And you'll have as much of a peaceful sailing as I can manage."

"Thank you. And… and Gaius will live?"

"He will. And he will remember you fondly." Apollo looked past him. "Cousin, your children are exceptional."

Morrigan smiled. "Thank you. Now, if I want them to remain exceptional, I need to take this one back. We'll trouble you no further."

Apollo bowed his head, then patted Lorcan on the shoulder. "Go on. Go back." He looked at Morrigan again as Lorcan crossed to his grandmother's side. "Cousin, visit me when you can. Your ways… that was most interesting. We have nothing like this healing touch. I'd be curious to learn more, to learn if this is something my priests might share."

Morrigan took Lorcan by the hand. "Once my own house is in order, then perhaps," she said. She looked Apollo up and down and smiled. "Perhaps."

Chapter Eleven

"Grandmother, may I ask a question?"

"If the question is how much longer are we going to walk, I don't know."

Lorcan chuckled. "It isn't. And honestly, I'm enjoying being with you. From what I remember Da saying, it's not something you do."

Morrigan glanced at him. "It isn't. But you're a troublemaker, and need more attention than all nine of my boys put together." She laughed. "And I find that I am enjoying that. What is your question?"

"Are you Corvina?"

Morrigan stopped walking. "You want to know if I'm your pet?"

"She's not a pet. She's my friend. And the priests said there's something called a…" Lorcan paused, frowning. "A *daimon*. A sort of a spirit."

Morrigan nodded and started walking again. "I see. Yes, there is, and we don't interfere with them. Remember, a *deamhan aeir* killed two of your uncles, your aunt, and your unborn cousin."

Lorcan bit his lip. "I didn't realize they were the same thing. Is Corvina a *deamhan aeir*? Do I need to worry?"

Morrigan chuckled. "Corvina is a raven. No more. No less." She stopped. "This is it."

Lorcan looked around. When they'd left Elysium, they'd walked into what looked like a tunnel. And this was still a tunnel, looking no different from any other part of the tunnel. "Here? Why here?" He looked around again. "It looks the same as the rest of the tunnel. There's no way out."

His grandmother shook her head. "It looks the same to you. Not to me. This is where you go back to yourself." She pointed a finger at him. "No more stunts, fledgling. No more heroics. Get out of Rome and go home." She paused, then cocked her head to the side. "And take the woman with you. You seem to care for her. Take her with you and save her life."

"Woman? Which… you can't mean Livia… wait. Do you mean Drucilla?" Lorcan blinked. "Save her life?"

Morrigan nodded. "You told them you are having visions. Tell them that you have seen this—if she stays in Rome, she will be dead in a year. Her place is in Eire. Bring her there."

Lorcan nodded "I'll tell them. I… I like her. I don't want her hurt." He looked around once more. "How do I go back?"

Her answer was a hand between his shoulder blades, and a firm shove.

* * *

Lorcan gasped and raised his head, panting. He was still kneeling next to the couch, his hands still resting on Gaius' chest and forehead. It looked as if no time had passed at all.

"Lorcan?" Drucilla sounded tentative. "Are you all right?" She reached out toward Gaius, but didn't touch him. "Did it work?"

Lorcan nodded, shifting to sit on the ground with his shoulder pressed against the side of the couch. "It worked," he croaked. Then he winced. "He'll be fine. I need something to drink."

Footsteps, and a hand the color of burnished oak holding a goblet moved into view. "It's safe," Tavi said. "It's from a new amphora, and I watched them open it. They've already poured out the tainted wine."

Lorcan reached for the wine, but his hands were shaking so hard that Tavi sat down next to him and held the cup to his lips. Lorcan sipped, then took the cup from Tavi and took a longer swallow.

"What's happened?" he asked as he drank. "What have I missed?"

"Missed?" Tavi repeated. "You haven't missed anything. The guards aren't even back with Galius yet." He looked around. "Marcus brought the real guards in, and Grandfather and my father are with them. Ennius and Nona came through once the guards went into the library, and they're with Yaroah and Manius. And Livia is in the garden with the Pontifex. He's a little shaky. The rest of us are here." He looked around. "Almost. I'm not sure where the Flamen Dialis or the Flamenica are… no, there they are. We're all here." He poured more wine into the cup. "Are you all right? That didn't seem to take very long."

"It took longer inside of it," Lorcan said. "If that makes any sense. It felt like hours. And… I…" He glanced around, then lowered his voice.

"My grandmother is angry at me, because I could have hurt myself badly. But your Apollo says I did him a service."

Tavi's eyebrows rose to disappear into his curls. "You... you spoke to one of *our* gods?"

Lorcan nodded and sipped more of the wine. "He's very nice. And he wants Grandmother to show him how the healing chants work. He wants it for his priests." He looked around. "Did Laris ever get here?"

Tavi shook his head, reaching over and taking the cup from Lorcan. He took a swallow, then passed the cup back. "He hasn't, and no one knows where he is. There are guards searching for him." He glanced over to the other side of the couch, where Drucilla was sitting. "We've all got questions for him, and I'm inclined to ask them with a club."

"Gaius gets to ask those questions first. And then I will, but I won't use a club." She looked at them. "Hairpins. I'll be using hairpins. Sharp ones."

Lorcan nodded. He waited until she'd turned her attention back to Gaius before turning to Tavi. "Grandmother says she has to come with us," he said, keeping his voice low. Not low enough, as Drucilla turned to look at him.

"Me?" she asked. "Are you talking about me? Your grandmother the Goddess wants me to go to Hibernia? Why?"

Lorcan took the cup back from Tavi and drained it. "Grandmother says you need to come with us. I don't know why." He sighed and closed his eyes. "I'm tired. And hungry. This was supposed to be a feast, wasn't it? Is there food?"

He heard a grunt, and opened his eyes to see Tavi getting to his feet. "I'll find something. Drucilla? Do you want to eat something?"

"I'm fine," she said. "I'm just going to wait for Gaius to wake up." She reached out and smoothed the front of Gaius' tunic. "When will he wake, Lorcan?"

Lorcan shook his head. "I'm not sure. He's sleeping deeply now, and he'll be fine when he wakes up. And probably starving." He looked up. "Bring enough for all of us, twice."

Tavi chuckled and leaned down to kiss the top of Lorcan's head. "I'll go and have food sent in. And I'll see how Livia is, and let her know you're done."

He walked away, and Lorcan set the cup down and closed his eyes.

"It is very hard?" Drucilla asked. "To learn to do what you did?"

Lorcan shook his head. "It's not hard to learn healing. At least, I don't think it's hard. But I've been learning from my mother since I was tall enough to see over her worktable."

"And the chants?"

"If you don't have the fire, you can't sing the chants." He opened his eyes and turned to face her. "Well, you can, but they won't do anything."

She nodded, and Lorcan knew what her next question was going to be.

"Is this something I could learn, if I went with you?"

Lorcan smiled. "You could start learning to heal tomorrow, the way that Livia or I would do it without the chants. But to know if you could learn the chants and how to use then, you'd have to come with us."

Drucilla nodded. She smoothed the front of Gaius' tunic again, then looked at Lorcan. "If I'd known this, would I have known that someone was poisoning me and killing my babies?"

Lorcan nodded slowly. "I... yes. I knew what that potion was by scent. You'd have been taught what *glechon* was and what it could do to you."

"That's what I thought." Drucilla licked her lips and looked around. "I'll talk to my brother. There's nothing in Rome for me anymore. Gaius has his Claudia, and he'll have the son he always wanted. I need to find what I want. And I think this may be it."

Lorcan smiled. "You'll be welcome in my family *baile*, Drucilla. My mother is an excellent teacher. And we'll talk to Livia—she can start teaching you on the way." He looked around. "Where's Tavi?"

Drucilla sat up straight and turned so she could see the rest of the *triclinium*. "I don't see him."

Lorcan got to his feet. He could see the Emperor and Decus near the doors, talking to guards. The *doctores* and Manius were near the door that led out to the gardens, which was where Livia and the Pontifex were supposed to be. And there was no sign of Tavi.

"Tavi?" Lorcan called, and saw every head in the room turn to face him.

"Lorcan, what is it?" Decus called, coming toward him. "Are you all right? Did it work?"

"Gaius will be fine," Lorcan said, talking quickly, not looking at Decus. "Tavi went to get something for us to eat and now I don't see him. Did he have to leave the room for it?"

"He didn't go out past us," Decus said. "But he could have gone by way of the garden."

Lorcan looked around again, and noticed the door that led to the library was open. Who had opened that? "Ennius?" he called. "Did Tavi go past you to the gardens?"

"No," Ennius called.

"And... did you leave that door open when you came back?" Lorcan pointed at the library.

Ennius came to join him, looked toward the door, and shook his head. "No. The guards told us to close it." He blinked. "Oh..."

"Get your weapons," Lorcan said softly. He looked around. "Are there swords I can use?"

"The boxes by Father's couch," Decus said. He turned and raised his voice. "Father!"

"What is it?" Lucanus joined them, accompanied by one of the guards. This one was wearing a far more elaborate set of armor than Lorcan was used to seeing. "What's wrong?"

"Tavi said he was going to find us something to eat, and now he's not in the room at all. He didn't go through the gardens, because the *doctores* would have seen him. He didn't go past you. And the doors to the library are open. The guards said to keep them closed," Lorcan answered. "I think something is wrong, and I'm going to look. But I need weapons."

Lucanus paled. "There were other traitors in the guard," he murmured. "Come with me." He turned and stalked toward the couch in the alcove. As he followed the Emperor, Lorcan looked around again. Someone else was missing.

"Where's Corvina?"

"The last I saw her, she was with your wife," Lucanus said. "So, I presume she's in the garden." He paused. "Manius, go and bring your daughter and the Pontifex in," he called. "If there are more traitors about, I want everyone where I can see them and they can be protected by guards I know I can trust."

"Can you trust any of them?" Lorcan asked softly. Lucanus scowled at him but said nothing, so Lorcan looked toward the garden. If they couldn't trust the guards, then at least Livia would be with her father and the other *doctores*, who Lorcan did trust. But Livia didn't appear; instead, Manius came back into the *triclinium* at a run.

96

"Lorcan!"

Lorcan met Manius before he'd covered half the distance between them. "What is it? Where's Livia?"

"Not in the garden," Manius gasped. "I can't find her or the Pontifex. I didn't even see Corvina."

Lorcan closed his eyes, trying to think, trying to keep from panicking. His head was still foggy from the healing, and he didn't feel at all steady, but he had to do something. His mates... "Give me the weapons." He turned, and Lucanus nodded, bringing him to the table and opening one of the chests. Inside was a pair of beautifully-made, matching *siccae*.

"Manius told me that he'd promised you a set made to your measure. I asked if he would allow me the honor," Lucanus said. "Use them well, Lorcan."

Lorcan nodded and picked one up, smiling slightly at the weight in his hand. "It's perfect." He met Lucanus' eyes. "I'll use them well."

"Go find them and bring them back safely," Lucanus said.

Lorcan picked up the second sword and looked at the other box. "That has a *dolabra* in it, doesn't it?"

"Two," Lucanus said. "A matched pair for my namesake."

Lorcan studied the box for a moment, then turned. "Yaroah, you don't have a shield. Think you can use a *dolabra*?"

Yaroah came over and watched as Lucanus opened the box to show the pair of axes inside. He nodded. "I will carry this, and I will give it to Tavi when we find him. That is your plan, Lorcan?"

Lorcan smiled. "You know me. Yes."

"Then let us go hunting." Yaroah reached down and picked up one of the pair, resting it on his shoulder. He looked around, then whistled. "Nona, Ennius!"

"Coming!" Ennius carried a pair of swords over, handing one to Yaroah. Nona followed, also armed.

"What's the plan?" he asked. "They have to have gone back to the library, right? Is there a way out of there?"

Lorcan nodded. "Into the Temple. If they leave the Temple, where would they go? I don't know this city as well as you do."

The other *doctores* looked at each other. "I..."

"I'm coming with you." Decus reached into the box and took the other *dolabra*, shouldering it the way that Yaroah had. "If Galius isn't still in the Temple, there's one place he might have taken them. He kept a house near the walls, and he doesn't know that I know about it. He'll think it's safe. He'll go there."

"How would he get there?" Nona asked. "He can't have planned for this. Now he may very well have hostages, and he'll have to get them across Rome without being noticed. How?"

Lorcan frowned, looking at the door. "Unless he's not planning on leaving the Temple," he murmured. "There's the other library." He pointed to a second door. "That one, it goes to the other library, doesn't it? The one with books in Greek?"

"Yes," Lucanus answered. "What are you thinking?"

"That he let Decus know about the house. That he had planned for something like this. Something where things have gone wrong. So he's laid a false trail to take forces loyal to you away from the Palace. Once we're gone, he'll come back and finish what he started. He has more guards following him than you knew. He's cornered, and a cornered dog will bite." He looked around. "Manius!"

"Lorcan?"

"Take everyone in this room to the *ludus* and bar the doors. We'll meet you there."

Lucanus looked startled. Then he nodded. He glanced at the door. "Good hunting, Lorcan," he said softly. "Bring them back safely." He looked at Decus. "I expect you to invoke your rights as his father, Decus."

"I intend to."

* * *

"What's the plan?" Nona whispered as they started down the corridor. Lorcan glanced back at him. Nona and Ennius were with him, while Decus and Yaroah had taken the other corridor to the Greek library.

"We're going to find them," he answered. "Then we'll see how many little pieces I dice Galius into." He paused. "The door at the end is open. No more talking."

They crept the rest of the way down the corridor, and Lorcan waited for a moment at the open door, listening. There was a soft sound from inside, almost like a moan. Then he heard a raven's angry hiss, and pushed the door open.

Julius lay curled up in the middle of a pool of blood on the floor. The moaning was coming from him, and stopped as Lorcan dropped to one knee next to him. "Julius?" he whispered, touching the guard's shoulder. Julius rolled onto his back—his throat had been slit from ear to ear. Lorcan shuddered, reaching out and closing the man's eyes.

"I'm sorry, my friend," he murmured.

"Is he dead?" Nona asked.

"Yes," Lorcan said, getting back up. "I don't understand. Why kill him?" He looked around. "Corvina?"

Another angry hiss, followed by a rattling sound that seemed to come from underneath a table. Ennius crawled underneath. "Well," he said, his voice muffled. "Lorcan, she's hurt. Come here, sweetheart. You know me. I'll help you." He rolled onto his back, and Lorcan could see Corvina resting against his chest. There was blood on the front of his tunic.

"Looks like someone tried to do for her what they did for Julius," Ennius said. "But there's blood on her beak. She probably gave as good as she got."

Lorcan crouched, picking Corvina up and putting her on the table to examine her. There was a gash over her breast, and one wing hung at a crooked angle.

"I think they hit her with something," he said. "She's not broken, though. Just cut. Nona, is Tavi's toga still on the floor?"

"Yeah. Need bandage strips?"

"Please."

By the time he'd finished bandaging Corvina and securing her wing, Decus and Yaroah had joined them.

"The Temple is empty," Decus said. "I don't know what happened to the priest."

Lorcan frowned. He moved Corvina to his shoulder. "Hold on," he murmured to her. She clicked her beak at him in response. "The temple is empty. They didn't go back to the Palace. Where are they? They can't have gone anywhere else. There's no way for them to get through the streets without being seen. They couldn't have had a *lectica* waiting. He wasn't ready for this. Unless… tunnels. Decus, are there tunnels under the Temple? Like the ones that go to the arena?"

Decus frowned slightly. "I… yes. Not directly, but yes. There's a tunnel that leads into the Palace, and that connects to the one that leads to the arena."

"Why have a tunnel when you could go through the library?" Nona asked as they followed Decus out of the library and through the empty

Temple. "Oh… because it comes out in the *triclinium*, and just anyone can't be in there. Never mind."

Decus opened a door and looked down the narrow flight of stairs. "They came this way," he said. "There's blood on the steps."

"We need a light," Ennius said. "A lamp, or a torch. We'll be feeling our way blind down there." He looked around. "If the priests were smart… there." He walked away, coming back with an oil lamp. "It's not much, but it's another weapon if we need it."

"Another…" Lorcan started. Then he shuddered. "That's horrible."

"That is not something I would have expected you to fear," Yaroah murmured. "You seem to have no fear."

"When you wear feathers? Fire is an enemy," Lorcan answered. "But I don't have mine now. Let's go."

Decus went first, carrying the *dolabra* in one hand and the lamp in the other. Lorcan followed, watching for movement in the tunnel ahead of them. Here and there, something glistened on the floor, patches of something wet that reflected the light. Water, Lorcan hoped, although the smell told him otherwise.

Who was bleeding? Galius, he hoped.

"Had a thought," Ennius said. "You're not going to like it."

"What is it?" Lorcan asked.

"Just… Livia fights. If someone attacked her and the Pontifex in the garden, we'd have heard it. There would have been a fight, and there wasn't. So, someone got her out of the garden without a fuss… which tells me that the Pontifex isn't another hostage."

"Oh, I don't like that at all," Decus said. "And we're coming to a junction. Be quiet."

They stopped at the crossing, and Lorcan looked down each dark corridor. "Which way?"

"That way goes to the Temple of Vesta," Decus said, pointing. "This way goes to the arena."

Lorcan nodded. "Which way would he go? The arena or the Temple?"

"Are we thinking the Pontifex is involved in this?" Decus asked. "If he is… they went to the Temple. But we should look for a trail." He started down the tunnel to the arena, then came back and went toward the Temple. He bent, and picked up something that glittered and shone in the lamplight.

Livia's necklace.

Once they moved further down the tunnel, there was a small trail of blood droplets every few feet. Lorcan had to fight to keep from leaving the group and racing down the tunnels. This was taking too long. Galius could have killed them already. Or worse…

Decus stopped and gestured for the others to come closer. "I'm not sure how far it is before we reach the Temple," he said. "From this point out, no talking. Lorcan, can Corvina stay on your shoulder if you're fighting?"

"I don't know. We'll find out." Lorcan looked down the tunnel. "Let's go."

They walked on in silence, and Lorcan noticed that the tunnel was getting brighter as it sloped upwards. He looked down, away from the light, listening. Faint birdsong, and… raised voices. He stopped, and the others stopped around him.

"This is out of control!" Lorcan recognized the Pontifex' voice. "I agreed to help you because you said that you'd rid Rome of the upstart! But it's all gone wrong!" Lorcan couldn't hear what was said, but he clearly heard the outraged response. "Murdering my sister was never part of the agreement! Murdering the Emperor and the heir was never part of the agreement! None of this was part of the agreement!"

Laughter, and someone screamed. Lorcan glanced at Decus, who grimaced and blew out the lamp. Then he gestured, and they started moving once more.

The tunnel opened out into an empty kitchen, and through the door they could see the back of the tall, round Temple of Vesta. Just outside lay the body of the Pontifex. Lorcan took a step toward him, but stopped when Nona touched his arm.

"You can't help him," Nona whispered. He looked around. "Where are the virgins?"

"What?"

"The priestesses of Vesta," Decus answered. "There are six of them. Daughters of the highest families in Rome. One of them is my oldest daughter, Decia Lucania." He looked around. "A day ago, I'd have said he'd never hurt them. The penalty if he so much as touches one is death. But now…"

"Find them," Lorcan said. "Find the priestesses and get them out. Yaroah, go with him. Nona, Ennius, you're with me. Which way?"

Chapter Twelve

"I've never been in here before," Nona whispered as they made their way down the long portico. "I mean… this is the House of the Virgins. We're not supposed to be in here!"

Lorcan clicked his tongue at Nona to silence him, and heard Corvina make an echoing click. They had gone down the left side of the courtyard, heading away from the Temple where Vesta's sacred flames burned. Decus and Yaroah had gone down the right side, which Decus said would take them to the hall where the Virgins slept, and where he hoped he'd find them. Hopefully, they weren't also hostages.

The entire place was oddly quiet. This side of the courtyard opened into a row of rooms and storerooms that were punctuated by staircases leading up. All of the rooms were empty. There were no servants, no priestesses. The only sound was the water spilling in the fountains at the center of the courtyard. A brick structure in the center of the courtyard partially obscured the view from one side to the other, and Lorcan kept looking at it as they passed, waiting for something to jump out at them. Nothing did, and the silence was making him nervous.

He paused when he heard a whistle, then Decus moved into view, leading six women dressed in white robes trimmed in purple. Yaroah followed behind them. He saw Lorcan and trotted across the courtyard.

"Decia Lucania says that they were here," he said as he reached them. "They locked her and the other priestesses in a storeroom off the bakery. She didn't see any other prisoners, and we have not found Livia or Tavi." He pointed to the end of the courtyard. "There are two courtyards there, and the priestesses' hall. The mill and the bakery are there, and they are all empty. We haven't yet searched the upper floors, but I do not think they would go up."

"If they did, they'd be trapped," Lorcan murmured, looking up at the opposite side of the courtyard. "Does she have any idea where else

Galius would have taken them in here?" he asked. "They haven't left. They haven't gone back to the tunnels. They have to be here."

"We will search. Decus is taking the priestesses to the tunnels. He'll meet us and—"

A woman screamed. Lorcan burst into a run, heading toward the sound, hearing the others behind him, feeling Corvina's claws through the fabric of his tunic as she clung to him to keep from falling. He started to skirt around the building in the courtyard, and saw movement inside just as he heard Ennius shout behind him: "Look out!"

Lorcan stopped, swords ready as one of the false guards dove toward him. Training took over, and he blocked with his left-hand sword, striking with his right, feeling the bite of metal on bone a moment before the man screamed and fell. Lorcan jerked his sword free, paused to make sure Corvina was safe, then kept moving, catching up with the others who had passed him while he'd dealt with the attacker. He could see Decus now, holding off two more of the false guards, and it was clear that Tavi's father had no idea what he was doing with the *dolabra*. Yaroah hit the guards first, then Ennius, dealing with them while Nona and Lorcan skirted around the fight. Decus had fallen back, panting, his arms streaked with blood.

"My son fights with this thing," he wheezed as Lorcan reached his side. "I never... I need to take it more seriously!" He shook his head as Lorcan tried to examine him. "I'm fine. I can wait."

"Yaroah said you didn't find him," Lorcan said. "Where would they take them?" He looked at the women. One of them strongly resembled Decus. "Lady, where would he have taken my mates?"

"Mates?" Decia Lucania smiled. "Oh, you're the one who turned my little brother's head. I've heard of you, Albus." She pointed toward the back corner. "I think they might be there. Those men came from there. There are five rooms through that door. When you go in, there is a staircase in front of you, but I don't think they would go upstairs. To the left there's an outer room, a storeroom, and the hall we use for lessons. You have to pass through the outer room to get either of the others. There are no windows, but there are ventilation holes up high. To the right is the *triclinium*." Decia Lucania looked thoughtful. "And to answer what I think your next question will be, I'm not sure how many he has now, but Galius only had five guards when broke in."

"That was my next question. Thank you," Lorcan said. He looked over at Yaroah and Ennius, and the two guards who were now motionless on the floor. "He has two guards left. And Galius himself. I want him."

"No, you're going to leave him for me," Decus said. "Lorcan, you heard my father tell me to invoke my rights?"

Decia Lucania gasped, and Lorcan glanced at her, seeing the horror on her face. He turned back to Decus. "Yes, but I didn't understand what he meant. What rights?"

"My right as his father to correct the mistake that I made by siring him," Decus said. He walked past Lorcan and picked up one of the discarded swords. "I'll give the *dolabra* to Tavi when we find him. This is my weapon."

Lorcan blinked. "You... you have the right to kill him?" he stammered. "Because you're his father? You..." He stopped and shook his head. "I need to stop trying to make sense of Rome. I was going to tell you to take the women to the tunnels and back to the Palace."

"And I'm telling you no," Decus said. "Lucania, you'd best go and find a safe place."

"We'll go to one of the upstairs chambers and bar the doors," Decia Lucania said. She looked at Lorcan. "I assume that's Corvina? Will she come with me?"

"Corvina, go with the lady and behave yourself," Lorcan murmured in Gaeilge.

Corvina coughed at him, but went to Decia Lucania without a fuss. She stroked the raven's feathers. "Be careful," she said. Then she gathered the women up and hurried them away.

"How are we doing this?" Ennius asked. "Two hostages. How do we do this so no one we like gets killed?"

Lorcan started walking in the direction Decia Lucania had pointed until he could see through the door to the staircase just inside. He stopped and turned around to face the others. "Watch my back. They're probably watching us. Someone needs to be on those stairs, in case it all goes wrong and he tries to get away by going up."

"If he's smart, he's got someone on those stairs, in case we try to come at him from above," Nona murmured.

"Fine. Decus, take Yaroah and take that staircase. Once you have it, wait. Don't engage. Not yet."

"When?" Yaroah asked.

"Once you hear fighting."

"Be careful," Decus said. He glanced at the door, and his mask slipped for a moment, letting Lorcan see the worry underneath. "Lorcan—"

"I'll bring him out. And if I can, I'll leave Galius for you." Lorcan waited until they were gone, then turned to look at the door. He could see the figure in the shadows. Galius.

"What do you want?" Lorcan called.

"Your head on a platter," Galius shouted back.

Lorcan snorted. "I've heard that one before," he muttered. "You want my head on a platter?" he called. "Come get it."

Galius laughed again. "You want your women? Come get them." He vanished back into the shadows.

"Lorcan..." The warning was clear in Nona's voice, but Lorcan shook his head, and Nona fell silent.

"You're going in there, aren't you?" Ennius murmured.

"Yes."

"And... what do you want us to do?"

Lorcan licked his lips and turned his back to the door. "Keep them inside. If anyone tries to get out this way, kill them. If Galius comes out, put him down, but leave him for Decus."

Ennius nodded. He took a deep breath and rested one hand on Lorcan's shoulder. "Don't do anything stupid," he said. "We want to be able to send you home in one piece. You're so close to getting on that ship."

Lorcan couldn't help it. He smiled. "I am getting on that ship, and I'll have both of my mates with me," he said. "Thank you, Ennius. My brother."

"You know, maybe we should go to Hibernia with you," Nona said. "Keep you out of trouble."

"Just watch my back now," Lorcan said. He turned back to the door and walked into the darkened hall. The stairs were in front of him, and he looked up to see Yaroah looking down at him. The big man nodded and moved out of sight. Lorcan looked to the right, but the *triclinium* was empty. He went left, into the hall. Galius was waiting for him, leaning against a table. His face was bruised, and there was a bandage wrapped haphazardly around his left arm.

He was alone.

"Where are they?" Lorcan demanded.

"You're going to deal with me first," Galius answered. Lorcan took a step toward him, and he held up an empty hand. "We're talking first," he added quickly. "I'm unarmed."

"Should I care? Tavi was unarmed. Livia was unarmed. And I don't care what you have to say." Lorcan paused, listening. There should be at least one guard. Where? "I know you've been lying. I expect you're still lying, and I don't believe you're going to stop lying. I don't care what you have to say or what happens to you when I'm gone. I want my mates. So get out of my way."

"That was… rather a long speech for someone I expected to gut me on sight." To Lorcan's surprise, Galius laughed. He sounded… almost relieved. "So… you don't intend to kill me?"

"Your father asked me to let you live," Lorcan answered. "I honor your father, even if you don't. So you get to live. For now. Now where are they?"

Galius frowned. "I… you're not what I expected. You were supposed to be a wild animal. A barbarian, like all the other barbarians. But you're not, are you?"

"Given what I've seen ever since I left Eire?" Lorcan snorted. "I'd rather be a barbarian than live with what you call civilization. So, if we're bargaining, then we're making a bargain the way we would in Eire. If my mates are unharmed, then I won't hurt you. I'll take them, and I'll leave, and you'll be your father's problem."

Galius glanced at the doors to Lorcan's left. "Do I still get to walk away if he's a little harmed? He was much more difficult to take than I thought he'd be. He didn't used to be able to fight like that."

"Where are they?" Lorcan growled, and watched as Galius went pale.

"He's in the first room. The woman is in the other one."

"And your guards?" Lorcan asked.

"I'm alone." Galius looked around. "No one else here."

Lorcan scowled slightly. He still didn't believe Galius, but he needed to get to Livia and Tavi. He pointed with one blade at the table. "Sit there."

"On the table?" Galius did as he was bid, and folded his hands in his lap. "Now what?"

"Nona!" Lorcan raised his voice. "Ennius!"

The two men entered a run. Ennius stopped and looked around. "Where are the guards?"

"He says he's alone," Lorcan said. "Take him to Decus." He waited until Nona and Ennius had escorted Galius from the room, then moved toward one of the doors. Was this the first room, or the other one? He wasn't sure. He entered, and saw that this was the storeroom, filled with casks and boxes. And Livia, bound to a chair.

She was blindfolded and gagged, and Lorcan saw her flinch as she heard him come toward her. "It's me," he said, going to his knees and laying one sword on the ground so he could remove the blindfold. "Livia, it's me. It's over."

She blinked rapidly as he tugged the blindfold off, focused on him, then looked past him and squeaked through her gag. Lorcan heard the scrape of a sandal on the stone floor and spun, sword raised. The last guard lunged at him, and Lorcan just barely dodged the attack. He staggered to his feet, moving away from the chair, away from Livia. His second sword was still on the ground at her feet, but there was no way he could reach it. Not without putting Livia into harm's way. He drew the guard off, letting himself be pushed, watching for an opening…

There! Lorcan blocked the guard's sword, pivoted, and punched the man in the face. The guard staggered back, blood streaming from a clearly-broken nose. Lorcan followed, driving his sword into the guard's belly. The man screamed as he fell, then lay still. He might have been dead, but Lorcan wasn't sure. He didn't care. He wiped his blade on the guard's tunic, then went back to his wife. He cut the ropes binding her to the chair, pulled the gag from her mouth, then pulled her into his arms and kissed her.

"Are you all right?" he asked as he pulled back. "He didn't hurt you?"

She shook her head. "No. I'm fine. You're not. Lorcan—"

"I'll manage," Lorcan said. "I don't have a choice." He let Livia go. "Tavi is supposed to be in the next room."

"The Pontifex—"

"Betrayed us. I know. He's dead. Galius killed him." He handed Livia one of his swords and took her other hand. "Did you see what they did to Tavi? Is he hurt?"

"I don't know. They had me blindfolded almost the entire time."

Lorcan nodded and led Livia out of the room. He jumped as a shadow moved near the outer door, but it was Yaroah.

"I came to help, and heard fighting," Yaroah said. "Livia!" He looked around. "Where's Tavi?"

Lorcan pointed. "There. Wait here. I may need you." He went to the door and opened it, walking inside. This was the hall for lessons—there were tables and more chairs, racks of scrolls. And Tavi, bound to another chair, almost bonelessly limp. His tunic was torn and blood streaked, and Lorcan could see the bruises on his dark skin. He crossed to the chair and crouched so he could better see Tavi's face. No blindfold or gag, which told Lorcan that Tavi had been unconscious for a frighteningly long time. Then Tavi opened one eye, winked at him, and closed his eye again.

Lorcan burst out laughing and started cutting ropes. "How long have you been faking being unconscious?"

"I'm not entirely sure," Tavi answered. He sat up. "I don't know how long I was unconscious before I woke up here. And I wasn't sure what was happening, so it seemed a better idea to stay limp and not be a target. If you don't react, he gets bored. Where is he?"

"Nona and Ennius have taken him to your father." Lorcan cut the last rope. "Can you stand? How badly are you hurt?" He glanced at the door. "Livia! Yaroah!"

Tavi leaned heavily on Lorcan's arm as he stood up, wincing. "I'm not sure. You and Livia can examine me later." He took a deep breath and winced. "Everything hurts. I feel like I fell out of a tree."

"How does that feel? Falling out of a tree?" Lorcan put his arm around Tavi's waist. "Lean on me, if you need to."

"You never... of course you never fell out of a tree. Birds don't fall out of trees." Tavi laughed, then winced again. Then he stopped. "Lorcan, why hasn't Livia come in yet?"

Lorcan looked toward the door, then stepped away from Tavi. "Stay behind me," he said, and started toward the door.

The outer room was empty, and on the ground were a *gladius*, a *sica*, and a *dolabra*. Lorcan walked out and picked up the *sica*, going to check the storeroom while Tavi picked up the *dolabra*. The body of the guard was where he left it, and he went back to join Tavi. Tavi nodded toward the door, and they peered out into the courtyard. They could see Decus, on his knees and with a sword held across his throat by a guard standing behind him. The *doctores*, all kneeling and surrounded. Livia, standing alone with a guard, a knife held to her throat.

"Five guards," Lorcan murmured. "Your sister told us he came in with five guards."

"He had more than five in the library," Tavi said. He moved back inside, his back against the wall. "I counted... there are six out there?"

Lorcan nodded. "That explains why he was so calm. He knew we were outnumbered." He looked back out the door, and heard Galius shout.

"I see you! Come out, barbarian. Come out or I'll kill all of them."

Lorcan scowled, trying to think. "Tavi, now what?"

"Can you keep him busy?" Tavi asked. He glanced at the stairs. "Challenge him to single combat or something. Bait him, like you did in the library. Keep him busy," he repeated, and ran up the stairs.

"What are you doing?" Lorcan hissed. No answer, and he took a deep breath, tried to steady himself once more, then walked out. "I'm here," he called.

"Where's your woman?" Galius asked.

"Are you blind? Livia is right there." He glanced back at the door. "How hard did you hit Tavi? He won't wake." Lorcan saw Livia's eyes widen, and knew he'd have to apologize for frightening her. "Let them go."

Galius laughed. "Go? Of course not!" He walked over to where a guard was standing next to Livia, trailing his fingers up her arm and laughing when she jerked away. "This little one is my passage out of Rome. And the others? They're the message to my grandfather that I'll be back." He smiled, waving the sword he held at the guard standing over Decus. "Kill him."

"Coward," Lorcan spat, the words falling from his mouth before he really thought about what he was going to say. "Getting someone else to do the deed. Killing with poison and guile, like the weakling you are. Have you ever even fought a real opponent?"

The barb struck, and stuck—Galius turned and stalked toward him. "You're calling me a coward? Weak? You craven little barbarian slave!"

"Prince of my own people and *semideus* recognized by your own gods as their kin, and I kill my enemies with my own hands and my own blades. Not by poison. Not by trickery. Not with hired swords and a knife in the back." Lorcan smiled at the look of pure fury on Galius' face. "I haven't seen you fight yet. Are you as hopeless with that blade as Tavi was before I taught him better?" He saw movement across the courtyard, as Tavi ran from the portico to the brick building. He needed to keep Galius' attention. Hopefully, he wouldn't have to keep it going too long—he could feel himself flagging. "Is that why you have other people do your killing for you? You can't do it yourself?"

"I killed Antius!" Galius shrilled.

"By surprise, with a knife hidden in your toga." Lorcan sniffed. "What skill does that take? You're a coward, and a fool, and no one will ever follow you... unless it's to your pyre." He glanced at the guards and raised his voice. "Do you all intend to follow this fool to death? You think six of you are going to take all of Rome? Against guards loyal to the Emperor, and people who love him? Are you all idiots?" He looked at the guards. "Do you think you're going to get away with threatening the Vestal Virgins? That's a death sentence, I'm told."

The guard standing with Livia tensed. "I..."

"Ignore him!" Galius snapped. "He's a barbarian and he knows nothing."

Lorcan shook his head. "I know you're not winning this. I know you can't win this. Because you can't hold it. Even if you kill me. Even if you kill everyone in this courtyard, you can't hold Rome. You think you're strong, but all you are is a bully who hurts people who can't fight back." Lorcan struck fast, slapping the flat of one blade against Galius' upper arm. The man yelped and staggered back, away from Lorcan. Lorcan followed him. "I can fight back. So, fight me, coward."

Galius stared at him for a moment, his face flushed red. Then he charged forward, and Lorcan fell back before his attack, drawing him away from the others. He was faster than Lorcan would have thought, and better trained, but Lorcan wondered if he'd ever fought a real opponent. He fought like a *murmillo*, holding his off-arm bent as if he held a shield. It was a tempting target, and an obvious mistake. A mistake that Manius would have beaten out of him on the sands of the *ludus*.

Therefore, it wasn't a mistake. What was he doing?

Galius struck overhand, and Lorcan blocked with his right-hand blade, slashing with his left and aiming for Galius' unprotected belly. It was a poor strike and he knew it—the blade glanced off something under Galius' tunic as Galius turned with Lorcan and lashed out like a *cestus*. Too late, Lorcan saw the glint of metal from the rod hidden in Galius' fist, right before Galius caught him in the left temple. Lorcan staggered back, feeling as if the side of his face had exploded. His ankle turned, and he fell. Dimly, through the roar of blood in his ears, he heard Livia scream.

"Oh, I'll enjoy gutting you." Galius' voice was distant, and Lorcan blinked, trying to focus. He could see the man standing over him, his sword raised; he fumbled for his swords, trying to force his head to stop spinning. Something moved behind Galius, approaching fast...

Tavi.

Galius heard him, started to turn, and the *dolabra* caught him under the chin, the sharp blade cutting through skin and muscle so easily that Galius took three more steps before his body realized that his head was no longer attached. It staggered, then fell, and Tavi stood still for a moment, panting, his eyes closed, his arms and the front of his tunic painted with blood. Then he turned and pointed the bloody axe at the man guarding Livia.

"Let her go."

The guard fainted.

* * *

"We're almost there," Nona said. "Ennius, go on ahead and bang on the door. Let them know it's us."

Lorcan grimaced. He couldn't walk a straight line, could barely stand upright. Livia said the blow had rattled his brains, and he needed to rest. But taking a litter through the tunnels wasn't anything Lorcan wanted to do. So, they walked slowly, and he leaned on Yaroah and Tavi the entire way. The narrow stairs were torturous, but then he was in the familiar atrium of the *ludus*.

Home.

For now.

"Lorcan," Manius breathed, putting his hands on Lorcan's shoulders. "What happened?"

"Lorcan got his bell rung," Ennius answered. "He needs to lay down."

"And Galius?"

Lorcan swayed as he turned to face the Emperor. "He's dead. Tavi killed him."

"Father, I'll tell you everything," Decus said. "But let Lorcan go rest. He deserves it."

Chapter Thirteen

Lorcan spent the next three days sequestered with his mates, sleeping and resting and recovering. The others told him about what was happening outside the *ludus*—the executions of Galius' surviving guards, and the uprisings that were put down with brutal efficiency. Lorcan would not have expected the complete ruthlessness that Lucanus showed in dealing with the traitors, but he also didn't disagree, and he was somewhat sorry to have missed seeing it. On the morning of the fourth day, a servant knocked on the door and asked if Lorcan was feeling well enough for a visitor.

"You don't have to," Livia warned as Lorcan sat up.

"I want to," Lorcan said. "I'm bored, I don't hurt as much. I can almost open this eye, and I'm not seeing double out of the other one anymore. I think I can even walk a straight line."

"Yes, but will you purge afterward?" Tavi asked.

"Not as badly as you did," Lorcan teased. Tavi grinned in response and held his hand out.

"You are feeling better," he agreed as he pulled Lorcan up. "You haven't teased me like that since we came back. I'll help you dress."

"I want a bath," Lorcan grumbled as he pulled a fresh tunic over his head. "Livia, am I hale enough to soak?"

"If Tavi goes with you," Livia answered. "I don't want you fainting in the *caldarium*." She pressed against his side and rested her head on his shoulder as he put his arms around her. Warmth at his back, as Tavi joined them, wrapping his arms around them both. For a moment, Lorcan didn't want to move. Surrounded by love and warmth, he was almost completely happy.

Almost.

"Visitor first, then a bath," he said.

* * *

"Oh, now that is a truly spectacular bruise," Gaius declared as Lorcan, Livia and Tavi entered the atrium. He stood up from his chair, wobbling just a little as he crossed to meet them. Once he was close enough, he reached out and tipped Lorcan's head to the side. "Can you see out of that eye?"

"Almost," Lorcan answered. "How are you feeling? You shouldn't be up yet."

"When I told him I was coming to see you, he insisted," Decus said. He came closer, and Lorcan wondered at his clothing—he was wearing a different toga, and had his head covered as if they were going to the temple.

"Father," Tavi asked slowly. "Why are you dressed like the Pontifex Maximus?"

"That would be because he's the new Pontifex Maximus," Gaius answered. Decus blushed.

"Father appointed me this morning." He looked down at himself. "We've been discussing it for two days, the three of us. He even brought Decia Lucania into the discussion. And... I agree with his logic. It makes sense for me to take this position, to better support Gaius when he becomes Emperor."

"And appointing him now means that he'll have time to learn his duties before that happens," Gaius finished. "Now, this is only part of what we came to tell you." He looked around, and Lorcan realized he was looking for a chair.

"Come to the garden," Livia said. "We can sit and relax. Lorcan shouldn't be standing."

"Either," Gaius added with a rueful smile. "I heard the word, even though you didn't say it."

They went out to Livia's garden, and Gaius sighed as he sat down on a bench. "I'm not used to this," he grumbled. "I know it will take time, but it chafes to be so... so weak!"

"Would you rather be weak or dead?" Decus asked. "That doesn't seem a choice."

"I know, but it means I can't help Lorcan."

Lorcan frowned, leaning forward and resting his elbow on his knee. "Help me how?" he asked.

Gaius smiled. "You saved my father and my inheritance, and all of Rome. I thought I would return the favor."

"Return..." Lorcan sat up straight. "You thought you were going to come to Eire with me? With no guarantee of coming back? And you thought I'd let you do that?" He laughed at the shocked look on Gaius' face. "I almost killed myself to save your life, Gaius. If you got killed in Eire, my grandmother would pull all my feathers out."

"Father told him he was insane, and that if he so much as thought about leaving Rome, he'd be locked in his rooms in the Palace for a month." Decus tipped his head back and sighed. "I can't get used to having my head covered all the time. It'll come. I know. So, the other thing we came to tell you is that the courier ship will sail from Portus at dawn two days from now. Which means that you should prepare to leave tomorrow. All your provisions are arranged. And Drucilla is insisting that she's going with you."

"Which raises the question of why," Gaius asked. "I think the farthest Drucilla has ever been outside of Rome is Ostia. And now she wants to go to Hibernia. And learn to be a healer. What have you done with my wife?"

"She's not your wife anymore," Livia pointed out. "She's divorced, and wealthy in her own right. She can do as she likes."

Gaius sighed. "I know. I know she's not my wife anymore. But I do still care about her. I want her to be happy. And... I don't understand why she's so set on going to Hibernia!"

Lorcan nodded. He tipped his head back and looked up at the sky. "My grandmother told me to bring her. She said that Drucilla has to come with us." He glanced at Tavi. He hadn't told the others this yet. "She said that if Drucilla stays in Rome, she'll be dead in a year. I didn't tell Drucilla that."

Gaius sat up straight. "Dead? What? How?"

"I don't know," Lorcan answered. "Grandmother didn't say anything more. Just to bring her with us when we left. That her place is in Eire. I didn't mean to say anything to her that night—she overheard me tell Tavi. And she asked me about healing and if it was hard to learn. She wants to learn to sing the healing chants. The only place she can do that is Eire. So..."

"So, she's going to Eire. And maybe she'll be happy there." Gaius nodded. "I can accept that. I wish I could go with you. Father won't let me ride even ride out to Pontus."

"Because you're not strong enough," Decus said. "I'm going to go with you and see you off."

The rest of the day was a blur of packing and instructions, and Lorcan almost forgot about wanting a bath. Then Tavi cornered him and took his arm. "We have time," he said. "Come soak."

"I thought we were having a last meal together," Lorcan said as Tavi tugged him through the halls toward the bath.

"We are, but Livia said we have time. And if I don't take you to the baths now, we won't have one before we reach the villa in Ostia. Livia has Corvina. Let's go."

"I thought… didn't Gaius say Pontus?"

Tavi grinned. "That's in Ostia. It's an easy trip from here. Not even a full day."

"West of here?" Lorcan asked. "I think that's where they brought me from." He grimaced at the memory and fell silent. They reached the bath, and Lorcan let the bath slaves fuss over him, smoothing oil into his skin and scraping it off, then helping him dress in light robes and sandals. As he sat down next to Tavi in the *caldarium*, he said, "I'm not looking forward to being sick for however long we're at sea."

"Livia has a tonic for you. It tastes good, she says, and it'll help settle your stomach. And, if the trip out is anything like the trip Father and I had here, then it'll be fairly smooth. Good weather. It'll be nice. And we'll have a tent—"

"We'll have a what?" Lorcan looked at him. "A tent?"

Tavi nodded. "Oh. I… right. You were in the hold when they brought you here. That's not how we'll travel. We'll have a tent on the deck to sleep, and our own food and drink." He stood up and tugged Lorcan's hand. "Want to soak here and get the oil off? Or move on?"

"Move on. The heat is making me dizzy."

In the *tepidarium*, Lorcan settled onto the bench in the pool and sighed, tipping his head back and closing his good eye. "We're leaving. It's been so long… and we're finally leaving. I can't wait for you to meet my family. My mother is going to love you both."

"Have you had any more visions?" Tavi asked.

"Not since I spoke to my grandmother last," Lorcan answered. "You'd have noticed—when I have visions, I wake up screaming. After the last time, Livia said that if I do it again, she'll put me on the floor."

Lorcan heard Tavi laugh, and the water splashed up onto his chest. Then Tavi straddled his lap; Lorcan looked up to see Tavi smiling at him. He didn't say anything. He just caught Lorcan's face between his hands and kissed him. Lorcan slid his hands up Tavi's thighs to rest of his hips. Neither spoke, and the only sounds were splashing water, and their increasingly ragged breathing as teasing touches turned to bold caresses. Lorcan could feel Tavi's arousal pressing against him, feel himself responding as Tavi started to rut against him. He reached between them and wrapped his hand around both of their cocks. Tavi whined and broke the kiss, panting as he started pumping harder into Lorcan's hand.

"Your hand is bigger than mine," Lorcan whispered. "Help me."

Tavi laughed and reached down, covering Lorcan's hand with his own and squeezing hard enough to make Lorcan gasp.

"Who is taking whose arse?" Tavi whispered. "Is it my turn to take yours?"

"Yes," Lorcan moaned. "Oh, yes."

Tavi shifted off his legs and they climbed out of the pool. Tavi walked away, and Lorcan knelt next to one of the benches and bent over it, presenting his arse to Tavi as he returned.

"Bent over the bench," he murmured. "You remembered!" He set a small bottle down on the bench. "There. Now we're ready."

"Then hurry, before someone comes looking for us." Lorcan held onto the bench as Tavi knelt behind him. He picked up the bottle, and Lorcan heard the pop of the stopper behind pulled.

"How long has it been?" Tavi asked.

"Before I was kidnapped and brought to Rome." Lorcan looked over his shoulder. "I won't break, Tavi."

"I don't want to hurt you." Tavi poured oil into his hand. "You're hurt enough as it is." He placed one hand on Lorcan's back, and Lorcan felt pressure against his arse. He took a deep breath and relaxed, moaning as Tavi's slick fingers entered him. Tavi laughed. "You don't need much opening."

"Told you," Lorcan grumbled, then gasped as Tavi slapped his arse. Fingers slipped free, and Tavi pressed against Lorcan, his cock hot against Lorcan's skin.

"Be nice," Tavi growled. "Behave, or you can't have it."

"Tavi!" Lorcan tried to push back, but Tavi's weight pressed him into the bench, and he didn't want to strain and possibly hurt himself. So he behaved. "Please, Tavi!" he begged, and heard a soft laugh.

"Put your hands behind your back."

Lorcan twisted to look over his shoulder. "What?"

116

Tavi blinked. Then he sat back on his heels. "I... fuck." He pushed up and walked away, leaving Lorcan alone and confused. He scrambled to his feet and followed his mate.

"Tavi?" He caught up with Tavi and took his hand. "What just happened?"

Tavi shook his head. "I... I made a mistake. I wanted... but I shouldn't have tried to be the *erastes*. Not with you. I didn't hurt you, did I?"

Lorcan frowned. "No, I'm fine. Just confused. Come soak, and we'll talk." He coaxed Tavi back to the pool, settling next to him. "Tavi... when I had you the first time, there was scarring. You lied, didn't you? When I asked if he'd forced you? He..."

Tavi nodded.

"More than once?"

Tavi nodded again. He glanced over his shoulder, then slumped down in the water. "I... I'm sorry. I didn't want to say it in front of everyone. In front of my grandfather. Yes."

"Does Livia know?"

Tavi nodded once more, seeming to sink deeper in the water. "She helped. A lot. But..." He turned to Lorcan. "I'm sorry. I... I didn't mean..."

"Tavi, I'm not angry at you," Lorcan said. He took Tavi's hand and raised it to his lips, kissing his fingers. "I want to help. And if helping means coaching you so that you don't treat me the way he treated you... well, we might both enjoy that. But not until you're ready."

Tavi nodded, looking back at the surface of the water. "I killed him. I... I cut his head off. And... I thought that it would make me stop hurting. I thought... I dreamed about killing him, and it being over. And then I did, and it wasn't anything like what I thought. It still... I still hurt." He looked at Lorcan. "You're the healer. Why didn't it stop hurting? He's dead! I killed him! He can't hurt me anymore!" His breath caught, and he crumpled in tears; Lorcan pulled him into his arms and held him as he wept. He heard the scrape of a sandal on the tile, and glanced back to see Livia. She hesitated, then came and knelt by the side of the pool, reaching out and running her fingers through Tavi's curls.

"He told you?" she asked softly.

Lorcan nodded.

"I should have told you sooner." Tavi's voice with thick with tears. "I should have trusted you with it. You wouldn't... not like the others..."

He gave a watery laugh. "But you keep telling me that I don't have to listen to how things are in Rome. Not anymore."

"And I'm not a Roman, no matter how much your grandfather and your uncle want me to be," Lorcan said. "I don't see things the way they do. You were a child. You bear no shame, and no blame for what he did to you."

"What would be done to him?" Livia asked. "To Galius, in Eire?"

"Huh." Lorcan shifted, keeping his arms around Tavi. "I'm not a *brehon*, and I haven't really studied the law, but there would probably be a body-fine. A big one, given Tavi's rank."

"A fine?" Tavi repeated. "That's all?"

"No. He'd also lose all his status, all of his rank. He'd have to earn that back. He could be sold as a slave. If he didn't pay the fines, he could be killed." Lorcan shrugged slightly. "We can ask my uncle, if you want. He's a *brehon*."

"Which uncle?" Livia asked. "You have several."

"Cuanu," Lorcan answered. "Third oldest."

"After your father and… Petran?" Livia smiled. "I'll remember. I hope."

"I like Petran," Tavi murmured. He shifted around in Lorcan's arms so that his back was against Lorcan's chest. "And his mate."

"Are you feeling better?" Livia asked.

Tavi shrugged slightly. "I'm… not as raw."

"What happened?"

"I was stupid and if you'd seen me, you'd have smacked me. Or poisoned me. Or both." He paused. "The only time Livia and I ever fought was when she saw me do that to one of our lovers. She was furious, and we argued and… well, I wasn't going to tell her. But it just sort of fell out and…" Tavi paused again, then let out a huff of breath. "I was doing the same thing. Only this time, I realized what I was doing, and it scared me that I was going to do to you what Galius did to me."

"There's a difference," Lorcan murmured, rubbing his cheek against Tavi's tangled curls. "I wanted it. I still do. But not until you're ready."

Tavi nodded. "I'll get there. Eventually."

* * *

Lorcan slept without dreaming, and woke in the darkness before dawn when one of the slaves came to fetch them. They dressed quickly and brought what they were carrying with them out into the atrium. The morning meal was quiet, and the air in the *ludus* was heavy with goodbye.

"You could still come with us," Lorcan said to Nona as they walked toward the atrium. Nona didn't smile.

"We talked about it, Ennius and I," Nona replied. He ran his fingers over the wall as they walked. "And… this is our place. Neither of us would know what to do outside the walls of Rome. You were out of place in Rome? We'd be just as out of place in Hibernia." He looked around. "It'll be strange, being here without Manius and Livia and Yaroah and you. But we'll take care of all the ones like you who come our way." He smiled. "Oh, I did what you asked."

"You did? And?"

"And Ercc says he's been here so long that this is his home. He thanks you, but he's staying with us."

Lorcan nodded. "Take care of him, will you?"

Nona grinned. "You know you didn't have to ask that, right?"

Lorcan smiled and reached out to rest his hand on Nona's shoulder. "I know. Be happy, Nona." He looked around. "Where is Ennius?"

"Helping Manius." Nona chuckled. "They're packing up the armor. Yours and Yaroah's. He figured you'd want yours, at least. He's leaving, and he's still ordering us around." He shook his head. "I'm going to miss him. For all that he owned me, he was still more a father to me than my own father was."

"Thank you." Manius came around the corner and stopped, looking around. "I'll miss this place. And you. All of you. I already said my goodbyes to Ennius. Lorcan, we're ready." He glanced back over his shoulder and laughed. "Yaroah is ready to leave without us."

Lorcan laughed with him, then turned to Nona. "I'm going to miss you. Not Rome." He paused. "Well, not much. But I'll miss you and Ennius."

Nona nodded, then pulled Lorcan in and hugged him. "You take care of yourself. And kick your cousin's arse. Or his tailfeathers. Or both."

"Definitely both."

Chapter Fourteen

Apollo kept his word.

The first part of the voyage—from Rome to Carthage—was quiet and peaceful, with steady winds and smooth seas, and Lorcan not only didn't get sick, he found himself enjoying the journey. He slept most of the first day, and woke feeling better than he had in a long time. It helped that he wasn't trapped below the deck, chained in the dark and stench with other frightened slaves. He was outside, in the air. Still recovering from his injuries, but free, and on his way home.

He leaned on the rail of the ship and watched as the sailors rushed around, doing whatever arcane things they needed to do as the ship came into port. He'd picked this spot because it was out of the way, and he could watch as they worked. Corvina seemed to especially enjoy watching the sailors from her perch on Lorcan's shoulder, and had become quite popular with them. She croaked gently in his ear, and he turned to see Livia and Tavi as they wove in and around the sailors to come join him.

"Yaroah is getting ready to leave. They'll clear him to go ashore soon," Tavi said. "You should come and say goodbye."

Lorcan nodded and followed them back toward the two small tents that were set side-by-side near the back of the ship. Manius, Yaroah and Tavi shared one, while Livia and Lorcan shared with Drucilla. Lorcan still wasn't entirely happy with having one of his mates sleeping away from him, but he understood the need to maintain discretion. He just didn't have to like it. He looked around, then took Tavi's hand. Tavi smiled and squeezed his fingers.

"I miss you, too," he murmured. He reached out and took Livia's hand, pulling her closer. "I miss you both."

"How long before we reach Alba?" Lorcan asked. "I don't know how long it took us to get here when I was brought to Rome. I know someone said, but I forget."

"From Alba to Rome is 15 days, roughly," Tavi said. "We have 12 days left." He leaned closer. "Once we leave Carthage, I'll start coming to your tent at night. I already spoke to Drucilla. She doesn't mind." He chuckled. "I think she's chafing at being guarded as if she was still married."

"I didn't think we were doing that," Lorcan said. "But I suppose it has the same effect." He looked around and laughed—Drucilla was waving at them. As they reached her, she waved one arm, taking the harbor and the entire city.

"Isn't it magnificent?" she gasped. "It's so beautiful!" She looked up at the sky. "And hot. It's hotter here than it was in Rome, isn't it?"

"According to Yaroah, it gets hotter still." Lorcan looked out at the curved wall of the harbor. The gates were closed today, so he couldn't see the harbor behind them. "When I was here last, that was open, and there's more harbor inside," he said, pointing. "I don't know how they did that."

"I could tell you, if you really wanted to know," Tavi murmured. "We lived here before we went to Britannia, and Father told me about the harbor." When Lorcan and Drucilla both looked at him, he laughed. "I was born in Thabraca." He gestured. "That way, about half a day from here by ship. When we sail west, we'll pass the port. Once we pass Thabraca, all the ports we'll pass will be Numidian. My mother's family was from Numidia, but I forget where."

Drucilla looked up at him. "How did I not know you were born in Carthage?"

Tavi looked startled. "I… did you even know my mother was from Numidia?"

"I don't think I did," Drucilla said. "I met you when you were 10, remember? I never knew your mother, or that you lived anywhere but Britannia. So is this coming home for you, like it is for Yaroah?"

Tavi shook his head. "Not really. I don't remember the villa in Thabraca, and I only remember the Palace here a little. Not enough for it to be home. It's just a place where we lived when I was very small. Britannia was my home. And now…" He put his arms around Lorcan and Livia. "Hibernia will be home. Because you'll be there." He hugged them both. "Now, you two knew, didn't you?"

"I knew. I don't know if Lorcan did." Livia answered. "But you told me ages ago."

"I didn't know you were born in Carthage," Lorcan admitted. "I think I always thought you lived in Britannia forever. You never told me about Carthage."

"Because I barely remember Carthage." Tavi led them to the rail by where the sailors would lay a ramp down to the dock. "I was… five? I think? Yes. Mother died when I was five, and we left Carthage and Father became Governor of Britannia. And I was cold for what felt like forever." He chuckled. "It'll take Livia and Drucilla a few winters to get used to the cold and snow."

Both women laughed, and Lorcan leaned into Tavi's side, enjoying his warmth. "That's what furs are for. And cloaks. And fires."

"And being bundled up in furs, and cuddling near a fire?" Livia added, shifting so that she was in front of Tavi and could touch both of them. Lorcan smiled and kissed her.

"That sounds like a wonderful way to pass the winter," Drucilla murmured. "Tavi, once we leave Carthage, I should start learning to speak… Lorcan, what is it? I would call it Hibernian, but that's not what you would call your language."

"Gaeilge," Lorcan answered. "You should start to learn it, yes. We can all help you. And you wanted to learn healing. We can start that as well."

Drucilla smiled. "It's so exciting. New places to see and new things to learn!" She laughed. "I never thought I'd do anything like this!"

Lorcan smiled at her infectious enthusiasm, then looked over his shoulder. Yaroah and Manius were coming toward them. Yaroah had a pack slung over his shoulder, but he wasn't smiling. Lorcan moved away from the others and went up to him.

"What's wrong?" he asked.

Yaroah shook his head. "I am here," he murmured. "And… I never thought I would see this again. I dreamed of this, for more years than you've been alive. And now it's here and I don't know what to do."

"You told me you'd know what to do when you set your feet on the land that gave you birth," Lorcan said. "Are you ready? And do you want someone to walk down with you?"

"You would do that?" Yaroah hesitated, then nodded. "Yes. Please."

They walked over to the others, and Yaroah put down his pack. He looked around, clearly uncomfortable. Manius clapped him on the shoulder, and Yaroah smiled slightly.

"I'm here. In spite of you?" he said.

Manius arched a brow, then laughed. "I don't think there's any spite left in Rome. You took it all with you. But I'm glad. You won your way free, and you're home. I wish you only the best, Yaroah."

Yaroah's smile broadened. "Thank you." He gestured toward Lorcan. "Mind this one, will you? Since I won't be there to watch his back, you have to do it for me."

"I don't need minding!" Lorcan protested, knowing that it would make the others laugh. Yaroah relaxed slightly and bent so that Livia could kiss his cheek and hug him tightly.

"I'll miss you, little sister," he murmured, his voice just barely audible.

"I'll miss you, too," Livia answered, her voice shaking more than a little. Yaroah let her go, then turned to Tavi. They spoke in Yaroah's own language, then Tavi hugged Yaroah. He stepped back and smiled, and Lorcan touched Yaroah's arm.

"Ready?"

Yaroah stooped and picked up his pack, and he and Lorcan walked down the ramp to the docks. Lorcan stopped at the bottom of the ramp and looked up at Yaroah.

"My brother," he said, and his throat suddenly felt tight. "I wish you all the good things. All the blessings of all of your gods and mine."

Yaroah smiled and hugged Lorcan tight enough that his bones creaked. "Ghost. My brother Ghost. You be careful. And win. Win your place back." He reached out and ruffled Corvina's breast feathers. "Look out for him, Corvina." He stepped back, smiled, then turned and walked away. Lorcan watched him. Watched him stop. Yaroah looked to his right. Then his left. Then he turned. He was frowning.

"What is it?" Lorcan called.

Yaroah came back up the dock toward him. He looked around again, then met Lorcan's eyes.

"There's no green," he said. He smiled. "I told you I would know what I wanted when my feet once more stood in the land that made me. Except… I am not the person who left Carthage. Not anymore. The person I am now wants to see all the colors of green that exist in the world."

Lorcan stared at him for a moment. His words didn't make sense. Then he remembered, walking through the cold tunnels to the arena. Waiting for the first bout, and telling the others that in the summer, all the colors of green in the world existed in Eire.

"You're coming with me?" he gasped.

"Someone needs to fight at your side," Yaroah answered. "Someone needs to guard your back. Manius is too old, and I've more experience at it than Tavi." He laughed. "I want you to tell me about the women of your country. Perhaps I'll take a wife there. But I have to learn to speak your language before I can woo someone." He put his arm around Lorcan's shoulders, and they walked back up the ramp.

* * *

Twelve days at sea, watching the distant shore slide by. Twelve days of a hundred different shades of blue. Twelve days of teaching and learning, of laughter and healing. Corvina recovered enough to fly up to the top of the mast, and Lorcan found pleasure in laying on the deck with Tavi and Livia, watching her circle and call.

On the twelfth day, they left the sea behind and sailed upriver. Lorcan stood at the rail and watched the shore. Forts. Settlements. People. Children who shouted and waved, then shouted again when Lorcan waved back.

"We'll reach the palace by sunset," Tavi said as he came up behind Lorcan. "The Tamesis is a long river. You could sail this way for days."

"Have you?" Lorcan asked. Tavi grinned.

"From the source to the mouth," he said with a laugh. "Father and I did it once. It took three days, and it was a wonderful trip. And in the winter, the river freezes solid, and we can skate on it."

"Yaroah is going to hate that," Lorcan said. He looked over toward where Drucilla and Livia were sitting with Manius and Yaroah. "Is there a temple to Apollo where we're going?"

"Yes," Tavi answered. "Why?"

"He promised us a smooth journey. I should thank him. I haven't been sick at all." Lorcan looked back at the shores. "We're so close. The air almost smells right."

Tavi chuckled. "I understand. Come and help us work on Yaroah's accent."

Lorcan followed him, taking a seat on the sun-warmed deck. Corvina hopped out of Livia's lap and bounced over to him, croaking and clicking. Lorcan picked her up as Livia shifted to sit next to him. He put his arm around her, joining the conversation.

"I don't think I will ever speak your tongue," Yaroah grumbled. "It is so different from the languages I know."

"You learned Latin easily enough," Manius said.

"Because I heard it when I was young. You Romans were already in Carthage. Then I had no choice but to learn it. Now? I again have no choice, but I am older now than I was then."

"You'll learn," Lorcan said in Gaeilge. Yaroah frowned, then nodded.

"Speak to me only in your tongue," he said. "Make me learn it the way a child would."

"I should do that, too," Drucilla said. "But not when you're teaching me healing. I want to be certain I understand properly when it's something that can kill someone."

"Then we'll do that," Lorcan said. "Tavi, tell us about where we're going. In Gaeilge."

They sat and talked and laughed for hours, sharing wine and the last of the loaves of flat bread that Tavi had bought when they had last been in port. Lorcan craned his neck to see over the railing, and yelped when Livia poked him in the ribs.

"We'll get there when we get there," she teased. "You act like you're going to dive over the side and swim."

"Not a good idea," Tavi said, tearing a piece of bread off the loaf and popping it into his mouth. "Current flows back the way we came." He grinned and looked over the side. "Ah. Keep watch ahead. We're almost there. You're going to see something I doubt you've seen before."

That something was a wooden bridge that spanned the river, and the ship sailed underneath it and started angling toward shore. Lorcan got to his feet and looked back at it.

"I've seen bridges, Tavi. There are bridges in Rome."

"Have you ever seen the underside of one?" Tavi asked. He pointed. "There's the Palace, right on the water." He pointed to another structure that was farther away. "That's the forum. I don't think we'll need to go there. The temples are upriver, there."

Lorcan nodded, watching as the docks grew closer. He could see people on shore gathering, watching them. Tavi laughed and pointed.

"See the man in the red tunic?" he said. "That's Arcus."

"He dresses like the people here?" Drucilla asked.

"It's better for the weather, he says," Tavi answered. "He'll wear the toga if he has to, but he'll find any excuse to avoid it."

"Sounds like someone I know," Livia murmured.

"Where do you think I learned it?"

The ship drew up to the dock, and the sailors ran here and there, securing the lines, putting down the ramp. Lorcan picked up his pack and took Livia by the hand, following Tavi down the ramp to where his brother waited. By the time they reached Tavi's side, he was engulfed in warm embrace.

"Arcus, this is Prince Lorcan mac Diarmuid mic Morrigan of Hibernia," Tavi said. "And I don't know if you remember Livia?"

"Livia?" Arcus repeated. He looked at her, then past her. "Manius! Then... no! Not little Livia!" He burst out laughing. "Who told you that you could grow up beautiful? Manius! You're allowing your girl outrageous liberties."

"She's her husband's problem now," Manius replied, stepping past them and hugging Arcus. "You're looking good, boy."

"Ah, you're never going to call me anything but boy, are you?" Arcus laughed. "And, Prince Lorcan, I'm pleased to finally meet you. We've heard much of you, and we've all been hoping for your safe return."

"We've got a lot to talk about, Arcus," Tavi said. "And plans to lay. I have letters from Father and Grandfather."

Arcus nodded. "And it's rude of me to keep you out here. It's late. We'll dine, and then we'll talk in the morning." He gestured, and a young girl came running. "Show them to their rooms, Illica. And to the bath. They're yours to take care of." He reached out and tousled her short, brown hair. "Once they're in the bath, come find me and I'll have more instructions."

"Yes, sir." She bowed, then gestured. "This way, please."

* * *

It became clear that no one had told Arcus about Tavi's relationship with Lorcan and Livia—they were assigned a room in what Illica called the guest wing. Tavi and Drucilla, they were told, each had a suite in the family wing.

"It's only for a day or two," Livia said gently as they changed into borrowed clothes. "And if anyone knows how to sneak through the corridors here, it would be our Tavi." She smoothed the front of the brightly colored gown she had been given. "How is this?"

"You look beautiful." Lorcan took a moment to steal a kiss before he slipped his own tunic over his head. He ran his hands over the cloth and sighed, looking down at himself. He looked… right. For the first time in a year, he was dressed properly. He picked up Livia's cloak and helped her to pin it, then put his own cloak on and pinned the brooch. Corvina fussed at him until he picked her up and settled her on his shoulder. Then they left the room. Illica was waiting, and she led Lorcan and Livia through the palace to a large feasting hall. There were long tables and benches on either side of the hall, and a third long table at the head of the hall. Lorcan saw that Drucilla, Manius and Yaroah had already arrived, while Tavi was in the open space among the tables, surrounded by a group of children. He looked up and smiled.

"Lorcan! Livia!" he called. "Come meet my nieces and nephews."

His voice rang through the hall, and immediately there was a commotion from behind Lorcan. Before he could turn, he heard a familiar voice.

"Lorcan?"

Lorcan turned so quickly that Corvina launched from his shoulder and flew to perch on Livia's outstretched arm. The raven grumbled and cursed at Lorcan, but he ignored her, focusing on the two men who had followed them into the hall. Two men who wore black feather cloaks.

"Uncle Petran?" he croaked. "Uncle Turlach?" He took a step, and was almost immediately swept up in a tight embrace.

"I knew you'd come back!" Petran whispered, his voice harsh. "I knew it!" He stepped back, cupping Lorcan's face with his hands, shaking his head gently as he rubbed his thumb over the scar on Lorcan's cheek. "Look at you," he murmured. He stepped back again, looking Lorcan up and down. Then he stopped. Blinked. Reached out and caught Lorcan's right hand, pushing his sleeve up to reveal the tattoos that ran up Lorcan's arm. "Oh, Mother." He looked up. "Is this… are these what I think they are?"

"I was sold as a gladiator," Lorcan answered, his throat feeling tight. "I fought my way free. And I've come home. Cormac didn't beat me before. He's not going to beat me now. I'm going to make this right. I'm going to stop him." He looked over his shoulder. "Livia, Tavi, come and meet my uncles."

"I've met them," Tavi said as he came up behind Lorcan. "It's good to see you both. I'm surprised you're still here."

"We left and came back," Turlach answered. "Hoping for news." He smiled. "Hoping for this."

Lorcan laughed. He took Tavi's hand, put his arm around Livia. "Uncle Petran, Uncle Turlach, I want you to meet my mates."

Petran shook his head. "I'm sorry… mates?" He looked at Tavi, then at Livia. Then he laughed. "I… this shouldn't surprise me. It honestly shouldn't. You've never done anything the way we expected you to. Why should it be any different with your mates? Welcome to the flock, the both of you."

"Three," Turlach murmured. "Or did you not notice?" He grinned. "Grainne is going to love being a grandmother." His smile faded, and he glanced at Petran, a quick glance that told Lorcan that his visions were already coming true.

"Tell me everything," he said. "I need to know."

Chapter Fifteen

"Not yet," Petran said. "Lorcan, introduce us to the rest of your friends."

Lorcan grimaced, then sighed and brought Petran and Turlach to where Manius and Yaroah were watching.

"Manius, Yaroah," he said in Latin. "My uncles, Petran and Turlach."

"These are the married ones," Yaroah said. He bowed to them and added in halting Gaeilge, "It is good to meet you."

"We both speak Latin, if it is more comfortable for you," Petran said, speaking Latin. "Where are you from, Yaroah?"

"Carthage, and I must learn your tongue," Yaroah answered. "I have only been learning since we left Carthage."

"Then you have excellent teachers," Petran said. He turned to Lorcan. "And so did you. You never learned that Latin from me. Or from Cuanu."

"Livia was my first teacher, and Tavi my second. And Yaroah and the other gladiators helped." Lorcan looked up at Yaroah, who laughed.

"Our Ghost learned quickly," he said, clapping Lorcan on the shoulder.

"Ghost?" Turlach chuckled. "That suits you."

"Which is why I don't mind Yaroah calling me that," Lorcan said. "We fought together, in the arena. He saved my life. I saved his. He is as my brother." He smiled up at the big man, who nodded.

"And we make a fine spectacle," he added. "Lorcan, where is Corvina? Have your uncles met her?"

Lorcan looked at Livia, who looked up. "She's in the rafters, I think. She decided she didn't like the fuss."

Lorcan chuckled and looked up, seeing Corvina overhead. He croaked at her, and held his arm out; she called back and flew down, landing heavily on his forearm. He drew her to his chest and stroked her feathers, turning to his uncles. They were both staring at him.

"This is Corvina," he said. "She came to me injured, and decided to stay with me when she healed."

"And… you're certain that she's…" Turlach paused and looked at Petran. "Pet, that's not…"

"She's not Grandmother," Lorcan said. "I've spoken to Grandmother twice since I was taken. She says that Corvina is just a raven."

Petran snorted. "Mother is pulling your tailfeathers," he said. "Wherever a raven flies, so does she." He walked over to look at Corvina, who met his gaze calmly, then shook all over and flew up to the rafters again. Petran watched her go, then murmured, "I don't think anyone has spoken to Mother since the day you were taken." He paused, then met Lorcan's eyes. "We… Bran had a hero's funeral, Lorcan. Your father made sure of it."

Lorcan closed his eyes, grimacing. "I wish that he could have had a hero's wedding," he murmured. "How is Caoimhe?"

"When last we saw her, she was well. But that's all part of what we need to tell you, and you have quite a lot to tell us, I'm certain." Petran nodded toward the others. "But it will have to wait. Arcus is making that face. We're holding up his hospitality."

"I would never say that," Arcus protested, coming to join them. "But I will insist that we wait for long discussions until we're fed. News, for good or ill, goes better on a full belly, no?" He gestured to the head of the hall. "You are all my honored guests, and welcome at my table."

To Lorcan's surprise, he was led to the seat at Arcus' side, the place of honor. He hesitated. "Sir," he asked. "Should this not be where my uncles sit?"

Arcus smiled. "I've heard a bit about your deeds, Albus Corvus Torvus Victorinus. My father, my uncle, and my grandfather all think the world of you. You sit in the place of honor, and you've earned it." He stepped closer and put one hand on Lorcan's shoulder. "Mates?" he asked in a low voice. "Should I be moving you to the family wing, or Tavi to the guest wing?"

"Which has the larger bed?" Lorcan asked in reply. Arcus laughed and nodded, then gestured to the chair. Lorcan sat down and looked down the table. Livia sat next to him, and Tavi sat on her other side. Then Manius and Yaroah. He turned and looked past Arcus, and saw Petran and Turlach seated on Drucilla's far side.

"Why are my uncles seated with the family?"

"Your uncle Petran has been acting as a tutor to my children while he's been in residence," Arcus' wife answered. "They adore him."

"Lorcan, you haven't been introduced," Tavi called. "We were distracted. My brother's wife, Deiana. Deiana, Prince Lorcan mac Diarmuid mic Morrigan of Hibernia."

"Also known as Albus Corvus Torvus Victorinus, and Corax Princeps," Deiana said. "I've heard about you. You made quite the impression on Arcus' father. And my children all want to meet you." She smiled. "They've never met a real gladiator before."

"They'll be able to meet three," Lorcan said. "Yaroah was also a gladiator, and so was Manius."

"Be prepared for them all to follow you like puppies for your entire stay," Arcus said. "Once they decide you aren't going to eat them, that is."

Lorcan chuckled. "I'll try not to scare them. They don't think that I'm a barbarian, do they?"

Deiana laughed. "They're part barbarian themselves," she said. "I'm not Roman."

"You're from Alba?"

"I am, although my tribe has been living alongside the Roman settlement since I was a little girl. Governor Decus was the first to come out to us and try to live with us instead of trying to turn us into Romans. Arcus does the same." She rested her hand on her husband's arm.

"How many of the children are yours?" Livia asked.

"All of them," Deiana answered.

Arcus nodded. "We have four sets of twins. Which runs in my family. There were two sets of twins in ours." He nodded toward Tavi. "Before I forget, Antonina sends her love, and you have a pair of new nieces. Cassius and Marcus are on the wall and will be sorry to have missed you."

"You mentioned Antonina to us," Livia said. "Remember? Should I worry?"

Tavi frowned slightly, "When did I mention... oh!" He laughed and shook his head. "No, you shouldn't worry. She finally settled down and married a few years ago. To one of the boys she stole from me, as it happens." He sighed and shook his head. "We all get along much better now. He adores her, and clearly, he wasn't the right one for me." He looked up the table at Arcus. "Has there been trouble with the Picts?"

Arcus sniffed and picked up a goblet. "The only time we don't have trouble with the Picts, it's because we're all having trouble with raiders and have to work together. Now, no more discussions of politics. You're all hungry."

* * *

After the meal, Deiana invited Drucilla and Livia to join her, taking the children with them as they left. Arcus led the men to a smaller room.

"This is my private suite," he said. "We can discuss things here. I've read the dispatches, Tavi. Father sent information already, and I've hired mercenaries as he bid me, but with this new information. I'm having a hard time reconciling it. Will you explain?"

"I'm not sure what was in the dispatches," Tavi said. "And there's a lot to explain. Where do you want us to start?"

"Start by sitting down," Arcus said. He gestured to the various benches. "And then… start with Lorcan. His uncles will want to hear this, and I want to know the whole of it."

Lorcan sat down next to Tavi on a fur-covered bench and leaned forward, resting his elbows on his knees. Corvina pushed between his arm and his body, settling onto his leg and croaking at him. He shifted to make more room for her, and rubbed one hand over his face. "Start at the beginning? All right." He looked at Petran. "How did Conor come through it?"

"Terrified," Petran answered. "And blaming himself. He'll be glad to see you. Now, we know Cormac took you in the cove. How?"

"They used a net. Brought me down, knocked me over the head. When I came back to myself, I was on a ship. They brought me to Alba, but I wasn't here very long." Lorcan paused, getting his thoughts in order. Then he started—being sold in Rome. The promise Manius made him. Training, and being attacked by Gnaeus. Winning his freedom, and the esteem of the Emperor. Becoming a hero of Rome by fighting alongside the heir, and being adopted into the Emperor's family.

"Albus Corvus Torvus Victorinus," Arcus interjected. "The freed slave who fought in the arena as the undefeated *rudiarius* Corax Princeps."

"That was you?" Turlach gasped. "Some of the traders told us about the gladiator who was called Prince Raven."

"We hoped it was you," Petran said. "And we hoped it wasn't. Thinking of you as a gladiator…" He shook his head. "If your father had heard those rumors, he'd have taken wing to Rome himself."

Lorcan nodded. "Once I was free, I stayed by choice. I needed to train. I needed what I learned there, so I can be good enough to beat Cormac once and for all. I'm only going to get one chance to beat him. If I fail… he's well past caring about Grandmother's judgment. He's already tried to kill me twice by sending people into the arena. If I don't stop him, then he's going to kill me. So I have to beat him fast, and completely, and do it before he knows I'm close. We're hoping he doesn't know that I'm here yet. I made a fuss about not coming back by ship, because I get sick. We made it known that we'd be traveling over land, so if he knows I'm coming, he won't expect me for weeks. There's a legion that will be arriving—"

"A legion?" Petran repeated. "You've got a legion at your disposal?"

"Not yet, I don't. And then only if there's no other choice. I have to do this without Rome's help. I have to be able to take what's mine and hold it alone." He glanced at Arcus. "No offense."

"None taken," Arcus assured him. "I understand. I'm not entirely certain what I'm going to do with a bored legion, but I understand."

Lorcan snorted. "The rest is… messy. Tavi's brother turned on the rest of the family, so that he could become Emperor—"

"Antius did what?" Arcus gasped.

"It wasn't Antius." Tavi clasped his hands and looked down at them. "Galius turned on us."

"Lucanus!"

Tavi shook his head. "It's over. He can't hurt me anymore. He was plotting from Thracia, for years apparently, and he came back to Rome to finish what he'd started. And…" He looked at Lorcan. "Do you want to finish?"

"We think Galius was responsible for poisoning Drucilla so that she couldn't bear a child. The healer who was giving her the potion was found murdered before we could question him, so we don't know for certain. But I believed Antius when he said it wasn't his doing. Galius came very close to murdering Gaius. He did murder Antius." Lorcan paused. "He tried to kill the Emperor, and he tried to kill me, Tavi and Livia. Tavi, what am I forgetting?"

"And he desecrated the House of the Virgins," Tavi added. "Oh, Decia Lucania sends her love, Arcus."

"I... see," Arcus breathed. "Now the dispatches make sense. And he's dead?"

"Tavi took his head clean off," Lorcan said, looking proudly at his mate. Then he turned back to Arcus. "He claimed to have men loyal to him working for Cormac, and that I would be his wedge to conquering Eire once he was Emperor. He was going to try and make it look as if I went mad and killed the entire family. Which... your grandfather swears that no one would have believed it. I think he's right. All of Rome knows that I think Lucanus is a good man, and that I love him as much as my own father. Gaius and Decus are like brothers to me." He smiled at Tavi. "And Tavi holds half my heart. I think all of Rome knew that, too."

"You've had a busy year," Petran said. "Now, where do I start?" He glanced at Turlach, then sighed. "Diarmuid sent us to Alba after you, but we missed you here. We met with Governor Decus, and we told him what had happened. He did what he could, but... we were too late. Days too late. He told us he'd try to find you himself when he went back to Rome. He hosted us here, then we went home." He paused. "Things were quiet when we returned to Dun Morrigan, but Diarmuid knew it wouldn't last. He knew Cormac was coming. He went to Dun Righ and met with Eogan, then met with Becc. The entire village of Scath is empty now. Eogan took them all in near Dun Righ, helped them rebuild their homes there. Maelan and Cait went with them, so they're still under our wings. Just... in a safer nest." He paused again. "I didn't realize at first what Diarmuid was doing. But he was laying long-range plans. Dividing the flock so that we'd all be safe. Just before he sent us back here in the spring, Cuanu and Fergus left to go and live at the druid college, and Cathal and Alis joined Maelan and Cait. And Ronan took Siobhan to mate and set up his forge in Dun Righ. Which... that happened before you were taken, didn't it?"

"Yes, but not long before," Lorcan said.

Petran nodded. "He's the High King's smith now. Niall stood down from his place. So, when we left, the only ravens still in Dun Morrigan were your parents, Niall, Sorcha and Niamh, and I have a feeling Diarmuid was trying to convince Niall and Sorcha to leave. But you know that Niall won't leave the *baile*."

Lorcan nodded. "Did the message reach them, at least?" He glanced at Manius. "You did send something, didn't you?"

"I did!" Manius answered. "After the wedding. It was written. I just… forgot to send it. You're distracting, boy."

Petran shook his head. "They haven't seen it. I have it. It arrived with the first dispatch ship after we came back the second time, and we haven't been back to Eire since." He glanced at Turlach. "Not long after we got here, Eogan sent a messenger and told us to stay here."

Lorcan stared at them for a moment. "What? Why…" He stopped and closed his eyes, once again remembering his visions. "Dun Morrigan has fallen. It fell before the snows melted." He opened his eyes to see both of his uncles staring at him.

"How did you know?" Turlach asked. "Cormac and his warband took the *baile*, and no one has seen or heard from your parents, or from Niall or Sorcha or Niamh since. No one has been able to approach the *baile*, not even to fly over. Eogan said Ronan and Maelan both tried. We don't know if they're alive or dead—"

"They're alive," Lorcan interrupted. "He has them caged."

Petran went pale. "How… how do you know that? How can you know that?"

"Visions. Grandmother started sending me visions. I think… maybe she thought it would get me back here faster if I knew what was going to happen," Lorcan answered. "They started over the winter. I saw the same thing, over and over. Flying over Dun Morrigan, with snow still on the *urla*. Seeing burned-out houses, and the damage to the gates. Looking into the hall and seeing them. Raiders, living in filth. Cormac sitting in my father's place. He had my parents and his caged as ravens. And Niamh was a slave."

"Snow on the *urla*," Turlach murmured. "There was still snow on the *urla* when we left. Pet, we missed being there by days."

Petran rested his hand on his husband's knee. "And… cages. That's obscene. How could he…" He stopped. "Diarmuid. In a cage."

"What?" Lorcan asked. "What about my father and cages?"

"He never told you?" Petran asked. He shook his head. "He's terrified of them. Always has been. It was worse after…" He paused. "We told you about the *deamhan aeir*. When it was released, when it killed your uncle Ronan, the witch that thought she could control it was going to feed your father to it. She'd caged him, and…" He stopped again. "We're talking far too freely."

"It's all in confidence," Arcus said. "And I don't understand half of it. Don't worry." He rose and went to a table near the wall, coming back with cups. "I consider you two part of my household. My children call you both uncle." He went back to the table and came back with two more cups, which he handed to Lorcan and Tavi. "And you two? My brother, and... his mate? Did I get that right?" He smiled. "Nothing you say will leave this room. I swear it."

Lorcan took the cup and sipped what turned out to be smooth, sweet mead. "Thank you."

Arcus smiled, then brought another pair of cups to Yaroah and Manius. "Now, did I understand correctly? Manius, you trained Lorcan. Does that mean you owned him?"

"Best investment I ever made," Manius said. "I thought I was getting a *tiro*. Turns out, I was getting a husband for my daughter, and a man I'm proud to follow." He raised his cup to Lorcan. "So, things seem dire. Do we have a plan? We can't stay here long. If we stay, there's too much of a chance that Cormac will learn you're here."

"You think he has ears in Londinium?" Arcus asked.

"He had ears in Rome and Thracia, and contacts with Galius. Enough that Galius did him the favor of sending a pair of killers after Lorcan. I'd be surprised if he didn't have ears in your city." He frowned. "You hired mercenaries for Lorcan. How do you know none of them were being paid twice?"

Arcus frowned. Then he went to the door, opening it and shouting. Guards came running, then ran off once Arcus gave them their orders. Arcus closed the door and came back to sit down.

"I should have thought of that," he grumbled, picking up his own cup. "I should have planned for spies. We know he has men on the seas—"

"He does?" Tavi asked. "Then how are we getting to Hib... to Eire?"

Arcus grinned. "Let me handle that. Now, tell me the boring news, hm? How's Grandfather? And why is Aunt Drucilla here and not with Uncle Gaius?"

"Ah... my grandmother said she needed to be here?" Lorcan answered. "And I don't know why."

"Well, we'll find out soon enough." Petran sipped his mead. Then he smiled. "Grainne is going to be shocked to see you with hair that short."

Lorcan smiled slightly. "Keep hold of that thought. That she'll see me with my hair short. Because I'm not growing it back out until Cormac is defeated."

Chapter Sixteen

"I like your brother," Lorcan said in a soft voice as he and Tavi walked through the halls. Corvina croaked her agreement, then leaned down and started to tug on the pin to Lorcan's brooch. He clicked his tongue at her, and she raised her head to look at him, then made a derisive cough. He laughed. "Manners, Corvina. Behave yourself."

"Come here, Corvina," Tavi said, holding out his arm. Corvina jumped from Lorcan's shoulder onto Tavi's forearm, letting him bring her to his chest. He stroked her feathers as they walked. "Arcus is a good man," he said. "A good father, too. I think he practiced on me. I was only six when he met me the first time, and he sort of... took over looking after me. He always had time for me when I was small, even though he didn't even know about me until Father became Governor of Britannia and sent for the others to join us. None of them knew—Father never told Grandfather he'd remarried."

"I remember Gaius saying that he didn't know about you until you went to Rome the first time."

"I was 10." Tavi paused, then added in a low voice, "Arcus always listened to me, even when Father was too busy. And he's the one who caught Galius. He noticed I wasn't acting the same, and he was worried."

Lorcan was about to ask a question when he heard his name. He turned and saw Livia behind him, with Drucilla and Deiana.

"I was wondering where you'd gone," Lorcan said.

"I thought that we all should become better acquainted," Deiana said. "And I'm so glad I did. We had a lovely talk, and now I'll leave you with your men." She turned to Livia. "The move will be finished shortly, if it's not done already. And you'll all be more comfortable if you're together."

"Thank you," Livia replied. "We can talk more tomorrow. I'd love to see your library."

"You mean meet my library." Deiana laughed. "I'll take you out to meet my grandmother and my aunts." She turned to Drucilla. "Will you come with us?"

Drucilla smiled. "Thank you. Yes, please. I came to learn, and now I want to learn everything!"

Deiana's smile broadened. "I love that you feel this way. We'll go tomorrow. I'll walk you to your room, Drucilla." She nodded to Lorcan and Tavi. "Good night."

She and Drucilla walked away, and Livia turned to Lorcan. "We've been moved to the family wing," she said. "Into Tavi's room. Deiana insisted. Servants are moving our things now."

"Oh, good!" Tavi said. "It saves me from insisting. She found out you're a *medicae*, didn't she?"

Livia nodded. "She's a midwife. That's something I actually know very little about, so she's going to teach me as much as she can while we're here. Lorcan, do you know anything about midwifery?"

Lorcan shook his head. "Not a thing. It's a woman's calling. Mother wouldn't teach me anything about it. Said it wasn't my place. She knows quite a bit, though. She learned from the High Queen's midwife after I was born. You can ask her to keep teaching you when we get home. Although I'm surprised that you don't know, to be honest."

"Because it's the same in Rome," Livia said, taking his arm. "Midwives aren't *medici,* and midwives aren't trained in Apollo's temple. So tomorrow morning, Deiana is going to take us to meet her teachers."

"Tomorrow morning, I'll be taking Lorcan to Apollo's temple," Tavi said. "Then we'll be making plans for travel."

"And somewhere in there, your nieces and nephews want to meet a gladiator," Lorcan added. "But right now, I want a bed that's not moving. Tavi, you're going to have to lead."

Tavi chuckled and gestured, leading them through the halls to another wing of the palace and all the way to the end of the corridor.

"This is mine," he said, opening the door. "Ours now. But this has been my room since I was a child." He gestured. "Welcome."

The room was smaller than Tavi's suite of rooms in Rome. The walls were colorfully decorated with scenes that Lorcan assumed were from stories. An alcove held a wide bed, and there was another, narrower couch along another wall. There were chests and baskets under the couches, and cabinets and shelves on the walls. The shelves and a small table tucked into a corner were all laden with scrolls. A stand over the table held small lamps, and a larger lamp stood close to the bed. Corvina launched herself from Tavi's arm and landed on a shelf.

"Don't knock anything off there," Tavi said. He went over and took a bowl off the shelf, setting it onto the table. "There. Is that enough room?" Corvina gurgled at him, and he laughed. "Good. I'm glad you like it."

"This is very nice," Livia said, moving from table to couch to bed. "It's very small, though."

"I was very small when I was given these rooms. And Father offered to move me to larger rooms when I got older, but I like this room." He pointed to a corner over the bed where the wall met the arched ceiling. "That's the outside wall. There's a family of doves that nests in the eaves there. I can hear them in the morning. You'll hear them." He looked around. "And it's not as if we'll be here very long. I don't anticipate coming back." He sat down on the bench. "Will we? Come back to Alba?"

"Let's get to Eire first," Lorcan said, joining Tavi on the bed. "And let me do what I need to do. Then we'll see where we are. I promised your grandfather we'd send word. And we'll have alliances to make at some point." He leaned into Tavi's side. "Now, we've been how many days with no privacy? Shall we do something about that?"

Tavi blushed. "I thought you wanted to sleep."

"I said I wanted a bed that didn't move," Lorcan corrected. "I didn't say that I didn't want to move the bed."

Tavi's blush deepened. "I… what do you want? We'll have to be quiet, because there are others on this hall."

"Lorcan doesn't mind a gag," Livia murmured, coming over to join them. She leaned down and kissed Lorcan, then kissed Tavi. "I'd like to see you take care of him. Properly."

Tavi sat up straight, nearly spilling Lorcan onto the bed. "What? But I… Livia… I don't… I…"

"You can, if you do as I say," Livia said. "I won't let you hurt him. And you have to learn."

"Please," Lorcan added, his voice cracking slightly. "I want that. I want you."

Tavi swallowed. "You're sure?" he asked. Then he looked at Livia. "And you'll help?"

"Of course," Livia said. She chuckled and ran her hand over Lorcan's short hair, making him shiver and sigh in pleasure. "If we're doing this, then you're both wearing too many clothes. Let me see if I have what we'll need." She walked away from the bed, and Lorcan stood up, fumbling for the pin of his brooch. His fingers didn't seem to want to work, and Tavi stood up and unfastened it for him.

"You really want this?" Tavi asked. He sounded nervous. Afraid. Lorcan reached out and tugged Tavi closer, resting his hands on Tavi's waist.

"I want this. I want you," Lorcan repeated. "And I trust you. I know you won't hurt me. You may have learned all the wrong things, but Livia and I will help you unlearn them." He smiled and repeated, "I trust you, Tavi."

"And when we're done with you, you'll trust yourself," Livia added as she came to join them. Lorcan held his arm out, and she stepped into the three-sided embrace, putting an arm around each of them. "I have something to use as a gag. Do you want to have Tavi do to you what you did to him?"

"What, be bound for him?" Lorcan asked. The idea was exciting, but he felt Tavi tense. "Perhaps not yet?" He looked up at Tavi. "Too much?"

Tavi nodded. "Not yet," he agreed. Then he smiled. "But someday."

"You're both still dressed," Livia pointed out. "That will never do. Strip."

Lorcan laughed and backed away, tugging his tunic off over his head. When he could see again, he saw that Tavi had done the same. There was a prominent tent in his trews, but he wasn't smiling.

"Lorcan, are you sure?" he asked. "You… you really want me to…" His voice trailed off, and Lorcan frowned.

"Tavi? I don't understand. You wanted this. You told me you wanted this," he said. "What's wrong?" He looked at the bed. Tavi hadn't reacted this badly when Lorcan had taken him back in Rome. He'd been afraid, but Lorcan understood why, now that he knew how Galius had abused him. Why was he doubting that Lorcan would want him to do the same?

"Did he tell you something?" Livia asked. Tavi blushed crimson in response.

"That because I'd let him…" He coughed. "Don't look at me like that, Lorcan. I know I didn't let him. He forced me. But he told me every time that I was his whore, that being the *eromenos* was all I was good for. All I'd ever be good for. And after… whenever I tried to be *erastes*, I was just… doing what he did to me. I was being Galius. Back at the beginning, back before I understood what I was feeling, it was… well, not fine, but… I knew I could have you without hurting you. But now… I don't want to do what he did. Not to you. I can't do that to you." He clasped his hands behind his back. "Maybe I should just… not…"

"No," Lorcan interrupted him, closing the distance between them. He rested his hands on Tavi's waist. "You're not going to let him hurt you anymore. You're not going to let him keep taking everything good away from you anymore. He's dead."

"And he was wrong." Livia pressed against his side, smiling as he put his arm around her. "You proved him wrong when you killed him. You stopped him from hurting you or anyone else ever again. You are a better man than he ever was or ever could have been."

"She's right." Lorcan smiled up at Tavi. "And there's one more thing. I love you. I trust you completely. If you ever hurt me, I know it will be an accident, and you'll feel worse than I do. You've already shown me that."

"I have an idea," Livia said. "You were doing things that you learned from what Galius did to you. Suppose we change it?"

"Change it how?" Tavi frowned. "Is there a way to change it? I mean… is there another way?"

Livia smiled. "I'm still in charge?" She didn't wait for an answer. "Lorcan, undress and lay down. On your back."

Lorcan laughed. "Oh! Yes."

"On… wait?" Tavi frowned. "We haven't done that."

"Because after that one time, you wouldn't try again. You were always *eromenos*," Livia answered. "And then you left. I never had the chance to show you. I didn't even think how it might help you. Lorcan, you've done this?"

"With Bran. It was a little too adventurous for him. He didn't like it, so we never did it again. But I enjoyed it." He stepped away and untied the waist of his trews, pushing them down and stepping out of them. When he looked up, Livia was coaxing Tavi out of his trews, gentling him much as Lorcan would a fractious horse. Lorcan let her work, and went to lay down on the bed, stretching out on his back.

"When you did this, who was on top?" Livia asked, coming over to sit at the head of the bed and looking down at him. From this angle, she was upside down, and Lorcan grinned.

"I was," he answered.

"And you figured this out on your own?" Even upside down, Livia looked skeptical.

"I…" Lorcan paused, biting his lip. "I… might have seen my uncles…" His voice trailed off, and Tavi burst out laughing.

"You walked in on your uncles and decided to try it yourself?"

Lorcan propped himself up on his elbows. "They were in the stables! Anyone could have walked in on them. And they never saw me. I… I don't think." He laughed. "I'm not asking them if they saw me. Uncle Petran will turn as red as Uncle Turlach's hair."

Tavi smiled and sat down on the bed, his hip pressing against Lorcan's. The laughter seemed to have relaxed him. "And… you like this," he said.

"I know that I liked being on top." Lorcan sat up and rested his hand on Tavi's thigh. "That's all I know. I won't know if I like being on the bottom until you actually put me on my back and show me." He looked down at the bed, at his hand against Tavi's dark skin. "This is different enough that I don't think you'll be copying anything. I think we'll be figuring this out together."

Tavi rested one hand on top of Lorcan's, and slid the other one up Lorcan's arm to catch the back of his neck, pulling him into a kiss that felt as if it was equal parts desire and desperation. Lorcan put his hands on Tavi's shoulders, falling into the kiss as he tipped back onto the bed, drawing Tavi down on top of him. Tavi shifted, covering Lorcan's body with his own, tilting his head slightly to deepen the kiss as he ground his hips against Lorcan. And through it all, Lorcan could feel Livia's touch, on his shoulders, on his arms, brushing against his hair. Then Tavi shivered, breaking the kiss as he arched his back and moaned. Lorcan looked up to see Livia's upside-down amusement. She was naked. When had that happened?

"Tavi likes his back scratched," she murmured. Lorcan laughed and reached up, wrapping his arms around Tavi and running his nails down both sides of his spine. Tavi whimpered, then reached out, grabbing each of Lorcan's arms in turn and pinning them to the bed. He smiled and lowered himself to kiss Lorcan again.

"So… what do I do now?" he asked as he raised his head. "What's next?"

"You're going to need your hands," Livia answered. "I can get a belt or a rope to tie him, if you've changed your mind."

Tavi mock-scowled at her, then let Lorcan's hands go. "No ropes yet. Next time, maybe."

"Next time," Livia agreed. "But for now…" She took Lorcan's wrists and pinned him down again. "How is this?"

Tavi sat back on his heels, his head cocked to one side. "Good. That's good." He smiled slightly, then slid his hands under Lorcan's legs, pushing them up until Lorcan was rolled into a ball. "This is why I need my hands?" he asked. "Lorcan, is this comfortable?"

"I'm fine," Lorcan answered, his voice sounding muffled to his own ears. Tavi ran his nails down the backs of Lorcan's thighs, making Lorcan moan. "Better than fine. Do that again."

"No, I think I'm doing something else," Tavi answered. "Livia, gag him."

The pressure on Lorcan's wrists vanished, but he didn't move. Livia left the bed, coming back a moment later with a length of something thick between her hands. She pressed it down over Lorcan's mouth. "Open. Then bite down."

He opened his mouth for the gag, biting down as she bid. The thick cloth filled his mouth, and he whimpered as she ran her fingers over his cheek. "Very good. Don't let it go." She moved back into position and pinned his wrists down again. "Go ahead, Tavi."

Tavi stretched up to a shelf over the bed, coming down with a small flask. He tugged the cork out with his teeth and spat it across the room, then poured some of the contents into his hand. Lorcan couldn't see what else he was doing, but he felt the pressure against his arse, and whined softly, trying to move. All at once, he understood why Bran had found this position uncomfortable—between Livia's grip on his wrists and Tavi pressed against him, he couldn't move. Bran had never liked being confined, had never liked small spaces. Lorcan hadn't put the two together before. But now… this was uncomfortable, but in a maddeningly arousing way. He was pinned and gagged, and his lovers could do whatever they wanted to him. He whimpered as Tavi's long fingers found their target, straining against them both, wanting more.

"I think he likes this," Livia murmured.

"I like this, too." Tavi shifted, rolling Lorcan into a tighter ball, pulling his fingers free. Something thicker, blunter took their place, and Lorcan tugged against Livia's hands, wanting to pull free, wanting Tavi's cock. They both laughed when he moaned, and Livia shifted, letting his wrists go and rising up on her knees. He couldn't see what she was doing, but he felt her hands on his legs, holding him in place as Tavi started to move, his thrusting shaking the bed and the sound of skin slapping against skin clearly audible. Anyone in the hallway was going to be able to hear that, but there wasn't a thing Lorcan could do. Nor did he want to—he wanted this, wanted more, but he couldn't move with Tavi, couldn't see what either of his mates were doing as Livia shifted to kneel over him. He could smell her arousal, and ran his hands up her thighs and over her arse—her answering moan sounded oddly muffled, and he wasn't sure why. Then Tavi started to move faster, and a hand closed around Lorcan's cock. He bit down hard on the gag, clinging to Livia as he crested and screamed, dimly hearing Tavi's gasps and whimpers coming to a peak with one wordless, strangled howl. His movement slowed, and whoever was holding Lorcan's legs up let them go; he hesitated, letting Tavi move away before lowering them to the bed. Livia shifted, stretching out next to Lorcan, her head toward his feet. Lorcan raised his head to see Tavi, his eyes closed, leaning one shoulder against the wall, panting as if he'd run a race. He smiled, and ran his hand up Lorcan's leg.

"I can hear you thinking the question," he murmured. "I'm fine. Better than fine. That was wonderful."

Lorcan tugged the gag out of his mouth and laid it down on the bed. "Good. Thank you."

Tavi opened one eye. "Why are you thanking me?"

"For trusting us," Lorcan answered. "For letting us show you that you could. For finally being with me—with us—completely. No fear. No regrets. Nothing but us loving each other."

Livia rested her hand on his stomach, humming softly. "Yes. Thank you."

Tavi blushed all the way down to his collarbone. "I… thank you for showing me I could. That was wonderful." He leaned down and kissed Livia, then crawled over to cover Lorcan's body and kissed him deeply enough that they both moaned. Tavi smiled, then tucked his head underneath Lorcan's chin and sighed happily, relaxing over him like a breathing blanket.

"Is that where you're sleeping?" Livia asked. "What about me?"

"She has a point," Lorcan said. "What about our Livia?" He turned to her. "And what about our Livia?"

She smiled. "I don't need sex tonight, Lorcan," Livia said. She shifted around on the bed until they were nose to nose to nose. "I'm tired. I just want to be close."

"Tavi, move over." Lorcan nudged Tavi off to his right, and the three settled down with Lorcan on his back, Tavi's head on his right shoulder, and Livia's on his left. He sighed and closed his eyes.

"I love you both," he murmured.

Tavi kissed him. "Let me get the lamps," he said, and stood up. A moment later, the room was dark, and Tavi pulled up a blanket as he lay down, warm against Lorcan's right side. Livia was already heavy on his left, her breathing soft and sleep-regular. Lorcan sighed happily once more. All the nights for the rest of forever could be like this.

It was something to look forward to.

Chapter Seventeen

Lorcan woke to the soft cooing of doves. He rolled onto his back to find himself alone in the bed. He sat up slowly, pushing the blanket down to his hips, wondering where his mates had gone. He looked up—the shelf was empty. Even Corvina was missing?

He'd just pulled on his trews when the door opened, and Tavi came inside. He smiled when he saw Lorcan.

"You were sleeping so hard that we decided to let you be," he said, putting a tray down on the table. "Livia went with Deiana and Drucilla, and she left a kiss for you. Corvina went with her, and my brother Decus is standing as their escort this morning."

"Another Decus?" Lorcan laughed. "How many is that?"

"Just my father and my brother, so two." Tavi took a cloth off the tray. "There's a nice loaf for you, and some roasted eggs."

"I thought there was more. I mean, your sister is Decia—"

"All my sisters are Decia," Tavi interrupted. "It just means that they're the daughters of Decus. My brother Decus is Decus the Younger, like I'm Lucanus the Younger."

Lorcan nodded and sat down, picking up an egg. As he started eating, Tavi poured something out of a pitcher, and the scent made Lorcan smile.

"Beer? Is that beer?" He took the cup from Tavi and took a long sip. "Oh, that's good."

"I'll tell Deiana you like it," Tavi said. He pulled another chair close and sat down. "Arcus never learned how to drink beer. He doesn't like the taste. She'll be glad someone other than me appreciates her work." He poured more beer into another cup and leaned back in his chair, stretching his legs out and crossing them at the ankle. He smiled as he sipped. "I enjoyed last night, Lorcan."

Lorcan swallowed the last of his egg and grinned. "I think you noticed me enjoying it."

"And I didn't hurt you?" Tavi asked.

"I'm not even sore this morning. Now, I won't be eager to mount a horse, though. Is the temple walking distance?"

"We'll go by chariot, and Arcus asked to go with us. Which means we'll go after he finishes his morning business. We have time for you to meet the children. Want to spar?"

Lorcan finished his meal, keeping it light, then picked up his practice swords. Tavi laughed when he saw that Manius had packed the wooden clubs, taking them instead of his *dolabrae*; the two walked through the halls and out through the atrium to the courtyard. Almost immediately, they were surrounded by children, all clamoring for attention and demanding answers to their questions. Lorcan laughed, and when the children didn't settle, stuck two fingers into his mouth and whistled. The shrill sound brought immediate silence.

"Now, if you want answers, you have to ask questions one at the time," he said. "And if you want to see us fight, then you have to show us where we can fight so that no one gets hurt."

"There's a practice yard," one of the boys called. "For the legion. Is that good?"

"That would be perfect," Tavi said. "Thank you, Luc. Will you show us the way?"

"Luc?" Lorcan murmured as he fell in next to Tavi, following the children. "Another Lucanus?"

"Actually, he's Luccus. He's the oldest of the twins. His sister is next to him now, and she's Lucilia."

"What are all their names?" Lorcan asked.

"Luccus and Lucilia. Doccius and Caratacus. Julia and Julilla. And Verica and Vasianus are the little ones." Tavi pointed to each of the children in turn.

Lorcan nodded. "I'll try to remember who is who. But I'll get it wrong. I know I will."

"Father never got it right," Tavi said. "And they'd all laugh at him. I think he did it on purpose, though. That whistle was fantastic."

"That's how Uncle Niall would get our attention when all of the cousins were rowdy like that."

"You have to teach me how to do it."

The children led them around the palace to a wide yard with an open space marked off by cords. Luccus turned to face them.

"This is it. Uncle Tavi, are you going to fight, too?" He frowned. "You never fight."

"I learned how," Tavi said. "Lorcan, you wanted me to show you that move?"

"Just don't put me on my back this time." Lorcan entered the practice field, setting down his wooden swords and stripping his tunic off over his head. Tavi followed suit, and they walked to the middle of the field. Lorcan looked back to see that the children were all sitting outside the cords.

"They're well-behaved," he murmured to Tavi.

Tavi snorted. "They don't know you yet, so they're on their best behavior," he replied. "And out here? They all know the rules. They stay outside the cords, or they can't watch their father practice. In Luc's case, if he breaks the rules, he can't practice with his father. The others aren't old enough to learn yet."

Lorcan nodded. "Good rules. My uncle Niall would approve." He turned to Tavi. "Show me that move, slowly."

Tavi grinned. Then his face went slack and he attacked, moving as if through deep water. Lorcan met his movements, studying them, trying to predict how Tavi would move. He'd always been taught to watch the eyes, that even the most skilled fighter would look before he moved. But Tavi didn't—his no-expression face gave away nothing of his thoughts or his intended movements. Until Lorcan blocked an overhand strike with his right-hand blade. Then Tavi grinned.

"Now, it's mostly momentum," he said. "Do you remember what you did?"

"My side remembers," Lorcan answered. He moved slowly, deliberately, and Tavi knocked the sword back and moved through the turn, dropping to his knee and tapping Lorcan's side with one of his clubs.

"All right. I see what you did." Lorcan stepped back, mentally running through the movements again. "Tavi, I think the main reason that works is that it's so unexpected. It was like what I did against Yaroah in my first fight against him, right after I got to the *ludus*. But with this, if your opponent is faster than you, they'll take your head off. You have no way to guard."

Tavi got up. "You think so?"

"Let's try it faster."

Tavi nodded, then struck. Lorcan blocked and flowed into the fight,

148

watching for the overhand strike. He blocked, struck, and as Tavi dropped to his knee, struck again, tapping his sword off the top of Tavi's head. Tavi obligingly sprawled in the dust, to the cheers and laughter of the children. Lorcan laughed and reached down, helping Tavi to his feet.

"It's a good trick, but it'll only work once, and then only if the person you're fighting has never seen you do it in practice. The minute you bury your axe in someone's ribs, everyone else you're fighting is going to be looking for the same attack," Lorcan said. "Tavi, if you're in a real fight, like the one with Galius, no tricks. Just fight to win." He stepped behind Tavi and started brushing the dust off his trews, noticing that they had an audience. Arcus was standing at the cord barrier, flanked by Manius and Yaroah.

"I'm dreaming," Arcus called. Tavi jerked in shock and turned toward his brother. "What sorcery is this?"

"That sorcery is Lorcan," Manius answered.

"It wasn't sorcery." Lorcan laughed. "It was experience. I told you. My cousin is tall like Tavi, and he kept on having to be shown where his feet were. Tavi just needed to learn where he was."

"Sorcery or experience, it's something I never thought I'd see." Arcus ducked underneath the cords. "And what are the sticks when they're real weapons?"

"Lorcan is a *dimachaeri,* and fights with paired *siccae*," Manius answered. "Tavi fights with *dolabrae*."

Arcus turned to Manius, then looked back at Tavi and Lorcan. His eyes were wide as he shook his head. "I appear to be losing my hearing," he said. "I could have sworn you said my baby brother is fighting with *dolabrae*."

Tavi laughed. "You're not hearing things. I fight with a pair of axes. Grandfather gave a beautiful set to me before we left Rome. I'll show you."

"I want to see them. But for now, if you want to go to the temple, you should get washed up." He looked past them. "And there are eight small people whose tutors and nursemaids are looking for them!" he added. "Off with you."

The children scattered like startled birds, and Arcus chuckled. "Axes. My little Tavi, using axes. Are you going to start him on your throwing axes in Hibernia, Lorcan?"

"My cousin makes the best throwing axes in Eire," Lorcan answered. "I think I will. Once Ronan gets Tavi's measure—"

"That would be Ronan mac Niall?" Arcus interrupted. "The High King's smith?"

Lorcan blinked in surprise. "Yes," he admitted. "You know my cousin? How?"

"I have an example of his work," Arcus said. "A gift from your uncle. Now, for that bath. We can go to the Roman baths, or we can heat water."

* * *

Lorcan took the folded bundle of white wool from his pack and heard Tavi cough behind him.

"You're going to wear your toga?"

Lorcan looked over his shoulder to see that Tavi had already put on his trews. His shoulders were still speckled with water droplets, and more clung to his curls. He picked up a clean tunic and pulled it over his head.

"You're not?" Lorcan asked. "I know you prefer not to, but I thought... Roman ways to stand before Roman gods. Should I not wear it?"

"You might be the only one wearing it," Tavi answered. "Arcus only wears his toga for official business and important holidays. He says that he doesn't think that the gods care what he wears, just that he serves."

Lorcan turned to fully face Tavi. "I just want to say thank you. What should I wear?"

"What would you wear if you wanted to say thank you to your own gods?" Tavi smoothed the front of his tunic. Then he laughed. "How do you dress when you visit your relatives?"

Lorcan grinned and picked up his trews. He dressed quickly, then followed Tavi out into the corridor and through the halls until they came out into a sunny courtyard.

"Lorcan!"

Lorcan turned to see Turlach limping toward them. He stopped and smiled. "Uncle? Are you coming with us?"

"I volunteered to drive," Turlach answered. "There's not much for me to do while Petran is with the children. I usually take Lady Deiana around on her errands, but she's taken your lady down to visit the women in her family, and Decus volunteered to take them. I think he's pining over one of Deiana's cousins."

Tavi turned and stared at Turlach. "Really? Who?"

Turlach shrugged. "I'm not actually certain. There are a lot of them, and my Alban isn't that good, so I'm not sure which of them are Deiana's kin, and which are just there because she's married into power and they want a part of that. Some of the women down outside the walls remind me of some of the women in the High-King's court." He paused, then shook his head. "Before you ask, it was back before you were born, Lorcan. When I first met your father, when he was going looking for a mate and found Grainne. I warned him about the women in court then, and I had words with Arcus about the women out in the village now. Told him to keep an eye on Decus and the twins."

"You think there will be trouble?" Tavi asked.

Turlach shrugged. "Not sure. But the women back in Eogan's court wanted a high-born husband, and they didn't care how they caught him or who they had to hurt. The women outside the walls remind me of that. Some of them got annoyed when they flirted with me and I didn't flirt back. They mostly ignore me now, and I'm fine with that." He nodded. "There's Arcus. Let me go see which team the grooms picked." He limped away and Tavi whistled softly.

"Is he always that… suspicious?" he murmured.

"He has reason, I think," Lorcan answered. "I'm not sure of the whole of it, but I think it has something to do with the High King's first wife, and why my cousin is the way he is."

Tavi stopped walking. "What did the Queen do to your cousin? And how old was he?"

"He was 11, and according to my father, he was already hurt from something that happened when he was small. She manipulated that hurt, twisted it into something that tied his entire self into being my father's heir. He's never forgiven me for taking that from him. In his mind, I destroyed his worth just by drawing my first breath."

Tavi folded his arms over his chest and frowned. "You're raising more questions than you're answering," he said. "What happened when he was small?"

"Something I'll ask Uncle Petran to explain," Lorcan answered. "They didn't tell me any of it until after Cormac challenged me the first time. I may be missing part of it still. Now, we're keeping the others waiting." He stepped closer to Tavi. "We'll sit down with Petran when we get back and I'll have him tell you the entire story."

Tavi snorted. "I don't like that no one told you the why of this until it was too late to stop," he grumbled as he unfolded his arms and took Lorcan's hand. "They could have stopped this years ago."

"And if they had, I'd still be in Eire, and you'd still be in Rome. Or here. Livia would be in Rome. We'd none of us have each other." Lorcan squeezed his mate's hand. "I can't change the past. I can't change the choices my family made before I was born, or the choices Cormac made. The only thing I can do is stop him."

They walked on in silence, meeting Arcus next to the chariot, one made to a Gaeilge design, not a Roman one. It still looked as though it would be tight for four men. As they approached, Arcus looked at them and arched a brow. "Quarrel?"

"Just questions that need answering," Tavi answered. "Things I don't understand."

"Oh, and I know how that vexes you." Arcus smiled and reached out to ruffle Tavi's curls. "Come on, then. We can talk while we go."

Lorcan stepped up into the chariot, taking hold of the rail as Tavi pressed up behind him. Arcus joined them, and murmured something to Turlach, who called to the horses and snapped the reins. The chariot lurched forward, out of the gates and into the streets of Londinium.

"Now that there are no ears to hear us that we can't trust," Arcus said, raising his voice slightly to be heard over the horses. "I've found three among the mercenaries who were suspect. If there are three, there must be more. We need to get you off to Hibernia with the next tide."

"And that would be when?" Lorcan asked.

"Tonight." Arcus grimaced. "As much as I hate having to send you on so quickly, if I don't, you'll never reach Hibernia's shores. Right now, we can say with reasonable certainty that there are no ships that answer to Cormac on the waters. We may not be able to say that tomorrow."

"There's no moon tonight," Turlach added. "That's in our favor."

"How long will it take?" Lorcan asked. "I'm not sure how long I was out of my head when they took me from Eire."

"I've never sailed to Hibernia." Arcus shook his head. "Turlach, how long did it take you?"

"Three days," Turlach answered.

"I wasn't sailing three days!" Lorcan gasped.

"Lorcan, they would have taken you to the port on the western coast," Arcus added. "There's a slave market there. Now, if you sail tonight, you may get ahead of them. Or at the very least, they won't have time to put obstacles in place." He sighed. "I could have wished for more time to know you and to spend time with my brother. But that won't win you your place back, or help your family. Manius is overseeing your packing, which is being done by my aide, my wife's maid, and Illica, who are all trustworthy. Once the women come back, we'll get you on board the courier ship and on your way."

"Livia will be disappointed that she won't have time to learn more," Tavi said. "But there are midwives in Hiber... in Eire." He looked ahead and pointed. "There's the temple."

"It's this close? We could have walked," Lorcan said. "Why the chariot?"

"Privacy," Arcus answered. "I never can be certain how many ears in the Palace are connected to mouths that spill whatever they hear outside the walls. In the chariot? Well, I trust Turlach, and the horses can't talk."

* * *

They stepped out of the chariot at the temple, and Lorcan walked around to the horses' heads with Turlach.

"You still remember how to drive?" Turlach asked. "You're going to need to. We'll have two chariots in Eire, and I can't drive both." He grinned. "I'm a good charioteer. But no one is that good."

Lorcan laughed. "I've been driving a little. Gaius would let me take his team out." He reached out and ran one hand over a glossy neck. "Did Beauty ever come home?"

Turlach sighed and shook his head. "We think Cormac took her. He wanted everything that was yours. That would include your horse. I just hope he remembered how to care for her. I taught him when he was young, same as you. I gave him his first pony." He shook his head. "I hate that he was set on this path. I hate that we couldn't stop it."

"I'm stopping it now," Lorcan said. "But first, I need to say thank you." He turned and walked toward the temple, where Arcus and Tavi were talking to an older man wearing a toga. Arcus turned, clearly looking for Lorcan, and smiled when he saw him.

"Lorcan, come and meet Hyacinth," Arcus called. "He's Apollo's priest here, and he doesn't believe Tavi."

"What did you tell him?" Lorcan asked as he joined.

"They tell me that you've met and spoke with Apollo," Hyacinth said. "That's not possible."

"It isn't?" Lorcan asked. "Why not? My family, we're part god. Your word for it is *semideus*."

Hyacinth's bushy brows rose. "You're a *semideus*?"

"Lorcan mac Diarmuid mic Morrigan," Lorcan said, and watch Hyacinth's brows crawl higher up his forehead. It was disconcertingly like watching fuzzy caterpillars, and Lorcan looked away before he started laughing.

"The Hibernian Battle Raven. You're her grandson?" Lorcan looked back to see the priest nodding. "That might be enough to protect you. And you want to thank Apollo?"

"He told me that he would make our journey as easy as he could," Lorcan answered. "And it was, so I want to thank him."

The priest nodded. "Come inside." He turned and started toward the Temple, drawing a fold of his toga over his head. Lorcan followed, but stopped on the steps.

"I don't have anything to cover my head," he said.

Hyacinth looked back at him. Then he smiled. "You're a respectful young man. That's good. Come inside. He won't mind." He turned and entered the Temple, and Lorcan followed him into the cool darkness. As his eyes adjusted, the first thing he noticed was the raven.

The white raven.

The *living* white raven.

Hyacinth chuckled. "That's Albus. Say hello, Albus."

"The Emperor named me Albus when he named me a Roman citizen," Lorcan said. "So, who says hello to whom?" He walked over to the raven's perch and croaked at the bird, who shifted from foot to foot, then croaked back. "I've never seen another white raven."

"Another?" Hyacinth said. "You've seen one before?"

Lorcan bit his lip and nodded. "Yes. I thought... well, I thought there was only one."

"There's never only one anything, Lorcan Albus." Hyacinth joined him and held his arm out; Albus hopped onto his forearm and started worrying at the edge of his toga. "Now, this Albus? Apollo's Albus? He was born here. His mother was the previous Temple raven, and her feathers were black as coal. But Albus? He's special." He ruffled the raven's feathers; the bird stuck his head into Hyacinth's toga, then climbed into the folds. Lorcan smiled.

"He loves you very much."

"I love him right back," Hyacinth said. "Come to the altar."

Lorcan followed, standing next to Hyacinth at the stone altar. A brazier filled with glowing coals sat on the surface, and a basket sat on the floor. Hyacinth reached down, prompting a squawk of protest from inside his toga. He was laughing when he straightened, and he handed a flat, round cake to Lorcan.

"Here."

"What do I do with it?" Lorcan asked.

"Speak your words to Lord Apollo, then break the cake and burn it." Hyacinth stepped back, and Lorcan considered what he wanted to say.

"Thank you," he finally said. "For the smooth journey. I wasn't sick at all. And thank you for helping me to save Gaius." He paused, looked down at the cake in his hands. "If it's not too much to ask," he continued in a soft voice. "Keep watch over them for me? If things had been different, I might have been happy staying. But… things are what they are, and I won't see them again. So, if you could watch over them for me? And help them to be happy?" He broke the cake in two and laid the pieces into the brazier. The pieces started to darken and smoke, then flames started to lick up the sides. Lorcan watched the fire burn for a moment, then looked up.

Apollo stood on the far side of the altar.

They can't see me or hear me, the god said. *This is for you. You're welcome. I will watch over them. You didn't need to ask that, but I am very pleased that you did. Gaius misses you. He truly thinks of you as a brother, and he is feeling the loss. He will be married soon, and looks forward to that. Lucanus is well. And Decus settles into his role as Pontifex Maximus.* He paused. *And faithful Valerius has resigned his position as Flamen Dialis.*

Lorcan blinked. "I… why?"

Because he can no longer hold the position without the Flaminica, and his beloved Cordelia rests in the Elysian Fields now.

Lorcan frowned. Then he remembered Tavi joking about the Elysian fields. About being dead. He went cold.

"No," he whispered. "I… How did she die?"

In her sleep. In her own bed. In her own time. She was at peace.

Apollo paused again. *Valerius mourns her. Their marriage was one of true affection and respect, and I think that he will join her before the seasons turn again.*

Lorcan's throat felt tight. "I… do you… speak to him? Ever?"

Apollo smiled. *I can.*

"If you do, tell him that we're safe. Tell him that I think of him fondly." Lorcan blinked away tears. "Tell him I miss him."

I will tell him. Apollo smiled. *Wipe your face, Lorcan. And be well. Good luck.*

Then he was gone. Lorcan scrubbed his hand over his face and sniffled, looking at the brazier. The burning bread didn't seem to have been consumed more than it had when Apollo appeared. How long had they been talking?

He turned, and Hyacinth smiled at him.

"Did you do what you needed to do?" he asked.

Lorcan nodded, not trusting his voice. He coughed, then coughed again, seeing Tavi look up in alarm.

"Lorcan?"

"I'm… I'm fine." Both Tavi's brows rose. Clearly, he didn't believe a word of it. "I'll explain on the way back." He turned to bow to the priest. "Thank you."

"Good luck, Raven's son."

Chapter Eighteen

Lorcan jerked awake, and lay still for a moment, wondering what had startled him. The boat was rocking gently underneath them. Livia was warm in his arms, and Tavi against his back. Moving slowly, Lorcan slipped out from between them, pulling his woolen cloak around himself as he got to his feet and left the tent. The wind grabbed at his cloak and his tunic, pushing him toward the front of the ship, past the horses that Arcus had insisted on giving to them. There were a pair of chariots as well—Arcus pointed out that they would need to move quickly once they reached Hibernia's shores. It had made the open deck somewhat cramped, but he was right. They would need to move fast to stay ahead of Cormac's spies.

Once at the front of the ship, Lorcan ignored the sailors and leaned on the rail, looking out into the darkness. The sky ahead of them was the purple-gray that heralded the dawn, while behind him, the sky was streaked with gold and orange. Turning back to the west, he could just make out something darker than the dark water on the horizon. Lorcan rubbed his eyes and squinted.

No, he wasn't seeing things.

Home.

"Lorcan?"

He turned back to the tent and saw that Livia had come outside, rubbing her eyes. She looked deliciously sleep-rumpled. He smiled and went to kiss her, taking her hand.

"Come and see!" he said, and brought her back to the rail. "Look!" He put his arm around her shoulders, pointing. She squinted into the darkness, then gasped.

"Is that Eire?" she asked.

"It is." He squeezed her shoulders. "We're almost home."

She looked up at him and smiled. "Good. Now, it's still dark. Come back to bed."

For a moment, Lorcan was tempted. But he looked back out into the darkness, at the darkness that he knew was growing closer. "I won't be able to sleep," he said. "Go tuck back in with Tavi. I'm going to watch the sun rise."

She nodded and turned toward him, putting her arms around him and hugging him tightly. He wrapped his arms around her and kissed the top of her head before letting her go and watching her until she disappeared into the tent. Then he went back to the rail, and watched the dark smudge of home.

The rising sun had revealed all the shades of green when Lorcan heard someone whistle behind him. Yaroah joined him at the rail, leaning easily on his forearms.

"You were not telling tales," he said in Latin. "I have never seen so much green before. And so many shades."

"Did you think I was telling tales?" Lorcan asked. Yaroah shrugged.

"I think that sometimes, the tales we tell others about the things we love do not always tell of what we see with our eyes," Yaroah answered. He looked at Lorcan and smiled. "They tell what we see with our heart."

"And here I thought I was the harper." Petran joined them at the rail. "I could make a poet out of you in a year, Yaroah."

Yaroah frowned slightly. Then he laughed and held up two fingers. "Two years," he said in Gaeilge. "I must... get good... to learn speaking first."

"You're coming along quickly." Petran smiled and stepped back. "I'm going on ahead," he said. "Turlach is staying with you, to get you to the High King's seat. I'm going ahead to tell them we're here. And that you're here. You should make it to Dun Righ by sunset. I'll see you then."

"Be careful," Lorcan said. Petran clapped him on the shoulder and stepped back. A moment later, a raven flew from the deck, circled the mast, and flew off toward land. Yaroah's jaw dropped.

"That was not a tale either?" he gasped. "You truly can become a raven?"

Lorcan laughed. "Yes, but we don't normally do it in front of people outside the flock. You know what that means?"

Yaroah frowned slightly. "What?"

"He considers you family. He trusts you as much as I do." Lorcan gently punched Yaroah's arm. "Is there food? I'm hungry."

"Come and eat. I want to know more about this."

* * *

Lorcan sat with the others and ate, and in a low voice told them the truth—about his cloak, about being able to take flight. About the constant fear that Cormac might decide that he didn't need to be anywhere near Lorcan to kill him.

"I think that the only thing stopping him from just burning my cloak at this point is that he doesn't just want me dead anymore. He wants to be the one to do it. Everyone he's sent has failed. So now he wants to be the one with the knife, so he can be sure it's done." Lorcan offered a piece of bread to Corvina. "He doesn't fear Grandmother anymore, nor any of the rest of our gods. He's leaving my cloak alone because he wants to kill me face-to-face. He wants everything I have, and he wants me to know that I've lost everything." He paused, looking from his left to his right. From Tavi to Livia. "Tavi… if I fall, take Livia back to Rome."

"What?" Livia gasped. "Lorcan, we haven't talked about that!"

"I just thought of it," Lorcan admitted. "But… he wants what I have. Everything that I have. He won't be happy until everything that's mine is either his or destroyed. He murdered Bran. He stole my place. Turlach thinks he even stole my horse. What do you think he'll do if he finds out I have a wife? A fledgling on the way? A second mate?" He reached out and took Livia's hand. "You wouldn't be safe."

"Lorcan, I can't promise that," Tavi said. His voice was even, solemn. He put his arm around Lorcan, and only then did Lorcan realize his mate was shaking as much as he was. "We've come this far. You're not going to fall. You're not going to fail. I'm not letting you. And if somehow you do fall… it's because he's gone through me to get to you."

"We wouldn't be safe in Rome, either," Livia added. "Not if he has the resources to put people in place to kill you in the arena. Not if he has allies in Rome and Thracia. Lorcan, you can't lose. If you lose… we're all of us dead."

"She's right," Turlach said. "Lorcan, you know the conditions of the mate bond as well as any of us. We don't survive the death of a mate. Even without your cloak, I can't see that being different. You know they're your mates. The bond is made." He took a deep breath. "Pet and I learned that the hard way. You know that."

Lorcan swallowed and closed his eyes. "I…" He shuddered violently, and Tavi's arm around him tightened. "It's all resting on me," he whispered. "The entire flock. All of Eire. All of it. If I fail—"

"So do not fail," Yaroah said. "Ghost, I watched you walk onto the sands so many times with your head held high. You faced down an army of mercenaries with… how many was it? Six?"

"Six," Manius confirmed. "Although with the knock you took, Yaroah? You probably saw 12 of us. You and me, Lorcan, Gaius, Nona and Julius. And we won that one by guile more than skill."

"Guile?" Turlach asked. "Guile how?"

"They were mercenaries," Manius answered. "We hired them. Paid them three times what they were getting from… that had to have been Galius."

"It doesn't matter. Because one of them took the pay so he could get close to me. Because Cormac was paying him." Lorcan swallowed. "I can't make mistakes like that again."

"You've learned from those mistakes," Drucilla said. She'd been sitting quietly next to Manius, her brow furrowed slightly as she listened. "You're not the boy I first met in the cells all those months ago. You've grown, and you've learned. I don't think you could have done this back then. Now? I know you can." She smiled. "You're a hero."

"Someone else called me a hero," Lorcan tried to think of who it was. "Nona. It was Nona. He said it first. By the time Livia and I were married, I was a hero of Rome. I never wanted that. I never wanted more than what I had." He snorted. "But your gods and mine had other ideas. And you're right. I don't have a choice. I need to be the hero, and I need to not fail." He swallowed and shivered again. "But it's hard."

"And we're all here with you, boy." Manius reached over and patted his leg. "You're scared. I know. But remember that you're not walking into fire alone."

"And perhaps you will be lucky," Yaroah added. "Perhaps he'll see the hero you've become and die of fright."

Turlach laughed and patted Yaroah on the shoulder, then got to his feet and looked toward the west. "I need to go start preparing the horses. We'll need to move as soon as we're on shore if we're to get to Dun Righ ahead of the news. Lorcan, come help me. And stop fretting. It'll all be all right."

"You seem very sure about that," Drucilla said. "Are you a seer?"

"Me? Turlach laughed. "No. No visions for me. No, I've known Lorcan since he defied all the odds, took his first breath, and howled his defiance at the world. He's been doing the unexpected since he was born. He'll do this, too." He smiled. "Come on. We're almost to port."

160

"Port?" Lorcan got up and followed his uncle.

Turlach nodded. "When we came first, Arcus asked permission to build a port on the east coast for trade. A messenger came back with us, and Eogan granted the permission. They started work… it's nearly a year now, I think. They were building it when we left. I'm curious to see what they've done since."

* * *

Lorcan knew Dubhlind, the fishing community on the coast—it was where Caoimhe had gone to live when she and her mother left Scath. He'd been there a few times. There had never been a port here before, but now Lorcan could see a quay and several buildings set apart from the village. The ship drew slowly toward the quay, and Lorcan saw men waiting on the shore. One of them looked familiar.

"Turlach?" he called. "Is that Diarmuid?"

Turlach came to the rail and laughed, waving. "It is! What's he doing here?" He sniffed. "He must have his warband out."

Lorcan coughed. "Diarmuid has a warband?"

Turlach smiled at him. "Diarmuid has had a warband since not long after you were stolen from us. And he's had a wife since not long after that. Her name is Eimear. You'll like her."

Lorcan sighed. "I've missed so much. And I have so much to tell the people who've missed me. Once the fighting is done, we'll be talking for the next year."

Turlach clapped him on the shoulder. "Here's hoping for a true vision there. A year of just talking? I think we'll all welcome that." He looked over his shoulder. "They're running the planks out. I'll start having the horses led off. Go see if your mates need you for anything, and tell them to be ready. We're leaving as soon as the chariots are harnessed." He paused. "You said you were keeping your skills up with driving. Now you get to prove it."

Lorcan nodded and walked back to where their packs were piled. Tavi was leaning on the rail, watching the shore.

"This is fantastic," he said without turning. "I never would have expected an outpost here. Rome has never been able to have any sort of settlement in Hiber… in Eire before." He turned to Lorcan and grinned. "I'll remember eventually."

"You have time." Lorcan turned to see Livia coming toward them, leading Drucilla by the hand. Drucilla looked... ill, and Lorcan touched Tavi's arm as he straightened. Tavi turned to look and drew himself up to his full height.

"What's wrong?" he asked before Lorcan had a chance to say the same thing.

"We have a complication," Livia said, coming close and pitching her voice so it wouldn't carry. She glanced at Drucilla, and Lorcan knew what she was going to say.

"Drucilla is pregnant."

* * *

"I need you to take Yaroah and Manius in your chariot. I'll take Drucilla." Lorcan looked over at where Livia and Tavi stood on either side of the still-too-pale Drucilla. "And I need you to not ask questions."

Turlach arched a brow, then nodded. "Not ask questions like why the lady has been feeding the fish most mornings before you woke up? Petran caught her. She told him she was seasick."

Lorcan grimaced. "Yes. No questions about that."

Turlach nodded. "No one will hear it from me. Your chariot is waiting." He looked at the quay. "And so is your cousin. Go show Diarmuid that you're you."

"What?"

Turlach just laughed and walked down the planks. Lorcan followed him, and headed for the tall, scowling warrior standing with his arms folded over his chest. The sun glittered and flashed on his armbands, and Lorcan looked closer as he drew near.

"Ronan made those, didn't he?" he asked. "That looks like his work. I'm supposed to convince you I'm me?" He grinned. "How am I supposed to do that? And why do I need to do that?"

Diarmuid stared at him for a moment, then laughed. "You just did!" he crowed. "You knew Ronan's work from that far away." He closed the distance between them and hugged Lorcan tightly. "And why? We've had two fake Lorcans show up at Dun Righ since the solstice. Idiots who thought we wouldn't be able to tell the difference." He stepped back and shook his head. "I honestly never thought I'd see you again, cousin. I'm so happy you're home!"

"Thank you." Lorcan looked his cousin up and down. "A wife and a warband? I could wish you didn't have need of the latter. I didn't mean to bring trouble—"

"You weren't the cause of it, Lorcan," Diarmuid interrupted. "You were the excuse. If anything, it was my mother and I who set the seeds for this." He paused. "Cormac... I played as much a part in making him what he is now as anyone could have, for all that I was a boy and that stupid. I repeated everything I heard from my mother without knowing what it meant." He shook his head, then held out his hand. "Whatever you need to do, I'm at your back."

Lorcan clasped his hand, then tugged him close and hugged him again. "I want you to meet my mates, cousin," he said as he turned. Tavi was leading Livia down the planks, with Yaroah and Drucilla behind them.

"Lorcan?" Diarmuid was staring openly. "That... that man. Is... how do I ask this? Is he like you... just... reversed?"

Lorcan looked up at his cousin, then laughed. "No!" he answered. "He's from Carthage. His people have dark skin. And it's always hot where he lives. Hotter than our hottest summers, I think."

"Carthage," Diarmuid repeated, nodding slowly. "That... that's near Rome? Isn't it?"

"A few days of sailing," Lorcan said. "Livia, Tavi. Come meet my cousin."

Diarmuid smiled, and in a soft voice asked, "Which one is your mate?"

"Both of them." Lorcan grinned at the expression on Diarmuid's face. "I don't know. But they are!"

Diarmuid snorted. "Well, if anyone would know, you would. If I get back to Dun Righ before you do, I'll make sure you have a large bed." He stepped forward. "Welcome to Eire," he said.

"We'll have time for a better family reunion once we're all safe inside the walls of Dun Righ," Turlach said. "Diarmuid, you'll ride with us?"

"We'll escort, yes. But I'll want to spread us out on the road. A large group is an obvious target. Let me go and arrange it. Cousins, you are welcome." Diarmuid backed up a step, bowed slightly, then strode away, shouting orders.

"Lorcan, you wanted your mates and Drucilla. Yaroah and Manius, we'll take the baggage with us." Turlach looked around, then met Lorcan's eyes. "The road through the bogs is still treacherous, and Uragh isn't as safe as it was when you last took that road. Stay with the escort and watch for the markers on the road in the bog."

"Yes, sir," Lorcan said, nodding. "I'll be careful." He looked at the chariot. "Are there javelins?"

Turlach frowned and turned to Tavi. "Can you use a javelin?"

"No, but I can drive," Tavi answered. "If it comes to trouble, I can take the reins while Lorcan uses the javelins."

"Fair enough. And you can take turns with driving so that neither of you pushes too hard. I doubt either of you have driven for a full day recently, and you'll both be exhausted by the time we get there." Turlach looked up. "Which won't be until after dark if we don't get moving. That one is yours, Lorcan. I need to have a word with Diarmuid." He limped off, and Lorcan took a closer look at the chariots.

"We'll be tight," he said. "Which may make us slow." He shook his head. "Can't be helped. We need to talk, and we need privacy. To quote your brother, Tavi, the horses can't talk."

Things were arranged and rearranged, Lorcan and Tavi's weapons were loaded onto the chariot, and then things were rearranged again. It took longer than Lorcan thought it should before he finally snapped the reins and the chariot started forward. It was just as tight as he thought it would be, with Tavi on his right, closest to the socket that held the javelins. Corvina perched on the rail in front of him, and Drucilla and Livia were on his left, crowded in next to him. Lorcan guided the chariot to join the others that would be their escort, and followed them out onto the road to Dun Righ. Once they were underway, he raised his voice slightly. "Now we can talk. Drucilla?"

"I had no idea," Drucilla said. "And... this is Gaius' child. It has to be. I've been with no one else. But if I go back to Rome, no one will believe me. They'll think it's yours, or someone else's."

"And by the time you got back to Rome, Uncle Gaius will have remarried," Tavi added. He glanced at Lorcan, who nodded, realizing that this could be why his grandmother told him to take Drucilla out of Rome. She and her child would become weapons to be used against the Emperor.

"Drucilla, Gaius may be the father, but this is your baby, too." Livia shifted to put her arm around Drucilla. "What do you want?"

Drucilla gave a wet sounding laugh. "Besides this baby? I don't know. I know what I don't want. I don't want to go back to Rome." She was quiet for a moment, and Lorcan focused on driving, on the chariot in front of him. Diarmuid's chariot, he noticed.

Then Drucilla spoke again. "I want to know who I am when I'm not associated with a man. Not my brother's sister. Not my husband's wife. Just… me. I don't know who that is. I think she'll be a healer. Maybe a midwife. But I need to know who Drucilla is, so I know who I can be going forward." She chuckled, and Lorcan glanced at her to see her looking down at her hand, pressed against her belly. "Before I become someone's mother."

Chapter Nineteen

Lorcan had taken the road through the bogs and through the forest of Uragh dozens of times, but this was the first time he was driving it without Turlach's guidance. He didn't relax into driving until they were nearly at the crossroads where the coast road met the road into the bogs, where Diarmuid called for them to stop.

"Tired?" Tavi put his hand on the small of Lorcan's back. "I can take the reins when we start again."

Lorcan nodded. He rolled his shoulders, cinched the reins to the railing, then stepped down from the chariot, wincing at the twinges in his stiff legs.

"You've forgotten how to drive, haven't you?"

Lorcan turned and smiled at his cousin. "I think I have. For long distances anyway. There aren't a lot of those in Rome. That, and it's the first time I'm driving this road without Uncle Turlach at my elbow." He looked around at the other chariots. "Where is he?"

"He'll be leading the next group," Diarmuid said. "We've split the warband into three, so that there's no clear target. I sent the first group out when your ship landed. There's us, and Turlach will bring the final group later." He turned and bowed slightly to Livia and Drucilla. "We'll only be here long enough to have a bite and see to anyone's needs. Will you ladies need a guard?"

"If you show me where it's safe, I'll guard," Tavi said. He reached into the chariot and picked up one of his *dolabrae*, resting it on his shoulder. He grinned at the stunned expression on Diarmuid's face. "Yes, I can fight with this. Where am I going?"

"I'll come with you. I want to know how you fight with a giant axe." Diarmuid laughed and clapped Tavi on his other shoulder, and the two of them escorted Livia and Drucilla into the brush near the side of the road. Lorcan walked around the chariot to the horses, talking to them in a low

166

voice as he looked them over, making sure that the harness wasn't irritating them.

They remained just long enough to rest the horses and have a quick meal before Diarmuid was calling for them to move on. Lorcan wondered at the urgency as he stepped back into place and took up the reins again. Then they were off.

"Keep a careful eye!" Lorcan warned. "The bogs are dangerous."

"I'll keep watch," Tavi said. Lorcan nodded and turned his attention to the chariot in front of him, and to watching for the markers that showed the safe path through the bogs. On the rail in front of him, Corvina shifted from foot to foot, then crouched and took to the air, keeping pace with the chariot. Lorcan glanced up at her, then turned back to the road.

They were nearly halfway through the bog when Diarmuid called another stop. Lorcan brought his chariot to a halt, then rested his hands on the rail. His legs were shaking. Tavi handled him a bottle, and Lorcan looked at it for a moment before tugging the cork free and taking a sip.

"Beer?" he asked. "Where did this come from?"

"Diarmuid gave it to me when we stopped the last time. Are you ready for me to take over?" Tavi asked.

Lorcan looked up at the sky, then down the road. He nodded slowly. "Make sure you follow Diarmuid," he said. "Have you seen the markers?"

"Little cairns?" Tavi pointed. "Like that one?"

"They're on either side," Drucilla said. "I've been looking for them."

Lorcan nodded. "Stay between the cairns." He looked up as Diarmuid whistled. "We're rolling." He shifted to the side, letting Tavi take his place at the reins. A moment later, they were moving again. Lorcan looked past Tavi to the two women. Livia smiled at him, but he could see that she was as tired as he was.

"We're almost to the forest," he called. "It'll be an easier road from there. And possibly a longer rest."

* * *

They passed from the bogs into the great forest of Uragh, and Diarmuid called for another stop. He came back to their chariot as Lorcan helped Livia down.

"We're almost there," he said. "We'll rest the horses and eat. Then one more push to Dun Righ." He took a deep breath and let it out, looking up. "Lorcan, where's your friend?"

"Corvina? She was flying over us through the bogs." He looked up at the trees overhead. "She'll find us." He turned as he heard a distant raven calling. "That's her." He cocked his head to the side, listening. A warning call… "And… something is out there."

Diarmuid growled. "I was worried about that." He raised his voice. "We're moving! Get ready to roll!"

"What is it?" Tavi asked.

"There have been raiders in these woods since autumn," Diarmuid answered. "Some of them answer to Cormac. I don't want word of Lorcan being back to get to him. Or worse, have one of them think to win Cormac's favor by killing Lorcan themselves. We need to move." He whistled again, then shouted, "We're rolling!"

Lorcan looked up at Tavi. "Driving or guarding?"

"I've seen you use the javelins. I'll drive."

And they were off. No longer needing to watch for the markers, Diarmuid urged his horses on as fast as they could, and Tavi followed his example. Lorcan took a javelin from the socket and held it in one hand, keeping the other hand on the rail. A dark shape flitted overhead, and he glanced up to see Corvina flying with several other ravens. He grinned and called to his family, then turned his attention back to the road.

Tavi didn't turn his attention from his driving. "Who's up there?"

"Corvina, three of my uncles and two of my cousins." Lorcan studied the trees at the edge of the road. The ravens weren't alerting to anything hiding out there, hadn't given any indication of anyone in the trees at all, but it never hurt to be watchful. But the drive was uneventful, and Diarmuid called another stop as they broke out of the trees. The chariot slowed to a stop, and Lorcan turned to see the men who had appeared on the ground behind him. Petran was grinning from ear to ear.

"I told you," he said to his brothers. "He's home."

Lorcan laughed and stepped down from the chariot, and was immediately mobbed by his cousins Oscar and Becc. The brief wrestling match ended with Becc on his back, looking stunned.

"You couldn't do that before!" he wheezed.

Lorcan offered him his hand, helping him to his feet. "It's been a long year, and I spent most of it fighting."

"Petran said you were a gladiator. Let me see that arm," Oscar demanded, taking Lorcan's right hand. He whistled softly. "It's true, then? Romans mark their gladiators like this?"

"It's true," Lorcan said, nodding. "But I won my way free, and I won my way back. And... come and meet my mates."

"Mates?" Becc repeated. "Three of them?"

"Two." Lorcan held his hand out to Livia, helping her down, while Tavi helped Drucilla out of the chariot. Lorcan put his arm around Livia's shoulders and pointed with his other hand. "This is Oscar, and the very tall one is Becc," he said. "And the uncles you haven't met are Maelan and Cathal. Everyone, this is Livia, one of my mates. Tavi is my other mate. And Drucilla is our friend."

"Welcome to Eire," Maelan said. "Lorcan, do they speak Gaeilge? Those are Roman names."

"Livia and I both speak Gaeilge," Tavi answered. "Drucilla is learning, and is coming along fairly well for someone who only started when we left Rome."

"Tavi is the brother of the Roman governor in Alba," Lorcan added. "If necessary, he can translate for Drucilla, or for our other friends. They're with Uncle Turlach."

"Where is Turlach?" Petran asked.

"He's leading the last group through the bogs," Diarmuid answered. "They're probably halfway through by now."

Petran nodded. "Right. You boys escort them on. We'll go bring the last group home. Then... then we can make sure Lorcan knows everything, and we can plan."

"I thought you told us everything," Lorcan said. "Uncle?"

"Things have happened while we were in Alba," Petran said. "Go on, and get safe behind walls. We'll talk when everyone is inside." He stepped back, gathered Maelan and Cathal, and three ravens took to the sky, flying off to the east.

"The roads were clear on the way here," Oscar said. "But there's no guarantee they'll stay that way." He looked up at the raven that still circled overhead. "Uncle Petran said that she's yours? A raven as a pet?"

"Closer to a friend. She had a broken wing. We helped her, and she decided to stay with me when she healed." Lorcan looked up. "I'll explain later. I'll tell you everything." He turned to Livia. "Do you need a moment before we start again?"

"I'm tired," Livia murmured. "How much longer will it be?"

"At the speed we're going? We'll be there soon." Lorcan kissed Livia's forehead. "I'm sorry. I know this is hard."

"I understand why we're keeping this pace," Livia said. She looked up as Tavi joined them. He handed a bottle to her, and she took a drink before passing it to Lorcan. He sipped the beer, then took a longer swallow before passing it to Drucilla. She sipped, then shook her head and handed it back to Tavi.

"Are we ready?" Diarmuid asked, joining them. "There'll be a feast waiting for us, and beds."

"The beds sound better than the feast," Livia murmured. Lorcan laughed, hearing Tavi translating softly for Drucilla.

"Oh, I agree," she said in Latin. "Beds sound so much better than food."

"Then let's move," Diarmuid said.

* * *

Lorcan took up the reins for the last stretch of the drive. Diarmuid set an easier pace, and Lorcan was able to point out things as they drove past.

"The druid college is down that road," he said as they passed the crossroads. "That's where I'll learn to properly use the healing chants, and where you'll be evaluated, Drucilla." He pointed. "And there's the High King's *baile*. Do you see it?"

"On the hill?" Livia asked.

"The hill is Tara, the seat of the High King's power. And the *baile* is Dun Righ." Lorcan smiled. "I lived there for two years, fostering with the High King."

"That's when you had the horrible teacher," Tavi said. Lorcan laughed and nodded. "And the High King is also your uncle."

"Yes, but that's not widely known," Lorcan said. "Most people think I call him Uncle out of courtesy, because he's so close to my father. There aren't many outside Eogan's court who know the truth of it." He glanced at Drucilla, then switched to Latin. "My father is Eogan's older brother. But he didn't know that until years after Eogan came to the throne. The Morrigan claimed her sons for herself. None of them knew their sires."

"Does that mean you have claim to the throne yourself?" Drucilla asked.

"I don't want it." Lorcan looked up at the *baile* that was growing closer. "My *baile* is a full day's flight from here, south and east in the mountains. My home is Dun Morrigan. That's all I want. I don't want to be High King. I want to be my father's son, and someday, perhaps I'll be the Raven King." He smiled. "My *baile*, and my mates. That's all I need. And we're one step closer to getting it back."

Things were more and more familiar as they got closer to the *baile*. The fields where the boys troop trained and fought and played hurley. The village at the base of the hill, and the wattle and daub houses where the people who worked in the *baile* lived. Then the long road up and around the hill, rising higher and higher, until they at last drove through the gates. Diarmuid was already out of his chariot, talking with an older man who Lorcan at first thought was his father. After a moment of shock, he realized it was the High King, who saw him and smiled.

"Lorcan!"

Lorcan cinched the reins to the rail and stepped down from the chariot and into his uncle's embrace.

"Oh, Lorcan," Eogan breathed. "Welcome home." He held Lorcan at arm's length, then hugged him again. "You're safe."

Lorcan shook his head and stepped back. "Not until he's stopped, Uncle. He's going to try against you. He's not going to stop with what he holds now. He wants all of Eire. And he has help. He was dealing with mercenaries in Rome and Thracia, and with one of the Emperor's grandsons. We stopped them in Rome, and his ally there is dead, but I don't know what Cormac has available to him now."

Eogan blinked. "I clearly need to hear all of this. But it will wait until tomorrow morning after you rest and once everyone is here. Oscar and Becc have gone back down to the village—did you know Scath is here now? You did? Good. It's on the west side of the *baile*, and I'm sure there are many people there who will be glad to see you. And the last of your uncles will be arriving tomorrow from the druid college." He smiled. "Petran says you've married?" Eogan paused. "Mated. I never remember. Your father teases me about it. And... two? Is that allowed in Rome?"

"We're not in Rome, and I don't care," Lorcan answered. He looked back to see Tavi and Livia standing near the chariot. He held his hand out, and they came to join him. "Uncle, my mates. Livia Corvina, and Lucanus Decius Octavian."

"Tavi." Tavi bowed as he came up next to Lorcan. "The only person who calls me by my full name is my grandfather."

Eogan paused, his eyes half-closed. Then he nodded. "Your most exalted grandfather, if I'm remembering correctly. Cormac's ally…"

"Was my brother, and I'm the one who killed him," Tavi answered. "He was trying to kill Lorcan at the time. And he deserved it. My brother, I mean. Not Lorcan."

Eogan chuckled. "You've had an interesting year, it seems," he said. "And I'm keeping you from your beds. Diarmuid, is this everyone?"

"There's one more group, Father," Diarmuid answered. "I split the warband in three. The others will be here shortly after dark, I think."

"Livia's father is in that group," Lorcan said. "His name is Manius. He trained me. And a friend. A Carthaginian gladiator named Yaroah. I call him brother." He looked up when Corvina called from overhead, and held his arm out for her to land. She looked at Eogan, croaked, then climbed up to Lorcan's shoulder. "And this is Corvina. She adopted me in Rome."

Eogan looked startled by the raven, but simply nodded. "I look forward to meeting them both," he said. "And hearing their stories. For now, come inside and rest. There's food, and the Queen is waiting." He paused. "Lorcan, it's on me to scold you about your manners. I know you're tired, but you didn't introduce the lady."

Lorcan winced. "I didn't, and I apologize—"

"You're forgiven," Drucilla said. "Do you think I can't see how tired you are? Honestly, you're swaying like you're still on the ship. Now, will you translate, please?"

Lorcan nodded and reached for her hand, bringing her forward. "Uncle, this is Drucilla. She's come with us because she wants to learn to be a healer."

Drucilla bowed. "It is an honor, your Highness," she said in Latin.

Eogan bowed his head slightly in response. "A pleasure, my lady, and you are welcome here," he answered, also speaking Latin, albeit much more slowly. "But could you not learn to heal in Rome?"

"Not the way Lorcan does it," Drucilla answered. "Our healers wouldn't be able to save a man who'd been poisoned with *koneion*. Lorcan did it. He saved someone that I care about a great deal. I want to know how to do that. I want to be able to do that." She paused, biting her lip. "I've never done… anything of any significance. My sole purpose was to be pretty, and to provide a man with sons. That was stolen from me, because my sons would threaten someone's ambition. Now, I want to be able to do something… important. I want to do something for me. So, I've come halfway across the world to learn who Drucilla really is, and what she can do."

Eogan nodded slowly. Then he held his hand out. Once Drucilla had taken his hand, he bowed over it. "I look forward to seeing who the Lady Drucilla is when she's not hiding in someone else's shadow. Come and meet my wife. I think she'll like you. And her Latin is better than mine." He led Drucilla toward the hall. Lorcan took Tavi and Livia by the hands and followed them.

"Am I really swaying?" he asked in a low voice.

"A little," Livia answered. "I thought it was just because we've been on a ship for so long. You did it when we got to Britannia, too."

"I did?" Lorcan looked at her, then at Tavi, who nodded. "Neither of you said anything!"

"I think we were all swaying by the time we got to Britannia," Tavi said. "It happens when you're on a ship for days. Your mind thinks you're still moving. It's worse if the sailing is rough."

Lorcan snorted. "And when were you going to tell me?" He braced himself as Corvina launched off his shoulder, watching as she flew up to alight in the thatch of the hall roof. They entered the hall, and he stopped to let his eyes adjust to the dim light. He saw his aunt Caírech near the firepit, and next to her was his cousin Siobhan. The cloak of black feathers Siobhan wore wasn't a surprise. Her advanced pregnancy was, and he wondered why no one had said anything. He looked around, but Ronan was nowhere to be seen.

"Lorcan!" Caírech hugged him and kissed his cheek. "Welcome home." She smiled at Livia and Tavi. "You're his mates? Petran said he'd taken two, and he wasn't certain why or how, but I certainly don't care. So long as you're happy. Welcome."

Lorcan smiled and introduced Livia and Tavi, then looked around. "Aunt, we'll need to speak to Gormlaith tomorrow. Is she…" He paused, not sure how to ask.

Caírech nodded. "She lives down in Scath, but she's here now. Your cousins have been keeping her busy, and Siobhan is near her time. And then it's your turn?" She laughed when Livia blushed.

"My cousins have what?" Lorcan smiled as Siobhan joined them. "More than just you and Ronan? Where is he?" He looked around, and looked back to see that Siobhan had gone pale.

"Oscar, Muirenn, Orla, and Becc all have married," Caírech said quickly. "And there are two babies, with another on the way."

"Aunt," Lorcan said, watching his cousin's pale face. "Where's Ronan?"

Siobhan closed her eyes. "We don't know," she answered. "He went out with a warband over a month ago, and they never came home."

Chapter Twenty

Lorcan stared at her. "Ronan… with a warband? What was he doing with a warband?"

"The warband was his guard," Eogan said as he led Drucilla over to join them. "He was bringing weapons and tools to Dun Carriag, to help them after they were hit hard by raiders. The warband never reached them." He sighed. "I wasn't going to burden you with that before tomorrow. You need to rest. There's a great deal of planning to do, and precious little information that we have to make those plans."

Lorcan nodded. "I want to wait for Manius and Yaroah. I need to know they're safe before I can sleep."

"That's understandable," Caírech said. "Come and sit. Eat."

Lorcan led Livia and Tavi to the long table, sitting on the bench with them on either side of him. Eogan brought Drucilla to join them, and Lorcan leaned forward as they were served.

"I'm sorry," he whispered in Latin. "I've forgotten all of my manners."

"You're forgiven," she whispered back. "Now, I missed most of that. What's wrong?"

"My cousin Ronan is the High King's smith. His mate is the High King's daughter, Siobhan—"

"The very pregnant young lady?"

"Yes." Lorcan looked over to the High King's seat. Siobhan sat next to her stepmother; she raised her cup to him when she saw Lorcan looking at her, but didn't smile. "He went out with a warband and never came back. He's not dead. Siobhan would know if he was dead. But…"

"Do you think your cousin has something to do with it?" Tavi asked.

Lorcan frowned, resting his forearms on the table. "Possibly. Probably. I remember talking with my father about how Siobhan's mother might have wanted Cormac to wed her. Back when she was poisoning Cormac's ear against me."

"The Queen?" Drucilla glanced at the high table.

"Not Caírech," Lorcan hurried to add. "His first wife. Diarmuid and Siobhan's mother."

"And you said things were simpler here," Livia murmured. "I know you did. Nona told me you did."

Lorcan laughed. "Fair. Better to say that they were complications that I understood." Overhead, he heard a raven calling an alarm. He looked up. "Was that Corvina?"

"Unless it was one of your relatives?" Livia said. Lorcan shook his head and got up, climbing over the bench and walking toward the door. Diarmuid caught up with him halfway there.

"What is it?"

"I'm not sure," Lorcan answered. He walked out into the growing dusk, and saw the chariots rolling into the yard as ravens landed and changed into men. Yaroah waved at him. He waved back, then looked up. He could see Corvina circling overhead. And further away...

"Uncle Petran?" he called, unwilling to look away. It couldn't be! "Uncle Maelan?"

"Lorcan, what is it?" Petran came running, Maelan and Cathal on his heels. Lorcan pointed. Petran looked, caught his breath, then took to the air, the others following him. Lorcan stood and watched them, wishing he could join them. They reached the pair of clearly exhausted ravens, circled, then started to escort them back.

"What is it?" Tavi asked, coming up behind him. He squinted. "Lorcan? Those are... who are they? Can you tell?"

Lorcan nodded slowly, but he didn't answer. He started forward, trying to predict where the ravens were going to land, watching as they circled lower and lower. Maelan landed first, and turned to catch the young man that fell out of the sky and into his arms, and who cried out in pain as he hit the ground. Lorcan broke into a run, hearing Siobhan's voice behind him.

"Ronan!"

For the moment, he ignored his cousin, ignored the tumult that had erupted behind him. He only saw the other raven—she landed hard, and for heart-stopping moment, didn't move. Then she changed, and Lorcan dropped to his knees next to her.

"Mother?" he whispered. Her dark hair had gone gray, and she looked too thin. Haggard and old in ways that his mother never should look old. He reached out and touched her arm, drawing back when she flinched. "Mother, it's me. It's Lorcan."

176

At the sound of his name, she looked up, staring at him. For a moment, she looked puzzled, as if she wasn't sure she knew him. Then she blinked, and raised one shaking hand to touch his cheek.

"Lorcan?" Her voice sounded rusty. "You... is it you? Am I dreaming?"

"It's me," Lorcan repeated. "I'm home. I'm here."

She frowned. "You cut your hair."

Lorcan stared for a moment, feeling tears starting. Then he laughed, pulling his mother into as tight an embrace as he dared. She started to cry, and he rocked her gently, hearing footsteps around him. Livia knelt next to him as Tavi came and draped a blanket around Grainne's shoulders. Then he sat down on Lorcan's other side.

"How is Ronan?" Lorcan asked softly.

"They've brought him inside, and they sent for the healer," Tavi answered. "He's hurt, and they might need your help."

"How bad?" Lorcan asked.

Tavi grimaced. "I'm not sure, but I think his left eye is gone. I didn't see any more before they took him inside."

"We should all go inside," Livia said. "It's getting cold."

Grainne looked up at the sound of their voices, and Lorcan nodded. "Mother, I want you to meet someone. Two someones." He waited until Grainne looked at him again. "Mother, this is Livia, and this is Tavi." She looked from one to the other, then back at Lorcan. He smiled at her puzzled expression. "They're my mates, Mother. The both of them. And we have a fledgling on the way."

"Two mates?" Grainne looked startled.

"I don't know why," Lorcan said. "But they're both mine."

"And a baby." Grainne paused. Then she smiled. "Your father will be so proud. You're home." She frowned again. "And he's still there. He's still caged."

"And I'm going to free him. I'm going to stop Cormac. I'm going to end this." Lorcan shifted. "Let me help you up. We'll go inside where it's warm."

Grainne looked up. "There was another raven. I don't know her."

"Corvina. She's my friend. She came with me from Rome." Lorcan stood up and helped his mother to stand. When she swayed against him, he stooped and picked her up. She weighed almost nothing in his arms. "Let's go inside."

Caírech met them at the door to the hall.

"Gormlaith is with Ronan," she said. "She says that once she's done, she'll come see Grainne."

Livia stepped forward. "I can help your healer," she said. "I'm a fully trained *medicae*. I can't sing healing into a person the way Lorcan can, but I can help."

"Aunt, just tell me where I'm going," Lorcan added. "Ronan needs help now, and Siobhan needs you."

Caírech nodded. "You know which guest house your parents usually have. That one. I'll send servants with blankets and food." She held her hand out to Livia, and they vanished into the hall. Lorcan turned and looked up at Tavi.

"Which one?" Tavi asked.

"The first one, near the wall."

Tavi nodded. "I'll see you settled, then I'll go and tell Manius and Yaroah what's happened," he said. He hurried on ahead of Lorcan and opened the door of the guest house. Lorcan carried his mother inside and laid her on the bed, kneeling on the floor next to her as a stream of servants carrying blankets and lamps appeared. One of them started a fire in the firepit.

"We'll need food," Lorcan said without turning. "Something easy for her to eat."

"I want a bath," Grainne murmured.

"After you eat something, Mother," Lorcan said. He heard Tavi talking to one of the servants, then the door opened and Caírech and Drucilla came inside.

"Lorcan, we can stay with Grainne. Livia would like your help," Caírech said. "I've brought clothes."

Lorcan looked up. "Is it that bad?" he asked. "I—" His voice trailed off as he saw the look on Caírech's face.

"I'll stay," Tavi said.

Lorcan nodded, picking up a blanket and spreading it out over his mother. "Go and get your *dolabrae*, and tell Manius and Yaroah what's happening," he said.

Tavi leaned over him and kissed his cheek, then smiled at Grainne before hurrying out.

Grainne smiled and covered Lorcan's hand with her own. "I'll be fine," she said. "Go do your duty, healer."

Lorcan kissed her cheek and got to his feet. "Aunt, how bad is it?"

"Very bad," Caírech answered. "He's very badly hurt, and very weak. I don't know how they made it here."

"Days," Grainne said. "It took us days. He wouldn't let me stop. I would have, but he wouldn't let me stop." Her breath caught. "He tried to free all of us. They discovered him. We barely got away." She looked at Lorcan. "Go help him."

"Yes, Mother." Lorcan walked out into the gloaming. Tavi and Yaroah were standing outside.

"Your mother?" Yaroah said. "She's hurt?"

"I don't think so," Lorcan answered. "She's been badly treated, but I don't think she's injured. I'm going to go help care for my cousin, and I'll be back with Livia as soon as I can."

Yaroah nodded. "I will help Tavi guard," he said, resting his hand on the hilt of his *spatha*.

"Thank you," Lorcan said, and ran toward the hall. Diarmuid was waiting by the door, and nodded as Lorcan reached him.

"Mother said you'd be coming to help. I think Gormlaith is out of her depths."

"I'll see what I can do," Lorcan said.

"They're in Ronan and Siobhan's house," Diarmuid said, leading Lorcan around the hall toward one of the houses tucked between the feast hall and the walls. He knocked on the door of one, then let Lorcan pass.

"Lorcan." Livia and Gormlaith met him at the door.

"How is he?"

Gormlaith sighed. "Beyond my skill, I'm afraid," the old midwife answered. "There's nothing I can do."

Livia frowned slightly, then answered in quiet Latin. "I don't think there's any saving the eye. It's also not what's worrying me. His right leg... come and see. I'm not sure what happened. It looks as if they crushed it. I think it's poisoning his blood. He's burning with fever."

Lorcan winced and went to the bed where Ronan lay, quiet and pale and far too still. His left eye was covered by a bandage, as were his hands and wrists. Siobhan sat on a stool next to the bed, holding Ronan's hand. She looked up at him as he went to one knee across from her.

"Lorcan, is there anything you can do?"

"I'll try."

At the sound of his voice, Ronan groaned and opened his eye. "Lorcan." His voice was raspy. "I knew you'd come back."

Lorcan smiled and rested his hand on Ronan's burning forehead. "He can't get rid of me that easily," he said. "He can't get rid of either of us. Can you tell me what happened?" He shifted the blanket covering Ronan's legs to reveal his twisted right leg. Someone had cut away the trews, and Lorcan could see angry, red streaks marring the skin. "What did he do?"

"I tried to escape," Ronan answered. "His men held me down, and he used a sledge... told me that the next time I tried, he'd be aiming for one of the cages." He coughed, and Siobhan held a cup to his lips. "He wanted me to make weapons for his men. Said I should follow him, that I'm supposed to follow him because he's my older brother. When I refused, he pulled feathers out of Niamh's cloak and burned them. The man who calls himself her husband laughed and held her while she screamed." He stopped and closed his eye. "She knew I was sick. Knew I was dying. She helped me escape. But I couldn't get them all. I couldn't get my parents. They'll never forgive me."

"They're not going to blame you, Ronan," Lorcan said. "And you're not dying. Not while I can do something about it. Siobhan, let his hand go." He looked up to see Livia standing behind him. "I might fall over."

She smiled, leaning down and kissing him. "Do what you need to do."

Lorcan turned back to his cousin, rested his hand on Ronan's knee, and started to sing.

The healing didn't seem as strenuous this time—not nearly as difficult as saving Gaius. And this time, he could feel the healing as it worked, as it forced the poison out of Ronan's blood and healed what was killing him. There was nothing he could do about the badly healed bones, or about Ronan's eye—both injuries were too old to do more than soothe. But Ronan would live.

Lorcan blinked hard, waiting for his eyes to focus. When he could see again, Ronan was asleep, breathing normally, and his forehead was damp with sweat. Lorcan touched his skin and found it cool.

"He'll sleep," he said, his voice hoarse. "And he'll be fine when he wakes. I couldn't save the eye. His leg needs to be splinted, and I'm not sure he'll ever walk without a limp again. But he'll live."

He heard Siobhan sob, and looked across to see her and Diarmuid. Diarmuid hugged his sister, then came around the bed and held his hand out to Lorcan.

"Let me see you to bed," he said. "You've had a very long day."

Lorcan took the offered hand and let Diarmuid pull him up. Livia came to his side and slid her arm around his back, steadying him.

"Where are we going?" she asked. "Before he falls over."

"I'm fine," Lorcan protested. "Just tired. It wasn't as hard as it was to heal Gaius. And I want to see my mother. I want you to see her. See to her. The Queen and Drucilla are with her now." He let Livia lead him outside into the night, and Diarmuid and Gormlaith followed them.

"We'll let them have some privacy," Diarmuid said as he closed the door. "Gormlaith, you may want to get some rest. I'm not sure how long it's going to be before you're needed again."

"Not too long, by the look of things," Gormlaith agreed. "It's good to see you home, Lorcan. And your mother couldn't have done that better. Well done." She walked away, and Lorcan turned to his cousin.

"Where are we going?"

"You'll have the guest house next to your mother." Eogan came to stand with his son. "Your baggage has already been taken there, and… Manius, is it? He's watching over it. His Gaeilge is very good."

"My mother taught him," Livia said. "She was from Eire."

"Manius is Livia's father, Uncle," Lorcan added. He frowned. "I just realized… where's Cian?"

"He's part of my warband," Diarmuid answered. "He was with the last group, the one with Manius and Yaroah. So by now, he's probably in the hall trying to eat his weight in whatever is edible." He grinned. "He's fascinated by Yaroah. Does he speak any Gaeilge?"

"A little, but he only just started to learn on the way here."

Diarmuid nodded. "Cian said that Manius translated for him. Yaroah was a gladiator?"

"Yaroah and Manius were both gladiators," Lorcan answered. "Yaroah and I fought as a pair."

Eogan looked startled. "You… fought. You were a gladiator?"

Lorcan held his tattooed arm out. "Manius was my owner when I was sold as a slave in Rome. He was a *lanista*, a gladiator trainer. He taught me to fight, and once I was free, he continued training me so I have a chance to beat Cormac."

Eogan took his hand and studied his arm in the light of a nearby torch. "Manius was your owner?"

"It started that way. But now he says that he thinks of Lorcan as his own son," Livia answered. "He's here to fight at Lorcan's side, and to serve Lorcan's father, if the Raven King will have him."

Eogan nodded. "I see. I'll speak with him tomorrow. Him and Yaroah both."

"Tavi can act as translator," Livia said. "He was serving his father as translator when Decus was governor in Alba."

"I will ask him." He shook his head and let Lorcan's hand fall. "I had no idea of any of this, Lorcan. Petran didn't say when he came to tell us you were back in Eire. A gladiator... a slave..."

"A freed slave, and a citizen of Rome. Patrician, and part of the Emperor's household." Lorcan smiled at the stunned look on his uncle's face. "Lucanus is... overly generous."

"What did you do?" Eogan demanded.

"I helped put down a rebellion."

"And almost died," Livia grumbled. "Twice."

Lorcan nodded. "And almost died. Twice. But I won my way free, and I won my way home. And there are mercenaries to fight in my name, and a legion at my disposal in Alba if it comes down to needing men to defend your throne, Uncle."

"I... see. This keeps getting more and more interesting."

"You should see it from this side," Lorcan quipped. Eogan laughed.

"No, thank you. This is interesting enough. And the woman? Drucilla? What interesting things do I need to know about her? Caírech is quite taken with her."

Lorcan took a deep breath. "Drucilla is the former wife of Gaius, the Emperor's heir. He divorced her because they thought she was barren. But we discovered that she was being poisoned." He paused. "She came with us partly because she wants to learn to heal, so that she can keep other women from the losses she's experienced. And partly because my grandmother ordered us to bring her."

"The Morrigan," Eogan said. "Was in Rome. As I said, more and more interesting." He clapped Lorcan on the shoulder. "Go to bed, Lorcan. Oh... those mercenaries will be here when?" Eogan asked.

"I..." Lorcan stopped. "I forgot to ask Arcus when they were following us. Tavi might know."

"You can tell me tomorrow," Eogan said, his voice firm. "We'll deal with those questions tomorrow. And we'll make plans. But you need to sleep."

"And see my mother." Lorcan added. He bowed slightly, then put his arm around Livia. "Let's go see if she's awake."

Chapter Twenty-One

Lorcan led Livia toward the guest where were Tavi and Yaroah were on guard.

"How is he?" Tavi asked.

"He'll live," Lorcan answered. "When Mother is stronger, maybe she'll be able to do something more with his leg. But you were right about his eye."

Tavi winced, then turned to Yaroah and translated. Yaroah sighed and shook his head.

"He is the smith you told us about?" he asked in Latin. "Will he still be a smith?"

"I think so", Lorcan answered. "I hope so." He nodded toward the door. "Has it been quiet?"

"There's been… giggling," Tavi said with a grin. "I think Drucilla is getting on just fine."

"Good," Livia said.

Lorcan nodded and knocked on the door. From inside, he heard Grainne's voice, "Come in!"

"Come and meet my mother properly," Lorcan said. "Yaroah, you, too."

Inside, the first person he saw was his mother. She'd obviously bathed, and was dressed in a clean gown, sitting on a stool near the fire. Her long hair was spread over her shoulders, and Drucilla stood behind her, combing it out. She smiled at Lorcan, then looked back down.

"Lorcan." Grainne smiled up at him. "I was certain that I'd dreamed you."

"I'm very real, Mother," Lorcan assured her, going to her side and kissing her cheek. "How do you feel?"

"Better now that I'm clean," she answered. She tipped her head back, then smiled. "Drucilla, stop fussing."

"I do not fuss!" Drucilla answered in broken Gaeilge. "I care." She looked at Lorcan, then switched to Latin. "Tell her that I want to help. And she has beautiful hair."

Lorcan translated, and Grainne turned to face Drucilla, taking the comb from her. "You're not a servant."

Drucilla hesitated, then replied, "Not servant. Sister."

"Mother, Drucilla came with us to learn to heal," Lorcan added. "So perhaps also student?"

Grainne smiled. "Is that so?" She placed the comb in her lap, then pointed to another stool. "Lorcan, bring that here?" Lorcan moved the stool closer to the fire, and Grainne gestured. "Drucilla, sit."

Drucilla smiled and took a seat, and Lorcan brought another stool for Livia before sitting on the ground at his mother's feet. She immediately started to pet his short hair.

"You're here," she said softly. "You're home. I've been hoping for this for so long. Your father never stopped hoping you'd come home."

"I'm sorry it took me so long, Mother," Lorcan said. "But I'm here now, and I'm going to put an end to this."

"That's a discussion for tomorrow," Grainne said. "You have mates." She looked up. "And a friend who is your opposite?"

"Diarmuid said the same thing," Lorcan said with a laugh. "Mother, this is Yaroah. He's been my friend since the moment I reached Rome. We fought together in the arena. We won our freedom together. And he came to help me win back what's mine." He gestured Yaroah closer, and Tavi translated what Lorcan had said.

Yaroah bowed deeply, then hesitantly said, "Mother Grainne, I... I help... brother Lorcan. Ghost raven brother." He paused. "I stay... then maybe go my home. Or maybe no." He turned to Tavi and asked in Latin. "Did I say that properly?"

"I think she understands," Tavi answered. Lorcan looked up at his mother, at the smile on her face.

"He calls you brother?" she asked. She stood up, holding her hands out to Yaroah. "Lorcan, will you tell him that I cannot wait to properly welcome him into our home as my son?"

Tavi translated before Lorcan could, speaking in Yaroah's own language. Yaroah's jaw dropped, and he took Grainne's hands, bowed over them, then kissed her fingers.

"Sit, Yaroah," Grainne said, sitting back down on her stool. "We'll practice speaking. You'll learn."

Lorcan shifted a little as Yaroah sat down next to him, and Tavi came to sit on his other side. "I can translate, Mother. Or Tavi or Livia can, if I'm not with you."

"Tavi and Livia." Grainne looked at them each in turn. "My other new children. My son's mates. How is it possible that you have two?"

"I don't know, Mother. But the mate bond is there for both of them. We all felt it."

"But your cloak—" She paused. "Do they...?"

"They know," Lorcan answered. "And I don't know. I've promised them that I am not going to choose one of them over the other. So, until I know, I'm going to live as a man among men, with the people I love. And if I never know? I'll spend the rest of my days with the people I love, and our children. I think that's all I can ask for."

"Mother Grainne," Livia said. "Lorcan told us that you're a healer, and a midwife. I'm a trained *medicae*, but not a midwife. I want to learn more of that art. Tavi's brother's wife was going to teach me, but we had to leave Britannia quickly to get ahead of the news that we were returning." She smiled at Lorcan. "I may not be able to sing healing the way Lorcan does—"

"You... you what?" Grainne turned to stare at him, her eyes wide. "Lorcan, you haven't been trained! You could have killed yourself!"

Lorcan felt his face grow warm. "I know. I just... if I didn't, a good man would have died. He'd been poisoned with *fealla bog*. What the Romans call *koneion*. The healing chants were all I could think of. I took a risk. A big one. And Grandmother already yelled at me for it." He took a deep breath. "Once this is over, I'll go to the druid college and learn properly. But now... I seem to have the idea of it now. It wasn't as bad when I sang over Ronan."

"You did it again? Just now?" Grainne blinked. "And your grandmother spoke to you? In Rome? She spoke to your father once, after you were taken. No one has spoken to her since."

"Uncle Petran told me. I spoke to her twice. Maybe three times," Lorcan said. "And she sent me visions. I knew something of what is happening in Dun Morrigan. I knew about the cages. I just couldn't get here any sooner. The weather and Cormac's mercenaries both kept me in Rome far longer than I wanted." He paused. "I'll tell you all of it, whenever you want. But not tonight. You need to rest, and so do we. When you're feeling stronger, I'm hoping you'll be able to help Ronan more than I can. I pulled the sickness out of him, but his leg, and that eye… that's beyond me."

"That's beyond any healer, I'm afraid," Grainne said. "He's been injured for too long. I will examine him once I've had a chance to rest." She reached out and ran her fingers over Lorcan's short hair once more. "This will take some getting used to. Why did you cut it?"

"Because one of Cormac's allies used my hair as a weapon against me," Lorcan answered. "To hold me down while he tried to kill me. I'll grow it back out once this is over." He looked up at his mother's horrified expression. "It's just hair, Mother."

"All of this… everything that's happened…" Grainne stammered. "It should never have happened. Cormac… he wasn't raised to be this. We tried to help him…"

"Some people don't want help," Tavi said gently. "Some people… can't be helped. And some people… it doesn't matter what kindness you show them. They'll never see it as more than a threat. Or proof that you're weak, and therefore prey." He smiled, but there was a sick feeling to it.

Grainne frowned slightly. "You sound very certain."

Tavi nodded. "Cormac was allied with my brother, Galius. I'm not entirely sure which of them was using the other. I suppose it doesn't matter anymore. Galius is dead, and all his plans to use Lorcan and Cormac as an excuse to conquer Eire are dead with him. But he was like that. Kindness only meant he was going to hurt you more. And weakness was something to exploit." He paused, then smiled slightly when Lorcan took his hand. "I know. He can't hurt me anymore. I know."

Grainne sighed and reached out to touch Tavi's shoulder. "I want to know more about you. All of you. But you need to rest. And I should rest." She paused. "*Fealla bog*. You saved a man from *fealla bog*. Lorcan, it may be that you're a stronger healer than I am."

"We'll find out when I go to the druid college to be tested. When this is over." Lorcan tipped his head back against his mother's knee and closed his eyes. "I'm not sure what the next step is. But Uncle Eogan says that the last of the uncles will be here tomorrow. That would be Cuanu and Fergus."

"And Cuanu knows Dun Morrigan better than any of us. He designed the new *baile* after…" Grainne paused. Then she sighed. "Tomorrow. We will talk tomorrow. Go to bed. Tavi, Livia, take him and put him to bed." Lorcan sat up to see her making shooing gestures. "All of you. Bed."

"Where's the Queen?" Lorcan asked, getting up off the floor and offering his hand to Tavi.

"She left before you and Livia came back," Tavi answered, letting Lorcan pull him up. "You didn't see her? She said that she wanted to check on Siobhan."

"If she went through the hall, we may not have seen her." Livia suggested. Lorcan frowned, thinking of the hall. Then he turned to Yaroah.

"Will you stay?" he asked in Latin. "Guard our mother?"

"You think you need to ask me?" Yaroah answered.

"Tavi, take Livia to our house. It's next door. Keep your *dolabrae* close."

"Lorcan, what are you thinking?" Grainne asked.

"I'm not sure." He glanced at the door. "Arcus found men loyal to Cormac among the mercenaries he'd hired to serve me. I wouldn't think it impossible that Cormac has ears in Dun Righ, too. And there's only one door in the hall, isn't there?"

Grainne stared at him for a moment, and all the color drained from her face. "Go find the queen," she whispered.

"Find my father and take him with you," Livia added. "Don't go alone."

Lorcan nodded. Then he grimaced. "My *siccae* are in our house. I'll walk over there with you." He leaned down and kissed his mother, then turned to Drucilla. "Stay here," he said in Latin. "I'm not sure if I'm right, but it might get exciting outside."

Drucilla nodded. "Is the queen in danger?" she asked. "I like her."

"I hope not, but I'll come back once I know more. While I'm gone, Yaroah will guard you both." He turned and hurried out, followed by Livia and Tavi.

"Lorcan, are you sure something is wrong?" Livia asked as he opened the door to the dark guest house.

"I don't know," he answered. "We need a lamp."

"I'll go back and get one from your mother." Tavi trotted back to the other guest house, coming back with a lit lamp. He entered the house and walked around the perimeter. "It's empty. And your *siccae* are here."

Lorcan picked up his swords and looked around. "Stay inside. I'll be back as soon as I can. And I'll find Manius first." He kissed Livia, then kissed Tavi. Then he went back out into the night.

"Lorcan!" Lorcan smiled to see Manius coming out of the next house. His *lanista* looked at him and frowned. "Why are you armed?"

"Maybe jumping at shadows, but I don't think so. I told Livia I'd come and find you. I think there may be something wrong. The queen left my mother, and we didn't see her even though she would have had to pass us to get to my cousin."

Manius nodded. He disappeared into the guest house, then came out with his own swords. "Lead the way."

Lorcan headed toward the hall, watching people moving through the darkness. One of the shapes was familiar—Diarmuid.

"Lorcan? What is it?" he asked as he came toward them. "What's wrong? Why are you armed?"

"Because your mother left mine while Livia and I were still with Ronan, and we didn't see her. She was going to see to Siobhan, but we never passed her." Lorcan answered. He nodded toward Manius. "Diarmuid, this is Manius. He's Livia's father and my teacher."

Diarmuid nodded toward Manius, then looked around through the darkness. "Father is in the hall. Let's go see if he's seen her." He turned and hurried into the hall. Lorcan followed him, and found all of his uncles sitting with the king.

"Father, have you seen Mother?" Diarmuid called. Eogan stood up.

"No. I thought she was with Grainne." His eyes widened. "Why? What's wrong?"

"My mother says that Caírech left her to go and see to Siobhan while Livia and I were still working with Ronan. We never saw her." Lorcan looked around. "Cormac had allies in Rome, in Thracia, and in Alba. Does he have men in Dun Righ, too?"

A look of complete horror washed over the High King's face. "The gates have been closed since Turlach and Cian brought the last group in. They have to be within the walls. Petran, tell me it's not too dark for you to fly," Eogan asked in a low voice.

"For Caírech? We'll fly." Petran got to his feet and hurried toward the door, his brothers and his mate following him. The rustle of clothing became the flutter of wings as the ravens shifted and flew out into the night. The High King moved past Lorcan, following the ravens. As he got out into the night, he raised his voice and started shouting for guards.

"What now?" Diarmuid asked.

"Take your brother and go guard Siobhan and Ronan." Lorcan said.

"Manius, you're with me." They walked out of the hall and separated. Diarmuid whistled sharply, calling for Cian as Lorcan led Manius across the *urla*.

"Where are we going?" Manius asked in Latin, keeping his voice low.

"We'll start at the gate," Lorcan answered. "And work our way inside from there. They can't have gotten outside the gates." He pointed toward the gates. There were torches on either side, and Lorcan could see that the guards who were supposed to be manning the gates were missing.

"There should be someone there, shouldn't there?" Manius asked. He broke into a trot, and Lorcan followed, searching for the guards. For anyone. He heard a raven overhead, and looked up to see his uncle Maelan.

"There are no gate guards," he called. Maelan croaked at him, then flew ahead and landed on the gate. Lorcan slowed to a walk, and Manius stopped, falling in next to him.

"I assume that was a relative," he said. "Was that Petran or Turlach?"

Lorcan grinned. "Neither. That was my uncle Maelan. I'll introduce you to the rest of my uncles tomorrow." He turned, trying to see through the shadows behind the houses. "Let's start that way," he pointed. They walked into the shadows, and Lorcan paused for a moment to let his eyes adjust. The passage between the houses and the wall was wide enough for three men to walk side by side, and there were normally torches burning at regular intervals. Tonight, the torches were all out, and Lorcan wondered if they just hadn't been lit, or if they'd been dowsed to hide something. How many, and where could they have gone? The gates were being watched now, so they were trapped inside the baile. He slowed, listening. The wind through the thatch roofs. His uncles, calling to each other, reporting that they had found nothing. They must be inside somewhere, out of sight. Where…

"The stables," Lorcan called. "Let me lead."

Manius fell back, and Lorcan picked up his pace, moving quickly behind the houses and the hall, hearing nothing but the voices of his uncles and the sounds of the king's guards as they searched. Someone stepped out in front of them, and Lorcan raised his swords, only to lower them when he realized it was Eogan.

"Anything?" The king frowned. "The torches were never lit?"

"Nothing, but we're going to check the stables," Lorcan answered. "My uncles say they see nothing, so whoever it is must be inside. And how were they going to get Aunt Caírech out? They'd need a horse, or a chariot."

Eogan nodded. "I ordered a search of the guest houses and the hall already. I'll come with you to the stables." He gestured, and they walked out between the houses and onto the *urla*.

The stables were on the far side of the baile, and by the time Lorcan, Manius and Eogan reached them, there were guards ranged around the building. Petran was with them.

"And?" Eogan asked.

"We've searched everywhere else. The stables are all that's left, and Turlach says that the horses are stirred up in there." Petran frowned at the closed doors. "They're in there, and they have a hostage."

"Albus, you are not allowed to risk your life the way you did in the Hall of Virgins," Manius growled. "Decus told me what you did."

"We may not have a choice," Lorcan said. "Uncle, see if they'll deal. See what they want in return for the Queen's life."

Eogan nodded and went to the doors, pounding on them. "We know you're inside, and we know you have my wife," he called. "You have no way out of this *baile* unless you release her."

"If we release her, we have no way out of this *baile*!" someone shouted back. "If you want her back, grant us safe passage."

"Tell them that if they release the queen, you'll grant them safe passage through the gates," Lorcan said softly.

"And that will do... what?" Petran asked.

"Get the Queen away from them," Lorcan answered. "And once they're through the gates... they no longer have safe passage."

Petran's eyes widened. Then he scowled, and a raven flew up into the thatch. A moment later, three ravens flew off toward the gates. Eogan watched them, then looked at Lorcan. He looked troubled, but he turned and went back to the door.

"Release the Queen," he shouted. "And I will grant you safe passage through the gates of the *baile*."

"Do you swear it?"

Eogan grimaced. "I swear. You will be escorted safely through the gates."

The stable door opened, and a man appeared. His tunic was torn, and a rough bandage was wrapped around his arm. There was another man behind him. The wounded man pointed at Lorcan. "He's to escort us out."

"Lorcan, do you agree?" Eogan asked.

"I'll escort them through the gates." Lorcan stepped back. "How many of you are there?"

The stable door opened further, and a third figure came forward, a boy who looked to be barely into his teens. His face was marred by old bruises, and he looked terrified. Lorcan went cold, and glanced at Manius. Manius nodded and backed away, turning to walk toward the gate.

"Where's my wife?" Eogan demanded.

"Inside," the wounded man answered.

"Bring her out."

The wounded man scowled, then spat, "Dara, bring her out."

The boy flinched at the sound of his name, then disappeared into the stables, coming back out after a moment leading the queen. There was a bruise on one cheek, her gown was stained, and she looked furious. She stumbled, and Dara caught her and steadied her, then said, "Da, I need a knife. I can't untie the knots."

"Just let me take her," Eogan said.

The boy hesitated, then led Caírech to him. He glanced over his shoulder as Eogan embraced his wife, then whispered, "I'm sorry." Then he went back to his father, standing behind him with his head bowed.

"This way," Lorcan said, gesturing with his right-hand blade. The men started walking, and guards fell in all around them. Up ahead, Lorcan could see the gates being opened, and Manius coming toward them. He fell in next to Lorcan and nodded once.

"He's going to kill you," the wounded man snarled. "Cormac. He's coming for all of you."

"And if you're the quality of men he has at his back, we'll all die old men," one of the guards scoffed.

"Enough," Lorcan called. "Don't take any threat lightly. It could be the last threat you face." He looked up at the gate, and could just barely make out the shapes of four ravens. He stopped at the open gate and gestured, "You're free to go. Or stay, if you wish to serve a better man than my cousin." He met the boy's eyes. "It's your choice. Stay or go."

The boy frowned slightly, then glanced at his father. "I…"

"Come on, boy!"

Dara flinched again, then nodded. "Coming, Da." He tucked his hands behind his back and turned to follow his father out into the night. Lorcan stabbed one of his swords into the turf and reached out to catch the boy's shoulder.

"It's your choice," he repeated. Dara looked at him. He looked at his father, who was already walking down the hill and hadn't turned.

"I can stay?" he whispered.

"Will you swear to the High King?" Lorcan asked.

"I… yes. I'm sorry I helped hurt the lady. I didn't want to."

"Dara!"

Dara flinched again, then shook his head. "No. I'm not going. I'm staying." He turned and ran back into the *baile*. Lorcan followed him, hearing the gates closing behind him, followed by the cries of four angry ravens.

Chapter Twenty-Two

Lorcan surrendered Dara to Eogan and Caírech. The boy stammered through swearing his fealty, swearing not to Eogan, but to Caírech. Then he burst into tears, sobbing even harder when Caírech embraced him.

"We'll find out his story tomorrow," Eogan said to Lorcan as the queen led the boy away. "You've had a long day, Lorcan. Go to bed." He looked past Lorcan. "And here come your uncles and Manius."

Lorcan nodded and turned to see Petran leading the other ravens toward him.

"It's done," Petran said. "Cormac won't know anything from them." He looked at Lorcan "You surprised me."

"I did?" Lorcan frowned, thinking over the evening. He remembered the look on his uncle's face. "Oh. With promising them safe passage, but limited it to the gate?"

Petran nodded. "That's not something you learned from your father."

Lorcan licked his lip and nodded slowly. "And… is that a good thing or a bad thing?" he asked slowly.

Petran hesitated, then shook his head. "I don't know." He looked off in the direction where Caírech had gone. "It saved the queen. But…"

"But what?" Lorcan interrupted. He scowled, then shook his head. "But what? What else is there? Their lives were already forfeit for their betrayal."

"Petran, he's right," Eogan said softly.

"It's just…" Petran stammered. "You lied to them."

"I did not!" Lorcan protested. "Safe passage through the gate. How was that a lie? That's exactly what they got."

"And he did not offer that," Eogan added. "I did. Lorcan just offered his advice. Good advice that saved the life of my wife. Petran, I don't understand this… animosity."

"You're not a raven," Petran answered, and Lorcan felt the words like a slap.

"Well, I suppose that's why I don't understand. I didn't think you agreed with Cormac on that," he said, and watched his uncle pale. "Good night." He bowed to the High King, then turned and walked away, not giving his uncle a second glance. He heard Petran call his name, but didn't turn.

His first stop was to see his mother. Yaroah nodded at him as he approached, then frowned. "What is it?" he asked. "You look... who are we killing?"

Lorcan smiled in spite of himself. "No one. It's over. Caírech is safe. I wanted to tell my mother."

"She sleeps, and so does Drucilla. I will stay here and watch, and make certain that there were no other traitors. I will sleep across the door, inside." He looked around. "Go to Livia and Tavi. Share with them what you won't share with me."

Lorcan nodded. "Tell Mother that I came to check on her, and that I'll see her in the morning."

"I will try," Yaroah promised, and Lorcan turned toward the house next door. He knocked on the door, and when no one answered, he went inside. The bedcurtain hadn't been drawn, so he could see a shape on the bed, and one on the floor. The one on the bed was Livia. Tavi was the shape sitting on the floor, his back to the support post and an axe at his side. Lorcan smiled slightly and went to sit by the fire-pit, staring at the embers.

Not a raven.

And there it was. He didn't understand what was wrong because he wasn't really a raven. He'd been born to his feathers, but he wasn't like them. Not like the others. Not like his uncles, or his cousins. He was different.

And your difference is what makes you so special.

Lorcan looked up at the woman who sat across the firepit from him. "Don't wake them."

The Morrigan smiled. *They can't hear me. I'm only speaking to you. My son can be a rare idiot at times. And he is wrong. I told you that already.*

"Is he?" Lorcan asked. "Grandmother, I'm never going to be like them. I'm never going to be a real raven—"

194

You are a real raven, she interrupted. *Or was the raven in the temple in Alba a fake? A dream?* She arched a brow. *You are mine, as much as they are. I told you; you are a worthy son of my line.* She snorted. *Don't disagree with a goddess, boy*, she added. Then she paused. *What are you thinking?*

Lorcan scowled at the embers. "I don't know. My thoughts are circling. I thought Petran was different. I thought he saw me, and not just my feathers. But now… if that's how he feels? Do the rest of them feel the same? Or will I always be the white freak?" He sighed, and the words fell out. "I should have stayed in Rome."

Should you?

The words were flat, uninflected, but Lorcan still heard the hurt in them. He looked up at his grandmother. "My uncles and my parents made this mess. They did it before I was even born. They failed Cormac, and by doing that, they failed me. In Rome, I was respected. I was honored." He snorted and looked back the fire. "I was a hero. They loved me."

I thought you said you had enough of their love.

Lorcan shrugged. "I wasn't a freak there. I was… I was accepted. I was part of something. And I am never going to have that here!"

So you'd turn your back on them? On your father?

Lorcan shrugged again. "They made the mess. They set this all into motion. They should be the ones to fix it. I can take Livia and Tavi and go back to Rome…"

"You'd do that?" Lorcan turned in his place to see Petran standing inside the open door. His uncle looked horrified. "You'd abandon us?"

"Don't wake them," Lorcan snapped.

They can't hear him either. Morrigan smiled. *Come in, close the door, and sit down, my idiot son.*

Petran came to the fire-pit and sat down, folding his legs under him, then folding his hands in his lap.

"I'm sorry," he murmured. "I didn't mean… I didn't mean you!"

Lorcan leaned his elbow in his knee and looked at his uncle. "You know, when you start throwing shit, you don't really get to choose who you splash."

"Lorcan!" Petran reared back, his eyes wide in shock.

"Too coarse?" Lorcan scoffed. "Too bad. I learned worse in the arena." He paused. "How much of what I said did you hear?"

"I came in when you said you should have stayed in Rome. When you said we did this, that this is all our fault." Petran sighed. "You're not wrong. We did fail Cormac. And we did fail you." He shook his head. "Maybe we could have done more. Tried more. I can't think what else we could have done, but… maybe. We were all still reeling, and that's I think the only reason we didn't. We were all… damaged by that monster." He paused again. "They were the first deaths. The first time death came for the Morrigan's own. Your uncle Ronan was my twin. And Oscar and Muirenn. She'd just learned she was pregnant. We lost Ronan when the thing was freed, and we lost Muirenn and Oscar within a day of each other. And I almost lost Turlach. That's why he limps." He stared into the fire-pit. "I told you about Cormac, when we got him home. We didn't know how to help him. Who to trust. We did… the best we could." He shrugged and looked at Lorcan. "And it wasn't enough."

"And now I have to risk my life, and my mates, and my child to end this." Lorcan rubbed his hands together, his guts churning. "Or I could take them back to Alba."

And be safe for how long? Morrigan asked. *How long until Cormac comes for you, Lorcan? For your mates and your child? For Lucanus' brother's children?*

Lorcan looked across at her. "You think he will?"

You know he will, Lorcan. He was not content to leave you alive in Rome. He will not be content until he destroys everything you love and defeats you.

Lorcan sighed and nodded. "I know. I just don't understand why he hasn't killed me already. He has my cloak."

"Are you complaining?" Petran asked. Lorcan snorted.

"Of course not."

He doesn't just want you dead, Lorcan, Morrigan said. *He wants to defeat you. He wants you to know that you've lost. Which means—*

"That he wants to be the one to do it," Lorcan finished. "I know that. I said it to Turlach, on the way from Alba. He wants everything that I have. He wants me to know that he's stolen it all. And he wants to be the one to stab me in the guts so I bleed out slowly while he laughs at my dying." He shook his head. "I know that. I just don't understand it. He could just kill me and have it be done."

"Do you have to understand?" Petran asked.

Lorcan considered the question, then shook his head. "I suppose not. I don't need to understand why. I just need to stop him." He took a deep breath and looked down at his hands. "I do need to understand why not being a raven means that Eogan won't understand why you reacted badly to what I suggested. Because I don't understand either, and no matter what you or anyone else says, I am a raven." He pointed at his grandmother. "She says so."

I don't understand your objections, either, Morrigan said. *I rather liked the specificity. It was very clever.*

Petran gaped at his mother. "You... you liked that?"

Morrigan nodded. *Explain why you did not.*

Petran frowned. "It was... manipulative. It's so close to what Niall told us about the witch who trapped him, all those years ago."

"I don't know what you're talking about," Lorcan said. "Is this another story that someone should have told me but no one did?"

Petran sighed. "Probably. It's why Niall has no voice. Your father never told you?"

Lorcan shook his head. "No. And I never thought to ask. Uncle Niall doesn't talk. Uncle Fergus is like a child. They just are that way. So tell me."

Petran took a deep breath. "Niall was `19, and we all thought Sorcha was dead. That was how all of this started." He fell silent, rubbing his hands together. Lorcan let him be, and Petran nodded before he continued, "He wrote this all down, so we'd know all of it. Pages and pages of it. He met a woman. He thought she was being attacked, and he protected her, brought her to her home. She promised him guest right from dusk until dawn, seduced him and bewitched him so that he couldn't leave before dawn. Then she took him prisoner. She claimed to be Eogan's sister, and she knew... half-truths and lies about us and our cloaks. She wanted the throne, and she thought that if she could steal our power, she would be able to challenge Eogan and win. She enslaved Sorcha, murdered Sorcha's father, and she cursed Niall to silence. She would have killed them both, but Fergus killed her first. By accident, but then there was no way to break the spell. Oscar tried for years." He paused. "I told you about the *deamhan aeir*. I didn't tell you that he was that witch's brother, and being cursed to be a *deamhan aeir* was his punishment for hurting Niall. I didn't tell you that your uncle Oscar cursed him. He created that monster out of anger. He'd never have said it, but he loved Niall, possibly more than the rest of us combined. What that witch did to him... I've never seen him so angry."

"Uncle Oscar created a monster that ravaged all of Eire, and you're upset that I limited the safe passage," Lorcan said softly. Then he laughed, a broken, bitter sound. "Uncle, you have no sense of proportion. None."

Morrigan chuckled, and Petran looked sourly at his mother. "I never entirely forgave him, either. The monster's first victim may have been his own mother, but his second was Ronan. And Oscar paid for it, in the end. It killed his mate and their child, and then it killed him. It called him Father... and it ate him while we watched. Then we killed it. But not before it hurt Cormac and almost crippled Turlach." He paused, picking up a stick and using it to poke the embers, sending a spray of sparks flying up to fade into the darkness. "So that's it. What you did tonight? It was very much in the same line of the manipulation that started this nightmare. And..." He took a deep breath. "And you were right. You saved Caírech. And that boy, who looks to have been just as much a victim. You did it with minimal bloodshed. I just..." He stopped. "I don't know. It felt like deception. But it wasn't, was it? You told them exactly the truth, and it was on them that they didn't hear what you said. And we never told you any of it, to know why that might stick in the craw. You never knew. So that's something else you were right about. We failed you." He poked the embers again, and when the sparks had faded, added, "I'll tell Eogan to prepare a chariot, if you're truly serious about going back to Rome. We'll handle Cormac ourselves, the way we should have. I'll send word when it's safe for you to come home."

"I am home," Lorcan said, and watched the shock and relief fill his uncle's face. "Eire is my home. Dun Morrigan is my home. I'm going to take back what's mine. And that will be the end of the questions about if I'm truly a son of the Morrigan's blood. I am as much a raven as any of you, and the color of my feathers doesn't matter. The only reason I didn't understand had nothing to do with my feathers, and everything to do with you and my uncles and my father deciding I didn't need to know any of this. And it came around and it bit all of us." He reached over and took Petran's stick, broke it, and tossed it into the firepit. "I didn't choose this fight. You all put it on me. And I can't run from it, or he'll come after me. I have to end it."

Petran nodded. He looked tired, and older than Lorcan could remember ever seeing. "We're all behind you, Lorcan. We all want to see this end. And you are one of us."

He is, indeed, Morrigan said. *He is my grandson, and a most worthy child of my line.*

Lorcan smiled. "Thank you, Grandmother." He closed his eyes and yawned, and when he opened his eyes again, the Morrigan was gone. Petran was looking at him, and there was an odd expression on his face.

"What?"

Petran smiled. "I just realized. She does favor you. That was the longest conversation I've had with her since she left me and Ronan with Diarmuid when we were children. She's never been... communicative. The last time any of us spoke to her was your father, on the day you were taken." Petran slowly got to his feet. "Lorcan, I am sorry. I was careless with my words, and I hurt you." He held his hand out, and Lorcan let his uncle pull him up to his feet. Petran rested his hands on Lorcan's shoulders. "You're special. I've always known that. Since you were born. I always thought you were special. I've never thought of you as less, or as a freak, and I'm sorry I made you think that, even for a moment." He sighed. "We can talk more tomorrow. You're tired, and today has lasted far longer than it should have."

"I don't think there's anything else to say, Uncle," Lorcan said. "Except that I believe you. And I forgive you."

Petran looked stunned for a moment, then pulled Lorcan into a tight embrace. He rested his head on his uncle's shoulder, closing his eyes. All at once, the day caught up with him, and he felt tears starting.

"It's all right, Lorcan," Petran murmured. "We'll get through this."

Lorcan nodded, his cheek scratching against his uncle's *leine*. "We will," he whispered, his voice harsh. "And we'll save them all."

"Yes, we will."

* * *

"Should we let him sleep?"

Lorcan rolled onto his back and opened his eyes to see Tavi and Livia looking down at him. He looked around—he was on the floor next to the cold fire-pit. What... oh.

"I didn't want to wake you," he croaked. "I came in late, and you were both asleep."

"What happened?" Livia asked. "Is the queen safe?"

"She's fine, and we dealt with the traitors," Lorcan sat up and rubbed one hand over his face. "I'm not even a little bit awake."

"Yaroah came to tell us that your mother is awake, and he was taking her to the hall to eat," Tavi said. "He asked for help, so I'll meet them in the hall to translate."

Lorcan nodded. "Livia, go with him. I want a bath. I'll go wash, then I'll join you." He got up and looked around. He barely remembered Petran leaving.

"What is it?" Tavi asked.

"I'll tell you over a meal," Lorcan said. "I'm starving. Find Manius while you're going."

Tavi nodded and offered Livia his arm, leading her out of the house. Lorcan followed them out, walking across the *urla* toward the bathhouse.

"Lorcan! It's Lorcan!"

Lorcan turned, and laughed out loud when he saw the big man running toward him, his arms outstretched, and his feather cloak billowing behind him. "Fergus!"

The big man reached him, scooping him up like a child and hugging him tightly. "You're home! You're home!" He turned and raised his voice. "I told you he was coming home! I told you!"

"I am home," Lorcan agreed, hugging his uncle. "I'm fine. I'm safe. Please put me down?"

Fergus laughed and set him on his feet. He cocked his head to the side, then took Lorcan's right hand in his. "Pretty raven. I like this. Cuanu, look at this."

Lorcan smiled at his other uncle, who had reached them. Cuanu looked at Lorcan's tattoos and nodded. "It is pretty work, if you don't know what it means."

"What does it mean, Cuanu?"

"I earned them fighting, Fergus," Lorcan said. "I... I'm not sure how to explain. I was a long way away from home, and people would watch me fight. And when I won, I got a new tattoo." He pushed his sleeve up to show the rest.

"You won a lot," Fergus said. "Did it hurt?"

"Yes."

"Did you cry?"

"It didn't hurt that much." Lorcan took Fergus' hand in his. "It's good to see you, Uncle. I want you to meet some people. I—"

"Grainne!" Cuanu gasped. "What? How?" He brushed past them and ran to embrace Lorcan's mother.

"Grainne! Grainne is here!" Fergus laughed. "Lorcan, did you know?" He paused, and frowned slightly. "Who is the pretty lady? And is that man a shadow?"

"Pretty lady? Shadow?" Lorcan turned, and saw Drucilla standing behind Yaroah. "Oh. They're my friends. His name is Yaroah. He's not a shadow. He comes from a place very far away, and all the people there are dark like he is. And her name is Drucilla."

"She's Cuanu's Drucilla." Fergus said, nodding emphatically. "Cuanu, the pretty lady Drucilla is here for you."

Cuanu looked at them, clearly puzzled. Then he turned, and saw Drucilla for the first time. His eyes widened, and his jaw dropped. Drucilla stepped out from behind Yaroah, met Cuanu's eyes, then looked past him at Lorcan.

"Drucilla," Lorcan said in Latin. "This is my uncle, Cuanu."

Cuanu looked at him. "You learned Latin?"

"I had no choice," Lorcan said with a grin. "Drucilla is learning Gaeilge. Maybe you could work with her?"

Cuanu turned back to Drucilla and held his hand out to her. She put her hand into his, and he bowed over it. "It would be my pleasure."

Chapter Twenty-Three

Lorcan slipped away to the bathhouse and hurried through washing up and changing his clothes, then went to the hall. He found his mates sitting with Grainne, Drucilla and Yaroah. He kissed his mother on the cheek, then kissed Tavi and Livia in turn before sitting down next to Livia.

"Where's Manius this morning?" he asked, taking a bowl of porridge from a serving girl. "Thank you." He nodded toward Corvina, who was sitting on the table. "Should she be on the table?"

"It's her breakfast, too." Tavi offered Corvina a piece of bannock. "And to answer your other question, he was here when we came in, sitting with the High King," Tavi answered. "I think they ate with your uncles, and they went off together."

"There are two more of your uncles," Livia added. "They came in with your mother, Yaroah and Drucilla. And one of them seemed quite taken with Drucilla."

Lorcan smiled. "My uncle Cuanu. He and Fergus just arrived. I saw them on my way to the bath. And yes, he is." He reached for a pitcher and poured a cup of beer for himself, then held the pitcher up. Tavi nodded and passed his cup to Lorcan. "Uncle Cuanu has never found his mate," he added as he passed the cup back to Tavi.

"Oh," Tavi murmured. "Is that why?"

"Is that why, what?" Livia asked. She looked from Tavi to Lorcan, then her brows rose. "Oh. Is that so?"

Lorcan nodded and sipped his beer, then turned his attention to his porridge. "I'll talk to Drucilla later. But for now, I need to eat, because all of my uncles are here, and we can start to plan the next step."

"I'm thinking you may want to show them what they can expect from you and from Yaroah," Tavi said. "Your uncles were talking. I'm not sure they all know that Livia and I both speak Gaeilge."

"Oh?" Lorcan switched to Latin. "And what did you overhear?"

"That they're not certain if you're going to be able to beat Cormac if it comes to a challenge," Livia answered. "Petran argued for you, but he had to admit that he hasn't seen you really fight yet."

Tavi nodded. "He wasn't there when we practiced in Hibernia. And you fought me, so I could show you that attack. So that wasn't a real fight." He looked down the table. "Yaroah," he called. "You and Lorcan should show them how the best gladiators in all of Rome fight."

Yaroah laughed. "Perhaps we should!"

"Let me make certain my uncle knows," Lorcan said. "So he doesn't think we're attacking him, or trying to kill each other." He picked up a bannock and broke it in half. "Once I finish."

Livia sipped from her own cup, then turned to Lorcan. "Who were you talking to last night?" she asked. "I woke up, and you were sitting with your uncle and a woman. I haven't met her yet."

Lorcan coughed. "You saw her? She said that she made it so that our talking wouldn't wake you. I didn't know you were awake, or I'd have introduced you."

Tavi looked at Livia, then at Lorcan. "Who... Lorcan, were you talking to your grandmother last night? And I missed it?" He frowned. "Why were you talking last night?"

"I... I'll tell you later," Lorcan said. "Uncle Petran... well, if he hadn't made it right, we'd have been leaving today."

"Why? What did Petran do?"

Lorcan turned to look past Tavi at his mother. "I'll say that I'd have expected a harper to have a better understanding of words and their meaning, and leave it at that. We settled it between us, and Grandmother let him know that he was wrong and she wasn't pleased with him." He ate a piece of bannock. "Mother, don't let it bother you. It's over."

"Good." Grainne folded her hands on the tabletop. "Livia, I'm going to be seeing to Ronan today. Will you come with me?"

Livia smiled. "Thank you, Mother. I'd like that."

"Will one of you translate and ask Drucilla if she'll come as well? My Latin isn't strong."

Drucilla's smile lit up the hall when Livia asked her. "Thank you!" she answered. "There's so much I want to learn. And... oh." Her cheeks colored, and Lorcan turned to see that Cuanu had come back into the hall. He came toward them, stopping and bowing toward Drucilla before turning to Lorcan.

"Eogan says that you have forces coming?" he asked. "Mercenaries? And possibly a legion from Rome? Lorcan, am I going to have to rebuild Dun Morrigan again?"

Lorcan chuckled. "Ah… it might not be a bad idea to plan for improvements and anything you might have forgotten the last time," he answered. "We'll sit down to plan later and I'll tell you everything. First, I'm told that there is some doubt about the strength of my arm?"

Cuanu frowned. "Not from me. I know what those tattoos mean. You survived to have a full arm of them. You've gotten better than any of us could have imagined."

Lorcan smiled. "Thank you, Uncle. Yaroah and I will be showing them what we're worth."

"Now, Ghost?" Yaroah asked.

Lorcan drained the last of his beer and stood up. "Now."

* * *

Eogan suggested the *urla* for the bout, and when Lorcan arrived with his practice swords, he found there was a larger audience than he'd expected. Eogan and Caírech, with Diarmuid, his wife Eimear, and Cian. Dara, hiding in Caírech's shadow. Lorcan's uncles and older male cousins were all there, which he was expecting. He wasn't expecting the rest of the raven flock, and spent several minutes being mobbed by his aunts and his younger cousins. He met the six newest members of the flock—the mates of his four oldest cousins, and two tiny babies. He introduced them all to Livia and to Tavi, and watched near-identical looks of surprise on all of their faces when he explained that they were both his mates.

"That's allowed?" Orla's mate, Fiachra, asked, and was promptly punched in the arm by Orla. He laughed and put his arm around her. "I'm not looking for you to add another mate! Truly!"

"Lorcan," Manius called. He came over and nodded to Fiachra and Orla. "Are you ready? I'll be watching and keeping everyone back."

"Let me take my shirt off," Lorcan said. He handed his practice blades to Manius, stripped the *leine* off over his head, then went and handed it to Livia, accepting a kiss in return.

"Be careful," Tavi warned, and leaned in for his own kiss. "The last thing we need is for either of you to get hurt."

"I'll be careful," Lorcan assured him. He reached up to Corvina, sitting on Tavi's shoulder, and stroked her feathers. "You stay with Tavi," he added. "This isn't serious. But I need to show them what I can do. That I have a chance of winning this."

Tavi nodded. "I understand. Maybe we can play a bit later, show them Roman axes." He looked past Lorcan and straightened. "Isn't that your cousin?"

"I have a lot of cousins," Lorcan said as he turned to see the last cousin he'd have expected at the *urla*. "Ronan? What are you doing out of bed?"

Ronan and Siobhan had joined the others, and Ronan was leaning on Diarmuid for support. His leg was heavily splinted, and he still looked pale, the linen bandage covering his eye only emphasizing that pallor. But he smiled, and it was as if nothing had happened. As if the past year hadn't happened.

"Diarmuid said you were going to fight," Ronan said. "I saw your last duel. I want to see how much you've changed. I mean… they tell me you were a gladiator. You have to have changed, and gotten better. I want to see."

"Then you're going back to bed," Lorcan said. Ronan laughed.

"Yes, Da."

Lorcan laughed and turned back toward the center of the *urla* where Yaroah was waiting with his wooden *gladius* and a shield. Manius handed him his blades, bent and picked up a long staff, then looked around. "Everyone stand well back!" he called, leveling the staff between Lorcan and Yaroah. Lorcan set himself, his blades ready, and watched Yaroah. Yaroah grinned at him. Then the staff dropped, and Yaroah attacked. Lorcan was ready for the overhand strike, blocking and catching Yaroah across the ribs with his other blade.

"That's going to get you killed!" he called as he skipped back, avoiding Yaroah's answering slash.

"Who here knows that but you?" Yaroah laughed as he followed Lorcan, the crash and clatter of their blades ringing through the baile. Twice Manius had to recenter them as they passed too close to the onlookers. Then Lorcan rushed Yaroah, ducking underneath the bigger man's strike, passing him and scoring two hits—one to Yaroah's lower back, the other to the back of his left thigh. The second strike drove Yaroah to his knee, and Lorcan tapped him on the back of the neck before he could rise, letting his blade rest there.

"Yield?"

Yaroah laughed, dropping his weapons and holding his arms out. "Yield. I will not lose next time!"

"Just stop opening with an overhand, so there is a next time." Lorcan tucked his right-hand blade underneath his left arm and offered Yaroah his hand, helping him up.

"Lorcan?"

Lorcan turned from helping Yaroah up to see Diarmuid had come closer. "Yes?" he said. Then he saw the look on his cousin's face. "Oh. Want to try?"

"If one of you are willing?"

"Wooden blades," Lorcan said. "Because Tavi is right. We can't risk one of us getting hurt. Not now."

"Of course!" Diarmuid smiled broadly and stepped back to unfasten the pin of his cloak, handing it to Eimear. Then he came onto the *urla* and went to Yaroah. "May I borrow your blade and shield?"

"Oh, you want to try me?" Lorcan laughed. "Manius, we'll go again."

Manius snorted and came back onto the *urla* with his staff. "Playtime for the children?" he asked. Diarmuid laughed out loud, then stripped his own shirt off, taking Yaroah's sword and shield. He swung the sword back and forth, then nodded.

"I'm ready."

Lorcan set his feet and raised his blades, watching the staff. Watching Diarmuid. It had been years since he'd last sparred with his cousin, and Diarmuid had always had the best teachers. He snorted—worrying about how a fight would go was a distraction he didn't need, and a habit that Manius had trained out of him. He didn't need to worry. He just needed to fight.

Manius dropped the staff, and Lorcan attacked, driving Diarmuid backwards. For a moment, Diarmuid was clearly stunned, confused by an attack by two swords, and unable to do more than defend himself. Then he gathered and fought back... and found himself flat on his back on the grass, that same stunned expression on his face.

"What... what sort of fighting was that?" he gasped.

"I'm a *dimachaeri*," Lorcan said, tucking his right-hand blade under his arm and held his hand out. "That's how I was taught."

"Show me!" Diarmuid laughed as Lorcan helped him up. "That... no one in Eire fights like that!"

"Manius?" Lorcan called. "Interested in a new student?"

Diarmuid turned to look at Manius, who was leaning on his staff, grinning from ear to ear. "You taught him this?"

Manius nodded. "I was also a gladiator, also a *dimachaeri,* and like your cousin, I also won my way free by the strength of my arm. It took me longer, but I didn't have a slave uprising to put down. Then I taught other gladiators. And yes, I can teach you. But first, we have other matters at hand. Are you done feeding your opponents to the grass, Corax?"

Lorcan laughed. "I suppose."

"Corax?" Diarmuid asked. "What's that?"

Lorcan sighed. "I'll tell you all everything when we sit down to start planning. You should know what I know, and what help we have available." He turned to look at the rest of his flock. "So, have I convinced you?"

Petran snorted and shook his head, pointedly not looking over his shoulder at the others. "I told you. You didn't want to believe me. But look at that arm." He smiled. "Lorcan, explain the tattoos."

Lorcan held his arm up, the back of his hand facing his family. "These are the mark of a gladiator. Mine started on the back of my hand with my first win in the arena of Rome. Every win was another part to the tattoo, because Rome both loves and is terrified of gladiators, and they need to be able to identify them at a glance." He lowered his arm and laughed. "After I was freed, I confused a lot of them."

"Why?" Oscar asked.

"Because I was adopted into the Emperor's household, and granted the status of patrician," Lorcan answered, and watched the shock land on his uncles and cousins. "In Rome, I am called Albus Corvus Torvus Victorinus. But in the arena, I was called Corax Princeps. Prince Raven."

All at once, Cuanu started laughing. "Patrician. That means you were counted as a citizen, and wore one of those draped togas. With a full arm of gladiator tattoos." He turned to the others. "Gladiators are not citizens. They're slaves or freed slaves. They are not allowed to wear the toga. That's why Lorcan confused them." He shook his head. "Lorcan, you're a wonder."

"And we have plans to lay," Lorcan said. He handed his blades to Manius, then took his shirt from Tavi. "Shall we?"

The crowd started to disperse—the men of the flock moving toward the hall. Under Caírech's direction, Diarmuid helped Ronan back to his bed, with Siobhan and Dara following behind. Grainne and Drucilla collected Livia and followed them, with Yaroah trailing behind them. Finally, the only one left was Eogan, who lingered at the *urla*, frowning.

"Uncle?" Lorcan asked. "Is something wrong?"

"There was a messenger this morning," Eogan said softly. "He rode through the night to get here." He shook his head. "There's no help coming from Alba."

"What?" Lorcan and Tavi both gasped. Lorcan waved Tavi still, then asked, "What happened? The mercenaries—"

"From what we know, the Governor sent them on the next tide after you left. Their ships were attacked. The messenger said there were a bare half-dozen survivors, and the Roman guards say that they can see strange ships on the horizon. They think that anyone who comes after you, or who tries to reach Alba, will be waylaid. We're on our own." He nodded toward the hall. "We'll have to tell them."

"How are we going to let Arcus know, so he doesn't send anyone else?" Tavi asked.

Eogan shook his head. "I don't know. I just know that we have to end this before any more innocents die."

Lorcan took a deep breath, then nodded. "We'll need to talk to Mother, and have Ronan in to tell us what he knows. We need to know how many men Cormac has. What kind of weapons. If he has done anything to reinforce the *baile*." He closed his eyes. "Manius is right. Playtime is over. Time to plan."

* * *

Lorcan settled at the stable with Tavi on one side and Manius on the other. His uncles were already at the table, as were Oscar, Becc and Orla. She smiled at Lorcan when he saw her.

"I've taken up arms," was all she said. He nodded.

"My Livia's mother was a gladiatrix, and Livia fights as well. I'm glad to see you with us, Orla." He looked around. "Uncle Eogan and Diarmuid are—"

"Coming," Diarmuid called. Lorcan turned to see him helping Ronan into the hall. Eogan and Cian were behind him. Once they were seated, Eogan nodded toward Lorcan.

"We'll start with what I know. Then we need to know what Ronan and my mother know," Lorcan said. "Then we can plan." He paused. "Cormac spent the time where he ran away after he challenged me and lost making allies among the raiders and mercenaries. He had men in Rome and Thracia who answered to him, and he sent men to try and kill me in Rome. Then his ally in Thracia planned to lay the murders of the Emperor and his family at my feet, in order to have an excuse to invade Eire." He looked at

208

Tavi. "That ally… isn't a threat anymore." He paused again. "There were supposed to be mercenaries loyal to me joining us, and there's a Roman legion coming to Alba that the Emperor sent to support me. But… Cormac's people now control the waters between here and Alba."

"Oh, no," Petran breathed.

"A messenger arrived this morning," Eogan added. "The mercenaries who followed you… few of them survived."

"There's no way to send word to my brother in Alba, to tell him that Cormac controls the sea," Tavi said. "There's also no way to send for the legion. Unless one of you can fly that far?"

Cuanu chuckled. "No, lad. It's too far. A good thought, but too far. You'll learn your limits once you have a cloak of your own."

Tavi nodded slowly, reaching out and resting his hand on Lorcan's. Lorcan smiled slightly. Then he took a deep breath. "So… our forces are the warbands under the High King's command. Ronan, what do you know? Has he reinforced the *baile*? How many men does he have, and how are they armed?"

"I know less than I'd like, and I asked Aunt Grainne when they told me you wanted my help. She doesn't think she can help at all—she didn't see anything outside the hall until we escaped," Ronan answered. "When they took me, they brought me into the *baile* hooded, and chained me up in the forge. I didn't see the outside. It smelled, though. I could smell rot and damp. I don't think he's been doing anything to maintain Dun Morrigan at all. There were holes in the thatch of the hall, and rust in the forge."

"Rust? In Niall's forge?" Maelan repeated. "Oh, he'll be furious."

"I'll help him put it to rights once it's his forge again," Ronan said. "What else? Ah… how many men? I'm not entirely sure. The *baile* felt crowded, but I can't say I got a good count. And how are they armed?" He took a breath and blew it out. "Some of them with my work, scorch his feathers. If I refused… well, I refused one too many times." He shook his head and rested his hands on the table. "What else can I tell you?"

"What does he do when the regular ravens fly over?" Turlach asked. "I know he attacked Maelan and Ronan. But what does he do when it's not one of us?"

Ronan frowned. "I…" He drew out the sound, then shook his head. "I don't know. I heard ravens, but I couldn't see outside the forge. I don't know if he ordered his men to shoot them down the way he tried when Uncle Maelan and I tried to fly over."

"Turlach, what are you thinking?" Petran asked.

"That if we send the fastest fliers out with Corvina, they might be able to get more information," Turlach answered. "Lorcan, would she do it?"

Lorcan looked at Corvina, who was still sitting on Tavi's shoulder. "I… don't know," he said slowly.

"Wait," Cuanu said. "You have a pet raven?"

"I think she'd object to being called a pet," Tavi said. "She's not exactly tame."

Cuanu blinked. "Not tame," he repeated. "And you let her that close to your eyes?"

"She knows Tavi and Livia are part of her flock." Lorcan clicked at Corvina, who shifted from foot to foot on Tavi's shoulder, jumped down to the table, then hopped onto Lorcan's arm. "Who would go?" he asked, bringing his arm to his chest, and stroking Corvina's side as she rubbed her bill against his chest.

"The fastest?" Turlach looked around the table. "Orla? Could you be away from Fionn overnight? He's still so small."

"I talked this over with Fiachra, because I thought I might need to be away from them. This… I need to help stop this," Orla answered. "We can bring in a wet nurse."

"And you're the fastest," Oscar added. "Aife can take him, I'm sure. He's the same age as our Neasa."

Orla smiled at him. "Thank you." She turned back to Turlach. "Who else?"

In the end, it was Orla, Becc and Rhys who would take wing to Dun Morrigan. Lorcan looked down at Corvina. "Will you go with them?" he asked in Latin.

Corvina croaked at him, then hopped off his wrist and across the table to Orla. Orla laughed and offered her own wrist.

"I think that's an answer," she said. "We'll be back tomorrow with numbers and news. Let me go say goodbye to my mate and our son."

"I'll come with you," Oscar said. "And tell Aife we've got Fionn for a day or two."

They left, and Lorcan looked around the table.

"What plans can we lay in the meantime?" he asked. "Cuanu, you designed the new *baile*. How would you attack it?"

Cuanu laughed. "That's the problem," he said. "When I designed the new *baile* after the Dun Morrigan was attacked by that monster, I designed it to be able to be sealed completely against an invading force. If the gates are sealed, the only way in or out is by air."

Chapter Twenty-Four

Lorcan stared at his uncle. "By air," he repeated. "I... well, I suppose it makes sense. But it doesn't help us at all now."

Cuanu nodded. "Believe me, I am aware."

"Is there another way?" Tavi asked. "Do you have plans? Drawings? What is the terrain like around the *baile*?" He paused. "Do you have books? Scrolls? I... that sounds like a horrible question. But in Rome, it's said you don't even have writing. And I know better than to assume they're right. I lived too long in Alba to believe some of the outlandish stories my people tell about you."

Cuanu looked confused. "Outlandish stories? When we have time, I want to know some of these. Yes, we have scrolls. And writing. Why do you want to see the land around the *baile*?"

"I'm not sure," Tavi admitted. "But I also don't know anything about Dun Morrigan. I'm at a disadvantage, especially compared with the rest of you who lived there. But that may also give me the benefit of seeing something you all don't see..."

"Because you're looking at it with new eyes," Cuanu finished, nodding. "Do you read Greek? I have the plans for the *baile*, but they're in Greek."

"I read Greek," Tavi said. "I'm a bit surprised that your records are in Greek. Why not your own tongue?"

"Because Greek is the language of the scholars," Cuanu answered. When Lorcan and Tavi both started laughing, he arched a brow. "Why is that funny?"

"Because the Pontifex Maximus told us the same thing," Lorcan answered. "That's the High Priest over all religion in Rome."

"Right before he betrayed my grandfather and helped to try and kill all of us," Tavi added.

Cuanu paused, studied Tavi for a moment, then asked, "I appear to be missing something. Who is your grandfather?"

Tavi hesitated, then answered, "The Emperor. I'm the youngest son of the Emperor's younger son, and my father is now the Pontifex Maximus. He was governor of Britan… of Alba for many years, and my brother is governor now."

"The Roman Emperor's grandson?" Ronan gasped. "Did… am I the only one who didn't know that?"

Lorcan chuckled, then looked at Tavi. "Ah… did we tell my mother that?"

"We'll tell her later," Tavi answered. "I had some training, even after we'd all but given up on the plan for me to become a soldier because I was hopeless with weapons. At least, I was until I met Lorcan and he taught me what I was doing wrong."

"What about tactics?" Cuanu asked. "You've been trained in tactics?"

"Not really trained in tactics," Tavi said slowly, making a dismissive gesture. "But I've learned about the great battles, and I've had some of the training as a centurion. Which is why I want to see the *baile*, and hear about the terrain."

"I'll get my case—" Cuanu started to stand, but Fergus was faster.

"I'll get the tube!" He jumped up. Lorcan watched him go, but his mind was elsewhere. Something… then he remembered.

"The gates are broken," he said. "Grandmother sent visions to me, over the winter. And I saw the gates are broken. So, an attacking force has a chance to get in."

Fergus came back in, carrying a long tube. He handed it to Cuanu, smiled, then sat down.

"Thank you." Cuanu stood up and opened the case, taking out a roll of parchment that he unfurled over the table. Tavi whistled softly, standing up and leaning over to better see the drawings.

"This is lovely work," he murmured. He reached toward the page, but didn't touch it, his fingers skimming over the surface as he traced lines, studied the plans, read the notes. He scowled slightly, and the scowl deepened the longer he worked.

"The gates are broken," he finally said. "An attacking force can get inside, with some effort. But there are hostages, and Lorcan's cloak. If we attack the front, the hostages are as good as dead, and we have no way of knowing what Cormac will do with the cloak." He looked up. "What's here?" he asked, running his fingers along the curve of the wall. "Terrain, I mean. What's the ground like? And is there cover?"

The rest of the flock leaned in, pointing and talking over each other. Tavi straightened, folding his arms over his chest, his eyes narrowed. He nodded slightly, his eyes distant, his fingers moving every so often. Planning the attack, Lorcan realized.

"For someone who hasn't been training," he murmured, "you're doing very well."

Tavi snorted. "I'm making it up as I go along," he whispered back. Then he straightened as Petran reached out and tapped the parchment.

"The area here is bare ground," Petran answered. "No trees or brush. Nothing that could provide cover. Although in a year, that might have changed—"

"Not enough to make a difference in bringing an attacking force to that section of the wall," Cuanu argued. "Tavi, why that section?"

"Lorcan told me about his visions, and that his father and Ronan's parents are being held in the hall, here," Tavi said, pointing. "And this building here is...?"

"A storehouse," Turlach answered.

Tavi nodded. "And it blocks line of sight of that section of the wall from quite a few angles, it looks like?" He traced a wide arc on the drawing, then looked up at the others. "Yes?"

"Yes, but..." Cuanu came around the table to look at the plans from the same angle. "Yes. Why? What are you thinking?"

"Tell me how deep the timbers of the wall were driven?"

Cuanu blinked. "The height of a man. Why?"

Tavi grinned. "You fly. So does Cormac. You go over walls. In Rome? We dig under them." He studied the map again. "How far away would be we have to go to be under cover?"

Cuanu scowled, then tapped the page. "About here."

Tavi took a deep breath, let it out through his nose, then sighed. "It would take days to tunnel that far. We don't have days, do we?"

"Not if we want to keep Cormac from noticing that we're there. We also don't have Roman engineers," Cuanu said. "But we do have one thing that you Romans don't."

"What?" Tavi asked.

"Sorcerers." Cuanu stepped back from the table. "Turlach, I'm going to need a driver, if you're willing? We'll be a few hours, if that. I'd fly, but I think I'll have people coming back with me."

"A driver to go where?" Turlach asked as he stood up.

"The druid college." Cuanu looked around the table. "Keep working. I'll be back as soon as I can."

"Keep working," Tavi repeated as Cuanu and Turlach left. "Right. Any plans we make will assume that we can undermine that wall in something under a day. That's a very large assumption."

"Cuanu is up to something, and it involves sorcerers," Lorcan said. "So, assume that we can. What then?"

Tavi nodded, then looked across the table at Eogan. "Your Majesty? How many warriors in a warband? And how many warbands do you have?"

"Twenty-seven in a warband," Eogan answered. "And how many would you need?"

"I'm not entirely certain," Tavi admitted, looking back at the map. "This... this really isn't anything I've done before. I know the strategies, but I've never been a soldier. I don't know enough to even know what I don't know." He tapped the map, and the drawing of the *baile* from overhead. "Tell me about the approach," he said. "If we bring forces against the *baile*, how would they attack?" He looked up and grinned. "I know how a legion would do it. I don't know warbands."

Diarmuid got up and came around the table to stand shoulder to shoulder with Tavi. "It's been a few years since I was fostered at Dun Morrigan," he said. "But the approach was narrow. Carts went up to the gates in a line, so I'd say it isn't good for more than two chariots across."

"And on foot?" Tavi asked. "If we brought infantry in?" He paused. "You don't have infantry the way we do, though. Or do you?"

"Foot soldiers, you mean?" Diarmuid asked. "Yes and no. I've read about Roman battles, and our warbands aren't as... structured as your legions. But our warriors fight on foot as well as in chariots." He tapped the map. "For this approach, there's one major problem. If Cormac has archers, our men would be easy targets."

Tavi looked down at the plans, and Lorcan could see the surprise on his face as he turned back to Diarmuid. "Your shields are similar to ours. I've seen them. You don't *testudo*?"

"I... don't know what that is," Diarmuid admitted. "Da?"

"I don't either," Eogan answered. "Tavi, would you explain?"

Tavi nodded. "It's... well, it's sort of a shield wall. Your men form ranks. The first rank holds their shields in front of them, like this..." He held up an imaginary shield. "The shields stay edge to edge, and form a

214

wall. The second rank hold their shields overhead, and edge to edge." He raised his imaginary shield. "The third and fourth ranks do the same, and men on the outside of the ranks keep their shields to the side. It's… a box made out of shields, and it protects the men against archers and spears." He lowered his arm. "That's a *testudo*. Ah…" He frowned and looked down at Lorcan, asking in Latin, "Is there a word in Gaeilge for a *testudo*?"

Lorcan shook his head slowly. "I… what is it? Other than a shield wall?"

Tavi laughed and switched back to Gaeilge. "I see. A *testudo* is an animal, and it has a hard shell that it wears like armor. When it's in danger, it can pull its head and limbs into the shell to protect itself. You don't have them here?"

"We do not. So, the shield wall is named after the animal that protects itself," Eogan said. "I see. Tavi, will you show my men how this shield wall works? And drill them on it? We won't have much time, but if they understand, then we have a better chance. Cormac's men won't know how to defeat it."

"I hope not," Tavi said. "And… let me see. Assuming we can undermine the wall, then the forces at the tunnel will signal for an attack at the gate. Which will be the diversion keeping Cormac and his forces busy while we send a group in under the wall to rescue the hostages, and once they're safe, more men to take the *baile*." He took a deep breath. "All right. That's something that might look like a plan in poor light. Tell me what I've gotten wrong."

"Tavi," Petran said slowly. "Excuse me, but I might be remembering wrong. Weren't you your father's *translator*? You're a scholar. You're not a soldier, or a warrior. This… this isn't something I'd expect you to know."

Tavi bit his lip. "I… I was supposed to be a centurion. I'm the youngest son, so I was supposed to follow the examples of several of my older brothers and be a soldier. But… Lorcan, which cousin was it? Who had to learn how to stand every time he grew?"

"That was me," Becc answered. "You're tall like I am. Same problem? You grew too fast?"

"With the added complication of being told repeatedly that I was never going to be able to fight, that I was hopeless with a sword, that I shouldn't even try because I was worthless." Tavi's voice was flat, but his face was flushed. "So, yes, I was my father's translator, because there was no one who could deny that I was good with languages, and it didn't matter how many times I tripped over my own feet. I made a place for myself that no one could take from me. And I never looked for more, because I'd been told that I didn't deserve more. Until I learned otherwise. Until I learned I could fight. So now I can, and I do. It wasn't Lorcan who killed Galius. I did. Which makes me a scholar who fights." He folded his arms over his chest. "Do I have to go and get my *dolabrae* and take them out onto the *urla* for you to take me seriously, too?"

Lorcan rested his hands on the table as the flock shifted uncomfortably in their seats. He started to get to his feet and saw Petran turn pale.

"Lorcan—"

"Petran, Mother says you're an idiot, and you need to apologize. Again."

Silence, as everyone turned to stare at Fergus, who was looking down at the tabletop.

"Uncle Fergus?" Lorcan said, settling in his chair. "What did you say?"

"Mother says that Petran should have learned his lesson about talking without thinking last night." Fergus raised his head. "What happened last night, Petran?"

"Nothing you need to worry about, Fergus," Petran said slowly. "And… yes, she's right. I need to slow down and think. I… Tavi, I'm sorry. What I meant to say was that you were wasted as a translator. Your father should have seen your worth as a strategist."

Tavi snorted. "That would have required my father to see me. I'm the youngest of 11," he said. "There were days when he called me all by my sibling's names, including my sisters. Then by the names of the three dogs we had when I was a boy before he remembered which one I was. There were days he didn't see me at all. And he didn't know…" He stopped, and bit his lip. "Never mind. I accept your apology. Just… don't do it again."

"I won't. I am sorry." Petran took a deep breath. "I think my brains are going. That's twice in under a day I've made a mess of things."

"Fergus?" Cathal said. "Are you talking to Mother?"

Fergus smiled. "I always talk to Mother," he answered, and tapped his temple. "Here. She talks to me a lot. She told me Lorcan was safe, because I was scared that Cormac hurt him bad, and that he wasn't going to come home ever again, like Ronan and Oscar and Muirenn. And she told me I had to go live with Cuanu away from our mountain, but we'd go back when Lorcan came home. And he's home, so we're going back to our mountain."

"Fergus, you never told us that," Maelan said. "You never said Mother talks to you."

"You never asked me!" Fergus laughed, then looked distant. "Cuanu knows. He asked me. Mother says that since the bad thing happened, she needs to look after me. Because you all have your mates and your fledglings, and you can't always watch me. I'll be her fledgling always, so I'll stay under her wing. Always and always." He smiled brightly. "And she says you're doing a wonderful job, Tavi. And that Petran is right. They should have seen your worth."

Tavi blinked and sat down slowly. "She… will you tell her thank you?"

Fergus nodded. Then he laughed. "She says you don't need me to tell her. She hears you."

Tavi nodded. He looked stunned, and when he turned to Lorcan, there were tears in his eyes. Lorcan put his arm around Tavi, then turned back to the table. "Well? How is the plan? Is there anything that needs to be changed? Anything we overlooked?"

"Where will we be?" Cathal asked. "With the men in their armored wall?"

"No," Tavi said. His voice cracked, and he cleared his throat and tried again. "No. You'll be at the tunnel. You'll be the ones getting your kin out of the *baile*, and leading the forces against them from inside after the hostages are safe." He looked across at Ronan. "Your parents and your sister, and Lorcan's father, they're not going to know random fighters. They'll know you." He gestured widely with one arm, taking in the entire flock. "They'll go with you. And it will keep you all out of sight until they're safe. Because if Cormac suspects this is anything but the High King trying to remove a thorn from his side, then it will all be for nothing."

Eogan nodded. "Which means I should do something to start him thinking this is all my idea. Which… since my daughter's husband has returned to us nearly crippled, I have every reason to do." He leaned back in his chair. "I'll have to send a warband. He'll murder a single emissary."

217

"He has no respect for our laws," Diarmuid said, nodding his agreement. "Anyone you send will be sent back in pieces, because he's not going to respect *oigidecht*."

Tavi sat up. "That... I don't know that word."

"Roughly, it means hospitality," Petran answered. "Or guest-right. Anyone, any stranger, has the right to claim welcome, a bed and a meal, and to not be harmed. Cormac... he won't honor that. Whoever we send can't get too close."

Tavi nodded. "We would call that *xenia*."

"Is that Latin?" Lorcan asked.

"No. It's Greek, but it means roughly the same thing." He looked thoughtful, then snorted. "Have someone on a fast chariot? Tie the message to a javelin, throw it at the gate and run?" He paused, then added, "Not Diarmuid. Which... I hope I didn't have to say that?"

"You didn't, but I still thank you," Eogan said. "I cannot hand him another hostage, which Diarmuid would be." Eogan scowled. "I'll handle this part. You worry about the actual attack." He rose and left the table, and Tavi leaned forward, resting his arms on the tabletop.

"I don't think there's any more we can do here." He trailed his fingers over the plans. "We really can't plan more until we know if we can actually tunnel under the wall."

"Show us that shield wall," Diarmuid said. "Give us an idea of what we're doing."

* * *

That set the course for the rest of the morning—Tavi enlisted the help of Manius and Yaroah, and they demonstrated the *testudo* by taking a dozen warriors, showing them how to hold their shields, then leading them on a mock attack against another dozen warriors. The ravens watched the first few bouts before Orla insisted on trying. Before long, the mock battles were the ravens against the shielded warriors, and all of them were laughing.

"They'll need to practice," Tavi said as he walked over to stand with Lorcan. He was breathing hard, and there was dirt on his face, but he looked very satisfied. "But if they can remember to stay in formation in a real battle, it could work."

"And if we can't tunnel, then perhaps we can still do this," Lorcan offered. "I was thinking about it. If we can't tunnel under the wall, then my uncles and cousins can go over once the High King's warbands attack. Same outcome, just a different way of getting in."

"I hope it will be the same outcome," Tavi replied. "But there's no way to get more men in through the tunnel once the hostages are free." He scowled. "I'll think some more on it." Then he straightened and looked past Lorcan. "There's Drucilla."

Lorcan turned to see Drucilla coming toward them. "Grainne is taking a nap," she said. "I like your mother very much, Lorcan. And Livia is with the Queen and... oh, what was her name? Gormlaith? I'm to go and join them in a moment, but I wanted to take a moment." She shaded her eyes with one hand and looked out at the fighters. "Is Cuanu out there?" she asked. "I wanted to talk to him."

"He's not," Lorcan answered. "He had to go back to the druid college. He'll be back today."

She nodded. "I'm curious about him," she said. "I've known attractive men before, but none of them ever caught my eye the way he has. Not even Gaius did that. And he looked at me like he knew me. And did I understand the big man—Fergus?—correctly? He said I was Cuanu's Drucilla. Why did he say that?"

Lorcan smiled. "Fergus is... well, he's like a child. But he sees a lot. And one of the things he saw was something Cuanu saw as well." He heard the rattle of a chariot, and looked toward the gate to see that Turlach had returned, and that there were three old men in the chariot with him. Cuanu flew overhead, and called a greeting down to Lorcan. Lorcan called back, then turned back to Drucilla. She was looking up, smiling softly.

"That's him, isn't it?" she murmured. "Lorcan, I... I'm no blushing maiden to go all giddy when a handsome man smiles at me. But your uncle makes me feel that way. I don't understand."

"Do you remember what I told you on the way here, about the cloaks and the promise for when we find our mates?" Lorcan asked. Drucilla turned to stare at him, and he smiled. "Cuanu has never found his mate. Because just like me, his mate wasn't in Eire. She was in Rome."

"Me?" she breathed. "He wants... me?" She blinked. "Does... does he know? About the baby?"

"I haven't told him," Lorcan answered. "Do you want me to? Do you want me to talk to him?"

219

Drucilla hesitated, then nodded. "Please? I didn't... I didn't think I was coming all this way to find a new husband!"

Lorcan took her hands, then pulled her into a hug. "Of course. I'll talk to him. I'm fairly certain it won't make any difference to him."

"But what will it mean for the baby?" Drucilla asked. "The baby isn't going to be a raven. Or... or will they?"

"I..." Lorcan frowned. "I think we'll need to ask Grandmother." He looked up as Cuanu circled, then came in to land. "Now, go have a lesson with Livia. Gormlaith is the midwife who helped me into the world. And she taught my mother. You came with us to learn. Go learn. I'll talk to my uncle."

Drucilla smiled. She kissed his cheek, then went back the way she came. A moment later, a hand closed on Lorcan's shoulder. He turned and looked up at his uncle.

"Where is she going?"

"To have a lesson with Gormlaith," Lorcan answered. "Walk with me a moment, Uncle?"

He started walking, and Cuanu fell in next to him. "Are we talking about Drucilla?" Cuanu asked.

"She's your mate, isn't she?"

Cuanu smiled. "Yes. I never thought I'd find my mate. You brought her to me, and I'm in your debt."

"She's fragile, Uncle. Go carefully with her."

Cuanu stopped, turning to face Lorcan. "Tell me."

Lorcan took a deep breath. "Drucilla was married to the Emperor's heir. Gaius is a good man, and he's told me that he thinks of me as a brother. He'd be here if he could, helping us. The only reason that he divorced Drucilla is because she couldn't give him children—she miscarried every pregnancy—"

Cuanu shuddered. "No wonder she and Grainne get along so well."

Lorcan paused. "I hadn't thought of that." He shook his head. "Gaius loves her, and she loves him, but they agreed that she was never going to give him a child, so they divorced right before we left Rome. And then we found out that Drucilla was being poisoned, and that's why she lost her children." He paused again. "And... she didn't know she was pregnant again until we had already left Rome."

Cuanu's jaw dropped. "A... a baby?" He smiled. "I have a mate and a *child*?"

"Uncle, she's worried," Lorcan said. "She asked me what would happen to the child when she becomes your mate. Will they share Grandmother's gift?"

"Oh," Cuanu breathed. "Oh, I see. I... I'll go and ask Fergus if he can ask Mother. And then... she's with Gormlaith, you said?"

"Yes." Lorcan paused. "There's more, Uncle. Drucilla wants to learn to be a healer, and she wants to be tested to see if she has the healing gift the way Mother and I do. She wants to be more than what she was in Rome."

"And that was?"

"The way she put it was that she was a pretty ornament whose only purpose was to give some man sons. She's with us now because Grandmother said that if she didn't come with us, she'd be dead in a year. And she's with us to learn who Drucilla really is."

Cuanu nodded slowly. "I see." He smiled again. "I'll go and see how my lady would like her courtship to proceed. If she wants to go slowly, or if she wants to seal the bond between us quickly. I've waited for her this long. I can be patient. And we can learn who Drucilla truly is together."

Chapter Twenty-Five

"Lorcan, you remember Gaynor?" Cuanu asked as they walked over to where Turlach was helping the three old men out of the chariot.

Lorcan smiled. "It's been a long time since I last sat at the feet of the *Ard Ollamh*," he said, bowing deeply.

"It has been a long time." Gaynor smiled. "I am so very pleased you've come home safely. When this is all over with, I want to hear all about Rome."

"I have three people who can tell you more than I ever could," Lorcan said. He offered his arm to the old man, and they started slowly toward the hall. He saw Tavi approaching, and nodded to his mate as he fell in behind them. "And someone who can tell you about Carthage."

Gaynor slowed even more. "Carthage? You met someone from Carthage?"

"He's appointed himself my mother's guard," Lorcan said. He turned, not seeing Yaroah. "Where is he? He was here, helping the warriors learn to make a Roman shield wall. I... there he is. Yaroah!"

Yaroah turned at the sound of his name, waved, and came trotting toward them. "Lorcan," he called. "Queen Caírech called me over, and sent me to tell you that your cousin's wife has started her labors. She and Mother Grainne and Livia and Drucilla will be busy until very late. I am to tell this to your uncle as well." He looked around. "Which one is Cuanu?"

"I heard my name?" Cuanu called, coming closer.

"Siobhan is having her baby," Lorcan said. "Drucilla will be busy, and wanted you to know."

"Thank you. I'll find her later." Cuanu fell in on Gaynor's other side as they started walking again. "You can introduce one of your mates to the *Ard Ollamh*, and he can hear the plan and see what can be done."

"Your mate?" Gaynor repeated. "Ah, to be young again. But... Cuanu said one of? How many mates do you have?"

"Two," Lorcan answered. "Tavi is behind us, and Livia is with my mother."

"Two. Well." Gaynor paused, then sniffed, sounding amused. "I was never that young, I don't think."

Lorcan laughed. Then he gestured to Yaroah. "And this is my brother, Yaroah. His Gaeilge isn't very good yet, but I remember you speak Latin?"

"I do," Gaynor answered in Latin. "And I remember that you didn't. You learned?"

"I was in Rome. I didn't have a choice." Lorcan turned to Yaroah. "Gaynor is the *Ard Ollamh,* and head of the druid college."

"The… High Bard?" Yaroah said. "You told us this, in the bath in Rome. Before we left. Do you remember?"

Lorcan chuckled. "There's been so much that happened since then that I'd forgotten."

Gaynor smiled. "You've had quite the year, Lorcan. And I'll be interested in hearing all about it. Yaroah, when this is done, I also want to hear all about Carthage."

"I can tell you all about what it was before I was taken to Rome. I have been a gladiator in Rome for 20 years."

Gaynor looked shocked. "Well. You must be a very good one, then, to have survived so long. We'll talk. Even telling me about Carthage 20 years ago is more than I know now. And I doubt I will ever see it with my own eyes, so I'll appreciate seeing it through yours."

"Are you a sorcerer as well as being the *Ard Ollamh*? Is it the same thing?" Tavi asked from behind them. Gaynor stopped and turned around.

"I am, and it can be. And who are you? I don't recall seeing you before, and I'm here quite often." He looked at Lorcan, then back at Tavi. "Would you be Tavi, then? That's an interesting name."

Tavi bowed. "My full name is Lucanus Decius Octavian," he said as he straightened.

"Well, that is certainly a very full name," Gaynor said with a laugh. "I see why you go by Tavi. You're Roman. With a name like that, you'd have to be."

Tavi grinned. "I am. But I've lived in Britannia most of my life. My father was the governor there until last year."

Gaynor looked Tavi up and down. "Well, it's not every day that one gets the chance to meet the grandson of the Roman Emperor. That's a new thing. At my age, new things don't happen all that often." He looked at Lorcan. "And you claimed an Imperial scion as your mate how?"

"He was my language tutor," Lorcan admitted. "One of them. It's a long story, Gaynor. May I tell you later?"

"Of course. Cuanu says that there's a plan to rid Eire of the outcast, and that you need our help." He gestured to the two other men. "What can we do?"

Tavi frowned, looked at Lorcan, then bit his lip. "I... don't want to be rude, sir. But... I'm not comfortable taking you into a dangerous situation."

Gaynor smiled. He raised one hand, and made a short, sharp gesture toward Tavi, who fell backward, stumbling and sprawling on his back on the ground. He looked up, stunned.

"What—"

"Does that make you more comfortable?" Gaynor asked. He walked over and offered Tavi his hand. "Don't underestimate an old man, my boy. And don't underestimate me. I failed the Morrigan's children once, and it cost me my daughter. I'm not making that mistake again." He helped Tavi up, then dusted off his back. "The *Ard Ollamh* before me refused to help in the fight against the *deamhan aeir*. He hadn't been in the position very long, and his predecessor had poisoned him against the Morrigan's sons. He ordered us to ignore Oscar's requests for help. And... to my shame, we listened. We did nothing to help Oscar find a way to stop the monster, and I lost two people I loved a great deal." He paused, looking distant and somehow even older. "I will do whatever you need me to do. Now, let's hear those plans."

"Gaynor!" Eogan came out of the hall. Laughing, he joined them, hugging the older man. "Come inside. Have a drink with me before you start. Manius! Come join us!"

"Thank you, Eogan." Gaynor followed the High King, with Manius trailing behind them.

"Who was his daughter?" Tavi asked softly. "And how did he do that?"

"In reverse order," Cuanu said from behind them. "Sorcery. And his daughter was my brother Oscar's mate, Muirenn."

* * *

The ravens took their places around the table, and platters laden with bread and roasted meat, bowls of cheese and of nuts were all brought to the table. Lorcan ate and watched as Tavi went over the plans once more, showing the *ollamhs* what they would need to do.

"For a legion, digging out a tunnel that long would take days," Tavi said. "We don't have that kind of time. We need to be in place as soon as the sun sets, and ready to move inside the *baile* before dawn. Because the warband will need to attack at dawn, and distract Cormac and his forces long enough for us to get the hostages out." He looked down at the plans once more. "We'll have more information about the *baile* and how many men Cormac has… when, Lorcan?"

"Tomorrow evening, or possibly the morning after," Lorcan answered. "It's a full day's flight from here to Dun Morrigan. They should be back tomorrow, late."

Tavi nodded. "We'll be able to make a solid plan once we have that. For right now, this is what I have." He looked across at Gaynor and the other two *ollamhs*. "Can it be done?"

Gaynor looked thoughtful, then turned in his chair to talk to his colleagues. Lorcan reached out and picked up a jug of beer, pouring a some into a cup and handing it to Tavi.

"You're doing wonderful," he murmured. "Eat something."

Tavi sipped from the cup and shook his head. "I'll eat when I'm sure I won't just purge. I feel like I've been training all day. Pretending to know what I'm talking about is exhausting," he answered. "When this is done, I'm going to go lay down. How do centurions do this?"

"They're used to it?"

"I don't want to get used to this. I'm going to be happy to be nothing more than your mate for the rest of my life," Tavi grumbled as he sat down. "I never want to be this tired ever again."

Lorcan heard a chuckle, and Manius came up behind them. "You're going to be more tired," he said, clapping Tavi on the shoulder. "We still have to do this. Your plan involves no sleep at all for an entire night after traveling for at least a full day. Did you not think of that?"

"No!" Tavi groaned, then looked around. "It's a full day's flight, you said. How long by chariot?"

"Three days," Lorcan answered. "There's no direct road between here and there. We have to go back to the coast, then south for a day. Then… well, Scath is empty. That should give us a place to stop and rest, assuming that there are no guards there, or anyone watching it."

"Also, a base of operations, and a place to bring the hostages once we get them out," Diarmuid added. "We'll need to bring a healer with us. Not your lady, Lorcan. Or your mother. I won't bring either of them anywhere near Dun Morrigan until it's safe."

"Thank you," Lorcan said. "We'll have to see who we can bring. Because I can't be the healer and stay back in Scath. I need to be at the *baile*. I need to be part of the attack."

Eogan nodded. "I'll arrange for a healer. What else?"

Gaynor turned back to face them, clearing his throat. "We've discussed this plan, and it's possible to clear a tunnel that length in a night," he said. "But not with only three of us. We would need six or seven. I'll need to return to the druid college, and we'll need a second driver or a cart."

"I'll take you back, Gaynor," Turlach said. "Eogan—"

"I'll send another chariot with you, and I'll send out riders to start calling in the warbands and bring in the healer. Tavi, I'll want you to lead the warbands."

Tavi looked startled. "I... you want me to *what*?"

Eogan arched a brow. "It is your plan. Who better to lead?"

"Anyone! Literally anyone!" Tavi blurted. "I'm not a soldier! I'm not a warrior—"

"I can think of several people who would disagree with that," Lorcan interrupted. "Some are in Rome. Some are at this table. And one of them is very dead because he underestimated how much of a warrior you really are. You can do this, Tavi." He smiled at the stunned look on his mate's face. "And it is your plan. You're using Roman strategy and Roman tactics. No one else here understands them the way you do. You have to lead."

Tavi nodded slowly, his face ashen. He looked down at the plans on the table, then frowned slightly. "We'll have the information tomorrow. I assume we'll need another day to finalize plans and to organize the warbands. The soonest we could set out would be the day after that. And we'll need to make certain that our plans stay with us—if there's anyone who gets word to Cormac before we're in place, the plan is doomed before we even get there." He frowned and looked around the table. "That's going to be for the ravens to do," he said. "Set up a watch schedule among yourselves. We have to make sure no one tries to sneak off. We've already had too many spies, too many traitors. Cormac has more followers and more connections than I think any of us gave him credit for, and we've come far too close to disaster too many times. We can't run that risk." His frown deepened. "Which means we can't drill all of the warbands in the *testudo*. Is there one warband that we can be certain will not betray us?"

"Mine," Diarmuid said. "Mine are all former fosterlings. Four of them fostered in Dun Morrigan when I was there, and they think of Uncle Diarmuid as family. None of them have any love for Cormac and what he's done."

Tavi nodded. "Bring them, then, and I'll teach them what I know." He looked around. "Yaroah, will you help? Manius?"

"Of course," Manius said. He stood up. "Let's get to work."

Lorcan started to stand, then stopped, hearing a distant wail. "Is that... ?" He smiled. "That's a baby!"

Eogan rose, smiling broadly. "It is. Let me send the riders out. Then I should go and meet my grandchild."

* * *

Lorcan took advantage of the commotion of riders and warbands to take Tavi back to the house where they were staying.

"You said you wanted to lay down," he said. "We'll be busy enough soon. Come and rest." He tugged Tavi by the hand into the house and closed the door behind them. Tavi sighed and slumped down onto a bench.

"I'm not going to be able to rest. I don't think I'm going to sleep until this is over," he said. "Lorcan, no matter what you said, I'm not a warrior. You know that. I'm not a strategist, or a centurion. I'm... what if this all fails? I could be killing your family!" He looked up. "This... this is terrifying! My guts are churning. If I eat anything, I'll just vomit it back up. I... Lorcan, I can't do this!"

"Grandmother says she likes your plan," Lorcan pointed out. "And she says you're doing fine." He sat down next to Tavi, taking his hand. "Is that all that's bothering you?"

"I" Tavi grimaced. "I keep hearing Galius' voice, telling me that it's all going to go horribly wrong. That I'm wasting my time trying to be something I'm not, and that I'm going to get people killed." He glanced at Lorcan, then bit his lip, tugging his hand free and wrapping his arms around himself. "That... that you won't... won't want me anymore, because I'm going to get your family killed."

227

Lorcan sighed, leaning into Tavi's arm. "That's not going to happen. This plan is the best chance we have to get my family free. The *ollamhs* think so, the High King thinks so, and so do all my uncles. And my grandmother. This will work." He rested his cheek on Tavi's shoulder. "And, just so you know, I'm scared, too."

"That doesn't help," Tavi grumbled. "Because sometimes it feels like nothing scares you. You regularly walked out into the arena like it was a game. You looked death in the face every other day! Sometimes twice! If you're scared? Then it's all going to go wrong and... are you laughing at me?"

"No," Lorcan answered, swallowing his laughter. "I'm not." He smiled as Tavi scowled at him. "Fine. I'm not laughing much. I do like that you think I'm not scared. It means I've been hiding it really well since we got here. Tavi, I told you I was terrified, on the ship. Remember? You told me that you couldn't bring Livia back to Rome if I fell, because if I fell, that meant you'd fallen first?"

Tavi sniffed. "I'd forgotten that." He lowered his hands to clasp them in front of him. "I... you think I can do this?"

Lorcan put his arm around Tavi. "I know you can do this. And so does everyone else at the table. Even Petran, who is going to get slapped if he doesn't stop saying one thing when he means another."

"You wouldn't slap your uncle!" Tavi gasped.

"Not me," Lorcan assured him. "I think Grandmother will. You can do this, Tavi. You're going to lead the warbands, and you're going to do wonderfully."

"But I don't know anything about warbands!"

"Then make Diarmuid your second, and he'll help you with anything you don't know." Lorcan rested his cheek on Tavi's shoulder. "Think of it as the first step in an alliance between Rome and Eire."

Tavi's brows rose. "You think?" He cocked his head to the side. "No," he murmured. "No, it's not the first step. You were."

"Me? How so?"

Tavi smiled. "Your uncles came to Britannia to try and find you, and met with my father. That led to the port at... what was the name of the village?"

"Dubhlind."

"Yes. There. There would never have been a Roman port in Hibernia if your uncles hadn't come to Britannia."

Lorcan shook his head. "That's not something I did, though. If we're saying that the alliance between Rome and Eire is because of something someone did? Then we should be thanking Cormac. He set all of this in motion, and we've just been riding the winds." He chuckled. "Livia already says that I have to thank him before I kill him. Because if I hadn't ended up in Rome, I'd never have found either of you. I wouldn't have my mates, or a child, or any of the people I've come to love. So… yes, I'll be thanking him. Right before I kill him."

Tavi grinned in response. "Oh, maybe you should leave him alive, just so your gratitude can fester."

Lorcan shook his head. "It's tempting, but he won't stop being a threat. If not to us, then to our children and the rest of the flock." He leaned back on the bed, resting on his elbows. "As tired as I am of leaving bodies in my wake, there is no situation I can think of where leaving him alive makes him less of a threat."

Tavi nodded slowly, taking a deep breath. "Like Galius. I understand. Sometimes, the only thing you can do is end it. Like dealing with wild dogs." He looked thoughtful for a moment. "Lorcan, do you think… yes."

"Do I think? Yes. And if you finish your thought, I'll tell you mine."

Tavi grinned. "Sorry. Distracted. You said that there's a town? Scath? And we'll use it as a base?"

Lorcan nodded. "Yes."

"We need to send part of the flock ahead, to scout the town before we get there. We'll need to secure it, and we'll need to do that without Cormac knowing. So we need to know if anyone is there."

Lorcan stared at him for a moment, then laughed. "And you think you can't command?" he demanded. "Come on. You wanted to rest." He took Tavi's hand and led him over to the bed, lying down. Tavi stretched out next to him, a quizzical look on his face.

"I don't understand," he said. "What did I do? What's funny?"

"You, my love." Lorcan reached up and ran his thumb over one high cheekbone. "You're thinking of potentials. Possibilities. You're planning for them. Tell me again why you think that you can't do this?"

Tavi sighed and turned his head slightly to kiss Lorcan's palm. "Because all I've ever been good for is translating," he answered in a quiet voice. "Because I'm useless and worthless, the mistake who should never have been born, and who wasn't even very good in bed."

Lorcan sat up and looked around. "Where did he come from?"

"Who?"

"Galius. I could have sworn I heard him." Lorcan turned back to Tavi, who was gaping at him. "It was your voice, but those were his words."

"I" Tavi stammered. Then he swallowed. "You're right. Those were his words. I just... I don't... Lorcan, I'm my father's translator, your mate, and my brother's who... my brother's victim. I... I don't know who I am when I'm not... I don't know who's under that. I never was someone else other than that before." He paused. "Didn't Drucilla say something about wanting to learn who she was when she wasn't associated with someone else? I need to do that. I need to know who Tavi really is. Who I can be."

Lorcan nodded. "I'd say you're off to a fine start. And I'll help you however you need."

"I know. You and Livia both." Tavi smiled. "I'll be keeping the part about being your mate. I can lose everything else, but I'm keeping Tavi is Lorcan's mate."

"Did you think you had a choice?" Lorcan asked. He tugged Tavi closer, tipping back down onto the bed and pulling Tavi down with him. "You're mine. Always and always."

Chapter Twenty-Six

Tavi fell asleep draped across Lorcan's chest; pinned under his mate's warm weight, Lorcan dozed, waking when the door opened. He turned his head to see Livia, who stood framed in the doorway. Behind her, Lorcan could see his mother, who smiled when she saw him.

Livia came over to the bed and leaned down to kiss Lorcan. She ran her fingers through Tavi's curls, but he didn't move.

"Is he feeling ill?" Livia asked, keeping her voice low.

"Not ill," Lorcan answered, matching her volume. "He's worried himself sick, but he isn't ill. Uncle Eogan told him that he'll be leading the warbands—"

"What?" Livia gasped, loud enough that Tavi shifted and made a soft sound in his sleep. She stroked his back, and he settled into stillness again.

"It's his plan. And it uses Roman strategies and Roman methods," Lorcan answered once Tavi was quiet. "He's the only one who knows Roman ways well enough to lead and have a hope of having it come off properly. It's a good plan, and Grandmother likes it."

"She spoke to you again?" Grainne asked.

"No. She spoke to Uncle Fergus, and has been for some time, he says." Lorcan took a deep breath and held his hand out to Livia. "Come sit. Tell me. Boy or girl?"

"Yes," Livia answered. She sat down on the bed, her hip pressing against Lorcan's. "Siobhan and Ronan have twins. They haven't decided on names yet."

Lorcan smiled, closing his eyes. "Twins. We've seen a few of those recently. All of Arcus' children are twins. Do you think we have twins?" No answer, and he opened his eyes to see that Livia was looking at Grainne. "What?" he asked, raising his head. "Mother... I... do we?"

Grainne shook her head. "There's no way to tell. But Livia is carrying heavier than I would expect. I thought she was much further along in her pregnancy. Gormlaith agrees, and says that Siobhan was the same way." She came over, leaned down and kissed Lorcan's forehead. "You'll find out soon enough. Now, I'll let you rest."

"I can get up," Lorcan protested. "Mother... "

"You should rest," Grainne interrupted, putting her hand on his shoulder. "You're going to be very busy soon, and you need to rest. All of you do." She smiled and caressed his cheek. "I have my son home. Alive and whole, and he's grown to be a strong man. He has a man's responsibilities. He can spend time with me when those responsibilities are done."

Lorcan nodded. "I do want to talk to you about the healing chants. I need to know how to do them properly."

"This evening." Grainne straightened. "We'll talk tonight. And... Drucilla is to be tested, isn't she? We'll have to send to Gaynor—"

"He's here," Lorcan said. "Well, he was here. He'll be coming back. We'll have a team of sorcerers coming with us when we raid Dun Morrigan."

"Then we'll sit and talk with him and Drucilla later. He can test her for a healing gift, and we can discuss the chants, and how you risked turning your brains to porridge. Was it worth it?"

Lorcan smiled. "It was. I wish you could meet Gaius, Mother. You'd like him." He shifted slightly, putting one arm around Tavi, and resting his other hand on Livia's thigh. "If I'd been willing to stay in Rome, he wanted to adopt me and name me his heir."

"You could have been Emperor?" Grainne sounded amused. "That would have been interesting."

"For maybe about a month." Lorcan shook his head. "I'd have been assassinated before the throne was warm under me."

"Best for all of us that we're here now," Livia said, covering Lorcan's hand with her own.

"Yes. And you can tell me all about Gaius and Rome and everything once we're all safe and home in Dun Morrigan. Your father will want to hear all of it, and it will be a good way to pass the winter." Grainne smiled and leaned down to kiss Lorcan once more, then kissed Tavi and Livia before leaving. As the door closed, Lorcan tugged on Livia's gown.

"Lay down with us," he murmured.

Livia smiled and shifted around to lay with her head on Lorcan's shoulder. He put his arm around her and she sighed, putting her arm over both him and Tavi. "When will you be leaving?" she asked, her voice very quiet.

"Three days, I think," Lorcan answered. "And… Livia, you have to stay here. I can't put you within my cousin's reach."

"I know. I'll stay with your mother, and with Drucilla. But we won't like it. Mother Grainne tells me that your cousin Orla is a warrior."

"She is. And she's the one leading the scouting flight right now," Lorcan added.

"And she has a baby. A very young baby."

Lorcan chuckled. "I met him. He is very tiny."

"And she's still a warrior." Livia paused. "I want that. For myself. I learned to fight when I was young, because I was a gladiator's daughter, and I saw it all the time. But Father said I had to put it aside when I got older because proper women didn't fight."

"Your mother fought."

"My mother was a gladiatrix and a barbarian. You know full well that in Rome that's not considered something a proper woman should do," Livia said. "After Mother died, Father wanted something more for me than the arena. He didn't want to lose me to injuries the way we lost Mother, and he hoped I might marry someday. If I was a gladiatrix, I'd never be seen as a good wife. So I became a *medicae*. But… I can be both, can't I?"

"You can. And you will, if that's what you want. Once the baby is born." Lorcan hugged her to his side. "We'll be at Dun Morrigan by then, I hope. And we'll all be together. The entire flock. It will all be over."

"Let's hope that all the gods who can be listening are," Tavi mumbled. "And make it so."

"How long have you been awake?" Livia asked.

"Long enough to hear you say you wanted to be Bellona." Tavi raised his head. "How long was I asleep?"

"I'm not sure," Lorcan answered. "I was asleep for part of it. We should get up, though. We have work to do."

Livia shook her head. "No one is looking for us. The High King is still besotted with his grandchildren—"

"Grandchildren? More than one?" Tavi asked.

"Twins," Livia answered. Then she blushed, and Lorcan could feel the heat from her cheeks through his tunic.

"Livia?"

"Ah… maybe?"

Tavi laughed out loud. "Good thing there are two of us, then. Arcus always said he wanted another pair of hands with a set of twins." He ran his hand up Livia's arm. "And even if you only have one, there will be more. I don't see us as stopping with one, do you?"

Livia leaned across Lorcan to kiss Tavi, then shifted back to pillow her head on Lorcan's shoulder once more. "No, I don't think we'll be stopping with just one. I want children with both of you. I want to not be able to say who sired our children, because it doesn't matter. You're both going to be their fathers."

Tavi chuckled. "Except for this one. This one... this one will be special. They'll be just yours."

"You'll be their father, too," Lorcan protested. "Just because you weren't with us yet when they were made doesn't mean you're not going to love them."

"Oh, of course it doesn't!" Tavi agreed. "But I know full well that I wasn't there because I ran from what you were offering me." He sighed. "I'll be their father by courtesy, but they'll be your child." He raised his head and smiled. "And I'm fine with that. It's my own fault for running. Now, were we going out or staying in?"

"You tell me," Lorcan answered. "You both are on top of me. I'm not going anywhere until one or both of you move."

Tavi poked him in the ribs, then shifted on top of Lorcan entirely, pinning him to the bed. "I moved. Now what?"

"Now? I'm definitely not going anywhere." Lorcan smiled up at Tavi, then turned toward Livia, who was giggling. "You've got me. I'm trapped. Now what?"

"Well... as much as I'd like there to be a now what, someone is going to come looking for one, two or all of us," Tavi answered with a sigh. "We should save now what to be then what. Tonight."

"Definitely tonight. Assuming I don't fall asleep before then." Livia sighed and sat up. "I didn't know that I would be tired all the time, but Mother Grainne says that's normal."

Tavi shifted and let Lorcan sit up. He reached out and tugged Livia closer, pulling both of his mates to his sides. He took a deep breath and let it out, looking from Tavi to Livia, then back.

"Still scared?" Tavi asked.

"Still terrified." Lorcan chuckled. "Which you know. But this is what I've been fighting for. This is what I wanted. To come back and end this."

"If we're going to end this, we need to get the warband ready. Do you think they're here?"

"I think we're not going to be able to tell from here." Lorcan let him and Livia go. "Let's go. You need to eat something, Tavi. Then we'll see then what."

* * *

They walked out of the house into the gloaming. The *baile* was full of people, and Lorcan whistled softly.

"We were asleep longer than I thought," he murmured. "We missed all of this."

"We didn't even hear it." Tavi turned around, then jerked when someone shouted his name.

"Tavi!" Diarmuid made his way through the crowd. "There you are! Are you feeling better? You looked a little green before."

"I've gotten my head around the idea of leading the warbands," Tavi admitted. "Although the idea is—"

"Terrifying?" Diarmuid grinned. "I don't think there's a warrior in the *baile* who'd disagree with you. Your first raid is always terrifying. If it isn't, you shouldn't be going on a raid. Now, Manius tells me you use axes? Roman axes? I want to see. Will you show me?"

"Tavi hasn't eaten," Lorcan said gently.

"Then he can eat with us," Diarmuid answered. "My men and I are sitting down now. Come and eat with us and meet them, and then you can show me, and we can spar." He grinned at Lorcan. "I'll return him in the best condition. I promise." He draped one arm over Tavi's shoulders and led him away. Lorcan watched them go and laughed.

"Tavi's made a friend," Livia murmured. "That's good. I don't think he's ever had a friend. Other than me."

"No… what?"

"He's the Emperor's grandson. There aren't many who will look past that to see him," Livia pointed out. "Now, since he's gone off to meet his warband, where are we going?"

"To find my mother? We can sit down with her and Drucilla and Gaynor, and we can discuss healing and training." He looked around. "If I knew where she was. In the hall, maybe?"

"She's probably with Siobhan and Ronan," Livia said.

"Then we'll look there first." Lorcan turned toward the hall, leading Livia through the people, several of whom called him by name and welcomed him home. It seemed to take twice as long as it should before they reached Ronan and Siobhan's house, where Yaroah was standing by the door.

"Lorcan!" Yaroah grinned. "Where have you been?"

"Tavi needed to take some time to get himself settled to the idea of leading the warbands," Lorcan answered, speaking in Latin.

Yaroah nodded. "Mother Grainne told me that your uncle the King appointed him such. And explained some of your warbands." He smiled. "Your people and mine, we have this in common."

"We do? You have warbands in Carthage?"

Yaroah shrugged. "Yes and no. We have one. The Sacred Band. They are… the best of the best of our army. The rest… they're closer to what the legions are in Rome. But the Sacred Band, they are very much like what Mother tells me of your warbands." He nodded toward the door. "Mother has come to see the babies."

"Is Drucilla inside as well?" Livia asked.

Yaroah shook his head. "No. The last I saw Drucilla, she was with one of your uncles. Who all look alike, so I do not know which, nor where they've gone."

Lorcan nodded. "She's probably with Cuanu."

"Is he like you?" Yaroah asked. "To know his mate on sight? And does she agree?" He glanced away. "I like Drucilla. If he is bothering her, I will fight him. I want you to know that."

Lorcan laughed and clapped Yaroah on the shoulder. "Thank you. He's not. I talked to him already, and he wanted to talk to her to see if she was willing to let him court her now, or if she wanted him to wait, and how she would want him to proceed. And, just so you know, our mates know us, too. She knew him, and she talked to me, too."

"You know each other," Yaroah said slowly. He nodded. "I remember how it was after you and Livia first met." He grinned. "So perhaps I will be that lucky here?" He started to turn toward the door.

"Yaroah?" Lorcan waited until Yaroah had turned to look at him. "Are you coming with us to raid the *baile* and rescue my father?" He looked at Livia. "Or will you stay here and protect Livia and our mother?"

Yaroah's eyes widened. He turned and looked at the closed door, then at Livia. "I… had not thought I had a choice," he stammered. "I thought I would fight with you."

"And I'm remembering how you said you thought you were getting too old for this," Lorcan replied. "Yaroah, if you choose to fight with me, I'll happily have you by my side for this last fight. But if you choose to stay behind and protect the people we both love? That's fine, too."

Yaroah nodded slowly. "I… I will think about this. And I will tell you once I know myself. When does the warband leave?"

"In three days, I think."

Yaroah nodded again. "I will think about this." He turned and knocked on the door, which opened to reveal Grainne.

"I thought I heard your voices," she said. "Come in." She stepped back and out of the way.

The inside of the house was somewhat crowded, and Lorcan lingered by the door to let his eyes adjust to the cool darkness. Ronan and Siobhan were sitting side-by-side on the bed, each of them cradling a baby. Caírech sat next to Siobhan, and Eogan stood at the foot of the bed, beaming over them all with clear pride. Ronan looked up from his armful and smiled.

"Lorcan!" he called in a low voice. "Come meet my daughter."

Lorcan walked over to the side of the bed and knelt, the better to see the tiny, wizened face that was all that was visible in the bundle of blankets. Her hair was wispy, and as dark as Ronan's own.

"Have you decided on a name?" Lorcan asked.

"She's Fionnuala." Ronan answered, running one finger over her cheek. The baby yawned, and Ronan laughed. "And she's very opinionated already. You should see her when she's awake. Her face gets all scrunched and wrinkled and I swear to you, she already knows how to be mad!"

Lorcan smiled at his cousin. "And she already has you wrapped around her smallest finger."

"Completely," Ronan agreed. "Can you see across? Siobhan has Lachtna."

Lorcan sat down, hard. "What?" he gasped. "What did you say?"

Ronan turned his head and smiled. "His name is Lachtna. And his feathers are white, like yours."

Lorcan blinked. Suddenly, nothing seemed to make sense. "I… but that name was supposed to be an insult!"

"And you never took it as such," Ronan replied. "You turned the insult into a gift. Then you turned it into a weapon. You turned yourself into a weapon that's going to stop this nightmare. I thought it was the right name for my little white raven. I want him to know his worth, the same way his uncle does. I want him to know that he's part of the flock, no matter what color his feathers are. Livia said that she didn't mind if we used the name, because there's no way to know what color your child's feathers will be and you have a name picked already." He looked back at Siobhan and the baby. "I… do *you* object?"

"I just…" Lorcan swallowed, trying to make sense of his gyring thoughts. He shook his head and smiled. "No. I don't object. And I'm honored."

* * *

"Another white raven." Lorcan shook his head as he walked across the urla with Livia and his mother. "I spent most of my life being certain that I was the only one. That there was something wrong with me. Then… well, Tavi showed me that there were white Persian birds, and that they were normal. And he said he saw wild white ravens, in the north in Alba. And there was Albus—"

"Who?" Livia asked.

"I didn't tell you?" Lorcan turned, walking backward. "In Apollo's temple, in Londinium. The Temple raven there isn't a statue. He's real, and his feathers are as white as mine. The priest there told me that the raven's name was Albus." He stopped, turning and falling in step with the women. "In the rush to leave, I must have forgotten."

"I would have remembered a raven named after you," Livia said.

"Named after you?" Grainne repeated. "Your name isn't Albus."

"In Rome, it is," Lorcan answered. "The Emperor named me Albus when he named me a member of his household and granted me patrician status. Mother, it's a long story."

"And we said we'd save it until your father could hear." Grainne nodded. "I like it. Albus. It's a good name."

"Oh, there are Cuanu and Drucilla," Livia said.

Grainne stopped walking and turned to look. She smiled. "I don't think I've ever seen him smile like that," she murmured. "I don't think I have ever seen him look so happy."

"That's good," Lorcan murmured as they approached. "Because if he makes Drucilla unhappy, Yaroah will beat the feathers off him."

"He will not!" Grainne gasped. Livia smothered a giggle and Lorcan grinned at her. Then a thought occurred to him—Drucilla had told them that she'd slept with gladiators. That they were exciting. That Gaius had known, and had even arranged some of her meetings. Had Yaroah been one of those meetings? He glanced at Livia, wondering if she knew. If she'd tell him. Then he decided he really didn't want to know, and turned to wave at Drucilla and Cuanu.

"So," he asked as they joined them. "Are you Aunt Drucilla again?"

Drucilla laughed and looked up at Cuanu, who smiled and shook his head, putting his arm around Drucilla's shoulders.

"Not yet," he answered. "She will be, but I agree with her reasons for wanting to wait. Once this is done, she will be coming to live with me at the druid college. She can learn healing there, and once she is trained, we'll come back to the *baile*. We will wait until then, until the flock is all together."

"Sisters in truth, then?" Grainne asked, stepping forward to embrace Drucilla.

"Yes," Drucilla answered. She paused, then sighed and switched to Latin. "I've never had sisters."

"Nor did I," Grainne said. "Until I became part of the flock." She looked up at Cuanu. "Where's Gaynor? Drucilla should be evaluated, and Lorcan needs to properly learn the risks of using the healing chants before you've been properly trained."

"It was still worth the risk, Mother," Lorcan protested, following them toward the hall, where they found all seven of the *ollamhs* clustered around the table with Tavi and Diarmuid. Tavi looked up and smiled when he saw them.

"I thought you were going to spar?" Lorcan said, bringing Livia around to join their mate. "Are you done?"

"The light is fading too fast, and I didn't want to risk hurting anyone," Tavi answered. "We'll spar tomorrow. And drill the warband on the *testudo*. For now, we've been discussing tactics and how long it will take to tunnel under the wall."

"And we're all having a hard time believing that Tavi hasn't led men into battle before," Gaynor added. Tavi smiled, his cheeks darkening.

"Keep telling me that," he murmured. "All of you. I'm starting to believe it."

"Gaynor, would you have a moment to test Drucilla?" Cuanu asked.

"She wants to learn to heal, and she's seen Lorcan use the healing chants and wants to know if she can do the same."

"Of course!" Gaynor rose from the table and held his hand out to Drucilla. He led them across the hall to another table, where he offered Drucilla a seat and sat down next to her, taking her hand in his. "Healing is not easy work," he said. "It can break your heart. Grainne could tell you."

Grainne nodded. "There was nothing I could do to help save my brother's life. Nor any of Lorcan's brothers and sisters."

Drucilla winced. "That's why I want to learn. Did Lorcan tell you?" When Gaynor shook his head, she told him about Rome. About her life with Gaius. About the children she'd lost. She wiped the tears from her face, then added, "I was raised to be a pretty adornment on some man's arm. If I'd known how to be anything but a powerful man's wife, I might have known what it was that Laris was giving me. I might have recognized it. Lorcan knew it by smell."

"*Pulegium*," Lorcan offered. Gaynor looked horrified.

"Someone was feeding you *pulegium*? You're lucky to be alive."

"Galius didn't want me dead. He just wanted me barren," Drucilla said. "If I died, Gaius would have remarried." She took a deep breath. "As it is, he divorced me. He needed an heir. And I knew that I needed… to not be Empress. To be more than a pretty adornment. I didn't like who I was becoming. I lost myself in the trappings of the Imperial heir. I needed to find myself." She looked at Cuanu and blushed. "I just… wasn't expecting to find someone who saw me for me."

Gaynor smiled and patted her hand. "You're going to be a magnificent healer, my dear. And I'll be honored to help Cuanu teach you Gaeilge."

Drucilla blinked. "I… you can teach me? I have the… what did you call it, Lorcan?"

"The fire in the head," Lorcan supplied.

"Yes, you do," Gaynor said. "And, since we're all here, let's have a talk about the risks of using the healing chants without the proper training."

Chapter Twenty-Seven

Lorcan barely stopped moving the next day. From the moment he rolled out of bed, he and Tavi were moving. Planning. Training. Tavi drilled Diarmuid's warband in the *testudo* until they formed the shield wall without hesitation. When another warband arrived, there were mock battles waged in the fields outside the *baile,* testing the limits of the new shield wall, and letting the warband get used to taking direction from Tavi. Overhead, the ravens circled, watching.

And on the ground, Lorcan circled, watching. Watching as each new training battle increased Tavi's newfound confidence. Watching as his mate relaxed into command, teaching his men with the same patient tenacity that he'd shown when teaching Lorcan to speak Latin.

"He's very good," Manius murmured from behind Lorcan.

"He is," Lorcan agreed. "And now he knows it, too."

"I've been talking with Yaroah."

Lorcan turned to look at his mentor. "About?"

"About this raid. And about you asking him to stay here and guard your mother and your wife." Manius paused. "Take him with you. You need him at your back. I'll stay with Livia and your mother." He looked over his shoulder, and Lorcan saw Yaroah walking with Livia and Grainne. Manius waved at them, then turned back to Lorcan. "I think… no. I know that this sort of fighting is not anything I know. I fought in the arena. That's not the same thing as what you'll be doing."

Lorcan nodded slowly, then looked at Yaroah again. "Then why are you sending Yaroah? He fought in the arena for longer than I did. For longer than I've been alive, he tells me."

Manius looked at him. "Did he never tell you what he was before he was a gladiator?" he asked, sounding shocked. "Did he never tell you why he was a slave?"

Lorcan glanced over to where Tavi was working with several

warriors from another warband, showing them the *testudo*. "No, he never did. And I never asked."

"Yaroah was a soldier, Lorcan. From what I understand, an uncommonly good one."

"That... wait," Lorcan looked at Manius, then turned to where Yaroah was gesturing wildly. Whatever it was that he was saying had Grainne laughing. "He told us that the best soldiers in Carthage were in something similar to our warbands. Are you telling me that Yaroah was in Carthage's Sacred Band?"

Manius shook his head. "I'm not saying that. There are things I know that I swore not to tell. If he hasn't told you yet, it's not my place to do so. You can ask him, but... wait until this is all over."

"I'll talk to him." Lorcan glanced back at Tavi, then looked around again. Eogan and Caírech had joined Grainne and Livia, and Livia saw him looking at them and waved. Lorcan smiled and waved back, then said to Manius, "Keep an eye on Tavi, will you? Not that he needs it, but he might look for someone to help him show them a Roman technique."

"Of course." He patted Lorcan on the shoulder as he walked past him, moving to join the warriors who were watching Tavi. Lorcan paused, noticing chariots coming in through the gates. Another warband. He watched them for a moment, then went the other way, stopping behind Livia. She glanced back at him and smiled, stepping back to rest against his chest as he put his arms around her.

"Tavi is doing quite well," Yaroah said. "He is acting like he's been in command for years."

"He is settling in quite well," Eogan agreed. He smiled. "I'm getting quite a lot of practice in Latin these days. I don't think I've ever used it this much before."

Lorcan chuckled and turned to Yaroah. "Manius told me that he was talking to you about changing places. He says that you should come with me, and he'll stay."

Yaroah nodded. "We have talked. And... yes, I think he is correct. I say I am too old for this, but he is older. And I should be there to guard your back. One last time, we will walk out onto the sands?"

"Yaroah, Manius says you were a soldier before you were a gladiator?" Lorcan asked. "You didn't tell me that."

Yaroah scowled. "Manius talks too much," he grumbled, looking away.

Livia looked up at Lorcan, and spoke softly in Gaeilge, "Go talk privately."

Lorcan nodded and kissed her, then let her go and walked over to touch Yaroah's arm. "Walk with me."

Yaroah didn't move for a moment, then sighed. He bowed to Eogan, then followed Lorcan as they walked away. Once they were a good distance from the others, Lorcan turned and looked up at Yaroah. "My brother," he said. "What's wrong? How did I hurt you?"

Yaroah shook his head. "You did not. Memories… " He sighed again. "I was a soldier. Once. I was perhaps your age." He smiled. "You are young enough to be my son."

"I'd rather be your brother," Lorcan replied. "It lets me bully you until you tell me what's wrong. Now stop trying to change the subject."

Yaroah laughed. "Fine. Yes, I was a soldier. I was young, and new to the Sacred Band." He paused. "I do not speak of this. I have not, for years."

"You don't have to," Lorcan said. "It troubles you. I can see that. You don't have to tell me. And if you want to come with us when we raid Dun Morrigan, I'll welcome you at my side and watching my back." He smiled and playfully punched Yaroah's arm. "Just like you said. One last time on the sands, and then we'll be done. And you can decide if you want to stay, or if you want to go back to Carthage."

Yaroah smiled. "I like your home. I like your uncle, and your mother has welcomed me as her son. I think I may stay."

"Don't make that decision until you've had your first winter here. I remember someone complaining about the cold in Rome. It gets colder here."

Yaroah coughed. "Perhaps I will not stay. Or perhaps I'll find a wife to keep me warm." He draped his arm over Lorcan's shoulders. "Thank you for not pushing. I will perhaps tell you someday."

"When you're ready." Lorcan turned, hearing raised voices behind him. "What's that?"

"It's coming from where the warbands were practicing." Yaroah started moving, breaking into a trot as he headed back the way they'd come. Lorcan ran after him, coming to a stop near where the warbands had been drilling. Tavi had his back to them, facing a familiar man with long, pale braids.

"Bairre?" Lorcan gasped.

"Who is he?" Yaroah asked.

"A bully," Lorcan answered. "I've had dealings with him before, when I fostered here. I haven't seen him in years. What's he doing here?" He looked around, seeing the High King headed into the fray. "Go to my uncle."

Yaroah nodded, and they fell in behind Eogan, following him. Bairre saw them; he sneered at Tavi, then pushed past him toward Eogan.

"Since when do we have dealings with Rome?" he demanded. "What do we need from the degenerate Romans?"

"Since when do you think you have any say at all over who I welcome into my *baile*, Bairre?" Eogan asked. His tone was mild, but his clenched fists said otherwise. "Lucanus is mated to Lorcan mac Diarmuid, and is skilled as a strategist."

Bairre glanced at Lorcan, sniffed, then waved one arm at Tavi. "This is a strategist? And he will teach us… what? How to invade other lands? How to steal our women and children? How to become weak and degenerate, like the people in Alba under their Roman rulers?"

To Lorcan's surprise, Tavi burst out laughing. "Really?" he asked. "I'm more powerful than I thought, if I can do all that all by myself. It took my grandfather I don't know how many legions over I'm not sure how many years to take Carthage." He folded his arms over his chest. "I'm not here to do anything other than help my mate win back what's his. I have no quarrel with you."

"Bairre." There was thunder in Eogan's voice. "We have no time for this. If you are unwilling to follow Lucanus' command, you may return to your father and tell him that I've dismissed you."

Bairre stared at the High King. "You… you're letting a Roman lead the warbands? Not your own son? Have you already fallen to them?" He glared at Tavi. "He's not even a warrior!"

Tavi laughed again, and Bairre turned to face him fully. Tavi just shook his head. "You're that afraid of Rome?" he asked. "Of me?"

Bairre went white. "I'm not afraid of you!"

"Prove it." Tavi gestured to where he'd been drilling the warbands. "Meet me here. Bring your weapons. I'll go get mine."

Bairre stepped back, looking at Eogan. Tavi sighed. "He's not the person telling you to get your weapons. I am."

"You're challenging me?"

Tavi blinked. Then he looked at Eogan. "Your Majesty, is he really this much of an idiot? Or is this special for my benefit?"

"Tavi… " Lorcan growled the warning. Tavi just smiled at him.

Then he said something in another language. Whatever it was, Lorcan didn't understand it, but it made Yaroah snort.

"He knows what he is doing, Ghost," Yaroah murmured. "Let him be."

"Let him be?" Lorcan repeated in a low voice. "He may know what he's doing, but I don't." He started forward as Bairre advanced on Tavi, but Yaroah caught his arm.

"Let him be," he repeated. "Let him stand on his own."

Lorcan looked at Yaroah. "I… oh," he breathed as he finally realized what Yaroah meant. What Tavi needed to do. He nodded and stopped, watching as Tavi shifted his stance. He was relaxed, his arms hanging loose at his sides, his hands open as he watched Bairre move closer.

"Bairre!"

Bairre froze in place, turning toward the High King and bowing. "Sire?"

"Enough of this," Eogan snapped. "Get your weapons or refuse the challenge."

"He insulted me!" Bairre pointed at Tavi, sounding almost petulant in his anger.

"Then get your weapons!" Eogan turned to Tavi. "And you. Stop antagonizing your men."

"He's not mine yet," Tavi answered. "If he won't follow without fighting me, then he's not mine. I won't have him. We have no time for someone who thinks they're above following orders."

Eogan nodded. "Fair enough."

"I will not follow a Roman!" Bairre shouted.

"Then go home," Tavi answered, his voice even. "Because if you're going on this raid, you're following me." He stepped forward, moving close enough to poke Bairre in the chest with one finger. "And if you pretend to follow me, so that you can turn on me? And in doing so endanger my mate's family? Then I will kill you myself. Now decide. Follow, or leave."

Bairre slapped Tavi's hand away. "I accept your challenge. And if I win, then I lead the raid."

"And if you lose?" Tavi asked. "Will you follow?"

Bairre sniffed. "I will not lose."

"I said if, Bairre." Tavi folded his arms over his chest. "If you lose?"

"If I lose? I will follow."

Tavi nodded. "Good. Go get your weapons. I'll go get mine."

* * *

"What are you doing?" Lorcan demanded as Tavi came out of their house with his *dolabrae*. Tavi didn't look surprised to see the group waiting for him—Livia, Grainne and Drucilla had joined Lorcan.

"Making a point," Tavi answered. "He's not the only one asking this question, Lorcan. He's just the loudest. I've heard the whispers from the men about following a Roman, and what it might mean for Eogan's rule. I have to show that I'm his man, and I have to show that I can lead. I knew this was coming. It's just the direction that surprised me. I honestly thought it would be Dáire."

"You were expecting this?" Livia asked, coming up next to Lorcan.

"Either here or somewhere on the road," Tavi answered. "It's not a surprise. I'm a foreigner. I'm a Roman. Your people have no love of either. For me to lead a raid of this importance? There are going to be some who call it an insult."

"Yesterday, you were terrified that you wouldn't be able to do this," Lorcan pointed out.

"That was yesterday." Tavi hefted his axes up onto his shoulder. "Today, I need to show that I can." He glanced in the direction of where the men were waiting. "Looks like he's there. Let's go see if he pisses himself when he sees the *dolabrae*."

"Lucanus Decius Octavian!" Drucilla gasped. "What would your father think if he heard you talking like that?"

"My father?" Tavi grinned. "He'd wonder what took me so long. You haven't heard him when he really gets going. Remember, he was a gladiator long before he was Governor or Pontifex Maximus." He started toward the group of men, and Lorcan and the women followed him. The men parted to let Tavi pass, and the whispers started in his wake. They all fell silent as Tavi reached the center of the group and faced Bairre, who carried a sword in one hand, and had a shield on his arm.

"What are those?" Bairre demanded.

"Roman axes," Tavi answered. "I don't like swords." He rested the *dolabrae* on the ground. "Now, shall we repeat the terms for everyone to hear? If you win, you will lead the raid. If I win, you'll follow without question. First blood ends it, regardless of anything else, and I'll try not to kill you. I expect you to do me the same courtesy. The raid will need every man to be hale. Is that agreed?"

Bairre stared at him for a moment. "You… don't like swords?" he repeated. He sounded as if the concept had never occurred to him before. "How… *why*?"

Tavi chuckled. "Ask me again once we're friends," he said. "Now, are you ready? Do you need a moment?"

Bairre snorted and raised his sword. "I'm ready."

Tavi nodded. He raised his axes, and his face went slack. For a moment, the tension hung as thick as fog between them. Then Bairre struck… and Tavi disarmed him, blocking the blow, catching the blade of the sword with hook of the axe head, and throwing the weapon to the side. He stepped back and nodded toward the blade.

"Go ahead," he said. "You're not used to someone using an axe like this. So, we'll call that one practice and start over."

Bairre gaped at him, then stalked over, grabbed his sword off the turf, and rushed Tavi, screaming like a *bean-sidhe*. This time, Tavi blocked with both axes, catching the sword where they crossed, then pulling them apart with enough force that Bairre's blade shattered. Bairre staggered back, looking at the hilt and the remaining jagged stump of the blade. A rivulet of blood trickled down the back of his hand from where a shard had grazed him.

"First blood," Eogan called. "Bairre, you have lost. Will you honor your word?"

"I"

"Lorcan?" Tavi called, interrupting Bairre's stunned stammering. "How do I go about replacing Bairre's sword? I wasn't expecting it to shatter like that, and he'll need a new one before we leave."

"I'll talk to Ronan," Lorcan answered. "Are you done?"

"I'm not certain," Tavi answered. He turned to Bairre, who was staring at him. "Are we done, Bairre?"

Bairre nodded slowly, his mouth hanging open slightly. He licked his lips, then pointed at the *dolabrae*. "Will you show me those? They're nothing like our axes."

"I've seen your axes, and Pictish axes. I'm curious to try them, to really see and feel the difference." He held out one of the axes. "I may not have time before we have to leave to show you much, but I'll be happy to show you later."

Bairre took the axe from Tavi and nearly dropped it. "This is heavy!" he gasped. "And you use two of them? You're stronger than you look."

Tavi smiled. "Who else wants to learn how to use a *dolabra*?" he called. Other warriors clustered around him, hiding him from view, and Lorcan let out a long breath, feeling his shoulders relax.

"Your mate," Diarmuid said from behind him, "has more balls than anyone I have ever met."

Lorcan nodded, then heard a distant, familiar call. He looked up, and saw ravens in the sky. Corvina. Orla. Becc. Rhys.

"The scouts are back!" he shouted.

"Dismissed!" Tavi roared. "But stay close! I'll have orders for you soon!" He appeared out of the crowd and trotted over to join Lorcan, looking up at the sky as he rested his *dolabrae* on the ground. "Time to finalize the plans?"

"Once the scouts have a chance to eat and rest," Lorcan agreed.

As soon as the ravens were on the ground, they were swept away into the hall. Food was brought, and they sat around the table as Tavi rolled out the parchment that showed the plans for Dun Morrigan.

"What do we know?" he asked.

Orla looked up. She was eating with one hand, her other arm cradling her son to her breast. "He has between 30 and 40 men," she said. "It was hard to get a good count—he keeps them moving. The mood in the *baile* is… sour. We weren't there long, so it's hard to get a true sense of it, but I think he's losing them. The gates are broken, as Lorcan said. Several of the houses are burned, and the rest are in bad shape. And bringing Corvina was the best thing we could have done. Thank you for letting her come with us, Lorcan."

"You're welcome, but why?" Lorcan said. He offered Corvina a piece of cheese, which she took with surprising delicacy.

"She was the perfect decoy," Rhys answered. "And she found other ravens to mask our presence. Any time there was a raven in view, it was one of them. She kept his attention so we could get close enough to see." He looked at Orla. "Do you want to tell them, or should I?"

Orla sighed and shifted the baby from one breast to the other. "We got into the thatch of the hall. We could see in. And the only caged ravens we saw were Uncle Niall and Aunt Sorcha."

"No." Lorcan went cold, feeling as if a fist had grabbed his heart and was squeezing. "My father… "

"He was there," Grainne said, coming up and resting her hands on Lorcan's shoulders. He could feel them shaking. "When Ronan got me out, Diarmuid was still there."

"He's not there now," Orla replied. "There were only two caged ravens in the hall. And they were under guard. That's why we didn't try to get them out. We didn't even dare let them know we were there."

"Under guard," Lorcan repeated. "Because… why guard them if they're caged?"

"Because he expects another rescue attempt?" Tavi suggested. "There's been one, there could be another. If someone gets all his hostages, he has nothing to bargain with."

"He still has Lorcan's cloak," Orla said.

Tavi shook his head. "That's not a bargaining chip," he said. "That… Lorcan, I don't think you're right anymore. Before, he wanted to be the one to kill you, and that's why he didn't burn your cloak. But now… he can see himself failing. The cloak is a last resort. If everything goes wrong, if he falls, he's going to take you with him." He paused. Frowned. "We'll have to move fast and take Cormac alive," he said finally. "He's moved your father. Out of the *baile*, to someplace more secure. Orla, tell me about Scath? Did you scout it?"

"We did," Orla answered. "On the way out. There's no one there."

Tavi nodded, then looked down and studied the plans again. "This doesn't change our plans, except that we have to take Cormac alive. I'll tell the warbands. We leave at dawn, and we'll assemble in Scath under cover of darkness." He looked up, turning until he found Eogan. "By your leave?"

"Granted," Eogan said. "Bring them out, Lucanus."

Chapter Twenty-Eight

The rest of the day was a fog—Lorcan went through the motions of preparing, but he didn't remember a moment of it. He barely remembered the evening meal, and nightfall came as a complete surprise, as did Livia taking him by the hand and leading him to their house.

"You need to rest," she said. "You need your sleep. We both need to sleep—I'm going to be up to see you both off in the morning."

"Livia…"

"I know." Livia hugged his arm. "Lorcan, he's alive. Believe that. Your mother says that she'd know if he wasn't. He's alive."

He tugged his arm free and put it around her shoulders. "I know. I believe that. It's just… everything I've been working for. Fighting for. This entire year… and the end starts at dawn." He stopped and turned to look at her, rubbing his hands up and down her arms. "You've been with me since I started on this path, and you can't come with me any further than tonight."

"Tavi will be with you," she said. "And that's the only thing stopping me from sneaking into someone's chariot."

"That and your father?" Lorcan asked.

"He's already threatened to sit on me," Livia grumbled. "Twice."

Lorcan chuckled. "I'll thank him later," he said, and leaned in close to kiss Livia's forehead. "Someone will fly back with news once it's over. I won't leave you waiting."

Livia nodded, sliding her arms around his waist and holding him tight. "This is worse than the arena," she murmured against his chest. "In the arena, I could watch, and I was there if you needed me. Here… I won't know if you're safe for days, and I won't be there if you need me."

"You'll be here, and you'll be safe, and right now, that is what I need." Lorcan held her close. "I need to know you and the baby are safe." He closed his eyes, breathing her in. "It won't be long. Three days to Dun Morrigan. A day or two to finish this. Then three days to come back."

"Or we'll come to you, your mother and I." Livia tipped her head back to look at him. "It doesn't make sense for you to spend three days to come back here to spend three days to go back to Dun Morrigan. We'll come to you."

Lorcan nodded. "That does make sense." He looked around. "Where's Tavi?"

"He told you. He's gone to talk to the men before he comes to bed." She smiled. "You don't remember a single thing that he said, do you?"

"I don't even remember talking to him," Lorcan admitted. "Or... really much of anything since we left the hall." He frowned. "We ate. I remember that much—"

Livia grinned. "What did you eat?"

"I..." Lorcan started, then stopped and laughed. "I have no idea. Right. Are we going to bed?"

"Yes. And eventually, we'll go to sleep." Livia stepped back and took his hand again and led him into the house. The embers in the firepit gave the only light, and Lorcan went over to build up the fire, listening as Livia moved around the room behind him.

"Where's Corvina?" she asked.

"With Orla." Lorcan looked up. "Apparently, Corvina is taken with Fionn. She's nesting with him."

"That's sweet," Livia said, sitting down on the edge of the bed. "Nice to know that she won't be jealous when this little one arrives." She looked down at herself. "Or two."

Lorcan chuckled and got up, coming over to sit at her feet. "Or two. However many you have for me, now and in our future." He reached up and took her hand. "I know this is probably asking the impossible, but try not to worry too much about us."

"That is asking the impossible," she replied. "I worry about you every time you're out of my sight. Because the last time I looked away when you'd gone out to fight, you almost didn't come back." Her hand in his shook. "Lorcan, you said the end starts tomorrow. It could be. It could be the end, and not in a good way. I can't go with you, and I'm frightened you won't come back."

Lorcan shifted around to rise up on his knees. "I will always come back," he said, taking her hands in his again. He kissed her palms, then pressed them to his chest. "I promise. I will come back to you, my Livia." He reached out to cup her cheek, wiping away a tear with his thumb. "I'll come back, and I'll bring Tavi back, and there will be no more separations. No more fighting. Just us, and all our children. For however long we have together."

"Not forever?" There was a slight quiver in Livia's voice.

"I can't promise forever," Lorcan said. "I don't know if I can give you both forever, and I promised you both I wouldn't choose. So, I promise you for however long we have together." He looked up as the door opened, and Tavi came inside. He smiled when he saw them, but the smile faded immediately.

"What's wrong?" he asked, taking a pair of small axes from his belt and putting them down before coming over to the bed.

"We're leaving tomorrow, and Livia isn't," Lorcan answered. "And she's worried about taking her eyes off us."

"Oh," Tavi breathed. He sat down behind Livia, shifting until she was able to lean back against him. "I understand." He put his arm around Livia. "Livia, I promise that I'll take care of him."

"And I'll take care of Tavi," Lorcan added.

"And Yaroah will be there to watch both of us." Tavi rubbed his hand up and down Livia's arm. "We'll be back… " He paused. "When, Lorcan?"

"Eight or nine days," Lorcan answered. "Livia and I already talked about this. Three days there, a day or two to finish this. Then someone flies back and Livia and everyone comes to us. We could come back here, and it would be about the same, but then we'd have to spend another three days on the road back to Dun Morrigan."

"The travel won't bother me," Livia said. "Honestly, we've come this far!"

Tavi chuckled. "True. And soon we won't need to travel again." He kissed Livia's neck, then rested his forehead on her shoulder. "It's tomorrow. It's happening."

"Still scared?" Lorcan asked.

"And apparently getting better at hiding it." Tavi raised his head and sighed. "Bairre is… a handful. I think he's not as good a fighter as he thinks he is, but he responds well to support."

"You had axes. Gaeilge axes," Lorcan said, nodding toward the table where Tavi had put them. "Where did those come from?"

Tavi smiled, shifting around so that he was sitting with Livia between his legs. She leaned back against his chest and he put his arms around her. "Those came from Ronan," he said. "He asked Diarmuid to come fetch me and bring me to the forge. Ronan says that these will be good enough until he's healed enough to go back to his forge and make a set balanced for me. And I saw the babies. Another white raven?"

"They named him after me," Lorcan said. He shook his head, still unable to believe it. "Lachtna was supposed to be an insult."

"Ronan was right, though," Livia said. "You took the insult and made it a weapon. And when you get to Dun Morrigan, you'll throw that weapon in Cormac's face." She reached out and tugged on Lorcan's hands. "Come up here and be with us. It's our last night together, and I want both of you with me."

Lorcan nodded and got up, and the three of them arranged themselves on the bed—Tavi at Livia's back, as they'd been sitting, and Lorcan in front of her, facing them both. He propped his head up on his hand and ran his other hand up Livia's side. "I'm assuming you don't just want to go to sleep?"

She laughed, grabbing his tunic and tugging him closer, until he was pressed against her. "After tonight, I'll have an empty bed for days. No, I don't want to sleep. Yet."

Lorcan leaned down and kissed her gently, sampling her lips, hearing her hum in pleasure. He kissed the tip of her nose, then said, "You know, I haven't seen you ride Tavi yet."

"Oh?" Tavi reached around and ran his hand over Lorcan's hip. "Is that what you want? A show?" He nuzzled the back of Livia's neck. "It's been a long time."

She chuckled. "It has been. Do you want to be tied down?"

Tavi breathed out audibly, making a soft *ohhhh*. "It has been a long time. Do we have what you'd need?"

"Yes, I think so." Livia shifted. "Lorcan, help me?"

A few minutes later, Tavi was naked, sitting on a bench. Livia walked behind him, every so often reaching down to trail her nails over his skin, making him shiver.

"We'll keep this simple," she said. "Ankles and wrists, and a gag."

"Do I have to have the gag?" Tavi asked.

She laughed. "Tavi, I've heard you. Do you want the entire *baile* to hear you, too?" She gestured to the small collection of belts Lorcan had assembled. "Tie his ankles together, and his wrists in front of him."

Lorcan picked up a long belt and knelt in front of the bench, lashing Tavi's ankles together. "When will it be my turn to try this?"

"Once we're settled in Dun Morrigan?" Tavi answered. "Livia?"

"Yes. Consider it incentive." She smiled. "You've given me an idea. Once you have Tavi's wrists tied, help him to kneel."

Lorcan got up. "Cross your wrists." He quickly tied Tavi's wrists in front of him; Tavi tugged against the belt, then looked up.

"Why in front?" he asked.

"Because you'll be on your back soon enough, and I don't want you to hurt your hands," Livia said. She moved behind him again, running her hand down his chest. "Lorcan, he needs to be on the ground. And you need to be naked."

"Which first?" Lorcan asked, laughing. He helped Tavi down to his knees, then tugged his shirt up over his head and laid it aside. Then he bent, untied his shoes, and stripped them both off, standing up to look at Livia, who was still dressed. She smiled and gestured to the bench in front of where Tavi was kneeling.

"Have a seat."

Lorcan sat down, then realized what Livia had set up. "Oh," he murmured as she moved behind him. "We know Tavi knows how to speak Livia. Is it time to find out how well he speaks Lorcan?"

Tavi laughed. "I've been wanting to practice." He shifted slowly into a better position, then looked up at them. "Are you going to gag Lorcan, too?"

"Worry about what's going in your mouth, darling," Livia chided. "Let me worry about his."

Tavi grinned, then leaned forward. Lorcan saw the look on his face, and leaned in to meet him, running his hands up Tavi's arms to his shoulders, to his neck, cradling his face as he kissed him. His fingers tangled in Tavi's curls—he tugged gently, and Tavi whimpered into his mouth. Then Livia ran her nails down Lorcan's back. He gasped, breaking the kiss.

"Sit back and let Tavi work," Livia murmured. "Tavi, put your hands behind your head."

Lorcan sat up and Tavi raised his bound wrists and positioned them as Livia instructed, with his elbows wide. He leaned forward slowly, looking a little unsteady in his new position. As he got closer, Lorcan could feel his warm breath on his skin. He closed his eyes, jerking in shock as a hand cupped his chin, forcing his head back. Then he remembered how Livia had held Tavi when their positions were reversed, and relaxed.

"I won't hurt you," Livia said softly. She kissed him, and he sighed and relaxed even more, reaching up to touch her.

Wet heat surrounded his cock, and Lorcan's yelp was muffled by Livia's mouth on his. He felt Tavi's laughter, vibrating up and down the length of his spine. His tongue was doing something… Lorcan didn't know what, but it was nothing that Bran had ever done to him. Livia had done something similar, but this… there was sorcery in Tavi's mouth, arcane gestures in his tongue that left Lorcan straining against Livia's hand, screaming into her mouth as he crested and came, as Tavi drained him to the dregs and licked him clean. When he could breathe again, when Livia finally released him, Lorcan looked down to see Tavi had lowered his arms, and was resting his head on Lorcan's thigh, a soft smile on his mouth.

"I think I've acquired some fluency in the basics of Lorcan," he said. "But I may need to practice a bit more with the subtleties of the idioms."

"I have no idea what any of that means," Lorcan said with a laugh. He ran his fingers through Tavi's hair, making Tavi whimper, then moan as Lorcan tugged him gently upright and kissed him again.

"Where do you want him, Livia?" Lorcan asked. "The bed, or the bench?"

"The bench?" Livia repeated. She walked around the bench, studying it, then shook her head. "No, I don't think so. The bed will be more comfortable. Move him to the bed, please."

Lorcan nodded and stood, crouching and picking Tavi up. Tavi's height made it awkward, but Lorcan carried him to the bed without dropping him, setting him down on the furs and blankets before stepping back. Livia joined him, putting her arm around his back and leaning into his side. She was finally naked, and Lorcan kissed the top of her head before gesturing with his other hand.

"Here he is for you," he said. "Where do you want me?"

Livia cocked her head to the side, then held up a thick strip of cloth. "First, gag him. Then… fasten his wrists to the post."

Lorcan did as he was told, kneeling to use another belt to tether Tavi's wrists to the support post, then pressing the gag into his mouth. He looked up as Livia crawled onto the bed and straddled Tavi's thighs. Tavi raised his head, only to fall back with a muffled groan as Livia started to run her hand up and down his length.

"Once I'm in place, Lorcan, come and sit behind me," she said. She let Tavi go, then shifted onto all fours, crawling up his body, her breasts rubbing against him as she moved. She kissed his chin, then rose up on her knees and reached down, holding his cock still. Lorcan came around behind her, kneeling over Tavi's legs, pressing against her back. She sighed and slowly started to lower herself, gasping slightly, then laughing as Tavi whined.

"Missed this," she whispered. "Missed you. Oh!" She stopped moving, then leaned back into Lorcan, her hips starting to move as she ground against Tavi. Lorcan reached around and cupped her breasts, and she moaned, "Yes!"

Underneath him, Lorcan could feel Tavi straining, trying to move. He looked over Livia's shoulder to see Tavi pulling on his bonds, the cords of his neck standing out as he struggled to move, to thrust. Livia laughed and started to move faster against him, her breathing growing faster, more ragged. Lorcan ran his hands over her breasts, over her swollen belly and down, finding her *breall,* tracing slow circles with his fingertips until he felt her shaking, until her keening started. Then he used his other hand to turn her head to his, and feasted on her cries of pleasure. Her movements slowed, and Lorcan moved to kiss her shoulder.

"I finished too quickly," she said. "Tavi isn't done. Let me move. Stay where you are." She shifted, stretching out over Tavi, then rolling off to his side. She leaned down and kissed him, then wrapped her hand around his cock and started to pump. Tavi jerked, hard enough that Lorcan was almost knocked to the side. He sat down harder, bracing himself with his hands on Tavi's thighs. Tavi howled and shot, splattering Livia's hand and his belly and chest. She chuckled and let him go.

"I think that will keep me satisfied until we're all together again," she said. "Let's get cleaned up and go to sleep."

Chapter Twenty-Nine

Lorcan had never seen Scath so quiet. So empty. There were houses missing their roofs, the thatch blown away completely. Walls that had collapsed from wind and weather. The tavern seemed to be intact, but he didn't look too closely, and he tried not to look at the stables behind the tavern. Tried not to remember Bran, and that last morning. He stepped back behind a wall and waited for the other scouts.

"The tavern looks to be in good condition," he said. "We should set the healers up there."

Tavi nodded. "Makes sense. Which one is the tavern?"

Lorcan pointed. "That one." He looked around. "The town is secure. I'll take the *ollamhs* up to the *baile* and get them started. Rhys will come to you at dawn if we make it through to the timbers." He shivered. He didn't like this part, but he knew it was necessary. Tavi had to lead. "Be careful, Tavi. Diarmuid will watch your back. But still, be careful."

"You, too." Tavi looked around, then held out his hand. "See you on the other side?"

Lorcan grabbed his hand and pulled him into a tight embrace. "Tomorrow," he said. "This will be over tomorrow. I love you."

Tavi held on tightly, his nose buried in Lorcan's short hair. "I love you, too." He pulled back, then leaned down and kissed Lorcan, hard enough that for a moment, nothing else mattered. Then he let Lorcan go and gestured, gathering up the scouts and leading them back to the forest. Lorcan went with them, then left them to go to where Yaroah waited with the flock and the sorcerers.

"The town is secure," he told them. "Someone needs to stay down there to make sure that we have no surprises when we bring people back."

"Turlach and Cuanu volunteered," Petran said. He nodded to a tree branch overhead, and Lorcan looked up to see his uncles and Corvina. Corvina shifted, then flew down to land on his shoulder. The other two ravens flew off toward Scath. Lorcan nodded and took a deep breath.

"Right. Let's get into position and get started before it gets too dark. We have a long night ahead of us." He led the way through the trees to the place where the tunnel would start, looking around as the sorcerers started murmuring to each other.

"Set a shelter up there," he said, pointing to a hidden spot underneath a fallen tree. "So that the sorcerers can rest. We can't risk a fire this close to the *baile*, but they can at least have some shelter." He looked around again. "And sentries. We need to keep watch—"

"That's already done," Petran said, coming up to him. "I sent Rhys, Aodh, and Orla up to keep an eye. Becc, Cathal and Maelan will change with them at moonset, and Oscar and I will take the final watch." He nodded toward the sorcerers. "Yaroah is guarding Gaynor and his people. I think we're as ready as we can be right now."

Lorcan nodded. "Thank you, Uncle." He closed his eyes and took a deep breath. "Once we have the *baile* secure, we need to search it. All of it. Because from the moment we have Cormac prisoner, we'll be running out of time to find Da."

"We'll find him," Petran said. He paused. "What are you going to do with Cormac once we have him?"

"I don't know," Lorcan said. "We need him alive to tell us where he's taken Da, but after that... I don't know. I know I need to kill him. My children will never be safe so long as he's alive. But... honestly, I'm not certain if I *should* kill him." He frowned. "I mean... I know he says he wants me dead. And he could have. By all rights, I shouldn't be standing here. But he didn't. And I'm not sure anymore that he's going to. Because why wait?"

"He tried to kill you how many times in Rome?" Petran asked. "When we talked with Mother, you said you thought he wants to be the one to do it."

"Because I thought he needed to prove something," Lorcan said. "To me. To himself. But now I think Tavi is right. Cormac is keeping my cloak as a final weapon against me. If he fails, that's when he's going to kill me. But... he already knows he's going to fail. He knows he has no chance of winning anymore—his allies are dead or deserting him. There's no need for these theatrics. If he's going to kill me, why does it matter where or how? I'm not going to be any more or less dead. He's letting me live, and I'm not sure what is really driving him anymore. I don't understand why he's waiting." He looked at Petran to see the confusion in his face. "I'm not sure if any of this makes sense, even to me. You told me that he wants to be in control of everything so he doesn't get hurt anymore. But he's completely out of control now. And I know he thinks that I stole his entire worth because I'm my father's son, and his heir. But if he's trying to take that worth for himself, he's failing at that. Honestly, he's only given me more by pushing me to become more than I was." He waved one arm toward the *baile*. "Tavi calls him a wild dog. Says that you don't have a choice when you deal with wild dogs. But wild dogs… they have a reason for what they do. This is… unhinged." He frowned. "Uncle, has he gone mad?"

Petran frowned. "I… I don't know," he said slowly. "I don't know if we can go mad. I mean… there are some who'd say that we're all a little mad already, because we're Mother's children." He looked over his shoulder, toward the baile. "Maybe he is. Maybe… what happened to him as a child drove him out of his wits, and we just never noticed because he was so young. It's possible we didn't notice until it was too late." He frowned. "Gaynor." He turned and ran toward the sorcerers.

"What?" Lorcan took off running after Petran, catching up to him as he reached Gaynor.

"Gaynor, you told me once that Muirenn's mother was mad, that something happened to her that drove her wits away," Petran said. "Do you think Cormac is the same?"

Gaynor looked startled. "I… I've never met the boy," he stammered. "I have no idea. And Muirenn's mother? Her mind was shattered by sorcery gone horribly wrong. It's not the same." He paused. "But perhaps it is? I don't know."

"If we take Cormac alive, could you tell?" Lorcan asked. "Could you help him?"

"Again, I don't know." Gaynor folded his arms over his chest. "Now explain. From the beginning, please. Why do you think he's gone mad?"

"Because none of this makes sense!" Lorcan answered. "If he just wanted me dead, he could have killed me already. He has the means to kill me right now, and has since he took me and gave me to his men to sell as a slave. If he just wanted what I have, he has it all, except for my mates, and I don't think he knows about them. But even if he did want everything of mine, and want to control everything to protect himself, he's failed at it. All he's done has turn every man's hand against him. He wants to rule, but instead he's going to burn everything to the ground. None of this makes sense. And… I don't know if I should be killing him… or trying to help him."

259

"It's well past the point of helping him, Lorcan." Lorcan turned to see his uncle Maelan had joined them. Maelan looked toward the *baile* and continued, "You're a healer like your mother, so I understand you wanting to make it better. But how can you make this better?" He waved one arm. "He's tried to kill you how many times? He's tortured and caged his parents. Your parents. His brother. And Mother alone knows what he's done to his sister! Can you make any of that better?"

"Will killing him make it better?" Lorcan asked

"It'll stop this madness," Maelan snapped. "That's a start. Sometimes, you have to cut off the diseased limb to save the life."

"I know that," Lorcan said. He shook his head. "I know that. And I know that I don't really have a choice. I have to stop him, or this will never end. My children will never be safe while he lives. I have to protect my family, my mates. My family in Rome. I have to stop this."

"Then what's really bothering you, fledgling?" Petran asked.

Lorcan chased his thoughts around until he found the tail end of an answer. He took a deep breath. "I... he's done... so much. Hurt so many people. And yet... everything I have now is because of what he's done... if it wasn't for all this, I wouldn't be the warrior I am. The hero that Rome named me. I wouldn't have my mates. Cuanu wouldn't have his. There wouldn't be an alliance growing with Rome. Everything wrong that Cormac has done to me has turned into a gift, starting with the name he gave me. He's hurt the family so much... and I have to stop it all. But I can't help thinking that there's something I should be doing to help him. I'm a healer. I was a healer before I was a hero. Maybe I can make it right—"

You cannot. You are a good boy, Lorcan, but your hope for a better ending isn't enough. You want to make things right without spilling blood, because you've seen far too much of that for one so young, but you can't save someone who doesn't want to be saved.

The voice was unfamiliar, but clearly only to Lorcan. Petran and Maelan both gasped aloud, and Lorcan looked up to see two more figures had joined them. Two men, both wearing feathered cloaks. One was tall and very thin, with unruly curls that reminded him of Tavi. The other... it was like looking at Petran, only shorter. But Petran didn't glow—both of the strangers did, casting a faint light like moonglow in the growing darkness.

"Oscar?" Petran gasped. Then his voice cracked as he moaned, "*Ronan?*"

Lorcan stared at Petran for a moment, then looked up at the taller spirit. He swallowed. Then he bowed. "I… " he stammered. "It… it's nice to meet you, Uncle. Both of you."

Oscar smiled. *And polite, too. Tell Diarmuid I approve.*

"I…" Lorcan's mouth went dry. "He's… not with you, is he?"

Diarmuid lives, Oscar said. *You are right, though. Once you defeat Cormac, you'll have very little time to find where he's hidden Diarmuid. And before you ask, we don't know where.*

"It's really you, isn't it?" Gaynor said. "Oscar… oh, my friend. I'm sorry! I'm so sorry!"

Oscar turned toward Gaynor. *There is nothing to forgive, my friend. Nothing you could have done would have changed anything, and the attempt would have destroyed the druid college.* He turned and looked away, and held out his hand. A woman joined him, nestling under the shelter of his arm.

Father, she said. *I never called you that when I was alive, did I? I should have.*

"I always knew you meant it," Gaynor choked out. "Always."

I'm sorry I didn't get to say goodbye. She looked up at Oscar, who smiled down at her. *I am happy. Know that. And I miss you.*

"I miss you, too. Both of you." Gaynor looked back toward where the other sorcerers were working. "If you'd been here, this would be done by now."

Oscar looked sour. *I'm not allowed to help. Mother already told me no.*

Twice, Muirenn added.

Petran smiled. "Ronan. I…"

I like your man, Pet. Ronan said. *Good choice.* He shifted from foot to foot. *I'm sorry. I didn't mean to get my arse killed. I didn't mean to leave you alone.*

"It might have been nice to know you were there," Petran said. "To know that you could hear me if I talked to you."

We're not allowed. Oscar said. *This is a one-time exception. Lorcan needed to know that there's no healing Cormac, because there's nothing to heal. He isn't sick, and he isn't mad. He's made his choices. When the time comes, Lorcan, you cannot hesitate. You will have to act. But how you act is up to you.*

"I don't understand," Lorcan said.

Oscar nodded. *The injuries against the flock are many. Yours is not the only claim against him. Cormac must pay. But you don't have to be the one to exact that payment.* He turned sharply, as if someone had called his name. *We have to go back. You won't see us again. Not until you join us.*

"Uncle Oscar," Lorcan blurted. "I... I have a question. I have two mates."

Oscar nodded. *I noticed. And I'm intrigued by it. But that's not a question.*

"Can I share my cloak with both of them? Or do I have to choose one?" Lorcan looked at Petran and Maelan. "I... I can't choose one over the other. I won't choose one over the other."

Ah. I don't have an answer for you, Lorcan. I wish I did, Oscar said. *I don't know. You're the first. The first in so many things. So... I suppose that choice is also up to you.* He looked over his shoulder again. *Our time is up. Good luck tomorrow. We'll be watching.*

Then they were gone, and Petran crumpled to the ground like his bones had turned to water. "Ronan," he whispered. "I... that was Ronan."

"And Muirenn. My Muirenn." Gaynor looked around. "Is... does that mean my daughter is a goddess now? Or did they just visit us from *Magh Meall*? Petran, what does wait for the Morrigan's own when you die?"

"How am I supposed to answer that, Gaynor?" Petran asked. "I've never died before! I don't know!"

Gaynor chuckled. "Truth. How can we know what's waiting for us? When we do find out, it's too late to tell anyone." He rubbed his hands up and down the front of his robe. "Time to go back to work."

* * *

The sorcerers worked through the night, working in pairs as the others rested. The tunnel grew, but progress felt agonizingly slow. Lorcan paced, watching, wondering if they'd make it before dawn.

"Ghost, go rest," Yaroah said, coming out of the darkness. "You need to lead us in the morning. You need to sleep."

"I'm not sure I can, Yaroah." Lorcan tugged his cloak around himself and sat down at the base of a tree. He closed his eyes, taking a deep breath. "How much longer until dawn?"

"Hours yet." Yaroah sat down next to him. "Sleep. When you wake,

I will sleep. Your uncles are watching." He looked around. "So… " he paused, then asked, "Those were ghosts? True ghosts?"

Lorcan looked at him. "Yes. My uncles and my aunt."

"One of them looked like Petran."

"That was his twin, my uncle Ronan. The tall man was my uncle Oscar, and the woman was his mate Muirenn. Gaynor's daughter."

Yaroah nodded. "Ah. And… you have seen them before? This doesn't seem to bother you."

"No, I haven't," Lorcan answered, shaking his head. He looked at Yaroah again. "And I don't think we'll see them again. You could see them?"

"I do not think I was meant to, but I did." Yaroah shifted, rubbing his back against the tree trunk. "I saw glowing, and came to see what it was. I thought it might give away our position."

Lorcan nodded. "I don't think anyone saw it who wasn't meant to see it. So yes, you were meant to see them." He closed his eyes and tipped his head back. "I'm tired. But I'm not sure I can sleep."

"You learned to sleep in the cells, waiting to go on the sand. You can sleep now."

Lorcan turned his head and smiled at Yaroah. "This is easier with you here. I know you have my back, the way you did in the arena. Thank you."

Yaroah nodded slowly. Then he sighed. "I had a brother. Mago. He was younger than me by two years, and I was supposed to look after him. We went to war together. We went to the Sacred Band together." He tapped his shoulder. "Lean on me."

Lorcan leaned against Yaroah's broad shoulder and sighed. "The last time I slept on someone like this, it was on the slave ship. His name was Ivo, and that's all I know. We didn't share a language. There was a storm, and I was scared. He sang me to sleep. Then we were sold, and I never saw him again."

"If I sang to you, you would be more frightened than of any storm," Yaroah said. Lorcan laughed.

"What happened to Mago?"

Yaroah sighed. "I do not know. I never knew. The Sacred Band fell. The survivors were executed or sold. I was… I thought at the time that the dead were the lucky ones. Now? I think perhaps I am the lucky one. I lived to have a life. But I never saw Mago again." He looked at Lorcan. "If he fell in that battle, then perhaps his spirit found yours, and that is why you are as my brother. Or perhaps not. I cannot see your grandmother the goddess allowing a common soldier's spirit to inhabit one of her own."

"I don't think there's anything common about you, Yaroah. Which means there wasn't anything common about Mago. You're my friend, and my brother." Lorcan leaned against Yaroah again. "I'll try and sleep. You don't need to sing."

"If I sang, no one would sleep."

* * *

Lorcan woke with the scent of dawn in his nose, and scrambled to his feet, shaking his head. He heard wings overhead, then Petran landed next to him.

"Why did you let me sleep so long?" Lorcan croaked.

"Yaroah said to let you be," Petran answered. "You're leading us. You need to be sharp. We agreed."

Lorcan blinked his eyes and shook his head again. "I don't feel sharp. How's the tunnel?"

"We just reached the timbers," Gaynor said as he came to join them. He handed Lorcan a cloth bundle. "Eat that. I was coming to tell you that we're ready for instructions." He frowned. "We didn't dig deep enough to go under the timbers, and there's no more time. What is the next step?"

Lorcan took the bundle and unwrapped it to find a bannock and a piece of salted meat. He broke the bannock open and started eating. "Ah... if we can't get under the timbers, we need to remove them. Once we hear that the battle has started at the gate, we're going to set the timbers on fire," he mumbled around a mouthful. He swallowed and added, "Uncle Petran, send Rhys to Tavi and get the others ready. It's time." He ate another piece of bannock and looked around. "Where's Corvina?"

"I haven't seen her since it got dark," Petran answered. "Finish that so you can get ready yourself." He turned and hurried off into the darkness, and a moment later, Lorcan heard something flying overhead. He nodded and took a bite of meat, then went to find Yaroah. It was time to arm himself.

He finished eating as Yaroah unwrapped the armor that Manius had prepared for them—the same armor that they'd worn on that last morning in the arena. He helped Yaroah with his *manica* and *ocrea*, then stood still as Yaroah fastened the straps of his armor and helped him with the scaled *lorica* that he wore when he was fighting as a *dimachaeri*. As Yaroah picked up his shield, they heard a distant roar, and shouting from inside the *baile*.

"That's the signal!" Lorcan called. "Gaynor! Burn it!"

The sorcerers scrambled out of the tunnel and stood on either side of the mouth. Gaynor looked around. "Keep clear!" he called. Then the sorcerers started chanting, and Lorcan's ears started to itch. For a moment, nothing happened. Then flames appeared at the mouth of the tunnel, so dark they were almost blue. Lorcan went to the edge of the forest and looked out at the timbers that made up the outer wall of the *baile*.

Three of them were smoking, and as he watched, they tipped toward him and fell, landing with heavy thuds that seemed to echo through the forest.

"Go!" He started moving, running toward the gap, as a flight of ravens swooped over his head and into the *baile*. "Fast and quiet! Get them out!"

Chapter Thirty

Lorcan could hear the fighting from the front of the *baile*, and caught a brief glimpse of the gates open wide as he skirted around the hall to the doors. There were no guards, no one watching, and he and Yaroah slipped into the hall without any confrontation. The smell was as bad as his visions had led him to believe, as bad as the hold in the slave ship, and Lorcan almost gagged.

"Easy," Yaroah murmured. "Breathe through your mouth."

Lorcan nodded. He could see the others toward the front of the hall, and a body on the floor. Petran looked up as they came closer.

"There was just the one guard," he whispered. "Cathal?"

"Got it." Cathal broke open the cage door and swung it wide. The raven inside stepped warily out onto the table, flapped his wings, then changed—Niall crouched on the tabletop. He looked wild, and more than a little mad, ready to attack. Maelan stepped forward, his hands held up.

"Niall, it's us. It's me. It's Maelan. We're here. It's over. You're free." He glanced back. "Cathal will have Sorcha out in a moment. It's over."

Niall blinked, looked around again, and relaxed, climbing gracelessly off the table. He jerked as they all heard a roar from outside the hall.

"That sounds… promising," Yaroah murmured. He trotted over to the door and looked out, then came back smiling. "The fight appears to be over. I see Tavi."

A moment later, Lorcan heard Tavi's voice. "Spread out and search! Every house, every corner! Turn this entire place upside down and shake it!"

Lorcan turned back to see that the other cage was open, and that Niall had Sorcha in his arms.

"Uncle Niall?" Lorcan said. Niall faced him, and his eyes widened. He smiled. "It's good to see you, too," Lorcan said. "Ronan is safe. He and Mother made it to Dun Righ. He's recovering. And you have grandchildren." He turned. "Maelan, take Uncle Niall and Aunt Sorcha back to Scath to the healer. Stay with them."

"Grandchildren?" Sorcha repeated. Her voice sounded rusty. "What?"

"Siobhan had twins, and they're beautiful," Petran said. "Go with Maelan. He'll take you to the healers."

"No. Where's Niamh?" Sorcha looked around.

"We'll find her, Aunt." Lorcan turned when he heard his name, and Tavi came into the hall. He stopped and coughed.

"Oh, that's vile," he muttered. "Lorcan, we've taken the *baile*. What Orla told us about Cormac losing his men was true. The minute we got through the gates, they surrendered. We're securing things now, and searching for your father, and for anyone hiding away." He paused. "And for Cormac."

"What?"

"Diarmuid says that he's not out there. I have to take his word for it. And those men… they couldn't have been any more disorganized. There was no one leading them. As soon as the gates were open, they all collectively pissed themselves. There's maybe half as many as Orla said she saw, and no one can tell us where Cormac is." He looked back over his shoulder. "Come out of here, all of you. It stinks."

Lorcan followed Tavi back out into the open air. Across the *baile*, Diarmuid was directing warriors who were herding a small group of ragged and defeated men out through the gates.

"Diarmuid?" Tavi shouted.

Diarmuid looked over at them and shook his head. "He's not here!"

"Not here," Lorcan repeated. "Cormac… where the fuck is he?"

"Gone."

Lorcan turned, and all he could do was stare. Niamh. She was drenched in blood—her short tunic, her legs, her arms. There was probably blood in her cloak, but he couldn't tell. There was blood on her face, around her mouth, and he didn't want to think about why that might have been. He heard a moan behind him. Sorcha? Maybe. It didn't matter. Because in Niamh's arms was a cloak of blood-splattered white feathers.

"Niamh," he croaked. She came closer, then stopped and held out her burden.

"He's gone," she repeated. "Cormac. He's gone. There's a passage out behind the stable. He ran as soon as he saw the warband. Senach and

I were supposed to follow." She paused and looked down. "Cormac sent Senach to get the cloak. I stole it. And... I got blood on it. I'm sorry. But... he's dead." She looked past him. "You don't have to kill Senach for me, Da. I did it myself."

Niall brushed past Lorcan, walking toward his daughter, who froze and shrank back.

"No." Her voice cracked. Niall stopped. He nodded and backed away. Niamh hesitated, then held the cloak out again. "Lorcan."

Lorcan stepped forward and held out one hand. "Thank you," he said, his voice cracking. Her lips twitched, and she thrust the cloak into his hand. Then she backed away.

"I..." she started. She stopped and looked around. "Mother, Da. I'm sorry. I... I love you. Tell Ronan... tell him I'm sorry." She stepped back again, looked past Lorcan, and froze. Her eyes widened. "I... you. You. No. No. Not yet. No. I... I need time."

"Go," Sorcha said. "We'll be here when you're ready to come back. We love you."

Niamh nodded, tears tracing through the blood on her face. She turned, shifted, and flew away. Someone moved past Lorcan, following her for a moment.

Yaroah. He turned and looked at Lorcan, a look on his face that Lorcan couldn't remember ever seeing before.

"Is this what it is that you feel?" he demanded. "Is this... is this what you *have*? With Livia? With Tavi?"

"Oh, Mother," Petran breathed.

"I..." Yaroah turned and looked off in the direction of Niamh's flight. "Ghost, I am going after her."

"Yaroah, that might not be a good idea," Tavi said. "She... she's been hurt."

"I know." Yaroah said. "I know that look. I remember that look." He paused. "I had that look, once. I will keep my distance. But... " He turned and looked back at them. "I understand you now. I will follow her. I will be there when she is ready. And I will take care of her."

Sorcha came past them, looking up at Yaroah. "My Latin isn't strong. But he's Niamh's mate, isn't he?"

"Aunt Sorcha, this is Yaroah," Lorcan said. "My chosen brother."

Yaroah bowed deeply to Sorcha, then said in broken Gaeilge, "I will take care of her."

Sorcha bit her lip, then nodded. "Thank you. Take care of yourself, too."

"Uncle Cathal?" Lorcan called. "Help him get supplied. Help him with whatever he needs." He turned and raised his voice. "I need a horse! Now!"

"You have your cloak," Tavi said from behind him. "You could fly after him."

Lorcan looked down at his cloak. His skin. The urge to put it on, to *fly,* to be whole for the first time in a year was strong enough to choke him. But if he did it, he wouldn't be able to put it aside again. And he needed an answer more than he needed the sky.

"Hold this for me," he said, turning and holding the cloak out to Tavi. "I've never been a good flyer. I need a horse."

"We don't know where he's gone," Tavi said, taking the cloak. He ran his hand over the feathers.

"I'll find him." Lorcan looked up and saw Corvina circling overhead, calling. "And I think I know how. I need a horse—"

"Lorcan!"

Lorcan turned to see Petran leading a black mare toward him. He stared for a moment, then laughed and met them halfway, running his hand over her glossy neck.

"He took care of her," he murmured. "I'm amazed. He actually took care of her. Hello, Beauty. Let's go for a run." He looked at Petran. "Let Tavi and Diarmuid handle things here. Get Uncle Niall and Aunt Sorcha to the healers. And send Orla back to the Dun Righ to tell them."

"I'll wait on that until you bring Diarmuid back. I want to be able to tell Grainne her mate lives." Petran crouched and offered his cupped hands. "Go find him."

Lorcan put his foot into his uncle's hands, and swung onto the back of his mare. He grabbed the reins and turned Beauty toward the gate, goading her forward. He heard Diarmuid calling after him, wishing him luck, then he was outside the *baile*. He glanced up and saw Corvina banking and fly toward the east, toward the coast, and urged Beauty after her.

* * *

It was the cove. Of course it was the cove. Lorcan slid down from Beauty's back and let her graze, seeing another horse nearby. Cormac had ridden? He hadn't flown? That was odd. Lorcan drew his *siccae* and walked toward the edge, looking out into the cove. The water was halfway up the beach, the tide rising, and Lorcan could see an empty coracle bobbing in the waves, heading out to sea. He studied the horizon, but saw no ships. Where could Cormac have gone? Then he looked down.

Cormac was clinging to the rocks, caught in the middle of climbing down. Lorcan watched him for a moment, then coughed and saw his cousin flinch.

"What in Grandmother's name are you doing?" he asked, sheathing his *siccae*.

Cormac looked up and glared at him. "Why aren't you dead?"

"Because you hire incompetents and idiots. Why aren't you flying?" He looked down. "Your boat is leaving without you. You have nowhere to go, Cormac. Come up, tell me where my father is, and we'll end this."

"Let me go, and I'll tell you where he is."

Lorcan laughed. "Let you go? Go where? You have no followers left. Every man in Eire is against you. The Romans in Alba all know your name and your crimes, and the Emperor in Rome has no love for you. Nor does his heir. There's nowhere you can go, and your boat left without you. Come up."

"So you can kill me?"

Lorcan crouched. "Cormac, I give you my word. Come up and tell me where my father is, and I won't kill you yet. I'll take you back to the *baile*, and we'll end this there." He looked around. "It's not like you have a choice, Cormac."

Cormac looked down. Then he looked back up and started climbing. Lorcan backed away from the edge and waited, watching as Cormac dragged himself up over the edge of the cliff. He knelt there, panting, then looked up.

"You're not going to kill me. You swore it."

"Tell me where my father is, and I won't kill you yet. It's conditional." Lorcan cocked his head to the side. "So?"

Cormac scowled. Then he jerked his head to the side. "Down there. There's a cave. You know the one."

"The crab cave?" Lorcan looked down. "That... it floods. Cormac, how long has he been down there?"

"Five, maybe six days? He's still alive, last I checked. That was yesterday. Got his feet wet, but he's still alive." Cormac looked over the edge. "Not for long, though. The water has been getting higher. So how well do you climb?"

"Climb… There's a trail, you featherheaded idiot!"

Cormac stared at him, looking completely confused. "What?"

"Of course you don't know about the trail. Why would you?" Lorcan snapped. He went to Beauty and swung up onto her back. "Corvina!" he called in Latin. "Watch him."

Corvina landed on a nearby rock and hissed at Cormac, who gaped at her. "I… who is that?"

"Just stay there. Don't make me come after you." Lorcan turned Beauty toward the top of the trail, hoping that the water wasn't rising too fast.

The trail ended in a switchback, and Lorcan left Beauty there, stripping off his armor and his swords, and leaving them above the high-water mark. He splashed out into the water and headed for the end of the beach. By the time he'd reached the place where the cliff curved, he was swimming, aiming for the crab cave and hoping that Cormac had been telling the truth. The water was lapping at the topmost arch of the cave mouth, so Lorcan dove and swam inside, surfacing in cold darkness. "Da!" he sputtered, hearing water dripping around him. "Da, are you here?"

A raven called back, and Lorcan turned, trying to pick the source of the sound out from the bouncing echoes. "Da, keep calling."

The raven called again, and Lorcan swam toward the wall, then started to feel his way along it. His hand found a ledge, just below the water. Then a cage, and he almost cried.

"Da," he breathed. "I… I need to get you out." He felt the cage, finding the lock by touch. With his other hand, he groped along the ledge, coming up with a rock the size of his fist. He held onto the cage and smashed the rock into the lock over and over until he heard something splash, then fumbled for the lock again. The cage door swung open at his touch, and he heard splashing water and the scratch of claws on stone.

"I hope you can swim, Da," Lorcan said. "You're going to have to."

There was a heavy splash and a wave washed over Lorcan, making him sputter and cough. Then a hand touched his shoulder. His cheek. Pulled him into a tight, one-armed embrace.

"Lorcan." His father's voice was hoarse. Lorcan hugged him back.

"We have to get out of here, Da," he said. "Can you swim?"

"I can swim." Diarmuid paused, then chuckled. "And I desperately need a bath anyway."

* * *

271

Lorcan led the way back to the trail, splashing up toward Beauty and rescuing his armor and weapons from the rising waters. He turned to see his father standing up and stretching, and noticed that he wasn't moving his right arm at all.

"Da, what's wrong," Lorcan asked, coming closer. He touched his father's shoulder—Diarmuid winced.

"Swimming may not have been the best thing for me," he said. "But it was preferable to drowning. I haven't moved my arm or had a full spread of my wings in… how long has it been?" He looked at Lorcan. "You've gotten taller. How long has it been, Lorcan?"

"Just over a year." Lorcan gestured, and they started up the trail. "If you want to ride, I can help you onto Beauty."

"I'll walk," Diarmuid said. "Lorcan, your mother—"

"Is safe in Dun Righ," Lorcan finished. "Ronan got her there. And Uncle Niall and Aunt Sorcha should be on their way to Scath, to the healers we have there. We've retaken Dun Morrigan."

"And Niamh?" Diarmuid asked.

"She… " Lorcan hesitated. "She's gone off to be alone. She killed the man Cormac gave her to, and she's gone off to the forest. She'll come back when she's ready." He paused at the top of the trail, looking around. Beauty was grazing nearby, and he went to rest his hand on her neck. "She has something to come back for. Someone."

"Her mate? Who?"

"My chosen brother, Yaroah." Lorcan smiled at the stunned look on his father's face. "You'll like him, Da. He's from Carthage. He and I… cousin Diarmuid wanted to know if he was like me, in reverse."

Diarmuid laughed. "I can see almost hear him asking that."

Lorcan started leading them back the way he'd come. "There's so much to tell you, Da. But the important part… I've mated. Twice."

"I'm sorry?"

"Twice. I have two mates. No one can explain it. You'll meet Tavi at Dun Morrigan. He led the assault. And Livia is with Mother at Dun Righ." He looked up at his father, realizing that it wasn't as far to look anymore. "And by the time the first snows come, you'll be a grandfather."

Diarmuid slowed his pace. "I… two mates. How is that possible?"

"I don't know," Lorcan answered. "I also don't know what that means for Grandmother's gift. Which is why I'm not wearing my cloak. Tavi has it." He looked ahead, and saw Cormac sitting in what looked to be exactly the same spot where Lorcan had left him. "Well, there's a surprise."

"Why is he here?" Diarmuid asked. "Why is he still alive?"

"Because I told him that if he told me where to find you, I wouldn't kill him yet," Lorcan said. "I intend to take him back to Dun Morrigan and end it there, in front of the flock. I'm just not sure how I'm ending it yet." He looked back at Cormac, then noticed Corvina. As he watched, Cormac started to fidget. Corvina growled at him, and he moved back to his original position. Lorcan laughed.

"Who is that?" Diarmuid asked slowly.

"Corvina. She's a friend. She's been with me since shortly after I arrived in Rome." Lorcan looked at his father. "You have the oddest look on your face."

"I thought... you found her in Rome?"

"I think I know what you're thinking. Grandmother says that she's not Corvina. Uncle Petran says he's not sure she's telling me the truth, though."

"You've spoken to her?"

Lorcan nodded. "A few times. I'll tell you all of it later. Once this is done." He whistled, then called in Latin, "We're back, Corvina." The raven hissed once more at Cormac, then took off, flying to land on Lorcan's outstretched arm. She sidled up to perch on his shoulder and coughed once. Lorcan reached up and ruffled her feathers. "Yes, you're very fierce. Thank you."

Cormac got to his feet slowly. There was blood on his arms and on the backs of his hands. "You found him."

"And now I'll take you back to Dun Morrigan, and we'll end this." Lorcan looked around. "Go fetch your horse. Don't try to fly off."

Diarmuid snorted. "He can't. Mother cast him out for his crimes against you. She took away his gifts."

"And the horse ran off when your pet attacked me," Cormac grumbled.

"Then I suppose you're walking."

* * *

Lorcan helped his father mount Beauty, and they started walking. He kept one hand on Beauty's shoulder, and both eyes on Cormac. His cousin seemed... defeated.

"It seems odd to say this, but I owe you thanks, Cormac," Lorcan said.

"You what?" Cormac stopped walking, earning a warning growl from Corvina. He flinched and started walking again. "Thanks. You owe me thanks. Why?"

"Because my mates were in Rome," Lorcan said. "Uncle Cuanu's mate was in Rome. And so was Niamh's." Lorcan looked over Beauty's back to where his cousin was staring at him. "If I hadn't been sold as a slave in Rome, I'd never have found any of them." He smiled. "I was adopted into the Emperor's household because of you. And named a hero of Rome. If I'd stayed, I could have been Emperor myself someday."

Diarmuid chuckled. "I cannot wait to hear this entire story."

"You... could have been Emperor." Cormac shook his head. "You're lying."

"I'm not," Lorcan replied. "In the arena, I was called Corax Princeps. But you knew that. What you don't know is that the Emperor named me a hero, and granted me the rights of a Roman citizen. He named me Albus Corvus Torvus Victorinus. The victorious white raven warrior. And the Emperor's son asked if I would stay, and if I was willing to be adopted as his heir." He looked forward, seeing a chariot coming toward them, and ravens in flight. "I think we have a welcoming party."

"If you had all that in Rome, why come back here," Cormac demanded.

Lorcan met Cormac's eyes. "Because I didn't want it. Any of it. This is my place. This is my home. My family. You stole what was mine by treachery. You held it by terror, and you lost it by incompetence. Now you are going to pay for your crimes. This ends today." Lorcan brought Beauty to a stop and walked around to stand in front of Cormac. He held up his tattooed hand. "You know what these mean. You have to—you knew where to send Tierney, and you had Galius send the twins. Oh, you should know. Galius is dead. He failed, too."

Cormac paled. "You owe me thanks, you said," Cormac stammered. "That means... you can't kill me."

"My gratitude only means that if I kill you, I'll do it quickly," Lorcan said. "I haven't yet decided if I'm going to do it, or if I'm going to give you to my father, your father, the High King, or Niamh. No matter what, today you're going to answer for what you've done."

Chapter Thirty-One

Lorcan stepped back from a visibly shaken Cormac, turning to face the chariot, which was drawing to a stop. Turlach was driving, and Tavi was with him. The ravens landed, shifting to become Petran and Cuanu. Lorcan held Beauty still while Diarmuid dismounted. He walked forward, and was immediately mobbed by his brothers. Tavi smiled as he came past them, joining Lorcan and hugging him tightly.

"You're soaked," he said, letting Lorcan go. He looked past Lorcan, then switched to Latin. "He's still alive?"

"I told him that if he told me where he'd hidden my father, I wouldn't kill him yet. That I'd take him back to the *baile* and deal with him there," Lorcan answered. He looked at Tavi. "Where's my cloak? And how did you know where to look for us?"

"In order? In the chariot with Turlach," Tavi answered. "And we set out in the direction you left. Turlach guessed it might be the cove. With you being wet… it was, wasn't it?"

"Yes." Lorcan held his arm out, and Corvina sidestepped down to his forearm. She cocked her head at him, and he nodded and said, "Keep an eye on him."

Corvina croaked and took off, circling overhead. Tavi looked up at her, then arched a brow. Lorcan just shook his head. "Cormac, don't move," he called. Then he led Tavi over to Diarmuid.

"Da?" he said. "This is Tavi. Lucanus Decius Octavian, but we call him Tavi." He looked up at Tavi. "One of my mates, and the one who led the raid on Dun Morrigan."

"Do I still have a *baile*?" Diarmuid asked. He smiled, and Tavi chuckled.

"It's a little battered in places, and cleaning it might take some time," he drawled. Diarmuid laughed and held his hand out, clasping Tavi's wrist, then pulling him into a one-armed embrace.

"Welcome, my son," he murmured. "Welcome." He smiled and let Tavi go. "I can't wait to meet… Livia, was it?"

"Yes, Da."

Diarmuid took a deep breath and tipped his head back, then jumped when someone yelped. Lorcan turned to see Cormac waving his arms, trying to defend himself against an attacking Corvina.

"I told you not to move," Lorcan called. Cormac stopped flailing and scowled at Lorcan.

"I'll take Diarmuid back in the chariot," Turlach said. "And… are we taking Cormac back as a prisoner? I have rope."

"Given that the only thing keeping him from running off is Corvina? Probably a good idea. Give it to me." Lorcan took the rope from Turlach and went to Cormac. "Give me your wrists."

"No," Cormac replied, shaking his head. He took a step back, and Corvina dove at him. He waved one arm at her.

"If you don't want her pecking at you the entire rest of the walk, you'll give me your wrists." Lorcan glanced up at the raven. "I said I wasn't going to kill you out here. I didn't say anything about her not pecking your eyes out. She's not tame, Cormac. And by now you should have realized that neither am I." When Cormac didn't move, Lorcan growled, "Wrists. Now."

Cormac went pale. He held his hands out; Lorcan lashed them together, then tugged on the lead. "You can stand or kneel. But don't try and run." He turned back. "Da, take the chariot with Turlach. Tavi, you can ride with me. Beauty can take both of us."

"Give me the tether." Turlach held his hand out. "That way, he doesn't try and pull you off the horse."

"Don't kill him, Uncle."

Turlach snorted. "Not even a little?"

"Uncle!"

"Fine. He's yours." Turlach tugged the rope. "Move."

* * *

Back in Dun Morrigan, Lorcan jumped down from Beauty's back and helped Tavi dismount, then went to where the rest of the flock had gathered. Cormac was at the heart of the group, kneeling, with his wrists still bound. To Lorcan's surprise, Niall and Sorcha were there.

"They wouldn't go to Scath," Tavi murmured. "We brought the healers up after you left."

Lorcan nodded. "We'll need to search and see if we can find Uncle Niall's wax tablet."

Tavi blinked. "Oh! I forgot!" He trotted away, coming back a moment later with something wrapped in a piece of leather. "Ronan gave this to me, and told me to give it to his father," he said. He went on to where Niall and Sorcha stood and handed the bundle to Niall, who unwrapped it. He turned the metal tablet over in his hands, then looked up at Tavi and smiled. He opened the book and wrote something, then held it out to Lorcan.

What are you going to do with him? Niall had written.

"I'm not sure," Lorcan said. He turned back to where Cormac was kneeling and stepped forward; the murmuring around him fell silent.

"In Rome," Lorcan said. "There's something called the right of the father. If a child commits a crime, their father is allowed to kill them, to correct their mistake in siring that child. I could give you to Uncle Niall and let him determine your fate, and not lose any sleep over it. Or I could give you to Uncle Eogan, for your crimes against Eire. I could even send you to Rome, for your part in the attempted uprising against of the Emperor. At the very least, you'd end up a slave and be sent to the mines. Or you'd end up in the arena as a gladiator, bleeding out for the entertainment of Rome. Could you survive a year on the sands, Cormac? Could you survive what you put me through?" He watched the color drain from Cormac's face. "I didn't think so."

Cormac's eyes widened. "I... " He shook his head. "Just kill me. You win. You've always won. Anything that was ever mine, you took from me. I have nothing left but my blood."

Lorcan shook his head. "You're wrong, cousin. You threw away more than I ever took from you. You threw away this family. You threw away Grandmother's gifts. You threw away your skill as a smith and the respect that came from that. The things that you pinned your worth on were never yours to begin with." He drew his *siccae* and looked down at the blades, then stepped forward and cut the ropes binding Cormac's wrists. Cormac shook his hands and got to his feet, looking around at the rest of the flock. "Cormac, you owe Becc the debt of Bran's life. You owe the people of Scath and this family the debt of everything you've done to them over the past year. I'd say Niamh has the greatest claim to your blood, but she's not here right now. Ronan's claim would be next, I think. Then mine. But I think that the flock will agree that I speak for them on this?"

"He's yours to do with as you will, Lorcan," Diarmuid said. "Justice is yours."

"The ford, then?" Cormac asked. "I'll need a weapon."

Lorcan looked at the man in front of him and sighed. "No, you won't," he answered. "Because I don't want your life. I don't want anything of yours, and I never have. It was always you claiming what was never yours to begin with. And now? Now I am the man you forced me to become, and my road back to Eire is paved in the bones of the people I had to kill to get here. I am tired of killing, Cormac. I choose not to kill you. But I can't let you go, either. If I do, my children will never be safe." He paused, then looked at the others. "I think the person who has the greatest claim on your life is Grandmother. You twisted her gifts to us into something horrible, and you betrayed your blood and your flock. You betrayed her." He stepped back and raised his voice, "Grandmother, I yield his life to you."

From behind him, he heard a raven calling. Then another. More, until the cries of angry ravens filled the air. He turned, and watched as the feathered cloud grew in the air over Dun Morrigan. Cormac screamed, and when Lorcan turned back, it was to the sight of Cormac running for the open gates. Tavi started forward, but Diarmuid and Lorcan both caught his arms.

"No, Tavi," Lorcan said softly. "This... this is Grandmother's to do."

The cloud of ravens passed overhead, then dove as one. For a moment, there were only ravens, screaming and growling. Screaming from within the cloud that cut off abruptly right before the ravens took to the skies again, the cloud dissolving as if it had never been.

There was no trace of Cormac left behind.

* * *

The following morning, the rebuilding of Dun Morrigan began. The sorcerers repaired the burned wall and the gates before leaving with the warbands. Diarmuid promised to send assistance and supplies, and to pass word on the people of Scath that they could return to their homes if they so wished.

"Tell them that if they want to stay in Dun Righ, I fully understand," Diarmuid told his namesake. "And tell your father that I'll come and see him once my wing is up to the flight."

"Of course, Uncle." Young Diarmuid smiled and hugged his uncle. "Oh, Bairre has asked to stay. He says you'll need the help, at least until things are more settled."

"Bairre?" Diarmuid looked at Lorcan. "Wasn't he a troublemaker?"

"Tavi showed him that he wasn't going to take any nonsense. I think Bairre would follow him to the moon now," Lorcan said. "Cousin, thank you."

Diarmuid laughed and hugged Lorcan. "I'm glad you're home," he said. "Now, if Livia, Aunt Grainne or Drucilla want to come straight here, I'll escort them myself."

"We'll hopefully have a place for them to sleep once they get here." Lorcan looked around, his gaze stopping on the dead circle of grass just outside the gates. His cousin followed his gaze and grimaced.

"I didn't see a lot of what happened," he said softly. "What… what happened to Cormac?"

"Grandmother took him," Lorcan answered. "That's all we know."

Diarmuid nodded. "Best that we don't know, then." He looked around. "I haven't seen Corvina since. Where is she?"

"She's been here, but I think she's telling me it's time for her to move on and live wild again." Lorcan looked around. "I haven't seen her since yesterday."

"Well, if you do see her, tell her I said goodbye. I should be getting off. It's a long way." He hugged them both again, then bowed and turned, walking out the gates.

"Did Orla leave at dawn?" Lorcan asked. "I wasn't awake."

"Yes," his father answered. "And honestly, if I'd been up for the flight, I'd have gone with her."

"I'll work on that arm later, if you want," Lorcan offered. "For now, I promised Tavi and Turlach I'd help them with the stables. Turlach had some interesting things to say when he saw the state of it."

Diarmuid laughed. "Things that would have made your mother pull out his pinfeathers, I imagine? I'll go see what help Petran needs, and… " He stopped as the bright ringing of metal on metal filled the air. Then he smiled. "Niall fired the forge." He took a deep breath and closed his eyes. "We'll heal. We may not be entirely what we were a year ago, but we'll heal."

"We will." Lorcan looked back out through the gates, toward the forest. Diarmuid put his arm around his shoulders.

"She'll heal, too. Her mate will help her."

Lorcan nodded and looked up at his father. "Yaroah said something before he followed her. That he recognized the look of her, because he'd had that look. I... he's my brother, and there are things I never knew about him. I hope he heals, too."

"They'll heal each other. And they'll come back." Diarmuid looked around. "Where's your cloak?"

"In my house," Lorcan answered. "Grandmother isn't answering me, so I still don't know what it means that I have two mates. I'm not going to put it on until they're both here. And I'm not going to invoke the gift until I know for certain that it won't favor one of them over the other. I'm not choosing between them."

"I understand. It's just strange seeing you without it."

"I haven't worn it in so long, it feels strange to have it, and I haven't even put it on yet!" Lorcan admitted. "I'm not sure how it's going to be to fly again."

"If you do... when you do... we'll go up to the perch. Once I'm able to fly again." Diarmuid looked up at the cliffs. "I should find Petran and Cuanu and see what I can do to help. Go on to the stables."

Lorcan hugged his father, then trotted off toward the stables, entering the cool darkness. The horses had been turned out so that the stables could be cleaned, and Lorcan looked around the empty space, seeing no one. "Tavi? Turlach?"

"I'm up here!" Tavi called from the loft. Lorcan looked up and didn't see anyone, so he went to the ladder and climbed up.

"Where are you?" he called, looking around. There was a large pile of hay blocking his view; he walked over and around it, then stopped. Tavi had laid a blanket out on the straw, and was sitting on it, naked and smiling up at Lorcan.

"Turlach is going to coming back... " Lorcan stammered.

"Not for a while," Tavi replied. "He said he was taking people out to cut more hay while it was still early. He told me not to expect him until after midday, and I should talk to you about what to do." He grinned. "So, are you going to tell me what to do? Or do I get to tell you?"

"Tell me you brought oil," Lorcan said, dropping to his knees next to Tavi. Tavi held up a flask, and Lorcan leaned in to kiss him. "On your back," he whispered against Tavi's lips. "Let me show you stable games."

Tavi laid back, pulling his knees up. "Like this?"

"Oh, just like that." There was something almost deliciously frantic about the whole tryst—at any moment, someone could come looking for them. Someone could find them. Someone could interrupt them before one or both of them had finished. So Lorcan didn't bother to undress, tugging his shirt up and pushing his trews down to his thighs before covering Tavi, pinning him down and kissing him hard and fast. They were both moaning, both panting by the time he picked up the flask and poured oil onto his hand, coating his cock, coating his fingers, then driving Tavi into even more of a frenzy as he made sure his mate was open and ready. Lorcan looked at Tavi, saw he was muffling his moans with his own arm—he shifted again, rolling Tavi into a tighter ball, pressing against him, pressing into him, starting to move against him. Tavi squirmed and tried to move, grabbing at Lorcan with his free hand, locking his fingers tight into Lorcan's shirt as he tensed, as his muscles with rigid, as he shot hard enough that Lorcan felt the splash. Lorcan kept moving, the waves of Tavi's pleasure carrying him into his own—he barked his own orgasm, then bit his lip to keep from making any more noise, whining through his nose as he slowed to a stop. He shifted enough that Tavi could lower his legs, then stretched out on top of him, moving up his body to kiss him.

"Do you think anyone heard us?" Tavi whispered.

"I…" Lorcan looked around. "I'm not sure I care. That was wonderful."

"You're wonderful." Tavi kissed him again. "You should let me up. We have work to do."

* * *

It was midday when the sentries Bairre had assigned announced approaching chariots and carts, and all work in the *baile* stopped. They'd made quite a bit of progress, and Lorcan and Tavi had been working on rethatching the hall when the call had come in. Now they waited at the gates, watching as the carts got closer. A raven circled and landed, and Orla joined the group at the gates.

"That's a lot of carts," Petran murmured from behind Lorcan.

"There were more," Orla said. "Some stayed in Scath. Grandfather is looking forward to getting back to his tavern. Mother and Aunt Alis are with him, and will be here later."

"They're coming back to Scath? Oh, that's good," Diarmuid walked out to stand in front of the group. "Our people are coming home. That's very good."

"Diarmuid!"

Lorcan clearly heard his mother's voice, even at a distance. He laughed as a raven took flight from one of the coaches, streaking toward them. Diarmuid met her part way, catching Grainne out of the air as she changed and pulling her into his arms. The rest of the flock cheered as they kissed, and Lorcan leaned into Tavi's side.

"There's Livia!" Tavi murmured. Lorcan straightened, looking where Tavi pointed. He looked up at Tavi, who laughed—they both took off running down the path, toward a cart that had just stopped. Livia was smiling, but not waving, and as Lorcan reached the cart, he saw why.

She was carrying a baby.

He stared for a moment, then stammered, "I… thought I knew how to count."

"This is Lachtna," Livia said, laughing. "Siobhan has Fionnuala."

Only then did Lorcan see Ronan, sitting on Livia's other side, and with Siobhan next to him. His cousin was laughing at him.

"Didn't expect to see me?" he asked. "We needed to be with the flock for a time. We needed to be together. Come help me down?"

Before Lorcan could move around the cart, Niall was there. He helped Ronan climb down and steadied him as Ronan reached back into the cart and took out a walking stick. Then he stepped back and looked his youngest son up and down before arching a brow. Ronan sighed.

"I'm getting used to it, Da," he said. "I'm not flying yet." He reached up and touched the patch that covered his left eye. "I'm learning. But… I'm here. And… " He turned. "Livia, let me take him?" He laid aside his stick and took the baby from Livia. "Da, this is your grandson," he said, passing the baby to Niall. "His name is Lachtna."

Niall looked startled, staring first at Ronan, then turning his attention to the sleeping baby, gently parting the blanket to reveal pale hair and downy white feathers. Niall ran one finger over the baby's cheek and kissed his forehead. Then he offered Ronan his other arm.

Tavi helped Siobhan down, then stepped out of the way for Sorcha, who took charge of baby Fionnuala. Once they were gone, Lorcan reached up and lifted Livia down, pulling her into a tight embrace. A moment later, arms closed around them both as Tavi joined them.

"I missed you both," Livia said. "I knew you'd be fine. But I missed you." She tipped her head back. "It's over?"

"It's over. Grandmother took Cormac."

"He's dead?"

Lorcan frowned. "I... assume so. Grandmother took him, and there was nothing left behind. And she's not talking to me anymore. And Corvina has flown off. I haven't seen her in days. Yaroah... I'll have to explain about Yaroah. He's fine," he hurried to say, seeing the look on Livia's face. "He's followed my cousin Niamh into the forest." He looked around. "Is Uncle Fergus here? And where's Manius?"

"Father is staying in Dun Righ. The High King invited him to stay as a counselor, and he accepted. And Fergus is here somewhere," Livia said. She stepped back, out of their embrace, and looked at him. "You're not wearing it."

"I wasn't going to, until I knew." Lorcan looked up at Tavi, then back at Livia. "It's in our house. I'll show you." He held his hand out.

"After all that we've been through, I don't want to see it on a hook, Lorcan. I want to see you wearing it." Livia smiled. "I want to see your wings."

Lorcan blinked, then looked at Tavi. "I... "

"Go get it," Tavi said. "I want to see, too. But I wasn't going to push."

Lorcan nodded and turned toward the gates. Cuanu had Drucilla in his arms, just holding her. It felt almost as if he was intruding, and he hurried past them. When he came back out with his cloak over his arm, Tavi and Livia were on the *urla*. He joined them, then swung his cloak onto his shoulders, shivering as it settled into place. Livia came closer, running her fingers through the feathers.

"It's beautiful," she murmured. She slid her arm around his back, leaning into his side. Tavi came and joined them, petting the cloak with gentle strokes.

"I want to see you fly," he said. "Show us?"

Lorcan shook his head and put one arm around Tavi, the other around Livia. "No. Not unless we can all fly. Either we all fly or none of us do."

There was no warning—all at once, it felt as if something was rushing out of him, down his arms and out both hands. Tavi yelped, and Livia squeaked in shock, and Lorcan dropped his hands and jumped back.

Black feathers on Livia's shoulders.

White feathers that gradually darkened to gray on Tavi's.

Warm laughter filled the air, and Lorcan felt a brush of phantom feathers against his cheek. *My most worthy grandson. You've served me well. All of you have. Enjoy your reward.*

Lorcan licked his lips, hearing the rest of the flock approaching. "Thank you, Grandmother."

The laughter faded. Diarmuid and Grainne came forward, and Lorcan smiled. "Da, this is Livia. My other mate."

"Welcome, daughter." Diarmuid smiled. "I look forward to knowing you better. For now… Lorcan, why don't you take your mates to the perch?"

Lorcan grinned. "I can, can't I?"

Diarmuid laughed. "You most certainly can."

Lorcan turned to Tavi and Livia. "Shall we? You know how. It comes with the cloak."

Then he changed and took to the air, hearing his mates calling as they joined him to dance on the wind and touch the skies.

Research Notes

The healing salve that Livia used on Gaius consists of the following herbs infused in olive oil and beeswax. I've added the names by which Livia and Lorcan would have known them:

- Comfrey
  - Livia: Solidago
  - Lorcan: Lus na gcnámh mbriste
- Lavender
  - Livia: Stoechas
  - Lorcan: An lus liath
- Borage
  - Livia: Euphrosinum
  - Lorcan: Borrach
- Hyssop
  - Livia: Hyssopus
  - Lorcan: Isop
- Calendula
  - Livia: Acantha
  - Lorcan: Liathan
- Plantain
  - Livia: Arnoglosson
  - Lorcan: Deideag
- Willow
  - Livia: Itea
  - Lorcan: Saileach

Other herbs mentioned in the books:

- Opium
  - o Livia: Papaver
  - o Lorcan: Meilbhaeg
- Pennyroyal
  - o Livia: Glechon
  - o Lorcan: Pulegium
- Hemlock
  - o Livia: Koneion
  - o Lorcan: Fealla Bog
- Wormwood
  - o Livia: Apsinthion
  - o Lorcan: Searbh Luibh
- Mint
  - o Livia: Mentha
  - o Lorcan: Cartal

Information on the Latin and Irish names of the herbs was found in *De Materia Medica*, by Dioscorides (published 50-70 CE), and *The Gaelic Names of Plants (Scottish, Irish and Manx)* by John Cameron (published in 1883). Any research mistakes are my own.

Broken Feathers
A bonus short story

Yaroah had never before seen a forest like this one. He'd been told that there had once been forests in Carthage, but all of the trees had been used to build ships. They were all gone before he was born, before his grandfather had been born. This was all new and wondrous, and he was completely, hopelessly lost. He had no way of finding his way back to the wooden walls that the warband had just liberated. He had no idea how to tell what direction he was going, or if he was even going in a straight line. The keep... no, no the word that Lorcan used was *baile*. The *baile* was, he thought, somewhere behind him.

She was in front of him.

He might not be able to tell what direction he was going. Might not be able to find his way back. But his way forward was clear, and he knew in his bones that she was in front of him. Still moving. Still running.

He would keep following. He'd keep his distance. He didn't want her to see him as a threat. But he did want her to know that he'd be waiting for when she was ready for him. However long that took.

Hopefully, not too long. Lorcan said that his kin were immortal. She'd have time to heal, time to grieve.

Yaroah didn't have that much time. He looked up at the tall trees, then closed his eyes. Which way?

That way.

He started walking again. He could hear running water somewhere off to his left. A stream, or a river, perhaps. Might be a good place to stop for the night. Assuming that she stopped for the night.

He heard rustling overhead, and looked up to see that he was being watched. She was standing crouched on a branch, looking down at him with her head cocked to one side, one hand resting on the tree trunk. Her short tunic was torn and covered in rusty stains and dirt.

"What are you doing?" she said. "Why are you following me?"

Yaroah frowned and hesitated. He thought he understood her questions, but… answering was harder.

"I… follow," he said slowly. "I…" He paused, then sighed. "I… not speak… good."

She looked amused. "What language do you speak?"

"Latin," Yaroah answered. "Carthaginian."

She lowered herself to sit on the branch. "I don't know Carthaginian," she said in slow Latin. "I know Latin."

Yaroah smiled up at her. "I am learning your language," he said. "But it is slow. And I have only been learning since we left Carthage. Not even twenty-five days."

Her brows rose. "You're quick, then."

Yaroah laughed out loud. "I am slow. Old and slow. And I am Yaroah. I do not know your name."

"Yaroah," she repeated, and the sound of his name on her lips made him shiver. "I am Niamh."

He frowned slightly, and repeated it. He must have said it wrong, because she shook her head. "Say it again?" he called.

"Niamh. It means radiant." She ran her fingers through her short, flame-colored curls. "My father named me when I was born, because of my hair."

"It is accurate," Yaroah said. "You are radiant."

Her cheeks colored slightly. "Does Yaroah mean anything?"

Yaroah shrugged slightly. "It's an old name, and I think it originally was the name of a god of the moon, but I do not know for certain. I was named for a general who was my several times removed grandfather."

She nodded, then stood up on her branch. "How long are you going to follow me?"

"How long are you going to run?"

She scowled down at him, then started walking again. When the branch bowed under her weight, she changed into a raven, flew to the next branch, and changed back. Yaroah stared at her for a moment, then followed, trotting to keep up with her.

"I'm not running," she said over her shoulder before taking on her feathers again.

"You are," Yaroah called when she changed back. "I understand why you run. I would have run, if I had been able."

She stopped and crouched again, staring at him. "What does that mean? You would have run? When?"

Yaroah moved to stand directly underneath her, his head tipped back. "Will you come down?" he asked. "It would be easier to talk." He reached up and rubbed the back of his neck. "I am not used to speaking to someone taller."

She blinked. Then, incongruously, she grinned.

"I…" She straightened and looked around. "Not yet. There is a place where you can camp, this way. Follow me." She took wing again, flying to the next tree, leading him through the trees. As they went, the sound of running water got louder.

"We do not have trees like this in Carthage." He raised his voice so that she could hear him as he walked. "I come from desert and flatland and rocks. Trees like this… how can you find your way?"

Her call sounded very much like laughter, and he smiled. That she could laugh was a good thing.

He stepped out into a clearing, through which a small stream ran. He looked around and saw her sitting once more on a branch over his head, her bare legs hanging down.

"No trees?" she asked. "How can you live where there are no trees?"

"How can you live where you can't see the horizon?" he countered, and went to kneel by the stream. He scooped up some water to drink, then sat down and looked up at her. "We had forests, once, or so my grandfather told me. But they were all cut down to build ships for trade and for war. Now? There are no tall forests like this. Only single trees, or perhaps groves of small trees."

She shifted, flew to a lower branch, and changed back. "This will be a good place to spend the night. You can build a fire, and you can sleep safely." She stretched her legs out along the branch, putting her back to the trunk. "Explain. Tell me what you mean, when you said you would have run if you could."

Yaroah looked up at the sky, which was growing darker. "If I wish to sleep tonight," he said, "I will not speak of this now. Or I won't sleep."

She nodded. "Yaroah, if I tell you to go back to the *baile*, what will you do?"

"If you tell me to go? I will listen, but I will also get even more lost. I cannot find my way there." Yaroah stood up and walked over the tree to look up at her. "I can find you. You are my way."

She swallowed. "And if I tell you that I am not?"

"Then you would be lying to both of us, my radiant one." When he looked up again, she was gone.

He closed his eyes, picked a direction, and followed.

* * *

It was several days later when Yaroah woke with the sun in his eyes, and her voice in his ears.

"How long are you going to follow me?"

He rolled onto his side and looked up to see her perched above him on a branch. The sun was behind her, and turned her bright hair to flames. He smiled. "I was wondering when I would see you again. How long will I follow you? That depends. How long are you going to run?"

"You said you would have run, if you could." She flew to a lower branch and changed back. "Will you explain now?"

"Share my meal with me, and I will explain." He unpacked the remains of the supplies that one of Lorcan's uncles had given him, and looked up to see her sitting across the embers of last night's fire from him. This close, he could see the scattering of freckles across her cheeks. He nodded and held up something that looked like a bag. "I have been wondering. What is this?"

"Have you never cooked in a leather pot before?"

"This is a pot?" Yaroah studied it. "How does it not burn away?"

"I'll show you." Niamh held out her hand. "Give it to me, and build up the fire."

Yaroah held the bag out to her, and drew back without touching her, gathering twigs and sticks and bark from a small pile he'd made the night before. He started to build the fire back up as she got up, heading into the trees. She came back with a long branch, and a forked one. The forked one she planted in the ground near the fire, then took the bag to the stream.

"Is there meal?" she called over her shoulder.

Yaroah looked in the pack and pulled out a pouch and two rough wooden bowls. "Yes. I haven't done anything with it because I didn't know I had a pot." He set it on the ground next to the upright stick. When Niamh came back, there was a small blaze rising from the embers. She nodded and picked up the longer stick, hanging the water-filled bag from one end and resting it in the crook of the forked stick while she buried the other end in the ground.

"Pour the meal into the bag," she said.

"How much?"

"About two handfuls of it."

Yaroah nodded and did as he was told. "Will the bag not burn?"

"No, the water inside will keep it from burning." Niamh looked around. "That rock over there. Will you get it?"

Yaroah got to his feet and went to pick up the rock. It was easily the size of both of his fists together, and heavier than it looked. He carried it back and waited, and Niamh pointed to where the end of the stick was buried. "Here."

"Ah, so it won't come up." Yaroah set the stone down on the buried end of the stick, then retreated to the other side of the fire. "Do you mind doing this?" he asked. "I have never seen this done before. It will not be edible if I cook."

"I will cook if you will explain what you told me." Niamh picked up another stick and peeled the bark off, then used it to stir the contents of the leather bag. "You said you understood. How?"

"Because I was where you are now," Yaroah said. He frowned slightly and looked down. Looked up. Looked away. He couldn't look at her, or the words would dry up and lodge in his throat, the same way they had almost every other time he'd tried to tell this. "I… there is only one person living who knows all of this. The others… they're gone. I have not told this to Lorcan." He paused. "I was a soldier once. I was… perhaps as old as Lorcan is now. In Carthage, we had a warband such as the High King commands, such as the ones that freed your home. But in Carthage, there was only the one. It was called the Sacred Band, and my family was honored to have two sons who were deemed warriors good enough to serve. Myself, and my younger brother, Mago. He was two years younger than me." He paused again, hearing only the wind in the trees, the rippling water, and the birds. "We went to war. And we never came home." He closed his eyes. "I never saw Mago again. He died that day, I think. I hope." He swallowed, shook his head. "Death… would have been better. So I thought then."

"How long?" Niamh asked, her voice soft.

"I do not know. I didn't see the sun between the day I was taken and the day I was sold in Rome." Yaroah forced himself to look at her. "For however long it was, I was chained in the dark. The only time I saw light was when someone took their turn at me."

She met his eyes. "You do understand. How did you get away from them?"

"I gave up," Yaroah answered. "I stopped fighting them, and they grew tired of me. So they sold me in Rome." He held his arm out. "Can you see them? They're hard to see on my skin."

She squinted slightly, but didn't come around the fire to look more closely. "I... you have tattoos?"

"I have gladiator tattoos," Yaroah said with a nod. "I was sold in Rome as a gladiator. My captors sold me as a member of the Sacred Band, as a fierce fighter. My owner bought me unseen. He swore for nearly an hour when he saw the beaten man he'd actually purchased, and he never repeated himself once." He leaned back and watched Niamh as she stirred the porridge. "It truly doesn't burn."

"If I keep getting distracted, it will," she said. "There's a patch of *sú talún fiáin* over there. Go see if there are any ripe. It's early, but you may find some."

Yaroah got up and picked up a bowl. "What do the ripe ones look like?"

He caught a slight, fleeting smile. "Red. Small berries, about the size of your fingertip, and they'll be red."

Yaroah nodded and walked in the direction she had pointed. He saw the patch of green, dotted with white flowers like stars.

"Oh! *Fragum!*" He knelt and started searching for ripe berries. "Livia grew *fragum* in her garden," he added. "I don't know what it does, but the tea is very good."

"Bring some leaves, then, and I'll make tea."

It took some time to find enough ripe berries to fill the bowl, and by the time Yaroah came back to the fire, Niamh had shifted the leather pot off the flames. He handed her the bowl, and she portioned out the berries and the porridge, then took the pot down to the stream, coming back and hanging it back over the fire.

"Put the leaves in, and we'll have the tea," she said, sitting down and picking up her bowl. "Who is Livia?"

"Lorcan's mate," Yaroah answered. "One of them."

A single brow rose. "One of them?"

"He cannot explain it, so don't even think that I can." Yaroah scooped some porridge into his mouth, swallowed, and smiled. "This is very good. Thank you. Livia is the daughter of the man who bought me. She was a baby when I came to their *ludus*." He paused for another bite. "That is a place where gladiators are trained. Her father is Manius, and he was our *lanista*. Our trainer and owner. Mine and Lorcan's."

Niamh held up one hand. "Wait. I'm confused."

"I was sold as a gladiator," Yaroah repeated. "I was sold to Manius, who was a somewhat successful *lanista* in Rome. My captors sold me to him under false pretenses—they bribed his agent, I think. He thought he was getting a fearsome warrior. What he got was a broken slave."

"But you're not broken now," Niamh said. She set down her empty bowl. "How?"

Yaroah finished his porridge and set his own bowl down. "Time. Distance."

She nodded. Then she rose, and without saying another word, changed and took to the air.

Yaroah didn't see her for two days. But he could feel her as he followed her through the woods.

* * *

It was nearing sunset when she finally showed herself to him again. "Tell me more," she said as she landed and changed into a woman. "About time and distance."

Yaroah smiled. He gestured to the fire and the leather pot. "I'm learning," he said. "I haven't burned anything yet."

"You came close," Niamh said. "I saw you." She sniffed. "What are you making?"

"There is fish in clay in the coals, and I found more *fragum*, so I am making tea. Eat with me."

She sat down across the fire from him. "Time and distance, you said. Is that all it is?"

"Not entirely," Yaroah answered. "There's also having the right people to help. Manius helped, as did his wife. Dareen was also a gladiator, but she was something of a healer as well. She helped. And there was Gebal. He was *primus palus* in the *ludus* when I came to them. That means he was first among the fighters. He was from Carthage, like me. And he refused to let me lay down and die." He sniffed, smiling a little at the memory. "He stood me up on the sands as soon as I was strong enough to be there, and he challenged me. I lost. Badly. The next day, he did the same. And the next. Until I finally said no more and fought back. That night, he told me that I was no longer a whipped dog. That I was on my way to being a man again. I learned to stand on my own again. I remembered who I was." He looked across at Niamh. "You found that path long before I did. And you did it alone."

"I—"

"The one who did this to you. You killed him. You took yourself back." Yaroah shook his head. "It's more than I ever did. Is the fish ready, do you think?"

Niamh sat quietly for a moment. Then she shook her head. "I don't know—"

"Is that about the fish, or about you being stronger than I am?" Yaroah asked. She made a face at him, and he chuckled. "You are!" he insisted. "You can laugh. I can't remember how long it was before I truly laughed. Before I truly was..." He paused, uncertain of the word he wanted.

"Happy?" Niamh asked. She drew her knees up to her chest. "I was happy. Before. I... I don't think I'll ever be happy again."

Yaroah nodded. "I know. I remember. And... no, not happy. I wasn't happy as a slave. Not knowing that any fight could be my last. Being at the beck and call of anyone who wished me in their bed and had the coin to pay for it."

"What?"

"Gladiators were in much demand among the women of Rome. And some of the men, but Manius held to his promise not to sell me to them. It's the one promise he kept to me." He closed his eyes, listening to the wind and the birds. "The first time I won a bout against Gebal, I laughed." He opened his eyes. "Relief. I was... relieved. I wasn't broken. I was... closer to whole." He sighed. "So, it takes time. Distance. Patience." He paused again. "Lancing the wound."

"What?"

"That's what Dareen called it. She said that the wound in my spirit was poisoning me, and that I had to lance it to let the healing start." He looked across at Niamh. "She was the first one I told. Everything I am telling you. Possibly more, because there are things I no longer remember. She cried with me. And when it was done... I felt... empty.

Lighter. As if a weight were taken off my shoulders. It wasn't long after that that I laughed again." He paused again, then grimaced. "And it wasn't long after that Dareen took a wound in the arena that poisoned her blood. The *medicos* could do nothing to save her. Or so they said. It's possible that they just didn't care. She was a foreigner, and a gladiator, and a slave." He reached out and picked up a stick, tearing the bark off and throwing the pieces into the fire. When he looked up, Niamh was staring at him.

"They let her die?" she whispered. "That…"

"In Rome, if you are not one of them, you are not worth the trouble." Yaroah broke the branch into pieces. "Ask Lorcan about how a *medici* treated him, because he was a barbarian and a gladiator. And that was in spite of him being favored by the Emperor."

Niamh was quiet for a long moment. Then she shook her head. "I don't understand that."

"Lorcan said much the same," Yaroah said. He tossed the pieces of branch into the fire and nodded toward the pot. "The tea should be done. Will you serve? I'll get the fish."

Niamh shifted onto her knees, then froze, looking over her shoulder. A moment later, Yaroah heard something coming through the trees. No, several somethings.

"Go!" he whispered. "Change and go!"

She turned, stared at him, then shifted and flew away. Yaroah reached over and unsheathed his sword, laying the bared blade down next to him where it would be hidden from view. Then dipped his bowl into the leather pot, filling it with tea, then carefully pulled the clay-wrapped fish out of the coals. He settled back down and sipped the hot liquid as three men in ragged clothes came into the clearing. They gaped at him, and Yaroah wondered if they were some of Cormac's men—hadn't Orla said something about men deserting the *baile*?

"Are you lost?" he called in careful Gaeilge. "I am… lost. Much lost."

"Ah… a bit, yes." One of the men came closer. "You… you're not from Eire."

"I am of Carthage." Yaroah sipped his tea. "I came," he paused, thinking of the translation, "to see all the colors of green in the world." He smiled and gestured with his bowl. "But no forests like this in Carthage. So, I am lost." He held up his bowl. "*Fragum* tea?"

295

"Fragum? That's not Gaeilge," one of the other men said. "That's Latin. You're a Roman? You came with them?"

"I am from Carthage, where we speak both," Yaroah switched to speaking Latin. "My Gaeilge is still new. I understand more than I speak." He laid down his bowl and rested his hand loosely on his thigh, watching as the second man came closer.

"You didn't answer me," he said in Gaeilge. "Did you come with the Romans?" He glanced back over his shoulder. "You're a long way from the Roman port."

Yaroah shrugged one shoulder. "A few days of walking along the coast? Not so far. I had no trouble until I came inland." He smiled and gestured with his other hand. "How do you find anything when you cannot see the horizon? I couldn't find the coast again if I tried!"

The third man, who'd been silent until then, snorted. He looked around, then nudged the first man. "You know Latin. Ask him," he said in Gaeilge.

"We're looking for someone." The first man looked around. "A woman. Bright red hair. She's a slave. An escaped slave."

Yaroah shook his head. "I've seen no slaves." He sipped his tea, and the second man stepped closer.

"You have tattoos," he said. "Your arm. Isn't that... those are gladiator marks, aren't they?"

Yaroah nodded. "They are. I won my freedom last year. After spending half of my life in the arena, I wished to see the world." He looked around. "It's very green. And confusing."

The second man stepped away and turned his back to Yaroah, whispering something to the other two. Yaroah shifted onto his knees and rested his hand on his sword, watching as the first man turned back to him. His hand was resting on the hilt of his own sword.

"Carthaginian gladiator. Freed last year. Is your name Yaroah?" When Yaroah nodded, he frowned. "I know of you. You fought with Corax. You came here with Corax." He nodded over his shoulder. "Your people took the *baile*. We saw the fight. Stayed out of it."

"And you should continue to stay out of it," Yaroah said. "I have no quarrel with you, and I want no trouble," Yaroah said. "If you walk away, any trouble ends before it starts."

The first man shook his head and looked around. "The woman is mine. Where is she?"

Yaroah shrugged. "As I said, I have seen no slaves."

He snorted. "Then why do you have two bowls?" He walked over to where Niamh had been sitting and bent, picking up a single black feather. "Where is she?"

"Not here." Yaroah raised his sword from the ground, resting the point on the turf. The other two men backed away. Yaroah nodded. "Your friends have the right idea. Walk away. You'll live longer that way."

"The woman—"

"Isn't here. And she isn't yours." Yaroah stood up slowly, watching the man blanch as he realized just how tall Yaroah was. "What's your name?"

"Odhran."

"Odhran. Turn around and walk away, Odhran. Find a woman who wants you, in a place where you won't be throwing your life away." He looked past Odhran to see that the others were near the edge of the forest. "Make better choices than to throw yourself against the gods. That way does not end well."

Odhran scowled at him. "She is my woman."

"She ripped the last person who thought that to pieces." Yaroah watched Odhran's eyes widen. "Do you really want to die?"

Odhran backed away from the fire, his scowl deepening. "You want her yourself. Admit it. You won't have her. She's mine." He turned and stalked into the forest, followed by the other two men.

Yaroah waited until he could no longer hear them, then sat back down. He cracked open the clay and ate, watching the forest. There was no sign of the men coming back, and no signs of Niamh. Good. He finished eating, wrapping the rest of the fish up in a piece of leather. He poured the remains of the tea onto the flames, dousing them, and buried the rest of the embers. When the ground was cool to the touch, he packed the bowls and the leather pot. He swung the pack over his shoulder, paused, and closed his eyes. His heart tugged at him, pulling him toward the trees to his right. So he turned left, walking away from the need he could feel in his bones. Odhran and his men were watching him, and they would follow him. He was certain of that.

He was not going to lead them to Niamh.

* * *

The direction he went lead him deeper into the trees on the far side of the stream, and before long, he could no longer hear the sound of running water. He could, however, hear the sound of something moving in the trees above him, keeping a steady pace with him.

"They are following me," he said, hoping she'd hear him. "You should not. I will find you when it is safe."

The response was a derisive croak. He chuckled and glanced up to see her sitting on a branch overhead.

"Fine," he said. "But stay out of sight."

Another croak. When he looked up, he could no longer see the raven. He nodded and kept walking. He had no idea where he was going, but that wasn't the point. He paused, looked to each side, and continued to his left.

"If I could find it, I would go back to the *baile*," he murmured. "It would be safer."

From above, he heard another croak. He looked up, and saw her fly ahead of him, leading him in a different direction. He followed, noticing that the ground was sloping downward. The trees opened up, and he looked out over a lake… and the *baile*, tiny in the distance. He laughed.

"I was so lost that I didn't know how lost I wasn't," he said, shaking his head. He studied the sky and the heavy, dark clouds, flinching as lightning chased above him. "Tomorrow will be soon enough to start back," he added. "We need to find shelter."

A cold hand slipped into his, and he looked to his right to see Niamh standing next to him. He smiled as she looked up at him, raising her hand to his lips to kiss her fingers. She blushed slightly, but didn't pull away. He lowered their hands and looked around.

"You know this area. I do not," he said. "Where can we shelter?"

She pointed. "There's a small village near the lake. We can go there."

Yaroah squinted, finally seeing the small houses that almost blended into the landscape. He nodded, then looked back over his shoulder. "As much as I like this, you shouldn't be here now. They're following me—"

She blushed harder and squeezed his hand, then changed and took to the skies, flying toward the lake. He followed, watching the storm build overhead. Fat raindrops started to fall, plopping loudly into the dirt, and hitting his skin with enough force to feel like thrown pebbles. He ducked as thunder rolled overhead, and started to run. By the time he'd reached the edge of the little village, he was soaked and shivering. Niamh was waiting for him, her hair plastered to her forehead.

"There's no one here," she said as he reached her, raising her voice to be heard over the storm. "The houses are empty. They've been gone for some time."

"Get out of sight," Yaroah replied. "I'll build a fire in... which?"

She pointed. "The roof is intact on that one. Yaroah, I'm not sure we should stay here."

"We cannot stay out in this storm, and there's no other shelter." Yaroah looked around. "If they are wise, they went to ground. We will wait out the storm. Then we will keep moving." He flinched away from another peal of thunder. "Inside."

Niamh led the way to the house, and Yaroah had to duck underneath the low doorsill to follow her. The inside of the dark house was damp and cold, and it took a moment for Yaroah's eyes to adjust enough to see Niamh kneeling next to the empty firepit, laying out kindling. He joined her, fumbling through his pack for the flint and steel that he'd been given. His hands were shaking too hard to strike a spark, and after a moment, she took them from him.

"Are you that cold?" she asked as she worked, gently blowing on smoldering tinder until a tiny blaze emerged.

"I am very cold." Yaroah held his hands toward the small fire. "This would be extremely cold where I come from."

Niamh looked at him. Then she chuckled. "You're going to hate winter here," she said. "Did Lorcan warn you about that?"

"He did," Yaroah said. "Is there wood?"

"There's peat. Those bricks, there." She held her hand out. "Pass one to me."

Yaroah looked over to the side, seeing a pile of small, brown bricks. He picked one up and handed it to Niamh, feeding her more of the bricks until there was a sizeable fire burning.

"What is peat?" Yaroah asked, holding his hands to the fire.

"It's..." Niamh frowned slightly. "It's a sort of dirt. It burns longer and hotter than wood."

"Dirt?" Yaroah picked up a brick. "This is *dirt*. Your dirt *burns*?" He tossed the brick back onto the pile. "I will never understand Hibernia. Your gods walk among you and your dirt burns."

Niamh stared at him for a moment. "I... do those things not happen in Carthage?"

Yaroah shook his head, laughing. "They do not!" He rested his hands on his legs and sighed. "As much as I am enjoying talking to you, my radiant one, it's not safe for you to be here with me. Not with them following me. You should fly back to the *baile*. I will meet you there."

"It's not safe for me to fly. Not in this." Thunder punctuated her statement. "This storm is going to last until after nightfall, and I can't fly in the dark." Niamh handed the flint and steel back to him. "And... I don't want to leave you." She smiled slightly. "I want to know more about Carthage. Does it get very hot?"

Yaroah nodded. He put the flint and steel back in the pack and moved closer to the fire. "Rome is hot. Carthage is hotter. Lorcan complained about the heat in Rome, even when it was not hot. Not hot to me, I mean." He looked across at her. "I will take you to Carthage, if you want to go."

She coughed, then stared at him. "Go? Leave Eire? And go... really?" She frowned. "I... I could do that?"

"If you wanted," Yaroah answered. "If you wanted to see Carthage. See Rome. I would be happy to take you. We have friends in Rome, Lorcan and I. They will want to know that he won. That this is all over." He paused. "And it will let you rest, for a time. You will be away from the memories. Away from where things happened. It will give you some distance."

"And time?" She shifted, moving closer. "I... I never... I've read about Rome. My uncles have told me stories. But I never... " She paused, then looked at him, gnawing on her lower lip. It made her look younger than her years. Finally, she asked, "We could really go there?"

"If you wanted to, I would be proud to take you there. Show you the place where I was born, the places that made me." He yawned, suddenly tired. "We can do whatever you want to do. But for now, we should rest." He stretched out on the ground next to the fire. "Will you change and sleep in your feathers? It will be safer. And probably warmer."

He closed his eyes, listening as she moved around. Footsteps came closer, stopped, and he opened his eyes to see her standing over him. She knelt, rested one hand on his chest, then laid down next to him, her head on his shoulder.

"Niamh, are you certain?" Yaroah turned to look at her, his nose brushing against hers. "I don't want you to be uncomfortable."

She smiled. "You're very comfortable. And you asked me if I was certain. That makes me even more comfortable." She sighed softly. "You are mine," she murmured. "I know that. And you've told me enough that I know you won't hurt me." She put her arm over his chest. "And this is nice and warm." She paused. "You're mine. I know that. I knew you were mine from the moment I saw you. I know you will never hurt me. I know this. I *know* it. But—"

"You're still afraid."

She nodded, then raised her head. "I don't want to be. But... "

Yaroah reached up and ran his thumb over her cheekbone. "Lorcan said that once he gave his mates cloaks of their own, they would have a share of his immortality. I assume this will be true for us?"

"Yes."

"Well, then. We have time. I am patient. And I have a wondrous imagination." He smiled. "Just being with you is enough, my Niamh."

She settled back down with her head on his shoulder. "What about children?"

Yaroah considered the question. "I never thought I would have children," he answered. "A slave and a gladiator does not plan for a future. A family. So I do not have an answer to that." He rested his hand on top of hers on his chest. "Do you want children?"

"I don't know anymore," Niamh answered softly.

"Your brother has children now," Yaroah said, and Niamh raised her head again.

"Ronan? Children?"

"Twins," Yaroah answered. He smiled. "A boy and a girl. They were born right before we left Dun Righ. So when we go back, we can go and see them. Spend time with them. And you can decide what you want." He yawned.

Niamh laughed. She raised her head and kissed him gently. "Yaroah, go to sleep. We'll go back to the baile in the morning." She settled against his side and sighed. "And then we will talk about babies and about going to Carthage."

Yaroah shifted, putting his arm around her. "You have surprised me."

"Have I? Because I'm this close?"

He rolled to face her, putting his other arm around her, running his hand underneath her cloak of feathers. "Because you think I'm going to be able to sleep with you in my arms," he answered. Then he kissed her, pulling her closer. She tensed, and when he pulled back, her pale face growing even more pale.

Yaroah bit back a curse and rolled away. "I'm sorry," he said. "I should not have done that. Not without your leave." He looked back, but she was gone. "Niamh, I am sorry. I made you uncomfortable and that was wrong." He heard rustling from above, and sighed. "Sleep well, my radiant one. I am sorry."

More rustling from above, then silence. Yaroah fell asleep trying to find her in the darkness.

* * *

Years of sleeping during Rome's summer storms meant that the thunder didn't wake Yaroah. It was the attack that woke him, although not soon enough to ward off the kick that nearly tumbled him into the fire. He barely had a chance to catch himself and roll onto his knees before another kick caught him in the ribs. This one was from the other side, and was hard enough to nearly lift him off the ground. He wheezed and coughed, unable to catch his breath around the shooting pain in his side. A blow to the side of his head made the world go dark for a moment, and he came back to himself to hear laughter from above him.

"And you're a gladiator?" Odhran scoffed. "Really? I doubt it. That was too easy. Get him secure."

Hands on his arms, dragging him across the floor. He tried to pull away, only to be hit from behind hard enough to make his head spin and his vision go dark again. When he could see, he was bound with his back against one of the support posts. He tugged against the cords binding his wrists behind him, but there was no give—they were already cutting into his skin. He shook his head, but his vision blurred and danced, making him see doubles and triples.

A pair of Odhrans crouched in front of him, a long knife in their hands. Yaroah blinked hard. Still two of them, who demanded, "Where is she? We saw her with you. Where did she go?"

"Away," Yaroah answered. "I was stupid. I behaved horribly towards her, and she left me. I do not know where she went."

"What did you do?" one of the other men asked.

"Behaved like one of you," Yaroah growled back in Latin. He couldn't think of the words in Gaeilge, could barely think of the Latin. He tugged against the cords again. "And now she is not here. She thinks I am like you, and she is gone." He let his head fall, wondering if it was true. Was she gone? Or was she watching from above? She said she couldn't fly at night, but she could have gone to one of the other houses.

Apparently, the same thought occurred to Odhran. "Go search the rest of the village," he said. "See if she took shelter in another house. In this storm, she can't have gotten far."

The other two men left, and the pair of Odhrans sat down in front of Yaroah. "She's supposed to be mine," he said.

"She doesn't want you. And the last person who thought he owned her… she tore him to pieces. I saw her."

They both looked startled. "You said that before. So Senach really is dead?"

Yaroah would have shrugged if he could. "I never knew his name. I only know that the first time I saw her, she was covered in his blood, and she told her father that she killed him. Why do you want to share that fate?" He blinked hard and looked up, but the world refused to focus. "If you touch her, I have no doubt that she'd rip your heart out with her nails and your throat out with her teeth. There are other women in the world. I have seen them."

"I bet you have," Odhran leered at him. "The stories about gladiators true? Women fall down at your feet?"

Yaroah grimaced. "Not so much. Gladiators are slaves. Highly prized slaves, but slaves. It was… a mark of status as a matron in Rome to be able to pay for a gladiator in your bed. If you refused… well, you did not refuse. You could not refuse. Our services were sold to the highest bidder." He snorted, shaking his head again, and wincing when it made the twins turn into triplets. "You are welcome to it. I prefer to be free." He closed his eyes and tipped his head back against the pillar. "What do you want?"

"Her, for one. You out of my way for another."

Yaroah snorted again. "I was never in your way. Your way does not include her. She does not want you." He heard a soft, rhythmic slapping sound, and opened his eyes to see both Odhrans tapping their knifes against their hands.

"She wants you," Odhran said softly. "She went to you. She held your hand. She doesn't run from you." They got to their feet. "You kissed her. I saw you. You're in my way."

"She did run from me," Yaroah repeated. He tipped his head back to look up at Odhran. "She's not here. She left, and she isn't going to have either of us. And you killing me will not change that. Let her be." He paused. "And let me be. I've done nothing to you."

"I told you. You're in my way." Odhran smiled. "I'm going to enjoy taking you apart. Killing a gladiator? I'm not likely to have the chance to do that again." He walked around Yaroah slowly. "How to start? An ear, maybe. Ears are easy."

Yaroah felt the cold tickle of a blade against his skin, tracing a line underneath his left ear. He jerked away, and heard Odhran laugh.

"Oh, no. You have to stay still for this." Yaroah heard the sound of cloth tearing, then something dropped over his head. Odhran forced the long strip of cloth into his mouth, then tied the gag tightly behind the post. "Better. Now I can work." He paused. "Where are those two? They'll miss the fun." He rose and walked away. Yaroah couldn't turn to watch him—he struggled and tugged against the cords that were making his hands go numb, fought against the gag, but he couldn't move. Movement faded away in the sound of rain and wind in the rushes above. He closed his eyes again, feeling a warm trickle down the side of his neck.

"Well, they're just going to miss it," Odhran said as he came closer. "Now, where were we…?" More cloth tearing, and Yaroah jerked as his ankles were bound. Now there was only a single Odhran, who laughed as he knelt over Yaroah's legs, tapping the point of his knife against Yaroah's cheek. "I don't think I'll start with the ears," he murmured. "I'll leave them. Leave them so you can hear me when I make her mine. No, I'll take your eyes first. Then… your lying tongue."

Yaroah growled behind the gag, twisting and trying to throw Odhran off, sending another wave of pain through his side. The other man just laughed, grabbing Yaroah's chin with one hand as the point of the blade hovered in front of his left eye. There was a flurry of movement, a flash of bright hair, and Odhran gasped and jerked, the blade falling from his hand. He leaned back, and Yaroah could see the tip of a blood-streaked blade—Yaroah's own *gladius*!—piercing Odhran's tunic. Behind him, Niamh growled, set her feet, and tugged—Odhran screamed as she pulled the sword free, and offered no resistance as she pushed him over and off Yaroah's legs. She stood over him for a moment, water and blood running from her tunic and over her skin. Then she brought the sword down, and Odhran stopped moving. Niamh rose, glaring down at the body. She spat, and Yaroah wouldn't have been at all surprised if the body had burst into flames. It didn't, and she turned back to Yaroah, straddling his legs and picking up Odhran's knife to cut the gag.

"Niamh—"

She didn't let him say more than her name. The moment the gag was gone, she dropped the knife, caught his face between her hands and kissed him. There was nothing timid about the kiss, nothing hesitant. She was claiming him, and Yaroah moaned and surrendered to her completely... except for one thing.

He broke the kiss and croaked, "Niamh—"

"I'm sorry," she murmured, her lips brushing against his. "I should have stayed closer. I should have warned you before—"

"Niamh, I can't feel my hands... ."

She drew back, frowning slightly. Then her jaw dropped, and she scrambled off his lap, grabbing the knife. A moment later, his arms fell loose, his hands dangling useless at his sides. He shook his arms out as she came back and cut the bonds on his ankles.

"Did he hurt you?" she asked. "I should have warned you about him. I knew he was dangerous. I just didn't think he was that bold. Or that stupid." She took one of his hands and started rubbing his wrist. "Can you feel anything yet?"

"Nothing yet. Orla told us that there were men abandoning Cormac." Yaroah nodded toward the body. "Was he one of those?"

Niamh kept rubbing his wrist. "Do you feel anything yet?" she asked. "And no. Odhran challenged Cormac and lost months ago. Cormac drove him out of the baile."

"And he went?" Yaroah asked.

"It was when Cormac was still in control of everything. Still in control of himself. Before the men who followed him starting hearing about his failures. The others, they followed Cormac because he promised them gold and land, and they left when they realized he was never going to give it to them. Odhran just wanted someone to hurt." She frowned. "Let me have your other hand."

"It's prickly," Yaroah said as he gave her his other hand. "Did he hurt you?"

"He tried." She paused. "It was the only time I was grateful to Senach." She met his eyes. "The monster Cormac called my husband."

"The one you killed."

She bared her teeth at him. "Ripped his heart out with my nails and his throat out with my teeth."

"You heard that?"

"Right before I went hunting for the other two. They'd have come running if they heard Odhran shout, so I had to take care of them first. I didn't want to risk you, and I can't take two at a time."

Yaroah chuckled, gingerly flexing the fingers of his right hand. "Little radiant one, where did you learn to fight?"

"My father taught me." Niamh let his hand go. "How badly are you hurt?"

Yaroah closed his eyes and opened them again. The room wobbled slightly. Breathing sent a sharp pain through his chest. "I cannot see properly, or take a full breath."

"It's that bad?" Niamh pushed on his shoulder. "Lay down. You can't walk back to the *baile* like this!"

Yaroah caught her hand and kissed her palm, "Niamh, I've fought in the arena with worse. And if I'm to lay down, we need to build up the fire and take that out of here." He gestured toward the body. "It was bad enough here with him alive. Dead, he's less threat, but more stink."

Niamh snickered, then looked at the body. "I'm not sure I can move him."

"We can," Yaroah said. He staggered to his feet, then swayed in place as the room pitched and rolled. Niamh jumped up and took his arm to steady him.

"You can't," she said. "There's another house with an intact roof." She slid her arm around his back. "Let's go."

She refused to let him walk unsupported, so Yaroah took the pack in one hand and put his arm around her shoulders, letting her lead him out into the rain.

"Sit down," she said as they entered another of the little houses. He sat down next to the firepit, and she knelt next to him, starting to pile up kindling. He rummaged through the pack and pulled out the flint and steel. Once the fire was burning, she shifted, learning against him and putting her arm around him once more.

"This doesn't hurt, does it?" she asked. "And don't tell me no just because you don't want me to move."

"It's the other side," Yaroah answered. "And I will not lie to you, my radiant one."

She nodded. "In the morning, once it's light, I'll fly back to the baile and bring someone with a chariot."

"I can walk!"

She looked up at him. "I could feel you trying to wander all over the village while we walked over here. You were trying to explore every bit of the ground. If I hadn't been guiding, you'd have ended up in the midden."

Yaroah chuckled. "It would not be the first time. How long would you be gone?"

Niamh tossed a peat brick into the fire. "I... a few hours?" She grimaced and shook her head. "I don't like leaving you alone that long. There are others of Cormac's people out here." She looked up at him. "I could... what else do you know about the cloaks? Did Lorcan tell you that you'll be able to change and fly?"

Yaroah stared at her for a moment. "He did not!" He laughed. "I should have realized, though. I have seen your uncles all change. I just hadn't thought about it enough to realize that I would be able to as well!"

"You would." Niamh hesitated. "I could give it to you now, but I don't know how you'd fly when you're hurt."

"Niamh, I am fine staying here and waiting for you to come back. I can defend myself. I am a gladiator."

"And how many of me are you seeing right now?" she asked in response.

He laughed. "You have a point. As much as I'm enjoying seeing a multitude of you, I think perhaps one would be better."

She chuckled and leaned into him. "We'll see how you're feeling in the morning. Lay down."

Yaroah settled down next to the fire, and she once again took her place next to him, her head on his shoulder. He put his arm around her and sighed. "Niamh—"

"I know. I heard you apologize." She rubbed her cheek against his shoulder. "It's going to take time."

"I know. I remember. And I am patient. And willing to do whatever you need." He turned toward her to see her looking confused.

"What do you mean?" She pushed herself up on one elbow. "I don't understand."

Yaroah smiled. "I will not do anything to make you uncomfortable. But I might make mistakes. Like I already have. Correct?" He waited until she nodded. "When I was bound, the first thing you did was kiss me. I enjoyed that kiss very much." He smiled as she blushed. "If it will help you be comfortable enough to kiss me like that again, you're welcome to bind me."

"What?" Niamh jerked up to a sitting position, staring at him. "I... what? I... I couldn't do that!"

"You could," Yaroah said. He reached up and stroked her cheek. "And if it helps you, then you have my permission. Just not so tight."

She caught his hand and held tightly to it. "Yaroah... that would hurt you."

He laughed. "Would you stop if I asked?"

"Of course I would!"

"Then I have no worries of being hurt." He squeezed her fingers. "My radiant one, come and lay down. You need to rest."

She settled back down next to him, resting her head on his shoulder. "In the morning, we'll decide what we're going to do. Go to sleep."

* * *

When Yaroah woke up, he wasn't certain for a moment why. The fire had burned down, and the storm had passed. The night was dark and quiet. He frowned into the shadows, but could hear nothing but the wind. The storm must have passed. Then what... ?

Niamh cuddled closer and ran her hand over his chest. That was it—she was petting him in her sleep. That's what had awoken him. He laughed softly and kissed the top of her head, only to hear her sigh softly.

"Are you awake?" he asked.

She nodded, her cheek rubbing against him. "I couldn't fall asleep. I've been enjoying laying here with you. You're very warm." She ran her hand down his chest again; he caught his breath and laid his hand over hers.

"If you keep on petting me, I will not sleep anymore," he murmured. She laughed, tugged her hand free, and tugged up the hem of his shirt, resting her cold hand on his stomach. He shivered.

"Niamh—"

"I don't want to be afraid anymore," she whispered. "I want to be happy again. I want—" She pushed herself up so that she was resting on one him, looking down at him. In the dim light, she was barely more than a silhouette. "I want to see Carthage, and Rome, and... anyplace else you can think of. I want... I want you. With me. Forever."

Yaroah smiled up at her. "You have that. You have all of that." He paused. "Most of that. Not being afraid anymore? That will come with time."

She smiled. "And distance. When can we leave for Rome?"

"I think your parents will object if I steal you away too quickly, so soon after you have all been freed, and for a year or more. Because it will be that long before we come back. We will not be able to travel in the winter."

She nodded. "I understand. I still want to go."

He laughed. "I still want to take you. Once Livia has her baby. Which… spring, probably. The baby will be coming in the winter. We will go to the High King, to see if there is any message he wishes to send, and then we will go Britannia, and see the Roman governor there. Arcus is Lorcan's other mate's brother. He will want to know how things fared, and he will help us with travelling on to Rome."

"Not Carthage?"

"Rome first. We will spend the fall and winter in Rome, at the *ludus*. Or at the Palace."

"The Palace?" Her voice ranged so high she almost squeaked. "The Emperor's Palace?"

"At the very least, we will visit them. The Emperor is very fond of Lorcan, and would have adopted him if he was willing to remain in Rome. The Emperor's son and heir calls Lorcan brother. They will be very interested in what has happened here. And they will want to meet you." Yaroah smiled up at the dark ceiling. "We will winter in Rome, and go to Carthage in the spring, before it gets too hot. Then we will come back here."

Niamh started petting him again underneath his shirt, stroking his skin with one hand. "Time and distance, and new places. What if we want to stay longer? Or stay… somewhere else?"

Yaroah shook his head. "We would be foreigners in Rome, and not citizens. It would not be wise. And in Carthage… we will see, but I think Carthage may be too much of Rome now. Again, we would not be citizens, for all that I was born there. I spent too long as a slave to be comfortable with being looked at as something less now. Here I have worth, and so do you."

Her hand stilled. Looking up at her, Yaroah could just barely see the furrow of her brow. "I haven't had worth. Not really. Not since… not since Cormac came back. I was a possession, not a person. Is that what being a foreigner in Rome is like?"

"That's what being a gladiator in Rome is like," Yaroah answered.

"To be a foreigner, you're not a possession, but you're also not a person. You're... less." He rested his hand over hers. "I never want you to feel that way again. I want you to always be cherished, always be loved. Always know that you are the most important person in my world. So we will not be staying in Rome for longer than we have to." He rubbed his thumb over the back of her hand. "You have one thing to be grateful to your brother for—if he had not done this, I would not be here. Lorcan would never have come to Rome. He would be forever alone, and so would you."

"Oh," Niamh breathed. "Oh, I hadn't thought of that. My uncle Cuanu—"

"He also has the same reason to be grateful," Yaroah interrupted. "His mate was also in Rome. Her name is Drucilla, and she is in the High King's baile with Lorcan's mother and his mate."

"It's so strange to think that anything good came out of Cormac betraying his family and his blood," Niamh said. "But Lorcan's mates. You. Uncle Cuanu's mate. What else?"

"Freedom for myself and the other gladiators of Manius' *ludus*. Nona and Ennius are *lanistae* there now, freed men of status and wealth. There are alliances building between Rome and Hibernia. The Emperor's heir has offered a marriage of his new step-son, if Lorcan's child is a daughter. If the child is a son, then perhaps that offer would be extended to Ronan's daughter. They want to make permanent the friendship that Lorcan offered."

"Is that why we have to wait for the baby?" Niamh asked. "So we know who is being promised?"

"And your brother and his wife will have to agree." Yaroah yawned and tugged against Niamh's hand. "Lie down. We should sleep."

"I don't want to sleep." She shifted, straddling him, bracing her hands on either side of Yaroah's head. He didn't dare move, and they stared at each other for a long moment before she lowered her head to his, kissing him again. Claiming him again, and it took every shred of willpower he had not to put his arms around her. Instead, he raised his arms over his head and crossed his wrists. When she raised her head, she looked at his hands, then at him.

"Yaroah? What—?"

"You are in control, Niamh," he said. "I will not move without your leave."

For a moment, she didn't move. Then, slowly, she smiled, sitting up so that she could slide her hands underneath his shirt, pushing the hem up.

"I want to see you," she murmured. "Up close. I watched you when you bathed in the stream, but I didn't see much. Now I want to see you."

Yaroah laughed out loud. "You watched me?"

She nodded. "I wanted to see you. I still want to see you up close in the sun. It looks like you have blue in your skin. I want to see if I was seeing things."

Yaroah smiled. "I will be happy to pose for you in the daytime, the nighttime, or any time you want me to. So long as it is not cold."

She giggled. "I will make certain that it isn't cold. Do you want me to build up the fire?"

"If you do that, I will undress." In answer, she shifted off of him and went to the firepit. As she added fuel to the fire, Yaroah stood up, stripping his shirt off over his head. He untied the waist of his trews, commenting, "The one good thing about the way Romans dress is no trews."

Niamh looked startled. "No… Really? What do they wear?"

"Long tunics. A *sublingcalum* in the arena," he said, hurrying to add, "I will show you what that is. There isn't very much of it." He gestured to his groin. "It covers… only here."

Her brows rose, as did the color in her cheeks. Then she smiled. "So… I would have to look very closely?" she said slowly. "If it's that small. I might miss it otherwise."

Yaroah stared at her for a moment, then started laughing, staggering and nearly falling as his trews slipped down. He sat down on the ground and took off his shoes, then got back up, stepping out of the trews and holding his arms out. She came closer, moving slowly, warily, as if any sudden movement might startle her into flight. He held perfectly still, letting her circle him, shivering as her fingers trailed over scars, down his spine, over his arm.

"I want to see you in the sunlight," she said as she walked around him. "I want to see the tattoos close up." She stopped in front of him, looking up into his eyes. "I haven't asked and I should have. What do you want?"

"To touch you," Yaroah answered. She nodded, and he ran his hands up her arms, feeling her shiver. "I want to make you happy," he continued. "I want for you to never be afraid again. I want to be by your side for the rest of our lives. That's all I want."

She stepped closer, resting her hands on his waist. "That's what I want, too." She slid her hands up his body, over his chest, and around to the back of his neck, pulling his head down to hers. As she kissed him, he felt a rush of warmth all through him, heady enough to make him whimper against her lips as something warm and soft wrapped around his shoulders and over his back. He pulled back, looking over his shoulder to see glossy black feathers.

"Oh!" he gasped. He looked back to see Niamh smiling at him. "It's done?"

"It's done," she agreed. "My mate."

He nodded. "My mate. I like that. I would have said my wife, but it means the same, doesn't it? I am yours, and you are mine. Forever."

She ran her hands over his cloak. "Now, guard this well. Do you know—?"

"That losing it will kill me? Yes. Lorcan told me about his fear that Cormac would kill him by destroying the cloak."

Niamh nodded. "I never understood why he didn't. Especially when we found out that Lorcan was returning to Eire. Senach pushed him to do it, but he refused. That was when the men started to leave."

"Lorcan believed that the reason was that Cormac wanted to be the hand behind the knife," Yaroah said. "So that Lorcan would know he was defeated."

Niamh shrugged. "Perhaps. But it doesn't matter now." She paused. "Do you think he's still alive?"

"Cormac?" Yaroah shrugged. "I doubt it. Lorcan would not let him live to threaten his mates or his child."

Niamh frowned slightly. She looked away, then looked back at Yaroah. "I would like to ask him one question. But I suppose his answer doesn't matter. It won't undo what he did."

Yaroah nodded. "Is that question why?" She nodded, and he ran his hands up and down her arms again. "I don't know if he'd be able to answer that question. He may not know himself."

"If he doesn't know, then we'll never have an answer." Niamh wrapped her arms around herself, and Yaroah gave in and tugged her gently into an embrace. She rested against his chest and sighed. "I don't know if I want an answer."

"I doubt it would help," Yaroah murmured into her hair. "In truth, I think it would make things worse. What logic would make a man turn on his own kin that way? Nothing that you need to burden yourself with, my radiant one. It's over. He will pay for his deeds, if he has not already. And you are free of everything but the memories." He cupped her cheek and raised her head to look at him. "And the memories will become easier to live with. I promise you that."

She smiled slightly, softening to wrap her arms around him, and Yaroah all at once remembered that he was naked save for the feather cloak. He swallowed, trying to think of something else. Anything else!

"Yaroah?" She looked up at him. "I still don't want to sleep. And neither do you."

"Sleep is the very last thing on my mind." He let her go and touched his cloak. "It seems wrong to lay on this."

In answer, Niamh unfastened her own cloak and laid it aside. Then she stripped off the short tunic she wore, standing before him as naked as he was. He sighed and smiled.

"You are so beautiful," he whispered. He took his cloak off and laid it with hers, then got back down on the ground. She stretched out next to him and ran her hand down his chest.

"You're a very beautiful man, Yaroah," she said. "Now, you were going to let me be in control?"

"And you may still bind me, if you wish," Yaroah said, nodding. He raised his arms and crossed his wrists, as he had before. "Do what you will."

She straddled him, stretching out over him and resting her chin on her folded hands. For a moment, all she did was watch him, intently enough that he had to fight the urge to fidget.

"I'm trying to decide what I want," she finally said.

"You can tell me what to do, or what you want," Yaroah suggested. "You are in control."

She nodded. "I want... I want it to be good again. I want to enjoy this again. How do I do that?"

"You let me show you?"

She nodded, and Yaroah sat up. He took her hands in his. "If I do anything, try anything, and it does not feel right, tell me and I will stop."

She nodded, and he ran one hand up her leg, over her hip, and down over her arse, pulling her closer, trapping his cock between their bodies.

He slid his other hand down her back, gently massaging her hips and her arse until she whimpered softly. He smiled, and ran his nails lightly up and down her back; she arched, and he kissed one of her breasts, then the other before starting to suckle. She gasped, and her nails dug into his shoulders, but she didn't tell him to stop. He sampled one, then the other, listening carefully as she whimpered for any sounds of distress. Her whimpers turned to moans, and she started moving her hips against him, grinding into him with maddening heat and pressure. There was a strong temptation to roll, to put her onto her back, but he fought the urge and let her build, let her set the pace. Let her take control as she pushed him down to the ground, rising over him, then sinking down onto his cock with slow deliberation that left him shuddering with want and need, desperate to move and unwilling to do anything to jeopardize her explorations into her own pleasure. A tiny, rational voice in the back of his mind wondered if she'd been a virgin before her brother had given her away. He pushed the thought away—it wasn't important. What was important was here and now, and the soft, little gasps of pleasure that were building to full-throated moans. He let himself run his hands down her legs, holding onto her thighs as her moans became screams, as her body clenched around him and crested. As she slowed, panting, to collapse over him.

She raised her head and looked at him, her brow slightly furrowed. "No, I have not," he answered the question he could see there. "May I?"

"Yes. Do you want me to move?" she asked.

"Roll with me." Yaroah guided her until they were on their sides, facing each other. He pulled her topmost leg over his hip, then reached between them to reposition himself. She rested her hand on his chest, gasping as he started to move. He sighed, feeling her heel digging into his arse as she tried to pull him closer. Then she grabbed his shoulder and pulled him, rolling onto her back. He caught himself on one hand, looking down at her in shock.

"Are you certain?" he whispered.

"Yes," she answered. He smiled and leaned down to kiss her, then started to move, rekindling the fire that had started to die in his surprise. She shifted underneath him, moving with him, gasping in time with his thrusting, her legs locked around him, her nails digging into his back as he started moving faster, driving her closer to the edge, following her every heartbeat of the way. Her gasps turned to keening, and she canted her hips, pulling him deeper as he harmonized with her. Soared with her, their voices breaking the still night air as they came, one right after the other. Yaroah slowly stopped moving, panting as he shifted off of Niamh and rolled onto his side, pulling her into his arms.

That was when he noticed the tears.

"Niamh?" he gasped. "What is wrong? What did I do?" He held her close, wiping her tears away with his thumb. She frowned, and he realized that, in his panic, both Gaeilge and Latin had abandoned him. He paused, trying to find the words. "I hurt you?" he whispered in Gaeilge.

She shook her head. "No. You didn't hurt me. That was… thank you." She buried her face in his chest, and he held her close as she sobbed. It took him a moment to realize what this might be.

Relief.

When she finally took a slow, shuddering breath and raised her head, he wiped her cheek and kissed her on the forehead. "Is better?"

She nodded. "I'm sorry," she whispered, her voice raspy. "I didn't mean to frighten you. Or make you think you'd done something wrong. You were wonderful. That was wonderful."

Yaroah licked his lips and nodded. "And you were not certain it could be wonderful again?"

She nodded again. "I didn't think… I wanted it to be. But Senach… every time… I hated it. Hated him." She rested her forehead against his chest, and he heard her muffled voice. "I love you."

"Since the moment I saw you, I have loved you," Yaroah said. "I wondered why I felt the need to come here. I wondered why when I got off the ship in Carthage, I knew I no longer belonged there. I knew I needed to follow Lorcan. I thought I was just… he told me that all the colors of green in the world existed here. I thought it was just that I wanted to see them." He kissed the top of her head. "It was you, bringing me home."

"Even though it'll be cold?" she asked with a wet sounding giggle.

"You're warm. It will be enough." He kissed her again. "Go to sleep, my radiant one."

* * *

The morning dawned bright and clear. Niamh decided that Yaroah was hale enough for his first flight, and she assured him that the knowledge of how to fly came with the cloak. Yaroah wasn't certain he believed her, and insisted on several smaller, practice flights before he was finally ready. Then they took to the skies, and he laughed as he soared over the tiny houses that disappeared into the turf. He'd thought he was free when he walked away from Rome. Now, he was truly free! He could see the entire world from this height, could see there were people in the village below the baile. The roofs on some of the houses were intact, and things were much cleaner than they had been. And… there was an odd circle of dead grass just inside the gate.

Niamh started to circle, spiraling down to the ground. Yaroah followed her, and by the time he took on his own form, there was a crowd waiting for them. As soon as his feet were on the ground, Lorcan grabbed him, hugging him tightly.

"I was worried about you!"

"I am fine," Yaroah assured him, laughing. "Better than fine. You never told me flying was so fantastic!"

"Isn't it?" Tavi joined them, hugged Yaroah. His cloak of feathers was white and gray, and his smile as wide as the whole sky. It faded as he studied Yaroah's face. "You're bruised. What happened?"

"Someone tried to challenge me for Niamh," Yaroah answered. He glanced over to see his wife, his mate, being welcomed by her parents. "He lost."

"You took care of him," Lorcan said. His eyes widened when Yaroah shook his head.

"Niamh took care of him, after he tried to break my skull."

"Lorcan, see if he has broken ribs?" Niamh called.

Lorcan stared at her for a moment, then looked up at Yaroah. "I want to hear this whole story. Once I check you for broken ribs. Come inside. We have a house set aside for you."

"A moment." Yaroah went to join Niamh, taking her hand. He bit his lip, then bowed deeply to her father. "I promise, I will do everything in my power to take care of her," he said. "I just… can't say it in Gaeilge yet."

Niall smiled. He held out his hand and pulled Yaroah into a one-armed hug. Then he took out his wax tablet and wrote something. He handed it to Niamh, who read it, then looked at her father.

"Da! Really?"

Niall nodded, then gestured. Niamh looked up at Yaroah.

"Da wants to know if you want to learn to be a smith," she said. "And don't say you're too old. You're immortal. You have the time."

"I…" Yaroah stammered. "I… " He looked down at the tablet, at their linked hands. "Yes. I have been a soldier, a fighter my entire life. It is time I be something else." He raised her hand to his lips and kissed her fingers. "You will help?"

"Of course." She gestured to the baile. "Welcome home."

About the Author

Elizabeth Schechter has been called one of the top erotica and alternative sexuality writers in the world. Her writing credits include the award-winning steampunk erotic romance *House of Sable Locks*, the Celtic fantasy series *The Blood of the Raven* and 2021 VIVIAN finalist *Written in Water*, the first book of the *Heir to the Firstborn* serial

She was born in New York at some point in the past. She is officially old enough to know better, but refuses to grow up. She lives in Central Florida with her husband and son.

Elizabeth can be found online at http://elizabethschechterwrites.com, or on Facebook at https://www.facebook.com/Elizabeth.A.Schechter. You can also find her on Patreon, at https://www.patreon.com/EASchechter.

Subscribe to Elizabeth's newsletter at https://www.subscribe page.com/k4u7k2

Other Riverdale Avenue Books/Circlet Titles You Might Like

Ravenborn
Book One of the Blood of the Raven Series
By Elizabeth Schechter

Ravenfall
Book Two of the Blood of the Raven Series
By Elizabeth Schechter

House of Sable Locks
By Elizabeth Schechter

Like a Breath of Flame
Edited by Cosmin Alexander and Cecilia Tan

The Siren and the Sword:
Book One of the Magic University Series
By Cecilia Tan

The Tower and the Tears:
Book Two of the Magic University Series
By Cecilia Tan

The Incubus and the Angel:
Book Three of the Magic University Series
By Cecilia Tan

The Prophecy and the Poet:
Book Four of the Magic University Series
By Cecilia Tan

Spellbinding: Tales From Magic University
Edited by Cecilia Tan

www.ingramcontent.com/pod-product-compliance
Lightning Source LLC
Chambersburg PA
CBHW020842020726
47497CB00005B/1223